A HITLIST OF PLUTOCRATS

I0639413

A HISTORY OF PLUTOCRATS

Ian McKinley

A HITLIST OF PLUTOCRATS

FICTION4ALL

A FICTION4ALL PAPERBACK

© Copyright 2025
Ian McKinley

The right of Ian McKinley to be identified as author of
this work has been asserted in accordance with the
Copyright, Designs and Patents Act 1988

All Rights Reserved

No reproduction, copy or transmission of the publication
may be made without written permission. No paragraph
of this publication may be reproduced, copied or
transmitted save with the written permission of the
publisher, or in accordance with the provisions of the
Copyright Act 1956 (as amended).

Any person who does any unauthorised act in relation to
this publication may be liable to criminal prosecution
and civil claims for damages.

ISBN 978 1 78695 910 2

This Edition Published 2025
Fiction4All
www.fiction4all.com

"The poor have sometimes objected to being governed badly; the rich have always objected to being governed at all."
G. K. Chesterton, 1908

"Today, an oligarchy is taking shape in America of extreme wealth, power and influence that really threatens our entire democracy, our basic rights and freedom."
Joe Biden, 2025

Acknowledgements

Thanks to Linda for putting up with me when I'm writing, Denis for technical and linguistic reviews and Jim for the cover illustration.

Chapter 1: Jim

It was a perfect day in late summer as I strolled along the Hasliberg Panoramaweg, a path that provided a breath-taking view across the Rhone valley towards Rosenlaui, the Schynige Platte and the more distant mountain complex that included the Eiger, Jungfrau and Mönch. *So perfectly Swiss, complete with cow bells in the distance, rustic wooden farmhouses and barns covered in flowers and, only occasionally, the distinctive smell of manure that has been recently sprayed on a field.*

Mid-week, the walking trails were relatively quiet and the mountain bars even more so. Basking in the sun, ignoring the dangers of high altitude UV, I had spent an overly long lunch in the Bidmi Bärgbeizli before heading back to the basic mountain chalet that I had rented for a month of R&R away from the bustle of the real world. I was thus at least an hour behind my usual schedule when I turned the last bend and caught the first view of my rustic holiday abode. This was just in time to see it explode in a gigantic blast that, even at a distance of about a hundred of metres, knocked me flat onto my arse.

Because it's what I do, the analysis of this attack was immediately running in the back of my brain. *No sign of any aircraft, so probably a drone with some kind of thermobaric payload. The poor man's cruise missile.*

My ears were ringing but, regardless, I managed to detect the vibrations of an incoming SMS in the phone that nestled in a breast pocket of my walking waistcoat. The message was straight to the point: *do not even think about fucking with us.*

Strangely, this caused my initial shock to transform into cold determination. It was less than 24 hours since I had been contacted by an attaché from the British embassy in Bern, requesting me to help them respond to some potential terrorist threat to their nuclear facilities. I had asked for time to think about it and, in the interim, decided that I was too old for this kind of intelligence work. I had actually been mentally drafting a polite email to get me out of any commitments when I just missed being blown to shit.

As the phone was already in my hands, it was only a few seconds before I texted the guy in Bern: *OK, I'm in.*

I was still cautiously approaching the scattered remnants of what had been my holiday accommodation, aware that at present my possessions were only what I stood up in, when my phone rang.

"Hello, Jim, this is Phoebe. We've got a bit of time before the bad guys spot that you weren't home when they blew your holiday digs to buggery."

The very British enunciation made it clear that the embassy team, probably MI5 or some similar organisation, were already aware of what had happened. This was rather scary and made me wonder about the threatening SMS. "The attackers already know that they missed. I'm not sure if they were just trying to scare me or if the SMS that I received was to check if the attack had been successful. In any case, what do you propose?"

"Extraction is en route. If you can just head downhill towards the field beside that quaint wooden barn, it'll make it easier for the chopper to pick you up."

"You've got me on a satellite image?"

"We could, but the local webcams make that a bit superfluous."

"So, I'm getting picked up by a helicopter..." I could already see a Swiss military machine approaching, "...and going where?"

"Canada."

"Canada! What the hell's that to do with the threat I heard about yesterday?"

"Absolutely fuck-all." I could almost detect a smirk in the voice. "Which is exactly why you're going there."

***

Less than 24 hours later, I was sitting on the balcony of my hotel room in the Inn at Laurel Point, looking over Victoria harbour. I had actually visited Vancouver Island once before, when in my early twenties, but nothing at all looked familiar. The coming and going of large car ferries provided a strange contrast to those of seaplanes, which had a base just opposite my hotel. The former, a very efficient way of moving any kind of materials from one coastal location to another, seemed to reduce any need for the latter, which were faster, but much noisier and far less cost-effective. Nevertheless, a dozen or so planes left for every one ferry. Of course, the justification of moving so many large vehicles – the smaller ones mainly SUVs and the larger RVs – from one place to another was also questionable. From my perspective at least, this was as bizarre as European control of assault rifles would be to most of the Americans using these ferries.

I heard my room door open and wondered for a few seconds if I had forgotten to put up the *do not disturb* tag on my door. I then remembered that I certainly had and thus realised that this was not room service entering. There is something about terror that causes some to freeze, whereas, for others, it provides a jolt that switches the brain to overdrive. Luckily, I am one of the latter. I was wearing nothing but a hotel robe and was armed only with a cup of coffee from the Nespresso machine. However, I had the advantage of being on the terrace when the intruder would expect me to be in the bedroom.

Moving very slowly to ensure that the chair made no noise, I stood up and moved to a corner of the balcony that was out of direct view from the room. As I expected, the intruder moved to check the bathroom after finding the bedroom empty and then crept stealthily towards the open door leading onto the terrace. Very cautiously, a head slowly emerged from the room, just placed where I could fling the lukewarm coffee at it and follow this up with a jab to the throat that, ideally, would collapse the windpipe of my attacker.

In the days of my youth, that might have been game over. Unfortunately, neither my strength nor reflexes were what they once were. The coffee seemed to have done a good job but, nevertheless, my opponent managed to twist away so that my hand hit only the side of a short-cropped head – probably causing more pain to me than to my victim.

My body may be feeble but, at least, my mind was fast enough to recognise my limitations in any extended conflict. I could have used my fists, knees, elbows, feet – but a younger, faster fighter would inevitably kick seven shades of shit out of me. So, I grabbed a pair of ears and smashed my bald head directly into a face that I only then spotted to be female. I felt her nose break, which was, as planned, accompanied by a gush of blood that splashed over my scalp.

I came from a generation that learned, on pain of a thrashing from your mother, that a boy should never raise a hand against a girl. This is probably what delayed my follow-up, which would have finished her off with a classic upper-cut to her exposed jaw. My hesitation was enough to provide an opening for her to knee my groin, leaving me rolling on the floor in excruciating agony, unable even to breathe. My brain was still struggling to come up with a counter-attack when I blacked out.

***

Waking up was a process of going from unconsciousness to pain. The agony in my groin dominated everything else. There was only a growing disconnect between the recognition that I was still alive and the awareness that the intruder could have done anything she wanted to respond to the damage I had inflicted on her. I slowly opened my eyes to see a face glaring at me from very close proximity: well within what the woke-crowd would call *my personal space*.

Blood was dripping onto me from her shattered nose and, already, it was clear that she would have a couple of spectacular black eyes. *Maybe one more hit to her nose…*

"Don't even think about it, you sad old git," she growled, the impact of the threat lessened by a snort and a messy spit to keep blood from running down her throat. "I'm supposed to take you to meet my Mum, my boss that is," she was clearly caught out saying too much. "Anyway, just do as I fucking tell you and maybe I won't mash what's left of your aged testicles."

"Miriam," I groaned, "don't let it be fucking Miriam."

"Fucking Miriam is probably what got you into this mess in the first place," my nemesis smiled maliciously, "don't you think so, Dad?"

Could it possibly be my daughter who was still staring into my eyes as she stabbed a hypodermic into my neck and I lapsed again into unconsciousness?

Chapter 2: Rachel

"Fuck, fuck, fuck, fuckity-fuck!" *How the bloody hell did that old bastard manage to break my fucking nose?* Miriam had warned me that he was more dangerous than he looked, but my mom could rarely be trusted to be telling the truth about anything. I wondered yet again why I ever agreed to join her in her dubious *national security* operations. A little voice in the back of my head reminded me: *lots of money, a glamorous lifestyle and regular opportunities to fuck-up bad guys. Yes, it has its positive aspects.*

Anyway, instead of walking this ancient fart out of here, I now needed to move to plan B. I already knew where the chambermaids kept the trollies that they used for moving used towels and bedding to the basement for pick-up by a laundry service van and had the app to summon such a van already loaded. Fundamentally, this should be a fairly straightforward extraction, but it now required that I avoid anyone en route. The clothes that I wore would not look out of place for service staff, but my bloody visage would certainly attract attention.

I had a quick look in a mirror and saw that my nose was bent to the side. *Supposed to let a doctor do this, but anyway...*

"Shite!" I cursed aloud at the shock of pain when I pulled my nose straight. The flow of blood increased markedly and I bent forward to stop it running down my throat. I held just below the bridge of my nose between finger and thumb of my left hand and then hit the wrist hard with my right. Another excruciating jolt of pain, but the flow of blood decreased considerably.

I spent five minutes in the bathroom, stuffing torn tissue up my nostrils to stem the residual bleeding and then washed the blood from my face and neck. There was, however, nothing I could do about my rapidly-bruising face and the blood-stains on my white t-shirt.

A quick rummage through my victim's luggage revealed a broad-brimmed hat and a grey cardigan, which was much too big but less noticeably so when the sleeves were rolled up. *Not ideal, but maybe enough to get by.*

Picking up a laundry trolley proved no problem, as the corridor outside the bedroom was presently empty and these were found at in a room beside the service elevator located at the end of the floor. Back in his room, all I had to do was lift my captive into the laundry sack. Unfortunately, in the process this revealed that the old bugger was nude below his bath robe. *What a truly awful sight! Euthanasia should be compulsory when your body looks as bad as that.*

As quickly as possible, I covered the body in a pile of bloody towels – hoping that these would divert attention from myself in case I bumped into anyone. As it transpired, this precaution was unnecessary. *Finally a stroke of luck.* My path to the service elevator and then through the basement to the waiting van was completely clear.

The van was autonomous and a simple hack redirected it to my extraction pick-up point, where

Miriam would be waiting. It seemed that I was finally getting a break until I climbed into the back of the dusty van and sneezed. Blood immediately started to pour from my nose. "Fuck, fuck, fuck, fuckity-fuck!"

Chapter 3: Jim

The next couple of days were a drug-addled phantasmagoria. Firstly, I seemed to be somewhere remote on the west coast of Vancouver Island, where I could see a young bald eagle perched outside my window. Then I was moved to Vancouver itself, the sirens at night a regular disturbance that seemed typical of the centre of this fentanyl-zombie-infested city. Then a move to somewhere in the middle of fuck-all. Osoyoos, it was called. Rather idyllic in a bizarre manner, but still in the middle of fuck-all.

There I met Miriam. While I stared at her in shock, she casually handed me a glass filled with a vile green fluid. "Drink this! It'll counter all the stuff that Rachel's been pumping into you."

I gulped the drink down and was amazed at how quickly the fog that I'd been living in for the last few days cleared. *Miriam fucking Isaacs seems to have a daughter called Rachel: how fucking biblical.* "Miriam – what the holy fuck's going on here?"

Typically, the grey-haired Amazon rolled her eyes to express her disdain at my ignorance. "It seems that the *Powers Above*", she provided emphasis with air quotes, "have decided that we need to work together to sort out one of their little problems."

"Absolutely no way! Go directly to fuck and do not pass go. There is no possibility that…"

"Well, to tell the truth," she grinned ferally while breaking into my tirade, "it's actually a really fucking humungous problem. In such a case, opting out isn't an option."

"Jesus suffering Christ on a bike!" I rubbed my face as if it would help me to wake up from this nightmare. "I know that you're linked into the alphabet soup that comprises international so-called intelligence, but I'm only a techy and retired to boot. So, you can just fuck off."

"It doesn't work that way. It's like your UK Official Secrets Act. Once signed, it always applies."

"It's decades since I ever did anything for the Brits and, even then, I never signed the Act."

"Ah, that's the wonderful thing about that Act, it applies whether you've signed it or not."

"Whatever, but don't forget that I'm Swiss now. This means that you can stuff your Official Secrets up your well-used arse."

"You've still got a UK passport, so it still works. And, anyway, you never had problems using my arse in the past."

"Mum, for fuck's sake, too much information!" Only then I realised that Rachel was sitting in a corner on the large sitting room.

For a moment I was shocked into silence. Then the surreal nature of this situation crashed in on me. "Yes, indeed, I remember that you had a very tight arse. But, whatever I got up to there could not possibly have resulted in a daughter."

"He isn't as thick as you said he was," Rachel sniped.

"And," I interrupted to prevent any further calumny, "the fact that I had a vasectomy at least a decade before our unfortunate encounter would suggest that your bastard offspring was fathered by other than moi, regardless of whatever else I might have gotten up to in my drunken state."

"Moi, moi," Rachel parroted. "Is this supposed to indicate that he's polylingual?"

"Actually, he is polylingual," Miriam smiled in her scary manner. "This doesn't, of course, excuse him for being a cunt, in whatever language you want to choose. Chatte, fica, kisa, fitte… I'm sure he could add a few more obscure versions. But," she glared at me, "your genetic contribution to your daughter is undeniable."

"No way, no chance, not at all. Before and after you, I've had sex with hundreds of women…" I was distracted by her snort, but realised that my exaggeration might have been a bit obvious. "Well, dozens…" Another snort. "Whatever. Lots of women without any protection, other than STD prophylactics of course, and not a single resulting pregnancy. It was more likely to be a virgin birth in your case."

"And the genetic evidence?"

"Which I haven't seen and, in any case, couldn't be obtained without my permission." Rachel's sneer made it clear that lack of consent wouldn't be a consideration in their case.

"Does this mean you're admitting there's a chance?" Miriam smiled. "Can't you see a little bit of yourself in your daughter?"

20

"Myself? You've got to be joking. This girl's a nutcase. She broke into my hotel room and assaulted me."

"Well, you did break her nose…"

I looked at Rachel and could see that she still had the traces of a couple of black eyes, even though her nose had been straightened. "She fucking deserved it! What the fuck was she doing in my room anyway?"

"Well, if you hadn't been such a tosser, she'd have explained this to you and saved a lot of grief on both sides."

I felt a cold shiver run down my spine. "Wait a minute, did you blow up my holiday place in Hasliberg?"

"Of course not," Miriam grimaced. "That was the opposition and they're the reason that we have to work with you in the first place."

"Ah, so this wasn't planned as a family-bonding experience?"

"If it was my choice, I'd bond the toe of my boot with your flabby arse." Strangely, Miriam smiled as she said this. "Anyway, the three of us have a job to do."

"The three of us? I know that you're tough as nails, but why bring the child into it?"

"Fucking child! I'll fucking child you…" Rachel erupted from her seat and flew towards me, exactly as I expected her to. I am old and I am slow, but a programmed reflex easily turned her attack into a throw that slammed her against the wall.

"As I said, why the child?"

"She's a lot better than you think, just as I'm a lot better than you."

Well, the latter was something I couldn't disagree about if the topic was gratuitous violence and grievous bodily harm. "But why the fuck am I involved in the first place? You're an aging spook and I'm an even older risk analyst. We worked together once, almost three decades ago, and that didn't go well."

"You identified the sources of materials that the IRA were using to build a dirty bomb and I neutralised the threat. It was a great success and the reason that I was fast-tracked into the Interpol anti-terrorist group."

"You bombed the house of the husband and wife involved, killing them and their six children."

"I did no such thing…"

"Okay, you provided the address to the UDF and implied that the bomb was targeted on Belfast Protestants rather than central London. The net effect was the same."

"The bombers were scum and a lot more families would have died if we hadn't stopped them in their tracks. In any case, the message was important. We had to show that any escalation of terrorist threats would be met by escalated responses. And it worked. They never attempted anything like that again."

"That's just when you had your wicked way with me, shagging me while the parents and kids were being murdered."

Miriam shook her head, but did not attempt to rebut the accusations. "There are times when hard decisions need to be made. That's what I do."

"This has fuck-all to do with your decisions. You get turned on by violence, the more extreme the better. I still remember it: you were completely on fire. I was two-thirds pissed, but you still managed to shag my brains out. It's burned into my mind. You know, I fell in love with you then, would have done anything for you."

Further hyperbole was avoided by Rachel making gagging noises while she pretended to shove her fingers down her throat.

"Anyway, that didn't last long. A couple of days later, I heard that you were shagging the UVF bastard who actually carried out the bombing. Of course, being the evil bitch that you are, you then betrayed him to the IRA and he was assassinated a week afterwards."

"You actually weren't supposed to know about that. But, anyway, it just tidied things up in a manner that both sides could live with. They may pretend to be adults, but the active members of these terrorist organisations are just kids having pissing contests in a sandpit. The grown-ups who run things behind the scenes are happy to manipulate them, but wouldn't touch any of them with a bargepole in real life."

"And you're an adult? You're a fucking psychopath!"

"Possibly so…" Now it was me snorting in response to her statement. "Probably so, but I do a job that needs to be done. I'd also much rather have it otherwise, but the best team for this option has been determined to be us and you."

"Mother and daughter psychopaths and a pensioner: what could possibly go wrong?"

Miriam grinned. "This is actually the good news. You haven't heard what our task is yet."

***

After this preliminary romp through parts of my history that I would rather forget, Rachel dug out some beers and snacks before we got down to the nitty-gritty. I could see that my nemesis and the munchkin from hell were waiting for me to start, so I slowly began to tease out the details that they seemed loth to put on the table.

Rubbing my forehead and flying by the seat of my pants, I started with the obvious. "It's terrorists again, with a nuclear component somewhere."

Two pairs of eyebrows raised, so it was clear that there was a bit of a communication gap between the Yanks and the UK embassy staff who had initially contacted me. "Not dirty bombs, as you already know how to handle these," I continued.

"Of course we do, Sherlock, you wrote the fucking book on those." Rachel was clearly unimpressed.

"But nuclear and risks for sure. You wouldn't have me here otherwise."

Miriam grinned. "See, I told you, he's not as fucking useless as he looks."

Rachel grimaced. "Maybe not totally useless, but we actually need someone useful."

"Yes, well, we'll come to that. But let's see what more he can deduce here." Miriam smiled in a way that sent shivers down my spine. "Why don't you outline the little problem that we've got to sort out?" She looked into my eyes and raised her eyebrows to emphasise the challenge.

"The Bern embassy crowd already mentioned nuclear threats, but I guess you've got some fuckwits targeting specific nuclear facilities. It was always going to happen, but that alone wouldn't be enough to force you to work with me." Rachel's look of surprise was reassuring in exactly the way that Miriam's smirk wasn't.

"Fine, you've got a group of loonies that you think want to bugger-up something nuclear," against my better judgement, I couldn't stop myself from going further. "They're not the usual terrorists, as you'd just fuck them over in your inimitable fashion." My glare in Miriam's direction had no discernible impact. "There are two options, therefore. Either you don't know who they are or you actually are fully aware of the bad guys involved, but can't touch them."

I gave them my most annoyingly smug smile, which caused Rachel to give the game away. A simple squirm was enough. "Okay, it's the latter. Why don't you just drop all the rest of this spook, posturing rigmarole and tell me exactly what's going on."

Miriam turned to her daughter with a grin. "I told you, he's the guy for this task."

"But he's too fucking old!"

"Old, yes, but he knows this stuff and age gives him decades of experience to draw on. And, by the way, he also just tossed your young, Marine-trained bod across the room."

"A fluke! No chance he'd be able to do that again."

"He also broke your nose…"

Rachel rubbed her face with her hands, clearly seeking a way out of her nightmare. "Two flukes…"

Miriam frowned. "Don't underestimate this old codger. He may look like a feeble pensioner: actually, in fact, he is a pensioner with a host of medical issues. But he's worked in the same counter-terrorist area that we do for his entire life. The fact that he's lived long enough to get a pension speaks for itself."

"Okay, ladies," I interrupted, "this is all very well, but I want to get back home and away from you lunatics ASAP. This is especially important as, despite all these peregrinations in the backwoods of Canada, you first need to convince me that you've got your mole nailed down."

"What mole?" Rachel sounded bewildered, although I noted that her mother did not seem in the slightest surprised.

I simply raised my eyebrows in Miriam's direction. "Okay, we certainly have leaks from our team. There's no way that you could have been targeted in Hasliberg otherwise. This is why there are now only the three of us involved here."

"And, of course, that's why you have me playing a critical role in this caper. An attack like that in Switzerland wouldn't have been considered if I wasn't a threat of some kind."

Miriam closed her eyes and grimaced. "Yes, right, this indicates that we do actually seem to need you. You scare the opposition, which has got to be a good thing. Why this might be, I haven't worked out as yet."

"Why do we have to go through all these fucking mating dances? Just tell me who's behind the threat. I can already guess that it's a Yank. We're in North America: not the US, but conveniently close to the border. So, it's either a politician or one of the mega-rich."

I laughed. "Miriam, you really shouldn't have involved the child. I can read her like a book. It's a mega-rich politician." Rachel's attack was so predictable that I had to do no more than twist to the side to allow her to barrel into her mother, with both of them ending up on the floor. "Do you want me to guess, or will you finally stop with these fucking mind games?"

She told me. My jaw dropped and the women burst into laughter. I really wouldn't have guessed that, although the profile certainly fit my expectations.

***

The Vice-president has a strangely invisible role in the US political system. The media concentrate almost entirely on the President and, depending on the constellations involved, the leaders of Congress and the Senate. This contrasts with the potential of this role, which can catapult the incumbent into being the most powerful person in the world, at least as far as the majority of the US electorate are concerned.

Although all Miriam's evidence was circumstantial, she had built up a strong case that Alice Beall was a woman with the ambition to go to the top, regardless of what the costs might be. Her political position was rather strange, being right-wing but strongly supportive of sustainable energy and rabidly anti-nuclear. She had, somehow or other, managed to make herself a poster-girl for green, tree-huggers. Of course, as always, there was a hidden agenda. Her family's wealth, built up by surfing the environmentalist wave, was increasingly coming under threat as the negative fallout of rushing into sustainable-energy projects without full life-cycle analysis became obvious.

The crux seemed to be that, in order to prevent a backlash against sustainables, she had decided to support terrorists with radical anti-nuclear positions in the hope of removing backing for this other key source of carbon-free power.

I frowned as I thought through this story. "It seems barely credible that a woman with so much to lose would get involved with something as risky as this."

"She's got a hell of a lot to lose if she does nothing. There's a class action going through the courts that could lead to legislation requiring that solar panels are at least 90% recyclable and also that costs for this are borne by the manufacturer – even retrospectively. This is going to be a huge financial hit for all those involved and, even if future costs are passed onto the purchaser, it'll certainly price solar out of the market for many applications. This requirement for recycling will also hit some other alternative energy options, in particular wind, but have minimal impact for nuclear as the quantities of waste per unit power generated are trivial for most reactor designs"

"Okay, I can see that and I imagine that there are many other vested interests supporting her. But would the Veep really sponsor terrorists with the aim of causing another Fukushima or Chernobyl?"

Miriam shook her head, clearly disappointed by my naivety. "That bitch would nuke Washington DC if it would further her political ambitions."

I smiled back at her. "It appears that you're caught between a rock and a hard place. If this plot comes to light and you've done nothing about it, your head will roll as you're where the buck stops in terms of anti-terrorist operations. However, if you're spotted taking any action against her, VP Beall will have your head on a plate."

"You don't need to sound so happy about that. By now, however, it's no longer just me: it's us. We're definitely caught between a truly massive rock and a really fucking hard place. As you spotted, my office is already compromised. Initially, I hadn't even decided that I was going to bring you in on this: you were just one on a list of options. Actually, fairly far down the list, due to your age. But the Brits thought I should at least talk to you and the opposition evidently picked this up and considered you enough of a threat to justify extreme prejudice. This in Switzerland, of all bloody places."

"And this tells you what?" I grinned in a manner that was sure to annoy her.

"That in terms of whatever action they're thinking about, they consider you a particularly serious threat…"

"God only knows why," Rachel contributed in a stage whisper.

"And that they have amazing resources at their beck and call," I added, seeing that this was a point not yet noted by my nemesis.

Rachel clearly spotted that her mother had been forced into the defensive and piped up. "So, your mission, should you choose to accept it, is to identify who we're up against, what their targets are and neutralise them ASAP. Of course, in this case, refusal to accept is not an option," she grinned in a distinctly evil manner.

"Not an easy job," Miriam conceded. "But there is the incentive that, if you don't get them first, they'll certainly kill not only you, but also me and your daughter."

"Me, I certainly don't want killed. You, on the other hand? Do you really think I'd go out of my way to save your psycho arse? I'd help them, given the choice."

"A bit harsh, but I can see where this is coming from." The object of my vitriol was typically unperturbed. "But have you got no feeling at all for your daughter?"

"Firstly, I don't believe that I have any genetic contribution to your bastard daughter. Even if I had, she must have 50% from you, so probably should have been drowned at birth for the betterment of humanity."

Out of the corner of my eye I caught a shocked look on Rachel's face and immediately felt like a complete arsehole. I hardly even knew the girl, but was saying things guaranteed to hurt her deeply. Despite the fact that she was clearly a total fruitloop, it was her mother to blame, not the girl. "Okay, right, whatever. I'll help, as I really don't seem to have any alternative. Give me a laptop with all the files that you have on this case and I'll look through them."

Miriam's look of relief was unusually obvious, so I decided to take advantage of it. "I've just realised that I'm starving, so get room service to send me lunch. A huge steak, medium-rare, with all the trimmings and a bottle of their best red wine would be just right. Both of you can now fuck off while I'm working. Just toddle off and strangle rabbits or torture kittens; whatever you usually do with your spare time."

I got a death stare from Rachel, but Miriam only smiled. "We've got connecting rooms, so we'll go through to the other one and raid the mini-bar." As she opened the connecting door, she turned and raised her eyebrows. "This is booked for a family: the parents' room and a bedroom for the mature daughter. Why don't you think about that?"

"Jesus Christ," I groaned. "I'd jump into bed with my granny before I'd even consider another encounter with you."

"Oh, so incest is your thing now. Should I bring in Rachel for a threesome?"

"My gran has been dead for a decade. So, if you think necrophilia might be my thing, you and your get are more than welcome to prepare for some action."

Amazingly, Miriam had no response, but Rachel slammed the door with unnecessary violence.

***

Apparently, our hotel was located in the grounds of a top-level BC winery. The steak was very good, as expected in Canada, but the Bordeaux-blend wine was truly exceptional. I had no idea that the Rockies produced anything of this quality, but global warming was inevitably buggering-up all traditional ideas of viniculture. Many of the Old World classics were being wiped out and replaced by New World wonders like this. I peered at the bottle: Nk'Mip vineyard. I had no idea of even how to pronounce the name.

I read Miriam's files while dining and a picture was emerging. This was helped considerably by the knowledge that our opponents were extremely worried about me being brought into the case. The attack on my humble abode in Hasliberg had been a major miscalculation on their part. If not for that, I would have simply refused to be drawn into anything that involved any sort of interaction with Miriam. This meant that, despite their mole in

32

Miriam's organisation, they certainly did not know our history in any kind of detail.

It would be easy to find out the old dirty-bomb story. Indeed, that would certainly be prominent in Miriam's CV. For a terrorist with nuclear ambitions, picking up that she was considering me to support an investigation of whatever the Veep's crowd were up to, must have rung alarm bells. However, the extreme over-reaction to this implied that they thought that I could be a serious threat.

I felt blocked for a moment, before the answer dawned on me. "Evil bitches! You've certainly got this room bugged, so get you arses in here now. I think I've got a lead. But, before anything else, order me another bottle of this wine along with a cheeseboard."

***

Before Miriam could say a word, Rachel couldn't contain herself. "What, you've worked it out already, over dinner? We've had an alpha team on that for weeks…"

"Calm down girl," Miriam looked like a cat who had just hit the cream jackpot. "He'll explain it to us in his typically annoying manner and then we can decide if he really has something or if his aged brain is no longer able to cut the mustard, as they put it in the land of his birth."

"Well, it should have been clear to anyone of the meanest abilities that…" I ground to a halt as I happened to be looking out of the window onto the

33

lake below us at this point. "Fuck! Does anyone else know that we're here?"

The ladies jumped to my side, so my concern was clearly evident. "Unless my aged eyes betray me, that's a military seaplane landing on the lake, which isn't something I'd expect to happen in a place like this."

"Fuck, fuck, fuck," Miriam mumbled while she fumbled with an over-large mobile phone.

Rachel simply grabbed me and dragged me into the interconnected room, before pulling a huge kitbag from the side of the bed. "You can shoot, I assume." A roll of her eyes conveyed that denial would have been laughable, while she pulled a wide assortment of weapons loose and threw them on the floor. "I'll find something for you here."

"I'm a pacifist and want nothing to do with the weapons of war," I said just to annoy her. "However, this compact SAM whatsit might be just the very dab."

"SAM means surface to air missile, you daft old tosser. Can't you see that it's already landed?"

"So what? It's actually just a place-to-place missile and, as such, doesn't give a fuck what medium the target is in." I opened the door onto the balcony, pointed the device in roughly the right direction and pressed *heat-seeker* on the firing pad. This would have been the perfect put-down if the recoil from the ejection mechanism hadn't knocked me backwards over a sun-lounger to send me crashing onto my backside. Luckily, the ladies were more intent on the missile's trajectory and so their gasps as the seaplane exploded in a fireball covered my struggles to get back onto my feet.

"Fucking hell, that's hardcore!" Rachel was clearly impressed.

"Christ on a bike! I hadn't realised that there wasn't a safety on that weapon," I confessed. "I was just going to lock on the target so that I could check for any obvious electronic counter-measures. Anyway, can I assume that you're sure that this was definitely full of bad guys?" I asked. "It could, potentially, have been a plane full of survivalist nutters who've purchased a military surplus machine."

Rachel looked worried, but Miriam laughed aloud. "You know this isn't the case and, even if it was, I can live with some collateral damage on this job. If it was the nutters that you mentioned, we have to fuck off ASAP before they start investigating what took out that plane. If it's our opponents, we should have been away long before that, as they'll inevitably have a satellite focused on us by now."

"And if it really was bad guys, your entire network is more compromised than you thought. How do we even start to defend ourselves against the resources that the Veep can call on?"

"Not easy, but get your shit together and we'll hit the road, heading north."

"Isn't that where the wildfires are at this time of year? Anybody leaving here who's halfway sensible will head east, west or south."

"Exactly, so we head north. The fires and smoke will make it a lot harder for them to track us."

"These are the fires and smoke that'll kill us if we get caught up in them," I pointed out.

"Exactly! It's a no-fly zone for anything but firefighters. So that's where we're going." I was exposed to a commanding glare that I remembered well from the past.

"I'm not happy with this," I tried my best glare back. "What good does it do to anyone if we end up as over-done barbeque along with the rest of the wildlife there?"

"Consider the options. I'm going north with your soon-to-be-beloved daughter. You can stay here, be captured and then be tortured to explain a plan that you don't actually know. The end result is that you get shot in the back of the head and disappear to a hidden grave."

"Or a pig farm," Rachel grinned maliciously.

"In any case, it's your choice."

I glared at Miriam. "Fuck! I hate you all of the time, but even more when you're correct! I'll carry Rambo-junior's hardware to the car that I assume that you have outside. As you know, beyond the clothes I'm wearing, I don't have any other personal shit at the present moment."

"Don't get your knickers in a twist, Dad," Rachel had to get in her penny's worth. "This is what we do: the difficult immediately and the impossible takes only a little longer."

"You may think that quote's a West Point thing, but Lady Aberdeen initially used it to support

36

prohibition. That actually did turn out to be impossible."

"For fuck's sake, stop the bon mot pissing contest and get your arses into the car," Miriam ordered. "We're out of here in ten."

Chapter 4: Rachel

It was actually eight minutes later when we drove off in Miriam's nondescript SUV. It had been parked beside an equally characterless panel van, which I had used to transport my kidnap- victim's drugged-up bod. I was driving, Miriam shotgun, with the old coffin-dodger slumped in the back. I simply followed Miriam's planned route, driving consistently 20 k above the posted speed limit, whatever it was. The route varied between dual carriageway, single roads with occasional overtaking lanes and simple roads where the overtaking option was indicated by broken central lines.

I just could not get my head around this Jim Forsyth guy. He manages to annoy me even more than my bitch mother does, and that was saying something. He also looked like a strong wind would blow him over and yet, after breaking my nose, managed to defend against a further two attacks that should have floored him. Of course, in retrospect, I could see that he had very deliberately provoked these attacks, but, even then...

Also taking out that seaplane. Was it really a mistake or was he actually trying to force us to run? If it had been loaded up with bad guys, then pre-emptive retaliation was a sensible move. But he couldn't possibly know for sure. Like Mum, I could live with collateral damage, but I'd want a bit more evidence of a threat before wiping out a plane that could be full of civilians.

He clearly hates my mother, which seems completely understandable if what he was saying is true. I've heard a different take of things from Miriam, but I know that she lies as a matter of course, whether it actually serves any purpose or not. In any case, it would fit her profile to be shagging a colleague while her victims were being murdered – and also later screwing the murderer before he was, in turn, taken out.

Well, at least he seems to be good at this profiling, risk-assessment shit. With a bit of luck, he'll find a way for us to re-can these worms and then we can get shot of him. *Or shoot him, should that be required.* I couldn't help grinning at the thought.

Chapter 5: Jim

Unlike most drivers on Canadian roads, Rachel took every opportunity to overtake. This often caused flashing headlights from oncoming traffic, although I didn't spot any case when this was in any way justified. Maybe my experience of regularly driving a sports car over the Swiss Alps had something to do this this. Gradually, I realised that Talking Heads were playing on the music system, certainly Miriam's choice. It was *Once in a lifetime* and I realised this completely summarised my present situation: *what am I doing here?*

"Okay, Miriam, we're now heading towards immolation. I guess there's some kind of hidden plan in here somewhere. How about letting me know what this is?"

"The plan in terms of where we're going is straightforward. The highway is closed by fires just north of the town of Barriere, so appropriately named for the current situation. We then take a dirt track that wends its way to somewhere that we can hide out for a bit. It's just south of the town of Clearwater."

"From what I've seen on the warning billboards, there are fires all around that area."

"Yes, but we'll be paralleling the railroad tracks, which should be protected. Probably." Her grin was obviously intended to annoy me. "We can hang out in this sleepy retreat for a couple of days. It's a place that makes Osoyoos look like centre of the universe. From there, we head on to Jasper when they open the highway."

"You're planning all this based on guesses of how the wildfires will develop? That's loopy!"

"Yes, isn't it? This is the only way that we're going to survive, given the forces being set up against us. Our advantage is that we're lunatics, who don't give a fuck. The opposition have no easy way to respond to that. They always assume that we'll behave in a logical manner."

Against my long-established, conservative nature, I couldn't help being attracted by this wild approach. I still worked after formal retirement, but that was just for something to do. I certainly didn't need the money or the inevitable stresses involved. Even if it was risky, something as inherently crazy as this op was certainly better than simply fading away into my dotage.

"Bugger it, but you can count me in. The next bit'll be tricky, though. Very tricky. But I think I can see a thread here."

Miriam grinned, so I wasn't sure if I should be happy or very worried.

"Anyway, as I started to tell you before our hurried departure from Osoyoos, the attack on me was definitely a mistake."

"Yes, I know. It confirmed my suspicions that I had a mole in my team. These suspicions are what finally led to my decision to bring you in. Against my better judgement, I should note."

"But there's more than that. Simply being aware that I might be approached was enough to justify a very public bit of overkill."

Rachel raised her eyebrows. "You really think that you're so much more important than the rest of us?"

"Clearly, or I wouldn't have been the first to be selected for assassination. Before Osoyoos, how many attempts on your life have there been in the last year or so?"

Rachel looked seriously pissed off, as if the lack of assassination attempts was a blot on her copybook. "Anyway," I continued after waiting to see if Miriam would jump in, "someone thinks I'm a threat to what they're planning and the possible seaplane-borne attack on the two of you occurred only after you were hooked up with me."

"So, what are our options?" Miriam looked as if she was chewing broken glass when she finally recognised that she was out of her depth here.

"The clever option, of course, is that you get me sent home and we never, ever, see each other again."

Miriam grimaced, but had to concede. "Not an option now. The fact that we're being targeted proves that the opposition are worried about us... about you," she corrected in response to my raised eyebrows. "The threat is so great that we've got to go for it, regardless of the risks."

"Who this we, white woman?" I struggled to get a Tonto kind of pronunciation to highlight the joke, but failed miserably even to my own ears. I decided to simply cut to the chase. "So, what's in it for me?"

"For fuck's sake, Jim, you know that you're going to do the job. This is just a typical, fucking-

42

about, mating-dance of the type that you said you hate! What do you want?"

"Well," I raised a finger to my chin as if deep in thought, "maybe a blow-job would be nice."

"Okay, whatever, let's just get this over and done..."

"Mum, what the fuck're you saying? You're not going to let him blackmail you like this?"

I burst out laughing. "Of course she would. It's what she is. She'd happily let me shag her senseless if it meant that I'd do what she wanted. Indeed, if this was to be followed by wholescale slaughter, it'd be her shagging me. Like the last time. But this time I want the BJ from the younger, prettier psycho, whether or not she's my offspring."

I basked in two basilisk stares while I thought back on the drugged-out misery that this pair had inflicted on me. *Sometimes life is really good.*

Typically, Miriam was the first to respond. "You're an evil bastard, but what the fuck's a blowjob in the greater scheme of things? She'll do it."

"Will I fuck! There is absolutely no way that I'd touch that smelly old fossil with a ten-foot pole. I'd rather gargle sulphuric acid that let that fucker put his shrivelled little willy into my mouth."

I was laughing so much at this point that I almost fell off my seat. "Do you think that I'm so far into my dotage that I'd let either of you bring your teeth anywhere close to my family jewels. I already have the option of internet porn and masturbation, which allows my very modest needs to be satisfied. Nevertheless, that was a nice thought, Miriam, prostituting your offspring to further your agenda. I would guess that this guarantees that your daughter, brainwashed though she may be, is going to really detest you now."

The looks of anger, disappointment and hate that the women exchanged only made me laugh louder.

Miriam shook her head and glared at me. "This is the *you* that convinced me that we'd never have a life together. You're a complete shit."

"Regardless of the *me*, I wouldn't have anything to do with a psycho like you."

"I think that you liked me, maybe loved me, but you've always had the talent to identify the weak points of everyone around you and exploit them for your amusement. Exactly as you did now. I actually wasn't going to do it, but the genetic data that proves Rachel's parentage will get downloaded to your laptop. I may be a psycho, probably am a psycho," she shook her head, "but that isn't what the source of the problem is. It's not that you can't live with someone like me, it's the hard fact that I wouldn't live with someone like you."

I was shocked into silence, then could only come up with a feeble rejoinder. "That's something that makes me feel like a reasonable human being, an idea that you just can't get your warped head around."

***

We arrived in a suitably-remote resort south of Clearwater and I immediately retired to one of the rooms in the cabin, locking the door behind me. I really couldn't fault Miriam's assessment and was haunted by the expression on Rachel's face after she'd presented it. I had always been aware that I was a bit of an insensitive shit – probably typical of alpha-males of my generation. But it was hard to have its impacts mirrored in front of me so graphically. *On the other hand, this might be just the incentive that I need to nail down my links to these terrorists.*

I set up an argumentation model on the laptop that I'd been provided with. It could be someone who simply knew my work, but that didn't seem compatible with the violence of the Swiss attack. Someone who knew me personally would be much more likely. Indeed, someone in a relevant technical area who really hated me would best fit the profile. Unfortunately, given my history, this didn't narrow down the field much. I knew that I was infamous for my tendency to speak my mind, no matter who might be hurt by it. I always believed that this was part of the scientific method, the essential critical assessment of what others had done. But that was certainly not appreciated by many at the top of ivory towers, who considered themselves above criticism. Unfortunately, it was also the case for many working in industry or consultancy, where any negative reviews could lead to decreased credibility and, more importantly, loss of income.

I put my head in my hands and tried to concentrate. The more I thought through things, the surer I was that pure academics could be discounted. However much some of them hated my guts, they would never have contact with the type of loonies that must be behind this plot. Most probably a consultant of some kind, as they make money out of their reputations and, in many cases, would provide anything the client wanted if paid enough. This was a smaller group but, nevertheless, over the decades that I'd been shitting on crap science, there were a significant number of the victims of my technical hatchet-jobs that would come into question.

Even then, most consultants, regardless how dodgy, wouldn't have services to sell that would bring them to the attention of plutocrats with an apocalyptic nuclear agenda. This was the key, so I couldn't help muttering to myself. "For the guys who're active in the nuclear remediation field, this'd be a win-win situation. They get paid megabucks to cause a nuclear catastrophe and, regardless of what happens to the future of nuclear power, they can be guaranteed big budgets for the subsequent clean-up and waste disposal."

Worldwide there were quite a few possible candidates but, if you narrowed in down to individuals who would be worried about me being involved, no more than a half-dozen or so. *Evenly split between those with their own consultancies and those embedded within huge organisations but with the flexibility to run their own little fiefdoms without any serious oversight. I really can't see how to get much further without more input.* "Okay, you've probably, let's get together to try and narrow down the bad guys a little," I shouted.

Seconds later the connecting door to the other bedroom opened and the women emerged, not even attempting to hide the fact that they had been listening at the door.

"Right, I've narrowed down options from the entire population of the planet to six reasonably-likely candidates. If we worked together, we could certainly get that down to two or three."

Miriam looked like the cat who had caught the canary, until I continued. "So now we need to discuss my honorarium. I may be retired with a good pension, but I've got a number of expensive vices that I'd like to indulge before I plop my clogs. As a techno-geek, I usually bill at around a couple of thousand Euros a day. Fucking terrible, if you think that lawyers and money traders straight out of Uni can expect much more, regardless of how fucking useless they are. So, ten kay a day: how would that work for you?"

"Fine, you've got it. Give me the names." Her grin really pissed me off.

I mentally kicked myself. I could have put another order of magnitude onto my rate and she'd have accepted it. But the bitch knew that, as a self-proclaimed *honest consultant*, normally a contradiction of terms, I'd stick to my offer once it had been specified.

"Okay, give me your e-links." Both women were now pulling out powerful-looking palmtops. I hit the key to transfer my argumentation file to the gruesome twosome. "I'd tend to go for the small consultancies, as they've less to lose and can be more avaricious. But look through the list for yourselves and see what you think."

After scanning my file, mother and daughter looked at each other in amazement. Miriam had her usual poker face, but Rachel punched the air. "That's it, we've got the fuckers now!"

Miriam frowned. "Don't get carried away, it could be a coincidence.

"What, six people in the world and one of these is the Veep's cousin?"

"Who is?" I hated to ask, but had no option.

Miriam couldn't stop her daughter. "Denis Buck! He's the senior technical manager of International Remediations Inc." She muttered something and then displayed a website on her palmtop.

"Denis? No, I doubt that he's really a credible target here. I included him for the sake of completeness. He fits the profile, but the guy's a moron. As I've repeatedly pointed out, this bloke is thick as a brick. Wouldn't know the scientific method if he fell over it. I can't believe he still uses his doctor title, after I showed that his thesis came from a mill in India."

Miriam grinned. "I take it from this that he hates you like death."

"Wouldn't piss on me if I was on fire," I agreed.

"So, he really does fit the profile, doesn't he?"

"He would, if he wasn't such a fuckwit. Organising piss-ups in a brewery? Not a chance! I bet he wears slip-on shoes because he hasn't managed the technical challenges of laces yet."

Rachel had been following my tirade while she paged through her palmtop. "Fuck, Jim, you actually put that in print as part of your review of one of his papers!"

"Well, I'm not renowned for being politically correct to technical bampots."

"Jesus, you weren't holding back in other reviews either. *Paper fit only to line the budgie's cage* or *should be burned and scattered to the winds*. Is this normal?"

I shrugged. "Nobody should send a paper to me for review if they don't want me to be completely honest."

"Honest? This seems to be gratuitously brutal."

I smiled at Rachel, amused by her naiveté. "Brutal is the only way to avoid getting into endless cycles of resubmission of modified versions of the same crap. The reason that I get such papers is that the editors know I'll get rid of technical bullshit as efficiently as possible. Actually, such review input for the editors used to be confidential, but the advent of AI-driven plagiarism forced these onto open servers."

"Even so, the guy you're verbally abusing here has a senior position in one of the biggest companies in this field."

"Yes, that's exactly why some editors bring me in. His papers are not only shit, but have a political agenda directly related to his company. The usual academics are too afraid to go up against an organisation that provides funding for many of them. I've got no such links, so can speak the truth."

"The truth according to Jim!"

49

"You know, girl, you're not totally thick, but have a lot to learn about the real world." I smiled in response to her glower. "In science – or anything else for that matter – there is no such thing as absolute truth. I've always said that if anyone found anything in my publications that they could prove was fundamentally incorrect, I'd happily admit to my error and retract the paper."

"And have you?"

I shrugged. "Of course. There are a couple of rather embarrassing cases, but most were relatively trivial. Importantly, this contrasts with a fuckwit like Denis, who has never admitted any of his numerous errors, many of them so fundamental that they repudiate the entire basis of the reported work."

Miriam broke in before I could add any more to defend my treatment of technical rivals. "So, let's say it is Denis Buck. What can we expect? He was a Marine. A major, no less. Served in a couple of North African hellholes between his first degree and going on for his doctorate."

"Actually, I knew about that. Seems like the Marines are a family tradition. Fast track to an officer position and thereafter into a senior management position in one of their companies. A lot of wank! He would have better using the time to learn the fundamental technical basis of the job he was taking on."

"Jim, you may think this man is a tosser," Miriam glared at me, "but can't you see that he's the most likely candidate. The Marines link could easily explain why we had a military seaplane in Osoyoos."

"Nope, you're barking up the wrong tree there. The loonies carrying out the attacks are military-trained, but not part of US armed forces."

"Why do you think that? Too disorganised, not professional enough?"

I smiled at Rachel. "You've been in the forces, that's clear. So if you were to characterise your experience, would it be organised and professional?"

"The Marines are the world's most professional group of elite soldiers. There's no doubt about that."

I couldn't help laughing. "Even Micky-Mouse nations like the UK have the SAS and SBS, who could walk though Marines without breaking a sweat. Then there are specialist groups in countries like Israel, who've been actually fighting terrorists for more than half a century."

"Can we just stop this bickering?" Miriam sighed. "From what we see here, this Buck bloke should be the focus of our attentions. If not him, who else should we consider?"

"I don't know, maybe Maria Sinclair?"

"Just a small consultancy, but stomped on by you several times. *As shown in this paper, unable even to spell uncertainty correctly* and *so fundamentally flawed that `not even wrong` seems the appropriate term to use.* She must really love you." Rachel was clearly enjoying her role as agent provocateur.

"Yes, but unlike Denis, not thick at all. Very smart, I'd reluctantly admit, but lazy as hell. Very

51

ambitious, but with too many irons in the fire. Despite the potential to be very good technically, her main aim is to be mega-rich, regardless of the cost to others. She spent a lot of time providing arguments to minimise apparent impacts of environmental pollution, while working with the polluters to ensure that, if they were caught out, the remediation work was done as cheaply as possible."

"I can understand why this woman isn't on your Christmas card list, but I'm not convinced that she'd be the prime suspect here." Miriam glanced at Rachel. "What do you think, love?"

"I'm sure that she'd carry out this kind of work without any hesitation whatsoever. A mega-bitch without the slightest trace of scruples."

"Sounds like your Mum," I muttered, drawing a pair of death stares.

"However, more to the point, I don't think she's got the contact network to get involved in something this extreme," Rachel continued. "She's carved out a niche market that involves helping mega-corporations escape the penalties for their past sins, and is making a fortune out of it. I can't see that she'd have an incentive to risk all of that by getting involved in something inherently more troublesome, especially if she got caught."

I shrugged my shoulders and nodded. "You could be right, but if I had to select someone who'd blow me to fuck in an instant, she'd be high on the list."

"I thought this Ozzy woman would be a fit for top of that long list. The rabid environmentalist."

"McCabe, yes, a true nutcase. Involved in lots of eco-terrorism, first with Greenpeace and then with more extreme loonies. She would, indeed, pay her own money to have a chance to stab me to death."

"How did you insult her? I don't see anything in open publications."

"She's not a publications person. More of a firebrand at rallies and demonstrations. She's an evil little shit who'll happily fabricate any kind of lies to motivate the great unwashed to support her crazy crusades. I've served a few times as expert witness in court cases against her. Actually got her jailed a couple of times, although not for as long as I would've liked. She was also heavily fined a couple of times, which must have crippled a couple of her campaigns."

"What about technically? Is she capable of doing this kind of work?"

"Probably, because she's got a very extensive network of eco-loonies, which must cover everything on the technical side that she'd need."

"So, if you were to choose between her and Denis, who'd you think would be our top priority?" Miriam frowned, clearly wanting me to make a decision that I thought was premature."

"Back off a bit now, this is completely ignoring all the other potential candidates that I listed. What about Smith, for example?"

"You've got to be joking!" Rachel grinned. "You've repeatedly pointed out that he's a butterfly who makes his living out of getting into the places that are hot with the media at any point in time, and then spouting, in your own words, technical gobbledegook."

"Okay, fair point. Right, if there had to be two options, I'd first choose evil McCabe and, reluctantly, would accept that fuckwit Buck also fits the profile."

"So, bottom line, you think it's McCabe?"

"Actually, the more I think about it, yes. She's not smart enough to do it on her own, but is very clever in the way she manipulates the idiots who think that the sun shines out of her arse."

"Okay, we've got a result." Miriam finally looked really happy as opposed to the simulations of this that her psychopathic nature generated. "So, we just need to take her out and the job is done."

"That's going to be tricky," I felt a surge of joy as I rained on her parade, "as Annie's already dead."

"For fuck's sake, Jay, what are you on about? Why would we ever be interested in a corpse?"

"Ah, that's the tricky bit. She's legally dead, literally hoist by her own petard if you believe the media. But I don't think that's credible. There's no way she'd build her own bombs when she's got cannon-fodder to do it for her. There was a lot of pressure on her building up at that time, so I think her sudden death was more than a little suspicious. Strangely – or not so strangely – the official records are thin and there is absolutely no hard evidence to show that the incinerated body they recovered was hers. That's why she's still on my list."

Miriam and her daughter looked at each other, before Rachel asked the question that they must have been exchanging by maternal telepathy. "And where did she die?"

"You're asking me, rather than just googling it? Maybe you've guessed the answer already. Houston, Texas."

"The Veep's home state and the city where her brother is chief of police!" Rachel danced around the room in delight. "We've got them now."

"Got them how?" I broke in. "Everything we have so far is circumstantial. Do you think you can go up against the heavy-hitters that the Veep has behind her with this chain of suppositions?"

"Maybe not, but it should be easy to take out living-dead McCabe, which would buy us some time."

I shook my head. No matter what any genetic analysis showed, this girl was 100% Miriam without the smallest traces of me. "Rachel, think about this for a minute. Firstly, we don't know where McCabe is, because she's legally dead. Then, even if we could find her, can we murder her based on mere suspicions?" I held up my hand to forestall any discussion of pre-emptive retaliation. "But, worst of all, without McCabe to interrogate, we still have not a Scooby who the technical guys and gals who will actually implement this plan are. To be blunt, this buys us fuck-all time and actually makes the job much harder."

My supposed daughter seemed unused to such harsh treatment, so couldn't help glancing towards her mother for help.

This was not forthcoming. "He's right, you know." Miriam screwed up her eyes as if in pain.

"Looking like someone who should be sent to EXIT as soon as possible, he lulls you into a false sense of security. He's a physical wreck who'll soon be drooling into his porridge and wetting himself every night, but there's still a remnant of the functional brain that was very scary in its time."

I fought to avoid a giggle, which might have added weight to Miriam's analysis, and so contented myself with a smug smile. "Old and past my sell-by date, I most certainly am. And this bothers me not a jot! Because, as you've already admitted, either of you would give me a blow-job to keep me supporting you on this mega-fuckup. Is it me who's sad?"

I leaned back and stretched, bathing in their detestation of me. "You know, I do my very best work when I'm relaxed and, thinking about it in that way, a really good BJ would be exactly what the doctor ordered. So, while I'm working on what we need to do next, I'd appreciate if you'd contact the nearest brothel and have them send round the girl with the best mouth. If she looked like one of you, that'd be a bonus."

Typically, Miriam was completely unperturbed, although her daughter looked scandalised.

"Not a problem, Jim. Rachel, you'll see there are escort services agency in my *contacts* file. When you're making the order, add a couple of fit young lads for us. You won't need to include any other specifications as, by definition, they'll be nothing like this old tosser."

I laughed out loud, pleased to see that this almost caused a crack in Miriam's façade, but then was surprisingly disturbed by Rachel's look of dejection.

He mother clearly noticed this, but showed no pity. "Come girl, hop to it."

Now Miriam was on the receiving end of one of Rachel's glares, while she quickly worked on her laptop. "I want nothing to do with this. I'll order a man for you and a woman for him. I hope he's got genital warts and she's an old hag." This last was muttered, but she plainly intended that we would hear it.

"Ah, so I'm getting the one that looks like your mother," I laughed again.

"You're treading on thin ice here," Miriam warned me. "I'm prepared to put up with your crap until I don't need you anymore. Then you're dropped, forever, for all time."

"Is that supposed to be a threat? If I never saw you again in the rest of my life, it'd be too soon,"

Then she leant forward and kissed me.

Shoot me with a Taser and I couldn't have been more shocked. I truly detested this woman but, when her tongue entered my mouth, it took me back to the first time this had happened. To be honest about it, she'd effectively raped me. I had started off drunk but, within a few minutes, had sobered up enough to know what was going on. She was wild for sex and I'd been happy to go anywhere she was leading. My experience with women prior to this was limited, but a young nympho being hot to rumble was beyond anything I'd even dreamed about. Even after all these years, she was the memory that brought life to many of my internet porn fantasies.

"Oh, Mum, for God's sake, get a room."

Suddenly, I was brought back to reality. "No, not again, I'm not going there."

Miriam only smiled, aware that I was almost caught once again in the threads of her pheromone-baited web.

***

It took a while, but eventually my prostitute appeared. Unfortunately, or maybe fortunately, she looked nothing at all like my in-house nightmares. A petit redhead, barely out of her teens, who was sharp and polite, but basically interested only in earning some cash. I learned her name was Karen and that she was a student, but that was all that was required in terms of introductions.

We stripped off and I was pleased by her lack of reaction to the sight of my decrepit body. I was happy to restrict the action to cunnilingus while she gave me a hand job, the latter probably a bit more effort than it would have been with someone younger. Then I simply cuddled her to me and told her that she had already earned her fee but, if she'd stay with me for the night, I'd give her a large bonus on top of her standard rate.

She looked happy with the arrangement, but then frowned. "Do you snore? If you do, I'll need to put in earplugs."

"I probably do, but this should be worth another 10% for you having to put up with it."

"Right, fine. But I've found that, when Johns snore, a bit of oral manipulation helps to sort the problem."

"You are indeed a smart young lady. Let me know if that occurs, and it'll be a further 25% on top."

"It's sure to happen, it always does with snorers."

"I'm sure it will, you little minx. I'm now thinking about 30%."

Her bonus was up to 100% before the next morning, but worth every cent.

Chapter 6: Rachel

Christ but I really hate that guy. He's not only a fundamentally horrible bastard, but he also brings out the worst in my fucking Mum, who has been a total cunt since she came in contact with him. More of a cunt than usual, that is. I couldn't help smiling at the thought, but then this turned to a frown. *Making me act as a pimp to sort out prostitutes for the pair of them is the final straw.*

Despite my annoyance, I couldn't help thinking about the whores. The young man had been a veritable Adonis and Miriam had offered to share him, happy to include her daughter in a bit of ménage-a-trois. After making it more than clear what I thought about this fucked-up suggestion, I retreated to the lounge that connected to the two bedrooms. Although there was a comfortable bed settee, I was now able to hear the noisy sex in both bedrooms. Although this didn't last long in Jim's case, my mother managed to keep a racket going for more than an hour.

For the first half hour, I tried to divert my attention by thinking over Jim's surprisingly rapid identification of likely actors in this plot. From what I had seen of their profiles, I would have no compunction about assassinating either or both of them. Denis Buck was the scion of one of the States' big-money families. Such extreme wealth bought the political influence to facilitate further money-grabbing. This was an autocatalytic process that was simply accepted as intrinsic to the workings of government in the USA, making it so similar to Autocracies arising from communism in countries like Russia, China and North Korea. Everyone may be able to vote, but political power remained within the hands of a small cabal. *God, but I'd love to put bullets through the heads of a load of these plutocratic fuckers.*

The Ozzie activist just seemed like a typical terrorist – of the non-raghead variety. A complete wingnut, who would happily bomb a kindergarten if she thought her cause would benefit from it. She seemed to have a family, so maybe threatening them would bring her out of the woodwork. *The bleeding-heart brigade would be up in arms, but nothing better than doing to others exactly what they'd like to do to you.*

Unfortunately, thinking about the most painful ways of removing these arseholes had the usual side-effect of building up my arousal, leading me to listen more closely to the sounds coming from Miriam's room while I absent-mindedly masturbated. *If that guy hadn't been a rent-boy, I'd have happily jumped his bones. Indeed, Jim's little bed-mate was very cute and I wouldn't have required much encouragement to give her a good seeing to.*

A threesome with my mother was a sickening thought, but I found myself wondering about possible combinations with the two prostitutes. As a member of a generation brought up with free access to internet porn, the spectrum of options I could imagine was very wide and enough to bring me to orgasm. Thereafter, however, my sad situation was only emphasised further by my mother's continuing screams of ecstasy.

Chapter 7

Karen refused my offer of breakfast, scooting off before I joined the rest of the team in the resort restaurant. Maybe she was forewarned. The buffet was completely naff in every possible way. Even the coffee was almost undrinkable. I was already settled in, sipping an orange juice, which might have had some real fruit components but most probably 100% synthetic, when my nightmare companions appeared. "What ho, ladies? How was your gigolo?" I asked in a voice that was just loud enough for the other hotel residents to hear.

"Actually, very fine," Miriam responded, while Rachel was clearly trying to distance herself from us. "Hung like a stallion and with the stamina of a bull."

"Yes, well, we can now add bestiality to the list of your perversions," I laughed, while ignoring the shocked looks on the faces of the other patrons of the establishment.

"And, so, how was your barely-legal hooker?"

"A doll," I admitted with a grin, "an absolute doll. We were going at it like rabbits on steroids for the entire night."

"Right! Do you think that's even slightly credible for someone of your advanced years?"

I grinned. "You're paying the bill, as I'm on honorarium and expenses. You'll be getting a fully detailed invoice from my little Karen. Mouth like a vacuum cleaner, that lass. I think I may be in love."

"For fuck's sake, will you two just pack it in for a bit?" Rachel was even louder than I had been, causing heads to turn. "Just stop trying to win points from each other and act like adults."

"Well, I guess the illegitimate daughter didn't get any last night." The words were out of my mouth before I thought about them. Conditioned reflex from my many verbal duals with opponents. I immediately wanted to apologise, but did not have a clue how to.

Rachel turned and stomped out of the room while Miriam glared at me. "Good one, Jim," she muttered before following her daughter.

I had been kidnapped and, somehow, it was me now feeling guilty. *Is this what Stockholm syndrome feels like? Fuck it!* I gave up on breakfast and decided to clear my head by having a swim in the lake. I'd been told it was cold, but that was maybe the kind of penance that I needed.

***

The lake was chilly, but not as cold as I had expected. I climbed down a ladder from the little jetty where several rowing boats and canoes were tethered, ignoring a tangle of weeds that rubbed against my legs, and then set off towards the far end of the little lake, maybe a distance of 500 metres or so. After the shock of first contact with the water, I swam breast stroke for a minute or two until I was sure that my head was not going to get chilled and then slipped into a slow crawl, which I could feel gradually relaxing the tensions in my muscles accumulated over the last few days. After about five minutes, I was mentally running through the case files, feeling the rather unique sensation of combining work with the pleasure of exercise. *Something I haven't felt for several years.*

I had just turned and was heading back when a helicopter raced over the lake at very low altitude, making a beeline for the cabin that we were staying in.

I was sure that I hadn't been spotted. *Not surprising. Who in their right mind would be swimming in the lake at this time in the morning?* I upped my speed to the closest that I could get to a racing crawl, well aware that the action would certainly be over before I got back to our digs.

I had actually started to clamber onto the jetty when I realised that I had a choice to make. The sensible option would be to head into the woods and work my way towards the nearest town – during which my greatest risk would be an encounter with a bear. Or I could check what was happening in the cabin, which could well be full of amphetamine-fuelled mercenaries with killing me at the top of their wish-list.

Despite this objective risk analysis, clad only in swimming trunks and sandals while carrying goggles and a towel, I slowly crept towards the cabin. The chopper sitting on the grass just below our cabin was military-spec: long-range, high-speed, but small. *For fully equipped soldiers, this'd give a maximum of four on board. Maybe fewer if they're intending to take someone – like me – back with them.*

In any case, there must be mercenaries in the cabin, presumably either torturing the women, if they're still alive, or holding them as bargaining chips for when I eventually show up. I should be shitting myself but, as usual, I went completely cold, slipping into what the younger generation would call my *zone*. Risk and threat management is my bread and butter and I have worked in this field for four decades. I was listing and rating possible response options in a subconscious manner while I dropped the towel and goggles and moved a large rock to a position by the corner of the cabin closest to the helicopter.

I then clambered into the chopper, which was more of a struggle than I had hoped due to the limited flexibility of my now-chilled knees. After a quick scan of the instruments, I flicked the switch that started the engine warm-up. The copter may be stealthed, but the warm up was inevitably noisy. I hurled myself back onto the grass and grabbed my cached boulder, aware of crashing noises within the cabin. As I expected, a burly figure raced around the corner towards the machine and straight into the rock I was swinging at his face.

A shock of pain shot up my arm, but I had the satisfaction of seeing my victim flying backwards in a curtain of blood. A helmet is very good idea but, with the visor open, doesn't do much against an attack like this. The guy must have been very tough though as, despite the damage I had inflicted, he was still conscious and scrabbling to pull a pistol from his shoulder holster. I easily beat him to it, battered his hand with the rock, drew the gun, flicked off the safety, and shot him between the eyes. Only then was it clear that the lad, or maybe a very butch lass, couldn't be much more than twenty. I am too experienced to get disturbed by this, but I still felt a loss of interest in getting any further involved. I simply slumped down and leant against the wall of our accommodation, ignoring the crashing noises from behind me. *This is a good test of the team. Now that I've provided a diversion, they should be able to do the tidying up. If not, we'll either die now or in the very near future.*

***

I was enjoying the sight of a bald-headed eagle circling above, maybe aware of the carrion lying beside me, when Miriam dropped down by my side. "We could have done with a bit of help in there."

"Come on, if you can't handle a couple of grunts who're starting to panic because their helicopter has just started up, then you shouldn't be here in the first place."

"Okay, we really didn't need you, but the gesture would have been nice."

"Why? This would've indicated that I give a shit about either of you. Which I don't."

"Harsh! But I did wonder if you'd high-tail it when this hit-team arrived."

"I thought about it, very seriously. But I think this nonsense needs to be brought to an end, one way or another. The fact that they found us here should show you that you can expect no support from your organisation. The Veep evidently has complete control there. That being the case, what do you propose to do now?"

"There isn't any choice, we run."

She glanced around and for the first time I was aware of several residents peering at us from a sensible distance. "I assume that one of you can fly a helicopter, so that's our obvious way out of here."

Miriam frowned. "Come on, I know that you've been flying choppers for decades."

"So what? I'm the brains here. I do the thinking while you and your nutty girl do the donkey work."

"What nutter is that?" Rachel emerged with blood, seemingly not her own, splattered over her clothing.

"The one that I'm looking at. Young psycho, get our shit loaded into the chopper. Old psycho, check through the bodies to see what arms we can scavenge."

"And, you, what do you do?" Psycho-daughter glared at me.

"I'm going to check out our transport and disable all potential tracking devices – a job that, given what's just happened, I wouldn't trust to either of you.

Rachel was clearly ready to respond, when Miriam grabbed her arm. "We need to get out of here, and fast. Any squabbling can be done later. Also, you should also shower and change, you look like a victim from the Texas Chainsaw movies."

"Actually, a bit more like Leatherface," I grinned. Unfortunately, the others missed my obscure fanboy reference.

Rachel flew, which I was glad about as my experience is at least a decade old. I had stripped out every electronic device that I thought could be used to trace us, which included everything that normally assisted aerial navigation. We thus had nothing other than a paper roadmap, which was fine when following smoke-covered roads at almost street-elevation, but a lot trickier when we had to divert from fires and follow rivers, with all their associated hazards due to power cables, bridges and other obstacles that continually emerged from the smoke in front of us.

Rachel was good, I had to admit. Maybe even really fucking good. I have flown choppers under fire a couple of times, but not above wildfires. This was an entirely different challenge. I tried to avoid looking out of the windows, as then I'd have to acknowledge how close we were to being toast. I had the map on my knees and was trying to trace our route, helped by a gyroscopic-compass function on my laptop that functioned without an internet connection. "Where was it you said we're going?"

"Banff."

I could not help being impressed how little dicing with death impacted Miriam's demeanour. "Okay, fair enough, where in Banff?"

"There's a resort above the town that I've used in the past. It's well out of town, towards the Sulphur Mountain gondola."

"Right, let's see." I looked at an animated wildfire map that I had downloaded earlier, along

69

with associated predictions of impacts on transport. "Fine, we need to head for Field."

"What field? There're thousands all around us," Rachel complained.

"It's the name of a little town – maybe a village anywhere else but Canada – about 60 kay north-west of Banff."

"And why the fuck would we be going there?" Our pilot did not seem to be very happy with my choice.

"Because it's just south of a wall of fire that's going to wipe it off the map in a couple of hours."

"That's why we're going there?" Miriam was cool and her concern was signalled only by a raised eyebrow.

"Of course, as should be obvious to even the grunt with her limited intelligence." Another death-stare from Rachel. "The fire will completely destroy this helicopter and it'll be days before anyone will be able to get in there to find out more."

"Brill idea, we lose the opposition but get burned to death! You really are a genius, Dad."

"Less of the Dad-shit, young psycho. According to the fire app, we can land just in time to jump onto a goods train that'll be passing through just before the line is closed. It won't be comfortable, but it'll give us a bit of breathing time."

Rachel rolled her eyes. "And just how are we going to get your aged carcass onto a fast-moving train?"

"Ah, child, you've never seen a PCR goods train going through a town! You can wait at a

70

crossroads for a quarter of an hour for one to pass. Walking speed. Even I could hop onto one of them."

"And this'll take us to Banff?"

"The way that it looks at present, this is the only credible option if we want to be subtle about it. As you may have spotted, the fires hereabouts are especially bad this year. We hop off again when it slows down to go through the Banff town centre."

"And how slow is that?" Miriam asked. "There usually aren't road crossings in larger towns like you'll find in hamlets like this Field place."

"Slow enough, as it's much easier to fall off than jump on," I grinned with a lot less confidence than I actually had. The arthritis in my knees and ankles made such manoeuvres anything but trivial.

Rachel seemed unconvinced. "I'm having enough problems staying safe from fires blowing away from us, but this old geezer wants us to land in front of one heading directly towards us. The viz will be totally fuck all."

"As you noted, *the impossible only takes a bit more time*," Miriam was at her most feral. "So, use your time well." She then settled back as if the problem was thus solved.

I grimaced. "Okay, young psycho, as you approach you'll need to be as close to the river as possible. The smoke will be less there, as the wind will be coming along the valley. You'll then be below cables but... Fuck!!!"

I was relieved to find out that I hadn't shat myself, but it had been a close thing. "Yes, well, bridges are also something that we need to look out

71

for. I'm following our route on this map and will try to give you some warning about them."

"And what about that last one?" The young bitch grinned. She was actually enjoying this. The fact that I was very close to a heart attack seemed to make it only more fun for her.

"Okay, top-gun, just do it your way. You don't need my help."

"I never did."

I really wished this was true, so that I could bale out as soon as possible. Unfortunately, I was sure that this was not the case.

The rest of the trip was nail-biting, although I did my best to hide the fact and Miriam seemed to be totally oblivious. We were following valleys to provide a much more direct route than the road but, with the map I had, this provided no information on most of the obstructions that could lie in our path – bridges, low-slung cables and even a swarm of drones that might have had something to do with the fire-fighting activities. I did detect a sudden intake of breath or two, but our pilot managed everything with impressive sangfroid, the epitome of the right stuff. I should have complimented her, but restricted myself to a muttered, "you can fly this thing."

"Is that an acknowledgement that, despite the decades of experience you have, I can do this better than you?"

"Of course, that's what we use grunts for. They do things. But we're the ones who tell them what to do. Bridge!!!"

An initial look of annoyance transformed immediately into one of pleasure. "You're the one giving the commands. Over or under?"

With a railway bridge directly in front of us, I could only scream. "Over, for Christ's sake!"

"Wrong choice, Dad," her amusement was obvious as she skimmed the surface of the river to pass below the obstacle in our path. "We were too close for over, so it had to be under."

"Fuck, girl, you know, I really hate you!"

"It's mutual, but I'm more likely to avoid a heart attack during our little trip here than you are."

"I really, really hate you!"

"You know, hate is very close to love," Miriam interrupted, silencing us both.

***

We landed in Field after flying for almost 2 hours, setting down in a meadow beside the railway tracks. This was just in front of the wildfire, which was blowing towards us with a noise that was almost enough to loosen my bladder. The goods train was already passing though the town, and moving much faster than I remember from my last visit, maybe two decades ago.

"They're running from the fire, so we need to get on board ASAP."

"It's not going more than about 10 k, so they're still crawling along," Rachel pointed out.

"10 kilometres in an hour may not be much to you, but think of your aged mother."

Unfortunately, the impact of my calumny was destroyed when Miriam jogged past me and jumped nimbly onto the back of a wagon containing ISO containers piled two high.

To add insult to injury, Rachel had loaded herself with a couple of large bags full of our kit and still managed to effortlessly jog past me and clamber up to join her mother. "He's barbequed roadkill," she grinned when she saw that I was slowly falling back as the train began to accelerate.

It was Miriam's look of disappointment that drove me to jump at a ladder on the side of a wagon two behind the one that they had boarded. The shock almost ripped my arms from their sockets. It was couple of minutes before I was able to slowly clamber up onto the flatbed and peer around the containers to see what the rest of the team were up to.

"That was truly feeble," Rachel radiated happiness. "So now you've got a choice, climb over the containers or edge along the sides. It'd have been easier if you had just got on this one with us."

"Why would I do that?" I shouted back, while the train was gradually building up speed. "The entire point was to have a few hours without any contact with you two nutcases. Job done!" I then slumped down and let the screams of agony from my various abused limbs amalgamate into a pain that was easiest to lose in unconsciousness.

Chapter 8: Rachel

Fuck, I really hope we need to kill him! Even if it isn't part of the plan, I'm going to kill the annoying old bastard anyway. Whether or not he's made a contribution to my genes, he can't just treat me like something that he scraped off his shoe. I'll gut shoot him so that he suffers as much as possible before he finally shuffles off his mortal coil.

I grimaced as I slumped against the lower container that formed a small component of this huge goods train. *How can someone as fundamentally useless keep pulling our collective coals out of the fire.* There seemed to be no logical explanation for it. I have been following Miriam's plans to the letter. Plans that we went over in detail before we set off on this bizarre road trip. Nevertheless, when the shit hits the fan, he is the one who takes command of the situation. *That fucking hit team! I could've handled them on my own.*

I closed my eyes while reviewing again the situation after the armoured mercenaries crashed into our cabin. I had been caught with my pants down. Literally, as I had been in the process of having an early morning download. I smiled involuntary. *At least I didn't shit myself with the shock. That had already been taken care of.*

So, pulling up my trousers while staggering from the loo to face three heavily armed assailants, what was I supposed to do? My mother, as usual, was no help at all. Clad only in bra and pants, she glared at them and told them to fuck off. The team leader only smiled and pointed a shotgun at her face. "Make me," he replied.

Mum and I just stood there while the other two fuckers searched the cabin. It did not take very long for them to determine that Jim wasn't there, but they then checked what little luggage we had for clues. By now, the boss of the group was seriously pissed off. He shoved the shotgun beneath my chin. What followed was etched in my mind. "Where's Forsyth, the Brit bastard?" he asked, just at the moment when the sounds of an engine kicking into life shook the cabin.

"Fuck, Dessy, what's going on? That's the chopper firing up!"

One of the heavy team immediately sprinted out of the door.

This distraction was all that I needed. I swiped the boss's gun to the side with my left hand while two fingers of my right plunged into his eyes, bursting his eyeballs. The idiot screamed and tried to back off, but my fingers were securely lodged, forcing him to drop the shotgun in order to grab a hold of my wrist. My knee to his groin transmogrified his scream into a choking splutter, which was silenced when my left hand smashed into his throat. He dropped to the floor when my bloody fingers pulled loose from his eye-sockets, giving a final grunt when I twisted his head and broke his neck.

The adrenalin surge of this fight had been enough to distract me from the rest of the action. I have no idea how she did it, but my mother was slowly pulling a thin stiletto out from just below the ear of our other attacker. Unlike the burly thug who I had dispatched, Miriam's victim was a slim young woman, whose eyes were wide with shocked surprise. The girl must have turned when her team leader screamed, leaving her open to Miriam's attack, although where my mum got the knife from I have no idea.

At that point I heard the shot from outside. "That'll be the old bugger taking care of the pilot," Miriam smiled and I noticed that her knickers had a distinct damp patch, which I was certain did not result from a loss of bladder control.

"Get your clothes on and grab a gun," I had shouted, rummaging for a machine pistol as I didn't have my mother's confidence in the ability of that old crock to handle an armed mercenary.

I was out of the cabin seconds later to find Jim, clad only in swimming trunks, sitting by the body of the pilot and simply gazing into space. He just hadn't bothered to see if we needed any help. *Fuck, but I really hope I get to shoot him. Ideally sometime very soon.*

Chapter 9: Jim

"Jump! Jump, you stupid old bugger!"

I spotted that the ladies were running along the sides of the track, before I worked out what that meant. I pulled myself up against the door of an ISO container while I struggled to remember what was going on. In a strange moment of clarity, I saw a grassy patch beside the train and hurled myself off, trusting that decades of aikido in the past would be able to handle the required breakfall. It was almost perfect. I flew through the air, hit the ground with a shoulder roll that brought me to my feet again – then ruined it all by staggering forward to fall flat on my face.

"Well done," Rachel giggled. "That was just about as elegant as I expected. I could throw a sheep out of the back of a pick-up and it'd land better than that."

I crawled onto my hands and knees and then forced myself onto my feet. "Bear in mind that a sheep my age would've been dead for five decades!"

"Then it'd be looking a bit like you do now," she sniggered. "Anyway, we reckoned this meadow was the best option, leaving us only a couple of kay walk into town. Then we can get a bus up to the place that we're going to stay in."

"Better idea, call a cab and then we'll ride up."

"I call a cab from here and any AI network crawler could pick us up," she pointed out with a smug grin.

"Okay then, so you just jog into town and then pick up the cab. You can pay cash and have us picked up here."

"Not so risky, but even cabs have GPS tracers and an AI search-machine might register the strange trip out to this pick up point. Just get your flabby arse up and moving."

"Again, that's a good point, but I seem to remember that, in these holiday places, they have bicycle rickshaw things for the super-fit types with families. Go and hire one of those for a couple of days, paying cash. Soon as you like, I'm choking for a beer." I waved her on her way in a deliberately annoying manner.

"Mum! I am so going to kill this arrogant old fucker…"

"I understand this, of course I do, having often had the same thoughts myself. But he's clearly wiped out, so it's better that you do what he suggests."

"Okay, right, that's me, Rachel the slave. So, are you coming with me?"

"Easier if you dump all your shit here and jog into town. While you're there, be a dear and pick up a couple of cans of beer. I must confess that I've also got a bit of a thirst." Rachel was getting a lot of practice with her |death stares and this one should have frazzled both myself and her mother.

Rachel dropped the massive kit bag that she had been toting and shrugged off the other bag, which was set up as a backpack. "Right, I'll do it. But, if come back and find the two of you fucking on the grass, I promise that I'll shoot you both. With the fucking pump-action shotgun. Many times."

Miriam smiled as she watched her daughter ran off at a pace that I could not have matched, even in my prime. "She does have funny ideas, doesn't she?"

I watched in amazement while she slowly started to strip off her clothes. "Just what the holy fuck do you think you're doing?"

"Well, we're stuck together here until the girl gets back and, at present, there's no smoke above us. So why not catch a few rays?"

Rachel had now vanished around a bend in the road and there was absolutely nobody else about. "Well, at my age, I'm much more likely to die of something else before a UV-related cancer does me in." I started to take my own clothes off like a rabbit in headlights, mesmerised by her still rather tight body. "Anyway, under no circumstances am I going to fuck you, so you can just forget about that ploy."

I couldn't turn away while she lowered herself onto a smooth area of grass and laid back with a sigh, very deliberately opening her legs and stroking her exposed genitalia. "That's just not going to work," I stated as I threw the rest of my clothes aside.

Off course, it did.

***

The deed was done well before Rachel returned in a four-wheeled, bike-based contraption. I rolled over onto my stomach as soon as she came into sight but, typically, her mother simply sprawled back with limbs akimbo. As soon as Rachel got close, she stood up to make a more theatrical figure. "Okay, girl, say what you're thinking."

Rachel grimaced. "Mum, you're such a hopeless, psycho slut. All someone has to do is kill someone else and you're ready to screw them."

"Yes, that's probably true. But it hasn't stopped me from being a caring mother."

"Caring mother? What the fuck? You had my gran look after me until I was in my teens. You also seem to have forgotten that you were prepared to let my father fuck me as long as it'd further your evil plans."

"Well, he isn't really 100% your father…"

"Regardless of whoever the fuck he is, you'd let an old geriatric fart like him shag me just to make sure that he supports whatever your evil plan is."

"No, love, that was never a risk. There was no way that he was ever going to touch you. He has many vices, but paedophilia isn't one of them."

"You've got to be joking! He was shagging a hooker half my age last night. He's actually just like you, no moral scruples at all."

Rachel was very near to ignition point, so I couldn't help putting out the fire with gasoline. "Well, the thing about young Karen, the professional lady that you refer to as a hooker, is that I never forced her to do anything against her will."

"You paid her to have sex with you, you sad old fuck."

"Actually I didn't, your mother picked up the tab. Nevertheless, she was paid to shag me, as she has screwed many before me and will certainly pleasure many more in the future. But, unlike a lot of her Johns, or Joans or whatever, I treated her with respect. I was mainly trying to annoy the two of you, so would have been happy with a night-time cuddle. She, the professional that she was, realised that I needed a bit of sexual stress-relief. Which, indeed, she provided – in a most professional manner. I wouldn't hesitate to recommend her, should either of you need such services in the future."

"I would never, ever, pay for sex!"

"Maybe not, but that's completely up to you." I turned to Miriam. "What about you? Have you ever paid for sex? Apart from last night, of course."

"Of course I have. Innumerable times. It's just like any other market: supply tailored to demand. As Jim has repeatedly pointed out, I'm a psycho slut and I can always find what I want without paying, but often it's just not worth the effort. If you want the release of sex, but don't want to go through the whole chatting-up shit, you really can't get better than a prostitute. Or two. Or several, if you need a lot of tension eased out. Specify the fantasy required and then, after appropriate payment – which is usually very well earned – you get to live the dream you were looking for."

Rachel looked shocked. "Jesus, you're even more cruel and heartless, not to mention sexually perverted, than I had imagined."

Miriam was listening, but was totally unmoved by this tirade. She casually rubbed an evidently very wet groin and then, possibly to shock her daughter, licked her fingers. "Yes, indeed, my girl, you don't know a fraction of what I've gotten up to in my time. However, this has nothing to do with the job. Jim and I just need to get some clothes on and then we're off to the hotel. Rimrock, it is. Unless, of course, you'd like to join us for a bit of pre-prandial nookie before we set off?"

"Mother, I really hate you. And Dad, Jim, whoever you are, for fuck's sake get rid of that feeble little erection. There's a stream down the hill that would do the job, I'm sure."

Miriam laughed. "I didn't think he had another one in him. I could give him a quick BJ now that'd solve the problem."

"Mom, I hate you more than death. I hate you more than that sad bastard. I hate you more than…"

I quietly escaped from this torrent of abuse, picking up my clothes and heading in the pointed direction, sliding the last bit on my arse down a steep slope and into an extremely cold spring. Immersion in this immediately turned me into Michelangelo's David, but I forced myself to have a good rinse, as if this was penance for the stupidity that Miriam had managed to encourage me into. I dried myself as best I could with my t-shirt, dressed and then slowly fought my way up the slippery bank to where the bike was parked.

"Okay ladies, the erection problem is now solved. Let's just get to whatever accommodation you've organised. Of course, when we get there, if you're up for some MFF action, then I'd be happy to oblige. I actually prefer a professional but, when it comes to amateurs, there's nothing better than fucking someone who really hates your guts."

"That's both of us," Rachel spat in my direction.

"What, you both want fucked?"

"No, you daft shit, we both hate you."

"That's the same thing. Look at your mother, dozing in post-coital bliss…" She had already dressed and climbed into the back of the rickshaw and was, indeed, gently snoring. "I have no idea why I shagged her. I used to truly hate her but, after all these years, maybe this has been tempered to extreme dislike. Despite that, she laid back with her legs open and there was nothing else I could do."

Rachel wiped her hands over her face. "She really is a psycho-slut. I think we both agree on that."

"She's the best, maybe that should be worst, manipulator that I've ever encountered. It's not just that she has a very good body, even after all these years, but she uses it like a weapon. It comes down to a cold-blooded attitude to sex. There's absolutely no romantic component to it as far as she is concerned."

"What, so there's a romantic component when you're shagging a hooker?"

"I always feel an emotional bond building during sex. In fact, I'm sure that's something which improved the kick for your mother when she first seduced me. And, I'm also sure that's what she expects now and is a reason that she made herself

84

available while you were picking up our transport. Of course, she was already soaking wet from the mayhem back in Clearwater – you know what she's like."

Rachel confined herself to a grimace, then started loading the kitbags into the back of our transport.

I checked to see that my nemesis was still dozing before quietly asking. "Do you know what your mother meant about me not being 100% your father? I've not had a chance to check the DNA report that she gave me, but I know that, despite the extremely low probability that I could have caused her pregnancy, this is something that's inherently 100% or nothing."

Rachel looked uncomfortable. "Mom says you're my father, but I know that it was a surrogate birth…"

I walked over to Miriam and slapped her hard on the face, shocking her awake. "You cunt, you evil cunt! You must have used material from my cells to fertilise the eggs that you stored before our last gig. The radiation exposure risk on the dirty bomb job was clear, so I remember that you said you'd done this as a backup."

"So what?" The surprise caused by her abrupt awakening quickly vanished. "I always fancied the idea of an offspring to follow on in my steps, so why not ensure that the best available genetic material was available for its conception."

"Apart from how fucked-up that unilateral decision was, what's with the less than 100% paternity?"

"Bugger! I hoped that you'd missed that slip of the tongue. Well, just then the technology was coming available…"

"You did a fucking mix and match! Your eggs and DNA input from more than one *father*. Tailored to create the monster that you were looking for."

"Jim, for fuck's sake, give the girl a break!"

"She didn't know about this? Of course, she wouldn't. Apart from being as loopy as her mother, she's an amazing result from such a risky procedure. So, how many of the other attempts were aborted?"

I actually felt scared when Miriam glared at me. Her daughter's death stares were nothing in comparison. "All of them!" she shouted, as close as I've seen to this sociopath losing her cool. "But, so what? Rachel's good, very fucking good. She may even be better than I was in my prime."

"You know, that's a fucking scary thought. But how much is nature and how much is nurture? Unless she's 90% you by nature, the psycho bit could result from being controlled by you from infancy." To my surprise, I noticed that I had placed my hand protectively on Rachel's shoulder. Even more surprisingly, she hadn't tried to break my arm.

"Whatever. But we need to get this job done before all of this angst is a thing of the past because we're already pushing up daisies. So, all aboard and let Rachel get her work-out for today. I think our destination is only about 12 k from here, but it's uphill all the way. Wake me when we get there."

Rachel and I looked at each other and raised our eyebrows and rolled our eyes simultaneously, which may indeed indicate a significant genetic

86

link. It was hardly a father-daughter bonding experience, but there was some kind of unspoken ceasefire in terms of sniping at each other.

As Rachel started to climb onto the driver's seat, she turned and grinned. "You were going to slap me on the bum, weren't you?"

"You do, indeed, have rather tempting buttocks and the thought did cross my mind."

"But you thought the better of it. Was this because you now acknowledge me as your daughter?"

"Actually, it was because I thought that you'd kick seven shades of shit out of me if I tried."

"Even better," she grinned.

"For fuck's sake, if you two want to go on with this, get a fucking room. And you'll only have that if my sprog finally gets her bloody arse in gear." Miriam had clearly been faking sleep, which didn't surprise me at all.

"You know, I really do hate her," Rachel's grin widened.

"Not any more than I do!" I patted her on the bottom and quickly jumped in the back beside the target of our mutual hatred. The smile that we shared just confirmed that our relationship had changed, and for the better.

Chapter 10: Rachel

The cycle ride to the hotel gave me a chance to clear my head. I already knew that Miriam had used a surrogate mother to carry me to term, but I hadn't thought on this further. The name of my father was never mentioned until, during the first briefing for this action, my mom accused Jim of the deed. Despite his earlier protestations, I only now really believed that Jim had no knowledge of his involvement in the pregnancy. Not only that, I find out that I was the result of a very risky procedure that was sure to be illegal.

I thought through what Miriam had let slip over the past couple of days, trying to work out who the other contributor of genetic material could be. Suddenly a shiver went up my spine. *The UDF assassin that she fucked on that operation, just before she had him wiped-out and shortly after seducing Jim. Jim for his brains and the other guy for his complete ruthlessness. Doesn't she know that mix-and-match genetics doesn't work like that?*

My fury was certainly helping me to slog my way up the hill towards our accommodation. *I wonder if Jim knows who else supplied genes, or if he even cares? Despite treating me like shit most of the time, I think he now feels a bit sorry for me, realising that I'm also a victim of Miriam's thoughtless megalomania. There was also a marked change in him after the chopper flight. He didn't say anything, but I'm sure I finally gained his respect there.*

This thought came as a surprise. Why would I care what he thought about me? Then it slowly dawned on me that it was because I couldn't help building up respect for him. He could have done a runner when the hit squad appeared, but he cleverly turned the table on our opponents by starting the chopper's engine. Although he left us to handle two of the team, he took out the other guy while armed only with a rock.

Of course, I was really fucked-off that he had shagged my mum while they had me fetching beers. However, I remembered how wet she was after knifing that girl and I was sure that she was ready to rock and roll at the first available opportunity. Any heterosexual man would be hard-put to turn an offer like that down. Matter of fact, anyone with the slightest interest in female flesh would be sorely tempted. I had been sure that she was just being annoying, but was almost certain now that, if I had shown any indication of being tempted by a threesome, then she would have happily gone for it. She claimed that Jim would never indulge in incest or paedophilia, but I would not put any sexual deviation past her.

Such thoughts made me uncomfortably aware that I also turned on by violence, although I knew well that this was not uncommon in the armed forces and, especially, in the elite units comprised of volunteers. Nevertheless, my responses could be at the extreme end of the spectrum, probably as a result of my mother's genes and those of the Irish terrorist, if he did indeed contribute to my conception.

Well, I just have to hope that we can avoid further combat until it's time for the bad guys at the top to be finally taken out. Hopefully, Jim will be well gone by then and I won't need to think any further about our increasingly ambiguous relationship.

Chapter 11: Jim

The *Rimrock* was a swanky hotel looking down over Banff, just below the gondola that took hordes of tourists to the top of nearby Sulphur Mountain. Despite our rather dishevelled appearance, check in was no problem. Miriam assured us that the suite had been prepaid from an untraceable Swiss bank account. When asked for photo ID, she merely smiled and slipped over a couple of $100 bills. "Just make it Smith, Mary Smith. Don't you think paparazzi are total bastards?"

The poor clerk was struggling to hide the cash while trying to work out which big name was gracing his hotel with her presence. It was clear that he thought it must be Miriam or Rachel, as he did not even glance in my direction. *Maybe that was why I'm so good in the intelligence caper, nobody ever notices me.*

We were on the 7th floor and, once again, had connecting rooms, each with two king beds. Miriam inspected both before selecting the one with the marginally better views of the surrounding mountains. "Fine, we'll have this one. You're next door, Jim."

"You can have this one, but I'll sleep next door," Rachel glared at her mother while I prudently retired into my assigned room.

"Rachel, are you off your *fucking* head? That's your father! If there is one perversion that's really bad for you, it's incest."

"Where's this coming from? You've already offered me to him!"

"But he wouldn't shag you, I know he wouldn't."

"Actually, I do know. That why I'm sleeping in there. Sleeping, mother, not shagging. Don't you know that there's a difference?"

In the moment of silence, I peeked into the room and mimed snapping a photo. "Rachel, ten points, zehn Punckte, dix points, diez puntos… You've struck your mother speechless, something that I'd never have though possible."

Rachel followed me but, before she could close the door, I caught her eye and winked. "Right, daughter, get your bare arse on that bed and spread them."

"Oh, father you're so rough…"

I quickly shut and locked the door, but was reasonably sure Miriam would have heard us pissing ourselves with laughter. It didn't make any difference, as she'd be seriously raked-off by her daughter's mutiny in any case.

***

After we got ourselves sorted out, an easy job given that our minimal luggage consisted mainly of Rachel's bags of weapons, we met up in the bar. This had the advantage of being less hormonally charged than the bedrooms. It was also clear that, if we wanted to eat, the bar was a better choice than the fine dining restaurant with its *elegant* dress code. We had ordered clothes over the internet, while Rachel also sorted out a couple of suitcases, but it would be a day or two wait for delivery. This was actually not bad, considering that we were in the middle of bugger-all and surrounded by wildfires.

Despite the general decline in tourism and the negative impact of increasingly frequent wildfires, the hotel had a fair number of holidaymakers. These were mainly Brits, but with a fair number of Asians and visitors from the Indian sub-continent. All evidently affluent, as the drinks here made Zurich seem cheap. In the bar, the tourists were, however, outnumbered – and drowned out – by a large North American group who must have been involved in some kind of meeting or workshop. They seemed to talk simultaneously, just shouting louder to make specific points. We managed to seat ourselves as far as possible from them, but they were still offensively loud.

Rachel was not pleased. "I think I'm just going to tell that bunch of fuckers to keep it down."

I had visions of her returning covered in gore, carrying the head of some *Brad* or *Rhona*. But, pleasant as a bit of quiet would have been, I caught her arm before she could stand. "Total wankers they certainly are, but they provide an excellent sonic barrier. With them boasting about their second houses, yachts and Ferraris, nobody is going to be eaves-dropping us."

"Nobody'll eaves-drop us anyway." Miriam placed a small object on the middle of the table. "Anti-sound generator," she noted smugly.

93

"Good bit of kit," I rolled my eyes theatrically, "but don't switch it on until we've got our drinks order in." Rachel smirked and nudged my ribs, which annoyed her mother in the way that she clearly intended it to.

After our drinks were served and the sonic shield switched on, I immediately jumped to the issue that was bothering me most. "Okay, Miriam, due to your crap security, we're in the cross-hairs of a bunch of mad assassins. We've been lucky so far, but that can't continue. We've got to remove this threat from the top."

"Take out the Veep?"

"If that's what it takes."

"She's not alone, you know. She may not even be the head of this conspiracy, as it involves some of the biggest names in commerce. Or politics. Although, in this regard, that's pretty much the same thing."

"She'll be high up in any case. We start at the top, then work our way down."

"There'd more disincentive if we wiped them out together with their entire families, pets, close friends – ideally at a party of some sort. Thanksgiving or Christmas, something like that," Miriam mused, probably to annoy me.

Thinking about assassinating the Veep reminded me about how difficult such high-profile wet-work could be, even in countries with less experience in countering assassins than the USA. "What about if we work through the middle? Not going for the top decision-makers, but the scum who actually implement the plans?"

Miriam looked at me scornfully. "There would be a half-dozen or so at the top. Go down one level and we have a score, maybe much more. One level below that, at least a hundred."

"Yes, well, it's clear now. There're about twenty evil bastards that aren't high enough on the totem pole to get the protection that the great and the good are provided with due to their political status. Because they are, by definition, totally evil, there's no reason why we shouldn't just take them out of the game. We just need a list, which my bitch nemesis will have already prepared, and then we can start wiping them out."

I was happy about my analysis, but rather worried about how aroused by it Rachel seemed to be. Her nipples were like acorns under the tight top she was wearing. Even worse, her mother was at least as turned-on, if not more.

I was relieved when our drinks arrived and we scanned through menus, trying to decide if this should be considered a late lunch or an early dinner.

***

After snacks and a couple of drinks, we moved back to the bedroom claimed by Miriam and sat by the picture window, sipping post-prandial drinks from the mini-bar while pondering how to extricate ourselves from our present pickle.

A starting point was a quick search to locate the Vice-president and the rest of our top-level targets. At my insistence, this ran through a super-TOR browser rather than using any of the agency tools that the women preferred. Under normal circumstances, the Veep would be in DC or Texas – as, indeed, would be many of our other assassination candidates. Thus, it was a surprise to find that Alice Beall was currently attending a NATO meeting in Brussels and, after that, was joining her cousin, Denis Buck, for a few days golfing in Scotland.

Rachel was bouncing on her chair like a hyperactive kid. "It's Buck, I knew it. This should be an ideal time to take them both out. How well can you protect someone on a golf course? It's a sniper's wet dream."

To my great surprise, Miriam looked at me and groaned. "Yes, if we'd just brought you in earlier…"

"I'd have had nothing to do with you. I still wouldn't have let you drag me in at any price if not for almost getting blown to buggery."

"But if you had, we wouldn't be as fucked as we are now, avoiding the teams aiming to remedy their previous error. Anyway, we live in the present, so we have to play the hand that we're dealt."

I could feel my cool, analytical side taking over. "Wait a minute, you should be happy about this news. Bugger! You've had a message from the bad guys, haven't you?"

Miriam grinned in a way that turned my blood cold, "God, but that was good. Very well spotted. Anyway, I would have told you sooner or later."

I glared at the evil cow. "Stop fucking tap-dancing! What was the message?

"If we don't give you to them, Europe will be a nuclear wasteland within 48 hours."

I looked into her eyes. "You cold-hearted bitch! So that's it, I'm now just the bait here."

"Why would you expect anything else?" Her grin widened.

"But... but... but...," I stuttered while my brain went into overdrive. "But why can't we just neutralise their threat..."

"How?" Her stare was pure *Cruella de Vil*.

I grimaced while I tried to put the pieces together. "It's the nuclear threat, you've heard more than once about it. Actually, I think I can now narrow down on the targets."

"How the fuck?" "You can?" The two women talked over each other, but they had obviously missed the point. "It's the nuclear wasteland in the threat, you muppets! Can't you see that?"

"How does that narrow it down?" Rachel frowned. Her mother clearly wanted to ask this question, but wasn't going to.

"Nuclear wasteland... Doesn't that help you a bit?"

"Well, if you attack any nuclear power plant..."

"Fuck all happens! Exactly! Even for the worst possible combination of impacts of an earthquake and a tsunami on an old plant like Fukushima Daiichi. It was a social and economic disaster, but there was never anything like a nuclear wasteland."

"What about whatever-it-was-called, in Russia?"

"Yes, Chernobyl in the Ukraine. The local operators had to work really hard to fuck that one up. And there are very old plants that are still vulnerable, so these could be possible targets. But, by global standards, the Chernobyl exclusion zone is buttons compared to the areas contaminated by non-nuclear disasters. Or, for that matter, even simple disregard for the impact of toxins released into the environment."

Miriam rolled her eyes. "Okay, let's forget all this pro-nuclear shit that you regularly use to annoy the tree-huggers. Where will the bad guys target if they're actually looking for a nuclear wasteland?"

To her evident surprise, I turned to Rachel. "Well, love, what do you think?"

The question evidently caught her off guard and she dropped back into her chair. "Nuclear, not a power plant," she muttered. "Maybe military, but that'll be tricky in so many ways... Fuck, fuck, fuck!" She turned to me and grimaced. "Or maybe a reprocessing plant?"

"Yes! Indeed! The fruit doesn't fall far from the tree – even if distantly related fruit in your specific case." I hastened to add. "Your mother is the ultimate black-ops agent: smart, sneaky, devious, whatever – but with no real technical background. She relies on sad gits like me to do the technical shit. You, however, actually understand a little of the basis of what we're doing here."

"Sellafield or La Hague!" Rachel's grin warmed me up inside, much though I'd never admit it.

"Why?" I couldn't help winking to show that she was on the right track. "There's also Mayak and a few other dodgy sites around the world."

"Well, if you want a nuclear wasteland, the best target is a reprocessing plant. There are a number of these but, in several cases, they're nuclear wastelands already, like Hanford or Mayak. Nobody gives a damn about them because this was all cold-war, military shit."

"Hanford, Mayak…" I nodded, "they're so fucked up that there's little you could do to make them much worse".

"…and there aren't many more targets like that, but I'd go for the ones where a contamination incident would have maximum impact. Hence Sellafield, La Hague or, maybe, the newer facilities at Marcoule."

"You're not as daft as you look." I dodged under a swipe that would have laid me on my arse. "No, seriously, the older plants are the most obvious targets. But…" Red laser sighting points started flicking about all over the room.

We all dropped to the floor, instants before the room was riddled with chain-gun devastation. Rachel beat me to the kit bag and, while I ripped it open, she pulled out a grenade-launcher and let rip.

The attack chopper exploded into a fireball, just in front of the window of our room. I had already rolled over Rachel and was able to protect her from the hail of glass shards that sheeted into the room. We cowered behind the bed until the blast of shrapnel had dissipated.

Rachel was bolder than me, hence first to lift her head above our shelter. Despite the ringing in my ears, I could just make out her shout. "Mum, are you okay?"

I was sure that the bitch from hell would survive any possible physical attack, so was shocked into silence when I saw her body splattered against the wall opposite the window with a part of a rotor blade protruding from her chest. "She moved into the wrong place, just at the wrong time," I mumbled, noting that her face had been shredded by the wave of blast debris.

I put my hand on Rachel's shoulder and shouted into her ear. "Come on, lass, we need to fuck off ASAP."

Watching her carefully, I saw a moment of grief while she wiped her hands down her face. This was quickly replaced by a look that could only be classified as scary. *Very scary. Actually, fucking terrifying.* At that moment, she was her mother's daughter. I would not want to be on the receiving end of the rage that this young woman was channelling.

She was ice-cold. With the help of lip-reading skill gained as my hearing degraded with age, I could just make her out. "So, Jim, what do you think? This could be all that they've got…"

I shook my head and again shouted into her ear. "Or more likely there's another couple of machines landing a team of heavies to finish the job…"

"Right, I suppose that's what I really expected. Pick up some tools." The kitbag with its assortment of serious weaponry was lying open at her feet.

100

"You know that this isn't urban combat shit? We could have quite a lot of collateral damage if we let loose with this kit."

"For fuck's sake, Jim, they've just blasted away with an attack chopper against a top-end tourist resort! Just shoot the fuck out of any dodgy targets and you'll be reducing the total collateral damage in this case."

I kitted up, including a protective vest that hardly fit around my chubby body. Rachel was still loading up with mega-death when I eased the bedroom door open, only to have it blasted from my fingers by a withering hail of automatic fire. The instant this stopped, I twisted outwards and used my shotgun to literally blow away the head of our attacker.

"Okay, we're..." I was shouldered aside as Rachel went totally Rambo. She had an assault rifle clenched under one arm and a grenade launcher under the other.

I stuck fingers in my ears to minimise further damage and waited for a few moments to ensure that I wouldn't get caught by friendly fire. Then it was just a case of following the trail of destruction. It was difficult to make an exact count, as many bodies were widely dispersed – grenades tend to do that – but there were about a half-dozen or so bad guys plastered around the path towards the elevators.

Rachel was waiting for me by the lifts, appearing to be completely calm despite the fact that the fire alarm was howling, almost drowning out instructions to leave the building immediately by the emergency stairs. "It seems that there are more coming up for us," she shouted, pointing towards the floor indicators, which showed all lifts were immobile except for one coming up towards our floor. I moved towards the doors of that lift and prised them open for the few moments that it took for Rachel to fire a grenade into the lift-shaft.

We automatically stood to the side as the blast dented the elevator doors. "Fuck, we've now got to walk down all those stairs."

Her hearing seemed to have recovered, so she nodded and her feral grin became even scarier. "No, we run down the main stairs, fucking up anyone who gets in our way. Any civilians will be clogging up the emergency exits, so anyone on this staircase is a bad guy. They must have come in on choppers, so we need to get airborne again."

My body sagged. "Again? We've done this helicopter shit before and it helped us not a jot."

"Yes, but there's a difference. Last time we were running away from our opponents, now we're running towards them."

Was that supposed to be reassuring? A couple of heavily armed bodies broke through the doors of the stairs at the other side of the elevators and, without thought, I blasted them at head level with my assault rifle on full automatic. Before the haze of blood had settled, I knew that I was committed. "Okay, Joan Wick, lead the way."

"What's this Joan Wick shit?"

I shook my head. "Movie, before your time, featuring a gun-toting psychopath. It was made for you."

I was speaking to a closing door, as Rachel was already pounding down the stairs. I followed more slowly, holding the banister and carefully stepping down. A fall now due to my dodgy knees was just what I didn't need.

To my surprise, Rachel was waiting for me two floors lower. "There's a group three floors further down. Probably just waiting for us." She pointed at a doorway into the corridor and then aimed down the stairwell with her grenade-launcher.

I rapidly bolted through the door and moved to the side, putting fingers in my ears. Rachel slipped after me and swept the empty corridor with her rifle before the door closed and another blast almost knocked it off its hinges.

As Rachel was about to charge along the corridor towards the other end of the building, I grabbed a hold of her sleeve. She immediately tried to shake herself loose. "There's another flight of stairs along there," she shouted.

I shook my head. "So what? As you've seen, the hit squads are already using them."

"What, you just want to make a stand here?" She was checking our armament as if this was a credible option.

"Don't be daft, we've got to get out of here – ideally without bumping into any more opponents."

"But, apart from the elevators, there are only 2 normal staircases and now we need to head for the one at the other side of the elevators. Unless, of course, you want to cram onto the external emergency stairs. Even at this time of day, they

103

must be crammed with panicked guests on the way down."

I pulled her in the opposite direction. "But there's a door marked *staff only* just a bit further along here. Want to bet there's a service elevator there?"

Recognising that this was a more sensible option, although clearly not pleased that she hadn't thought of it herself, Rachel followed along at my heels.

Just before we reached our goal, I saw that a guest room door was wedged open – presumably being cleaned before the evacuation order caused the staff to depart. I pulled Rachel in after me, while she frowned in confusion.

"Okay, kid, dump all the hardware and anything else that could possibly have been tagged." I was pulling sheets from the bag in a cleaning trolley to make space for them. Actually, we should also include any clothes that you've been carting around since the start of this gig."

"That's everything that I'm wearing. Actually, apart from these trainers, which I bought in Osoyoos."

"Fine, get rid of all the rest."

"Any what about you," Rachel looked bemused as she started to disrobe.

"I'm dumping this flack-jacket, but the rest of my stuff is what I brought with me to Canada, so it shouldn't be bugged."

I glanced at my supposed-daughter and noted that she was now down to a pair of very small knickers. "Get rid of the panties and also your socks. It's good that you'll at least have something on your feet."

"You're expecting me going off to fight a hit-squad like this, bare-handed and in the buff?"

"The entire point of this is to avoid any fights. Our opposition have been finding us far too quickly, so they must be tracing us electronically. Anyway, we don't want them to find out about us using the service elevator until it's too late, hence your exposed arse. I'll give you this t-shirt here," I quickly pulled it off and handed it to her, "and you can have my shorts when we have a bit of breathing space. Also, your wristcom has to go. I'll just hope that your gold chain and the nipple rings couldn't possibly be tagged."

To my amazement, Rachel did exactly as requested. I could only guess that she had quickly caught on to the anomaly of being found again so quickly.

I led the way into the service room, telling Rachel to let the bedroom door latch closed, and, after locking the door, called the elevator which had been parked at the ground floor. To my relief, it responded immediately and had arrived before I heard the first sounds of cautiously approaching footsteps.

Unlike the guest elevators, we could take the service lift down to a sub-basement level. I had worried that this might have been busy with staff, but they had evidently cleared out to an assembly area and we had the cavernous hall to ourselves. To one side there were lockers and a changing area, complete with shower rooms and toilets. There was also a laundry, a massive switchboard that monitored and controlled electrical services, and a small parking area for a half-dozen golf-carts. Ignoring a connecting hall that clearly served as a supply store, I made for a rack of e-bikes that could be rented by guests. Rachel diverted into the changing area to search for clothes while I set up bikes and helmets for us both.

I cracked open a small gate, located to the side of a large, roll-up garage door, and peered out at an extensive parking area holding a snowplough, 2 small buses and a number of private cars. This was strangely deserted, although a few people lingered on a ramp leading up to the level of the main road and the front entrance of the hotel. It seemed that most of them were smoking or vaping while they talked excitedly about the chaos that must be unfolding around them.

I left the gate open and returned to the changing room in time to see Rachel clambering into a black boilersuit with the hotel logo emblazoned on the back. "Sensible, I suppose, but I was just getting used to the sight of your bare bum."

"Stop waffling, you sad old git, and get into that other one," she pointed to a grey version that was lying on the floor beside her. "It seems to be about the right size, although you may have to suck in your gut to get it to close."

While I complied, Rachel evidently spotted the large wrist computer that I sported. "What the fuck! You said to dump anything that could be used to trace us and you've still got that ancient brute on your arm."

"Ah, my PASS, it's a personal assistant. What you call a wristcom in the states. Ancient it may be, but tailored to my requirements and hence useable without being traced. As I previously noted, the problem with your mother is..., well was..., that she just had no interest in technical shit. I'm sure that she just never seriously considered that her kit could be bugged. It could be that it was only her palmtop, but when the opposition have certainly found a way to trace us, it's better to take all possible precautions."

She shook her head. "Well, in this game, you can't be too paranoid. But I feel more naked without guns than I did without clothes."

"The advantage of being without weapons is that it encourages discretion, which is very much the better part of valour in these circumstances. Now, let's get our collective arses in gear and blow this joint." I strapped on a helmet and pushed a bike slowly towards the exit, stopping only to run to the switchboard and hit the emergency electrical cut-off switch which plunged the basement into darkness broken only by the light coming from the open gate. "I've sorted out a route, so just follow me."

As we cycled across the parking area, we were spotted by a couple of the smokers, who waved in a cheery manner. *Probably guessing that we're taking advantage of the chaos to slope-off early.* I raised an arm in response, but then had to concentrate on steering as we headed onto a track through the forest that was set up for mountain biking.

In absolute terms it was not very technical, but having had a few biking accidents in my past, I tended to be extra-cautious, which actually made things more difficult on a bumpy path. Nevertheless, the route was all downhill, so I did not need to try to work out how to engage the electric drive. It was only a little more than twenty minutes later when we emerged at a point at the edge of town where the path forked, with one option crossing the main road. This was also where a bus stop was located.

"Just leave the bikes out of sight from the road. There's a bus every fifteen minutes or so that goes into town."

"And you think these will be running, despite the zoo that the road in front of the hotel will be like now?"

"Yes, I've heard a lot of sirens going up in that direction…" Just on cue, I could see flashing blue lights approaching and we moved out of sight as an ambulance dopplered past. "But I guess that, if buses had been going up before the road was blocked, they'll be turned back at some point. Let's just wait for a bit and see."

"Why don't we just cycle into town, you lazy old bastard."

"Once more, that should be evident to anyone of the meanest intelligence," I smirked. "I'm sure that, when the bad guys spot that we've dumped the trackers, they'll hack into CCTV and any other accessible monitoring systems. With a bit of luck, the power cut will mask our exit from the basement and nothing will have picked up our trip through the forest. There will be plenty of cams around the hotel at present, but there seems to be no CCTV here, so

108

we should be able to make it to the centre of town without being spotted."

I had been prepared to give it an hour but, twenty minutes later, a shuttle bus appeared and stopped for us. I had expected to have to show a room key to get a free ride, but evidently our boilersuits were sufficient to get us waved inside. The bus was packed with other staff and we had to stand while a babel of speculation about the *terrorist attack* filled the vehicle.

Along with many of the others, we disembarked in the town centre. Although it was now almost 6 pm, most tourist shops were still open and I was able to use my PASS to buy a couple of mid-sized rucksacks and a selection of clothes for us both. We also picked out wide-brimmed canvas hats that we donned immediately. At Rachel's insistence, we also purchased a couple of large ceramic knives, a can of bear-spray and an ultra-compact hunting crossbow with a dozen bolts. We then took turns in a public toilet to change out of our boilersuits, which we dumped in a container for recycled clothing.

By now, the adrenalin that had been keeping me going was wearing off and I was beginning to feel my age, becoming aware of a number of aches and pains from injuries that I had not even noticed at the time. We needed to make a decision on how to proceed, with the best place to discuss this seeming to be a busy brewpub just off the main drag.

With our backpacks stored beneath a table on the patio, we were quickly served beers which we sipped in silence until our ordered burgers arrived. I fiddled with my PASS most of this time until Rachel eventually lost patience. "All right, mister smart guy, what do we do now?"

"The obvious options all involve getting the hell away from here ASAP. With a hire car, we can head in any direction. Public transport by bus or rail is also possible, but the services are very limited and would mean heading either west, back towards Vancouver, or east towards Calgary. Or, I suppose, there's also north towards Jasper, but that's a bit of a dead end."

"These are the obvious options. Why do I get the feeling that you'd prefer something else? Something less obvious."

"It all depends how smart our opponents are. They'll have found your mother's body and she'll probably have been considered the main technical threat. They wanted to get a hold of me, but I'm not sure whether that'll still be a priority or not, given that I no longer have access to the resources that she had."

"And what about me?"

"What about you?" I laughed. "You're just the daughter. Merely a bit of muscle for use as and when the thinkers might need it. They won't give a shit... Ouch! That was fucking sore." The kick under the table was not as serious as if it would have been had she been wearing combat boots, but I hammed it up anyway. "I'm an old man who's accused of being your sperm-donor, so I deserve pity rather than abuse."

"Stop your geriatric waffling and get to the point. What should we do?"

"Well, the best thing for me would be if we split up and I never saw you ever again."

"So, you'd just fuck off, abandoning me without any access to cash?"

"You'll manage fine. You'll be able to survive as a mugger until you can find a way back into the assassination business."

"You're wittering, you know. You've seen that there's a credible threat of a nuclear apocalypse in Europe and there's no way that you can ignore that. You also know that combatting such a threat will be easier if you have muscle to protect your feeble old corpse."

"Unfortunately, there you're not completely wrong." I shook my head. "I guess that means I'll have to look after you for the next bit."

It looked like Rachel was going to point out who was looking after whom in no uncertain terms, but she managed to rail herself in. "For fuck's sake, enough with this nonsense. What are we going to do?"

"Well, I've already booked us into a little Airbnb nearby. We can check in there and lie low for a couple of days until the dust settles a bit. This gives me some time to come up with a sensible plan, instead of all this rushing about when we're focused only on staying alive."

"Wait a minute, this won't work. Remember my mum said that the nuke attack will take place in 48 hours if you weren't handed over. We just don't have time to hang about here."

"Not even Miriam would have believed that threat. She was just using it to put pressure on me. We know for certain that we've got more than a couple of days. In fact, I'm sure that we've probably got at least a week or so."

"We know for certain?" Rachel screwed up her eyes in a grimace of concentration. "Fuck, yes, of course we do! The Veep's in Europe and nothing will happen until she is well clear of any fallout zone."

"Indeed. We now need to use this time to find out a lot more about possible threats and how to combat them. Luckily, this is my area of expertise. It's made more difficult without access to the search machines that Miriam has…, had at her disposal. But we can do some shopping for hardware tomorrow morning and then I can get started."

"And what do I do?"

"Oh, actually when I said *we* go shopping, I meant you, of course. Women are more suitable for that sort of thing, don't you… Fuck, that was really painful." This time the kick was much more vicious.

"Christ on a bike, you've really got a death wish, don't you? I have no idea how you managed to survive your encounter with my mad mother, short though it was."

"Well, it was touch and go," I admitted. "Anyway, there's other stuff that you can usefully do. For example, after we're checked in, you could get your flabby bare arse on that bed and…"

For an instant I thought I had gone too far when I saw my victim clench her fists. Then she burst into totally unexpected and uncharacteristic giggles. "Come on, Dad, you took every possible chance to ogle my bare bum and, even with your aging eyesight, you must admit it's not flabby."

I was totally caught out by this reaction and prayed that I wasn't blushing. "Well, perhaps I did, on the odd occasion, catch a fleeting glance of your posterior."

"You were salivating, admit it."

"Under the circumstances, I was too shit-scared to salivate. However, you do, based on a very quick glimpse, appear to have a toothsome rump."

"I knew it," she gave me a smug, Cheshire Cat grin. "You find me devastatingly attractive and, because you're my dad, you're forced to come out with all these insults in order to maintain distance. You poor old bugger, you're going to be suffering if I end up wandering around in the buff again."

I quickly responded to divert Rachel from this topic. "Well, the little cabin I've rented has a single bedroom, but it has an ensuite bathroom where you can change into your nightwear."

She scratched her head and, if possible, her smile widened. "Mmm, nightwear. Did we buy any of that? Did I miss fluffy pjs for you and a thick cotton nighty for me?"

As I have never worn anything in bed, this had not even occurred to me. "Bugger, I forgot. Maybe we've still got enough time to buy something."

"Don't be daft. I don't have any issues with nudity and, if you're uncomfortable, you can always close your eyes. On the other hand, after we finish here, we should probably pick up some toiletries and maybe a few beers. Your cheap cabin won't have the bathroom goodies and minibar that you're used to in your luxury hotels."

A good point. The girl definitely wasn't daft and her observations of my behaviour were very perceptive. *Just what I need, a provocative nymphet to add to my list of other threats.*

Chapter 12: Rachel

Jim had disappeared off to the toilet yet again. His third trip since we entered the pub an hour ago. *Probably a sign that his prostate's buggered.* I could not really get bothered by this, even though it meant that he could be waking me up throughout the night. I knew that I was tiptoeing around the fact that I had seen my mother slaughtered just a few hours ago. *Was this just classic post-traumatic issue-avoidance, or was I really so fucked-off with her that I actually didn't care?*

I closed my eyes and forced myself to relax, feeling my breathing slow down, getting deeper. The sounds from the bar around me faded into the background. This was an exercise that I had used several times after friends and colleagues had been killed in action. Or, even worse in one case, rendered paraplegic: a fate that I knew would soon result in her committing suicide. It should feel worse now, accepting that my mother had been murdered in front of my eyes. However, all I could feel was the last frisson of fear as a result of my lucky avoidance of the same fate.

Only now, I remembered that Jim had thrown himself on top of me, shielding me with his body. Not at all what I would have ever expected of him. And what had my fucking mother done? Without telling me, she had brought him into the game to act as a lure. Probably hoping that the attempts on his life would give her an angle against the Veep. It now seemed clear to me that she had been running another game in the background, behind our search for the planners of the nuclear attack.

So, I could find no traces of sorrow that the bitch was dead. If it had been me, she would have probably been more pissed off about the loss of her investment to create me, rather than anything else. No sorrow, but despite that an intense hatred of the bastards who had ordered these attacks. Although I might not be a high value target, they were happy to snuff me out just to clear their line of fire. This was something to remember when next I had one of these fuckers in my sights. I would shoot through a baby daughter to nail one them. Bomb the family car. Take out a wedding party. Whatever was needed.

"I hope you're not day-dreaming about me." Jim's voice shocked me out of my reverie. "I've seen that look on your mother's face a couple of times and it was never a good sign."

He really doesn't know the half of it. But no reason to mention anything other than my suspicions about Miriam's double-dealing. This is something I'll take care of myself. Up-close and personal.

Chapter 13: Jim

The little cabin that I had rented was an easy walk along Banff Avenue from the pub. En route we picked up basic toiletries, a six pack of beer, Rachel's choice of a Canadian craft gin and a large bottle of tonic water. Our accommodation was certainly basic, but clean and with a large bedroom containing a double bed, a table with two chairs beside a fireplace loaded up with logs, and a huge but very old-fashioned 2D TV. The en suite boasted a large bath in addition to the standard toilet facilities – a feature that had contributed to my selection of this option.

Rachel looked around and raised an eyebrow. "So, we're sharing a bed now, are we?"

"Your choice. There's a rug in front of the fire and you can sleep there if you prefer. In any case, I'm completely knackered and am going to have a long soak in the bath before I hit the sack."

Rachel frowned as I started peeling off clothes, grunting as additional aches and pains were encountered during the process. "I thought you said you'd strip off in the bathroom."

"I said that you could change into your nightshirt in the bog. However, I need all the space I can get, given the state of my arthritic joints. They were bad enough when we started, but jumping on and off trains, firefights, racing down stairs and cycling forest paths have just about finished me off."

"Oh, you poor old bastard," her smile of glee rather spoiled the effect of her consoling words. "Anyway, you seem to have forgotten shagging the bitch from hell as one of your energetic activities today." At the mention of her mother, I could detect a fleeting trace of a quaver in her voice, but she recovered quickly. "Anyway, I suppose I've already seen your wrinkly little dick, so there's nothing else that's going to shock me more than that."

"My wrinkly dick just matches the rest of my body, so it'd look strange otherwise," I pointed out.

"I can assure you that it looks strange under any circumstances, much like the rest of your sorry bod. How the hell did I end up with you on a mission like this? I should have someone who looks like James Bond rather than Gandalf the Grey," she sniggered.

"That's just your lack of imagination, girl. You think the job's all action and violence, the way it is in the movies. But, in real life, a bit of thought based on age and experience can make all that macho nonsense superfluous. When up against opponents with vast resources of cannon fodder, going against them toe-to-toe will certainly end badly. Miriam found this out to her cost and I'm sure that we escaped that trap by beating a careful retreat." Now in my birthday suit, I hobbled into the bathroom and started running hot water into the bath.

As I turned to close the door, Rachel blocked me and pushed through to sit on the toilet. "Okay, so you're the old, wise man. What could Miriam have done better?"

I kept my attention on the bath, adjusting the taps to make sure that the water would be as hot as I could stand it. "Well, for a start, she should have realised that we were targets and done everything possible to ensure that we couldn't be followed. Especially after Osoyoos, all your kit should have been checked for bugs and anything at all dubious dumped. Just as we did in the hotel this afternoon."

"If this was so obvious to you, couldn't you have mentioned it to us? You know that your head's also on the chopping block here."

"I admit that I was a bit caught out by the resources that the opposition have, coupled to their complete lack of concern about collateral damage. However, Miriam should have been better able to assess that risk. It's what she's supposed to do. Instead, she was too busy playing mind games to brief me properly. This is what should have happened in Victoria, instead of that kidnapping fiasco. You had me drugged up when I should have been analysing threats."

Rachel pondered this while I slowly lowered myself into the scalding bath. It was right at the limits of what I could stand and thus ideal for soaking out the aches in my muscles. "Okay, I suppose I should have realised that, at a technical level, Mum was well out of her depth," she reluctantly conceded. "But you're such an irritating old curmudgeon that it's difficult to take you seriously."

I lay back with a sigh and then realised that Rachel was waiting for a response. "Well, the old bit I can't do anything about, but remember that it was you that selected me in the first place. Curmudgeon: that's a good word and I can't deny that it's appropriate. However, I have subsequently realised that some of the things that I've said have been hurtful to you and I'm sorry for that. I just lash out when I'm annoyed. This is particularly the case when I'm being fucked about by a psycho like Miriam. You were just caught in the crossfire."

"Well, I actually had nothing to do with selecting you. In fact, when Mum told me, I was strongly against it. I may have been wrong there, though. I think you've shown today that you're not as totally fucking useless as I expected." Her grin took the bite out of her words.

"Well, from you, I'll take that as glowing praise." I grinned back.

"You know, I've been thinking about the way that my mum just happened to be have a link to the crowd who're searching for us. It seems to be a bit convenient..."

"Smart girl! I'm painfully aware that your bitch mother would, given the choice, be playing both sides of any conflict rather than simply doing her job as specified. In this particular case, her schemes backfired and she inadvertently ended up in the firing line. I can imagine how it might have gone. Miriam has dirt on the Veep and, although required to follow this up, makes some contact to see what would be in it for her if she helped the opposition a little bit. It probably wasn't anything more than letting them know that she had me under her control."

"And she was daft enough to assume that she could blackmail someone as powerful as the Vice-president?"

"I would imagine that she had lots of backups that she thought would keep her safe, but she was screwed by her lack of knowledge of the capabilities of modern technology to winkle us out. When we presented a clear threat, it was considered much easier to simply take us all out rather than get drawn into some cat-and-mouse game with your mother. Hence the total overkill at the hotel. But for a lot of luck, we'd be a melange of bits and pieces in morgue body-bags at the present."

Rachel looked shocked, but quickly recovered her composure. "So, what do we do now? I've been thinking through the travelling options and thought that buying a car would be the least traceable option, especially if we did it on-line. I assume that you've got enough funds for that."

"I've got plenty of untraceable e-money but, after you get a hold of a car, where would we go?"

Rachel scratched her head. "Well, I guess we need to get to Europe, so we head for an international airport. From here that'd be Calgary or, possibly better, Vancouver."

"Would these options be something that you previously discussed with the older psycho?" I grinned annoyingly.

"I suppose Mum was muttering something about this after we escaped from Clearwater."

"That's a good reason for doing something else. I think that we're safe to assume that whoever is organising these hit squads has all the intelligence that the Veep can access. Even if she wasn't already compromised, they'll now have everything on Miriam that can be obtained from Langley. They would also have all your military and CIA records and, probably, a limited amount on me. Although I've contracted to MI5 in the past, I've never been employed by them and make a habit of maintaining the smallest digital footprint possible."

"Okay, okay, we screwed up. But what are you going to do now?"

"Me? I'm totally shagged out and am going to flake out as soon as my head hits a pillow. You, on the other hand, can organise our travel out of here."

I was obviously being irritating and received a scowl. "So, I'm supposed to sort out travel without knowing where we're going?"

"Exactly! Now hop to it. You can work out the details using my wristcom while I soak for a bit more."

"Shit! You're as bad as my fucking mum is… was. How the hell am I supposed to do this?"

"You know what ride-sharing is, don't you?"

"Of course I fucking do! Ah, so that's how we get out of here without leaving a trace. Not a stupid idea. But where am I looking for a ride to?"

"Miriam's ideas were west or east and there's fuck-all to the north, so where do you think?"

"There's not much to the south… Well, not until you hit the US border. But can we risk a border crossing if there's some form of APB out for us?"

"Get a ride from any US citizens heading home, anywhere at all in the States. Ideally an old couple. In a US car, we can be fairly sure that 3 oldies and a girl will just get waved through. They'll be looking for you, in particular, so get a girly wig tomorrow and some clothes that'll make you look more like a teenage student than a battle-hardened squaddie."

"But there's still a risk that we'll be stopped for document checks. Are we just going to fight our way out in that case?"

"Don't be daft, that'd just draw attention to us. I'll sort out the documents. It'll be no problem, as we won't be checked leaving Canada, so don't need to show that we were registered when arriving. All I need is a retina scan from you and I'll sort out the rest for the US border."

"Jesus, you wander about with that kind of kit loaded on your wristcom, just on the off chance that you'll need it."

"Not at all, that's what the dark web is for. You can pick up the kind of material that we need for a couple of hundred euros, if you know where to look."

"Fuck, I didn't know that. The CIA geeks do all that kind of stuff for Miriam."

"One of many important things you don't know, lass. Such knowledge comes with great age – building upon the running start of a misspent youth. Anyway, shoo! Get things sorted out by the time I'm finished here and then the loo's all yours. And shut the door behind you."

Rachel did not seem like a happy bunny when she left – deliberately leaving the door wide open.

I soaked until the water began to cool and then climbed very carefully from the bath, aware that my creaking joints were putting me at risk of a fall. I then, equally deliberately, did not close the door before I had a noisy pee and then cleaned my teeth with much gratuitous gurgling and spitting.

Rachel pointedly didn't look up as I entered the bedroom. "This PASS thing of yours is total crap, you know. There's nothing modern in the way of apps available and it's so bloody slow," she grumbled.

"Yes, that's what you need to accept if you want to ensure that you can't be traced on the internet. Everything is going through re-routers and homebrewed search machines."

"But, for God's sake, a tiny touch screen! I'm surprised that it isn't steam-powered."

"Ah, I forgot to mention the voice control option."

"I've been trying that, but there's absolutely no response."

"Well, you need to switch it on first. It's that little button on the side. You need to hold it down for ten seconds. That'll also switch on the cam."

"But why? The entire point of voice-control is that you control it with your voice. Either a default *voice on* or a secure code phrase. You, however, have a physical switch. How bloody quaint!"

"Ah, the naivety of today's youth." To be especially annoying, I tapped her on the head – which could have been termed paternal had I been wearing any clothes. "Without a physical switch, a microphone is always on and hence hackable. This applies also to the camera, GPS and other traceable features. In my case, these default off and are accessed only when physically switched on. Because of the re-routers, voice commands are slow, so you'd be better using the virtual keyboard function, which will also work now that you're turned on full functionality."

"So, under normal circumstances, this is just an extremely bulky watch?"

"Under normal circumstances, I also carry a normal mobile phone. However, being a target for nutters who blow up chalets in Switzerland brings out my full paranoia, so I chucked it immediately afterwards. This is the kind of thing that Miriam should think... should have considered. Much better if she had been more paranoid and less of a psychopath."

"So, this thing doesn't even work as a phone?"

"It will do now, if you activate that function. But I'd strongly recommend staying well away from something so easy to trace. In any case, it pings a dark web site to check for messages whenever I'm online, so we're not completely cut off if someone wants to reach us. That kind of one-way communication is inherently untraceable."

"Fine, but what if the message is urgent?" Rachel finally turned to look at me. It was difficult to tell if her grimace of distaste was due to the hardware she had to work with, the state of my aged body, or both.

"It's just a matter of priorities. When I'm under cover, secrecy tops the urgency of anyone trying to contact me. It's an inevitable trade-off. You can see Miriam's problem here: she felt that she was so important that she always had to be instantly contactable. You can't have that without opening a vulnerability."

"Wait a minute. If you thought we were being tracked via Miriam's tablet or wristcom, why did I need to strip off and dump all my kit?"

"I was simply thinking about how I'd do it if I wanted to trace you. I'd certainly hack all coms, but I'd also place passive radio-frequency tags in any of your possessions that I could access. Actually, I wouldn't be surprised if these come as standard for most of the weapons that you had, assuming that these came from the Agency."

"Bugger! How could my fucking mother not know about this?"

"Too high up the management tree and no interest in techy stuff. That's the job of underlings, like you and me."

"Fuck! This isn't part of my military skill set. In the day, we didn't hide from anyone – it was our targets hiding from us. I knew that tame wonks provided tracking for our ops, but never had to know how this kind of shit actually worked."

"Well, this is something that you're going to have to learn fast. Luckily, it's high on my list of skills, so you might actually live long enough to pick up the basics. Anyway, I'm dead on my feet and am off to bed. You can get the ride share set up and then de-activate the PASS – again holding the button down for ten seconds. And try not to wake me if you decide for the bed rather than the rug. If you're like your mother, you'll now be panting for sex but, I can assure you, I've had more bonking in the last 24 hours than in the previous month, so it's going to take a while for me to recharge my batteries."

I noted that Rachel was mumbling something as I clambered arthritically into bed, but I didn't even try to make out what it was. Within seconds, I was fast asleep.

Chapter 14: Rachel

I quickly identified a suitable rideshare option and flagged it so that the old bastard could make a final decision in the morning. I then set up the best search tools available on this antiquated wristcom to dig deeper into Jim's background. While this was running, I prepared a large gin and tonic while I thought over the last couple of hours and, in particular, Jim's response to my worries about Miriam. I had to grudgingly admit that he was a very clever bugger and had picked up a lot of the issues that it had taken me so long to identify. Nevertheless, I was certain that he was missing something. Maybe something critical.

He was extremely disparaging about my mom's failure to identify hacking risks. Mom was no techno-geek, but she'd have to be brain-dead to miss this risk. So what if she was actually aware of it?

Here again, Jim's analysis seemed increasing weak when I thought through it in detail. That my mother would happily sacrifice Jim for any minor benefit to her plans was no surprise. But she would not so easily throw me to the wolves. Of that I was sure. Until this jaunt, I saw only that my mother wanted me to follow in her footsteps. But, now, I had a hint of something more. Getting in bed with the Veep was dangerous in the short-term but, if all went well, there could be long-term benefits. Miriam was close to retirement, but that would not change her obsessive need to be in the driving seat for international security issues. Now it was becoming clear that she did not really see me as a protégé, more as a glove-puppet that she could manipulate when she had been pensioned off and was formally out of the lamplight.

What she needed now was a huge success. Something that would put her in a position to nail down her legacy, serving her last years in a powerful role without any real oversight. I shuddered as pieces began to fall into place. *She didn't want to stop the nuclear attack. That was something that would be covered-up and the best that she'd get would be a congratulatory pat on the back and a minor promotion. On the other hand, if the attack went ahead and then she exposed all those responsible, she'd be golden – both nationally and internationally.*

It would have been a killer move if the Veep's team hadn't been even cleverer and spotted what she was up to. The attack on the Rimrock Hotel suddenly made complete sense. It was not Jim that was in the cross hairs, it was Miriam. Jim and I were just collateral and, if taken out, it simply made the subsequent clean-up easier.

The question was now whether or not I should mention this to Jim. We had been forced to work together, so letting him know this ASAP would be appropriate. However, I was sure that he had a number of cards up his sleeve, probably holding back until he saw how things developed in the future. Maybe it would be sensible for me to keep my analysis close to my chest for the same reason.

Chapter 15: Jim

I awoke with a sizeable erection just as first light was beginning to seep through the bedroom curtains. Unfortunately, this was not due to the naked girl sharing the bed with me, but the typical response to the pressure of an old man's bladder. With a groan, I rolled from the bed and almost fell due to the shock of pain from my knees. I held onto the bedside table for a moment to steady myself, then staggered to the bathroom as quickly as I could. Luckily, I had no bedwear to hinder me and was able to let loose as soon as I was within range of the toilet. I closed my eyes and sighed in relief. *Last thing I need now is to piss myself. Rachel would never let me live it down.*

Back in the bedroom, I spotted a capsule machine and set it going to produce espresso-strength coffee in a large mug. I noted that the growling of the coffee-maker was disturbing my sleeping companion, but slipped in a second capsule after the drips from the first stopped. When I started the machine for the third time, it must have passed her level of tolerance. "For fuck's sake, Jim, will you give it a break. It's the middle of the fucking night and I'm trying to sleep."

"Ah, an owl rather than a lark. Just shows your mother's blood in you. It's almost seven and I'm ready to hit the road, just after I get some caffeine down my neck. Want some?"

"Just fuck off, why don't you. I don't want coffee, I want sleep. I was up for ages sorting out our ride on that heap of shit that you call a PASS."

I was pleased to see that Rachel had deactivated the wristcom when she had finished her work. A quick flick though the keystroke log led me to her rideshare contact. "This seems to be fine, a retired American couple. Mister and Mister Harrington-Jones: looks like the very dab. About to head back to Spokane, again excellent. They're planning to leave today. I've already paid for this place for a couple of nights, but that isn't a problem. The drive is doable in half a day, but they seem keen to stop off in Radium en route, so would like to start early. Let me just confirm this... done! So, get your not-quite-totally-flabby arse in gear so that we can grab some breakfast before they pick us up. That'll be in just over an hour and a half." With that I pulled the curtains open to flood the room with early morning sunshine.

My companion seemed to be cursing me but, as she had a pillow over her head, it was difficult to make out. I ignored this distraction and activated my search engine. While sipping coffee, I had a look at how to set up a trip from Spokane to anywhere in Europe, as that was where the action seemed to be. In no time, I had identified a motel on the outskirts of Spokane that always seemed to have vacancies. I then sorted out a rideshare that would take us to Seattle early tomorrow morning.

Then, realising that I could postpone it no longer, I hacked into the RCMP major crimes database. Surprisingly, the Mounties had nothing at all about the Clearwater attack and hence there must have been a clean-up crew on site very soon after the incident. It appeared that we had another lucky escape there.

For Osoyoos and Rimrock, the events were reported, but details were hidden behind another firewall, locked in a database shared with CSIS, the Canadian national security agency. Hacking this was beyond my abilities, so I contracted it out to a dark web site, which provided instant access for a few hundred euros. From a quick scan alone, it was clear that these two actions had been linked and this was causing a diplomatic shitstorm for the Yanks. The exploding seaplane in Osoyoos had departed from the Seattle base of Exos, an often-renamed private military contracting company that was notorious for dubious work carried out for the CIA and some mega-corporations. The three helicopters involved in the Rimrock attack had no filed flight plans, but satellite images allowed them to be easily traced to a training camp in Montana, run by the same company. Although US Homeland Security claimed that they had no links to either of these actions, the Canadians were clearly unconvinced.

I shook my head in despair. *Someone high up in the Veep's team has screwed the pooch big time.* Osoyoos and Clearwater would have been planned as surgical strikes and, even if they failed, should not have led to significant collateral damage. The complete loss of both teams must have caused someone to panic, letting a heavily-armed hit squad loose on a high-end hotel. From the moment that the helicopter gunship open fire into a room in the

132

hotel, caught on video by a witness and posted immediately on a couple of news websites, the incursion had spiralled downhill. Only one of the two large troop-carrier choppers escaped before local police arrived, leaving almost a dozen of the attackers dead and as many seriously injured, before or while they were captured. Interrogations and forensic work were ongoing, but it was looking very bad for Exos. *Maybe time for another buy-out and name change.* I smiled with shameless Schadenfreude.

"What are you grinning about, then?" The voice in my ear caused me to jump, almost spilling the last of my coffee. "Don't tell me there's actually some good news for a change."

My attention must have been well distracted, as Rachel had showered and was now rubbing her hair with a towel. I couldn't prevent my eyes drifting lower to clock her naked body, realising as I did so that I was also in the nude. "Well, your boobs don't droop as much as I thought they did." I managed to duck in time to avoid what would have been a very painful slap. "But, seriously, it looks like the only casualties from yesterday were bad guys. There were only a few minor injuries to staff and guests, mainly from flying glass after the gunship exploded."

"And my mum," she pointed out, transforming my smile to a grimace as I realised that I had already forgotten this important detail. "I guess the survivors who managed to escape must have taken her body with them. Despite that, the remaining bad guys are going to be extremely pissed off. We

133

should have been an easy target and, during three attempts, they've lost the best part of 3 squads – not to mention 3 choppers and a seaplane."

"I think we've got little to worry about there. Some of your victims survived and are now in custody, while the intrusions into Canadian airspace have been traced back to Exos…"

"Fucking hell, someone's screwed up big time. You're right, though, the shit'll hit the fan in a most spectacular manner and everyone involved will be too busy trying to cover their own arses for them to have any time for us."

"And, with your mother definitely out of the picture, we'll probably fall off their radar anyway. Nevertheless, we should keep our heads down, just in case there's anyone higher up the food chain who bears grudges and also has access to black-op resources. Anyway, I'll brief you over breakfast. We're getting picked up at a café on the main drag, so we should get a move on. Some clothes would be good for a start…"

"What about you, with your shrivelled little willy on show? At least I look good in the nude."

I rolled my eyes and sighed. "Crass youths! Focus only on superficial appearances rather than appreciating the finer qualities resulting from age." Rachel was now pulling on knickers and a sports bra, so I deactivated my PASS and strapped it onto my wrist, ignoring her disparaging comments on my total lack of any kind of fine qualities. "We don't have time to pick up any more clothes, so you'll just need to work with what you've got. Anything that makes you look more airhead and less terminator."

Within ten minutes, we were dressed, packed and on our way out of the cabin. To my amazement, Rachel had done a great job on the clothing side, cutting the legs off a pair of jeans to make them so short that the lower parts of her buttocks were on display. Her tanga knickers were pulled high enough to present a classic whale-tail and the shirt knotted below her bra showed off her flat stomach. I knew that she had been using makeup to hide her black eyes, but the addition of fire-engine red lipstick diverted all attention from remnant bruises – and made her look a decade younger into the bargain.

I was about to compliment her, when I caught a glare that indicated that the girl was less than happy with her transmogrification. We simply lifted our luggage in uncomfortable silence and headed off. I left the key behind in the room, but hung up the *do not disturb* sign, in the hope that our absence would not be noticed until our check-out time tomorrow.

After we settled down to breakfast – a stack of pancakes and a strawberry smoothie for Rachel, coffee and a croissant for me – tension slowly eased from the air. We began to speculate about what Mister and Mister Harrington-Jones might be like. Rachel was hoping for some kind of Cage-aux-Folles, full-on gays, while I expected a completely ordinary couple of blokes. Indeed, I pointed out that we did not even know that they were married. They could, potentially, be brothers.

Rachel snorted inelegantly. "Brothers, no chance. Brothers would never, ever, refer to themselves as *mister and mister*."

"I suppose you're right," I conceded, "but we'll find out soon enough. We just need to watch out for the camper van they're driving."

Another snort. "A camper van? That'll really stand out, being that campers represent about half of the vehicles on the road hereabouts. Anyway, why're we getting picked up here? It would've been easier at the cabin, as we wouldn't have had to lug these rucksacks along with us."

"Just a standard part of making our spoor tricky to follow. If anyone thought to check ride-shares, this pick-up location would be a dead end. The cabin, however, could lead to the booking that was made last night."

"That's a bit overly paranoid. Do you really think anyone would be running such traces?"

"If I was in charge, I would. It's so easy to do with smart search engines if you just specify the task properly. In any case, it's minimal inconvenience for a possible benefit, so it's daft not to do it." I noticed her frown so continued. "Of course, you realise I should be billing you for all this on-the-job training."

"And what about me billing you for protecting your decrepit old arse?"

"That's not anything extra, it's just the job that you're already paid to do. In fact, I'm the boffin and you're the grunt, so I shouldn't need to get involved at all in any of the physical stuff."

"Well you haven't done so much. I took out the attackers yesterday."

"Most of them at Rimrock, I admit, although even then I had to blast a couple of them. But what about Clearwater? If I hadn't provided a diversion and then taken out the pilot, it might have been the end of the road trip for you."

"Shit, I'd forgotten that was yesterday morning. It was a busy day. Anyway, you just helped to speed things up. I'd have managed to overpower those muppets at some point."

"You didn't have much time. There must have been a clean-up team in there very quickly to ensure that there was no report of the action. They actually did a good job, as my hackers spotted that there was actually a record of us checking out that morning."

"Anyway, water under the bridge now. I can now see a camper double-parked across the road that's flashing its headlights."

"Okay, let's get moving." A touch of my PASS against the menu tablet was enough to settle the bill with untraceable e-cash.

By European standards, the motor home was huge: probably about 10 metres long and as wide as a coach. It clearly had off-road capabilities and these had been used recently if the mud splattering the lower half of the coachwork was anything to go by. A tall, heavily-built man, clad in shorts, t-shirt, trainers and a baseball cap, waved at us as we emerged from the café and directed us to a door on the pavement side of this beast."

"I'm Jim, although I usually go by Jimmy," he offered a large hand that looked well used to physical labour, "and I guess you must be the other Jim and this'll be Barbie." Rachel's initial contact had provided only an anodyne email address for her and I had felt free to expand on this when I

137

confirmed the trip. Of course, I could not pass up on the chance to select details for my travelling companion that were sure to annoy her.

"Jimmy, great to meet you." I was tensed for a hand-crusher, but his shake was surprisingly gentle. It was difficult to determine his racial background as his fine features and milk-chocolate complexion suggested Indian sub-continent while his physical build seemed much more Western or Central African. "And, yes, this is my better half, Barb."

I saw Jimmy's eyebrows rise while he shook hands with Rachel, clearly bemused by my companion's evident youth, but he covered this well. "Nice to meet you, Barb. Let's get you into the van so that we can stop blocking the street here."

"Sure thing," Rachel turned to give me one of her classic death stares. "I'll just help my old man up, as his legs don't work so well anymore."

Mainly to be more annoying, I scrambled up the steps into the huge vehicle as quickly as I could and then turned to my missus. "Will you be okay, dear. I can take your backpack if you like."

I received another look that would have killed, before she jumped up easily behind me. "Not a problem, honey. Just settle down now, so that you don't displace your truss."

Our banter was probably responsible for the smile on the face of our driver. "Hi, guys, I'm Leroy. Welcome aboard. Throw your bags in the back and strap into these seats up front and then we'll be on our way. We can do the rest of the introductions while we're rolling."

Jimmy slammed the door behind us and then climbed up into the front passenger seat. After buckling in, he turned to us with a smile, his seat pivoting so that it was at right angles to our direction of travel. "Leroy doesn't like to talk while he's driving, so I'll be doing the introductions from our side."

"Sounds good to me. Barb's a bit shy with strangers, so I'll be the spokesman for us. She'll certainly relax after a while and then you won't be able to shut her up." I coughed to cover my reaction to Rachel's painful nip of my thigh.

"Fair enough, Jim. So, as you can see, we're a real *Odd Couple*." This summed up well what I had already noticed. Jimmy was built like an ox while Leroy looked more like a mouse. Although Leroy was sitting, hunched over the steering wheel, I guessed he must be at least 40 cm shorter than his partner and weigh less than 50%. He had a tonsure of grey wispy hair and a grey goatee, with generally pallid skin apart from sunburn on his nose and forehead. "But looks can be deceptive," Jim added, eyes twinkling, "Leroy's the sportsman and I'm the bookworm."

Rachel couldn't help sniggering and I turned to frown at her. "Remember, looks can be very deceptive: just like in our case. Let me see now," I turned back to Jimmy, "Leroy's doing the driving and I've noticed how smooth it is. Even with power steering, cornering with something as large as this can't be easy. I'd guess his sport would be one that involves precision. Maybe snooker?"

Jimmy gave a deep belly-laugh and even Leroy quickly glanced back with a grin lighting up his face. "Maybe, in Europe, that's what he would have ended up doing. Here in the states, we have only games like pool that aren't so high profile. So shooting, pistol and rifle, is his sport. Semi-pro in his youth, but now just for fun. To earn money, his game is poker."

"Glad you warned us about that, Jimmy. We'll avoid getting drawn into any card games with him." I casually inspected our driver, who was wearing a baggy t-shirt, and noticed that his forearms and shoulders did indeed seem rather over-dimensioned compared to the rest of his body. *Fits well with pistol shooting.* "And, I suppose, having someone who can shoot could be useful if we encounter any bears."

Jimmy chuckled. "We both shoot, but only targets nowadays. Our hunting days are well and truly over. But don't worry none, bears aren't a problem, even in the forest. As I noted in my mail, we're planning on finding a hot spring about noon. There are a lot of uncommercialised ones just past Radium, so that'd be ideal for a picnic lunch. What do you think?"

"That'd be great for us," I looked towards Rachel, who nodded in a distracted manner. *Probably still annoyed at having to play my trophy wife.* "We'll need to stop at a store, though, to buy some provisions."

"Don't worry about that either. We've got a well-stocked fridge in this vehicle and there'll be more than enough for the four of us. Unless, of course, you've got special diets..."

"Not at all, we're both omnivores. We do have a few beers that we can contribute, but we should keep them cold."

"Just go into the back and shove them in the refrigerator. So, are those local brews?"

"Indeed, Three Bears IPA, very tasty."

For the next hour, Jimmy and I chatted about craft ales and the way microbrewery culture had expanded around the world. Leroy contributed only an occasionally nod or grunt of agreement while Rachel restricted herself to occasional grimaces and rolls of her eyes to convey how uninteresting she found this topic. Which, of course, encouraged me to draw it out as long as possible. *Definitely two benefits to this – annoys the girl while also deflects discussion about who we are and what we're doing.*

***

We drove for about twenty minutes beyond the town of Radium Hot Springs and then turned onto a dirt track just before Fairmont Hot Springs. "This pool isn't very well known," Jimmy explained, "but it's good for this truck as it's not far from the highway and beside an old logging camp with plenty of turning space." It was clear that this attribute would be important, as the camper took up almost the full width of the track.

"I just hope we don't come across anybody coming in the opposite direction." Rachel broke her long silence with this comment, leaning forward to get a better view of the road ahead of us.

"Not a problem," Leroy responded. "Even in the old days, the logging trucks had a system of mirrors to ensure that this didn't occur and now we've a high tech version of that. This may look like the land that time forgot, but there're now webcams at both ends of the road and we can check to make sure that nobody is going to surprise us."

Jimmy grinned. "Of course, this also assumes that anyone intending to use the road also knows about the webcams – but we haven't had a problem in the time that we've been coming here. In fact, over the last decade, I doubt if we've ever seen more than a couple of folk hereabouts at this time of the year."

"Anyway, I take it that the springs are swimsuit optional," I winked at an annoyed-looking Rachel.

"Of course. But, if you're uncomfortable with that, there're about a half dozen pools along the river and you can have one to yourself," Jimmy grinned.

"Maybe that'd be better, Hon," Rachel smiled. "Although the Old Man is really lovely as a person, he's not so pleasant on the eyes. And even worse without clothes."

Jimmy guffawed. "You're a hard woman, Barb. But we hang around with a lot of naturists and few of them are oil paintings. Anyway, as long as anybody's happy in their skin, there's no way that it'd bother us."

"Well, as long as there're no mirrors, I won't be bothered by anything that I'll see and, as you can imagine, Barb is very short-sighted," I smiled. "If we're having a picnic, though, it'll be easier if we're in the same pond."

"Sounds good to me. You can start getting yourselves together now, as we'll be there in five minutes," Leroy noted without taking his eyes from the road.

Jimmy undid his seat belt and twisted his way into the back of the camper. "I'll just put the food in a cool-box. Will you both be good with beer or do you prefer wine? We've got both real beer and alcohol-free for the driver."

"Beer is good for both of us," I answered before Rachel could respond. "I guess it would be easier to strip-off in the van and just head to the springs in sandals, if they're near enough."

"Yup, that's what we usually do," Jim responded while he dug around in the huge fridge. "I'll also sort out some towels if you don't have any with you."

"We've got these tiny camping towels, that wouldn't even cover my naughty bits, much less the rest of my aging corpse."

To my surprise, both Jimmy and Leroy exploded in laughter. When he had recovered, Jim wiped tears from his eyes. "You crazy Brits! How the hell do you ever come up with that stuff? *Naughty bits*, indeed." This set them both off laughing again.

Rachel was looking at me in a distinctly worried manner, clearly thinking that we may have ended up with a couple of insane cannibal killers.

Then it clicked for me. "Monty Python and all that off-the-wall comedy."

Leroy was still chuckling. "It's been decades since I first saw repeats of that stuff on public service TV. The originals were from a time when they bleeped out *strong language* to protect us from corruption. Dangerous terms like *naughty bits.* We had to search the internet to get a hold of the uncensored versions." For the first time he turned his view from the road and looked back at his husband. "We just can't get into a bath together without thinking about washing naughty bits." They both burst into laughter and I had to join in, leaving Rachel still completely bewildered.

"Well, you lads can do as you wish, but it'll only be Barb sorting out my naughty bits. Unless I get a much better offer," I grinned and reached over to slide my hand up Rachel's thigh, to her evident annoyance.

Jimmy shook his head. "I don't think we can offer much competition there, your Barbie is a very fine lady."

"You don't know the half of it," Rachel whispered as she loosened her seatbelt and started to strip off. She looked me directly in the eyes before she continued in a louder voice. "Anyway, you guys should go ahead and we'll follow after I've got this poor old sod sorted out." Her long-suffering sigh sounded very authentic.

"Righty-ho, here we are," Leroy announced as he drew into an empty parking area beside a dilapidated shed. "The path to the pools is directly in front of us."

The two men clambered down from the cab and joined us in the back of the camper, where they first stripped off and then started sorting out towels and the picnic cool-boxes – one containing food and another loaded with beer. We were also offered flip-flop type bathing sandals, which were more appropriate than the footwear that we had in our depleted luggage.

Leroy and Jimmy led the way, each carrying a coolbox, while we followed carrying towels. The contrast between the two men was even more obvious when they were naked: the short, thin, pallid frame of the former was emphasised when he walked beside his tall, muscular, brown-skinned husband. *I guess they're probably thinking the same about us, a flabby old pensioner and his well-toned young wife.* I grinned at the thought.

The hot spring was at the side of a rushing stream and the pool had been formed by a wall of large stones. "It looks natural, but was actually put together by lumberjacks almost a century ago," Leroy informed us while we stacked the picnic stuff together with towels and sandals on a bench formed by a halved tree-trunk, worn smooth by decades of weather.

The pool itself was large, about 5 metres in diameter, and about a metre deep. Smooth rocks around its circumference provided comfortable seating, allowing us to sink to chest-depth in thermal water that was just short of scalding. We each entered slowly, allowing time for our bodies to adjust to the temperature. During this process it was clear that, despite the heat, both men were turned on and were sporting sizeable erections. This was especially notable for Leroy, who was even better endowed than his much taller partner.

Jimmy grinned. "As you may have noticed, we're not at all shy and find sharing the pool with others quite erotic. If you're uncomfortable with this, there's another, smaller pond just a hundred yards or so further downstream."

"At my age, there's nothing about naked bodies that makes me uncomfortable and my little honeypie is a real free spirit – and short sighted to boot." I coughed to cover the shock of pain as Rachel nipped my scrotum. "Anyway, we're happy to watch, even if I won't be able to put on much of a show for you guys in return."

The exhibitionism was not as blatant as it might have been, the men taking turns on sitting on each other's lap. It was very obvious what was going on, but the direct action was out of sight. To help fit in, I pulled Rachel onto my lap, cradling her breasts in my hands, rubbing her nipples with my thumbs. Although it looked playful, the girl showed her displeasure by painfully biting my ear. Nevertheless, within five minutes I could feel her nipples hardening as her breathing became deeper. *Oops, this isn't at all what I intended to happen here.*

Unfortunately, once started, there did not seem to be an easy way of halting the action without it seeming very strange to the guys. Despite being on their second round of humping, they were both watching Rachel closely. *Voyeurs as well as exhibitionists. Not really surprising, I suppose.*

146

The only positive side of this was that my discomfort was sufficient to prevent an erection, although, with a writhing nymphet in my arms, I wasn't sure how long that situation would prevail. *Better bring this to a finish ASAP.* I pinched her nipples hard between finger and thumb and she came immediately and very noisily, writhing in my arms and painfully crushing my wedding tackle. This set the guys off, bringing them to simultaneous orgasms.

I couldn't help feeling a bit left out, but had certainly enjoyed pleasuring Rachel, who was still gasping and quivering in my arms. *Had to be a lot of built-up pressure there, so this'll have done her the world of good.*

Shortly thereafter we took turns clambering out for a quick splash in the cold water of the creek, before returning to sit on the edge of the pool, legs dangling in the water and drinking ice-covered cans of beer that Jim sorted out for us. This led on naturally to the picnic, which comprised self-service sandwiches and fruit – together with more beer. Here I made the mistake of asking Rachel, who had been very quiet until this point, to make up a sandwich for me.

"Ham and mustard," she commented while handing over the thick sandwich.

I bit into it and choked as the thick layer of hot mustard burned my mouth. I quickly gulped down a mouthful of beer while the lads looked at me in confusion and Rachel smiled innocently. "Your mustard's quite hot," I spluttered, before carefully nibbling at the edge of the sandwich.

147

"Yup, that English stuff has a bite to it," Jimmy nodded. "But, thinly spread on roast beef, you can't get better than that."

Yes, thinly spread. That little bitch did that deliberately. She's almost choking to avoid laughing out loud.

While I very cautiously finished my sandwich, requiring two cans of beer to get it down, Rachel chatted to our new friends, explaining that she was a bit shy and it took her some time before she could relax with people she did not know. Now she over-compensated by chattering nonstop, fabricating details of our honeymoon trip around North America.

After lunch, we had another short soak in the pool – without any fornication this time. Then, after an even shorter splash in the creek, we dried up and headed back to the van. *Now a straightforward run to Spokane – assuming that we don't get any surprises at the border.*

Chapter 16: Rachel

After we hit the highway, the guys started talking about their best road trips. Very good natured, but essentially a typical, alpha-male, pissing contest. I could now relax and try to work out what had just happened in the pool. *It's not as if I haven't skinny dipped with groups of friends or even, very occasionally, watched friends shagging. Somehow, the goings-on at the hot spring were completely different. Also, I haven't had an orgasm like that for yonks. I'm completely drained.*

Thinking about it, it was clear that the male-on-male action probably played a key role. It seems crazy that women being turned on by watching men making love is often considered strange, while almost every heterosexual male I have known would regularly watch lesbian porn. *Although this might be a Western attitude, I suppose.* I was well aware that large numbers of Japanese girls were addicted to Yaoi, *Boy Love,* manga and anime. There, it was considered completely unremarkable – even for teenagers. Nevertheless, a couple of acquaintances buggering each other while I watched certainly got my juices going. Especially when I knew that they were turned on by my voyeurism. Most especially Jimmy. He was staring directly into my eyes both times that he came.

Okay, but there's also the fact that I was sitting on Jim's lap at the time. Right, he may not be my father in a legal sense, but this is an old man who is genetically linked to me in some way or other. I think he was just being annoying when he started to touch my nipples, but that was enough to set me off. I started rubbing myself and then it was a positive-feedback runaway reaction. It felt uncomfortable, but there was no way that I could stop after I had started. The last jolt of pain as my nipples were squeezed hard just sent me over the edge.

I was still trying to get my mind around this when I noted that we had reached the border. For a moment I started worrying about the many options for things to go badly wrong here but, before I could list up all potential threats, we had already driven towards the *fast track* corridor and been waved through, without having to show any documents or even talk to the border guards.

My partner was impressed, even though he tried to hide it. "Fast track, that's nice, I guess you cross the border here regularly."

"Often enough," Jimmy nodded, "but Leroy's military clearance helps a bit."

Leroy cringed, evidently unhappy to admit to anything supporting his husband's claim. "I do a bit of work for the border control guys. Geek stuff, mainly programming recognition tools for the anti-terrorist guys."

"Holds the whole thing together," Jimmy contributed in a stage whisper.

"Whatever. The depressing thing is that we're running up a down-escalator. If we do well, we hold our place. But we're not doing well." Leroy shook his head.

"You know, we might be able to help you a bit here…"

I covered my face in my hands, dreading what the geriatric was going to come out with now.

"I guess you know who we are. You wouldn't have when we arranged this trip, but you're part of the system and I get the strong feeling that you pick up stuff quickly."

"You've got something to do with the terrorists who attacked the hotel yesterday?" Leroy phrased this as a question, but it felt like a statement.

"We're the folk that the terrorists were after. Come on, if we had attack helicopters, why would we be ride-sharing?"

"He has a point," Jimmy contributed. It seemed a response to Jim, but I could see that his attention was actually focused on me.

"I don't need this," I contributed sotto voce, before outlining our situation in a very measured manner, keeping my mother out of the story, downplaying Clearwater and neglecting to mention either Osoyoos or the Veep. *A masterful piece of disinformation.*

"So, there you have it," I concluded. "We're trying to prevent a bunch of terrorists fucking things up at an international level, where the damage could be horrendous."

"You think there'll be impacts as far as Spokane?" Leroy asked.

"Sure as shit, if you consider all the associated blowback. Remember 9-11, that didn't impact only the East Coast. The resulting chaos was global." I answered confidently, despite having little in the way of solid arguments to support this conclusion.

151

Jimmy looked at me in an ambiguous manner, that I guessed was a result of our time together combined with the revelations of the past few minutes. "So, why don't you stay over with us tonight? We can then try to see how we could work together on this."

Jim shook his head. "You're a nice couple of blokes, but we can't inflict this on you. There are seriously bad guys after us and they'd bugger-up anyone who was in any way associated with us."

Jimmy grinned. "Buggering, we could handle."

"Okay, in plain text, they'd take a chainsaw to your naughty bits," he added.

"Ouch!" Jimmy sobered up quickly. "I get it, this isn't a game."

"But you could help us a bit, hopefully without any risk to yourselves." My partner had the intense look on his face that seemed to indicate that he had some new idea of a way forward. "I guess Leroy has access to notice boards that contain identified terrorist threats. If he could post a note indicating that an NSA nuclear-threat team had evidence of an imminent attack on a target in the UK but was covering it up, this might be enough to both block the attack and make things very uncomfortable for senior government officials who have more interest in lining their own nests than national security."

There was several minutes of silence before Leroy replied. "You know, that's a very serious accusation with not a lot of evidence to back it up. It could cause a lot of disruption without doing any good."

"Well, I can be a bit more specific," Jim continued. "The target is Sellafield in England and the attack will be from the air. A wide-bodied cargo-jet flying from the west. I don't know the exact date, but in about a week or so and probably at night. The compromised NSA team was led by Miriam Isaacs, who was killed in the hotel yesterday."

"That's pretty damn specific," Leroy responded, "but why don't you just post this yourself. There are sites where whistle-blowers can provide security-relevant information completely anonymously."

I could see the problem here, so spoke up. "Do you really think that these sites are secure? Especially when there's an NSA team who know that we're a risk. They'll intercept any such message, wipe it and do everything in their power to trace it back to us."

Leroy nodded, without taking his eyes from the road. "You're right there, now I think about it. However, I could slip something onto an internal military notice board that'll be widely distributed before NSA pick it up. I'm pretty sure that this couldn't be traced back to me – especially as any attempts by NSA to do this on an army server would be likely to draw more attention to the message."

I let the others talk further through this, baffled by the details revealed. *How the hell did the old bastard managed to work all this stuff out? He seems to have unearthed everything that I suspected about my mother's role here and gone further to*

flesh out the planned attack. How in the Goddess's
name is that possible?

Chapter 17: Jim

As we approached our destination, I tried to get Jimmy to accept a contribution to the fuel costs. He was adamant that the pleasure of our company was quite enough and would not accept any payment. He did, however, compromise by accepting Rachel's almost-full bottle of gin.

After declining yet another offer of accommodation with them for the night, the Harrington-Jones couple dropped us off at the rather tired-looking motel that I had booked. It seemed like about half of its forty rooms were occupied, but we stood out as the only guests without a car. Indeed, check-in featured logging of the car's registration and a driving licence. Thus, the teenager at reception seemed at a loss for what to do with us. I convinced him that all he really needed was a photo-ID and got him to scan one of the Swiss-rail cards that I had available, as I claimed not to have a driver's licence. To the youth, this was even more bizarre than being without a car. The name on the rail-pass – Sean Connery – was accepted without comment. The deciding factor, however, was my offer to pay for the room up-front, in cash and with a large tip. This quickly convinced him that this would be okay and I was fairly sure that the entire cash payment would vanish into his pocket.

The room was close to reception and, although faded, was clean and included a small sitting area and a well-equipped kitchen niche. Probably less important after our trip here, but the bathroom also featured a large Jacuzzi. Rachel rolled her eyes when she spotted this feature. "I hope you don't think I'm getting in that," she glowered in my direction. "I've had more than enough hot water to last me until the end of this jaunt."

I feigned innocence. "Oh, well, at least you certainly seemed to enjoy your last soak."

"That was completely out of order." I received a now-familiar death-stare. "I know that we had to fit in with the profile that you had invented, but that didn't give you the right to openly grope me like that. You really are a pervy old bastard."

I grinned in my most annoying manner. "Old, I certainly am. I have also been called a bastard many times, even though I can prove that this isn't true in a literal sense. I suppose pervy is also justified, but it seems a bit unfair considering that watching the guys buggering each other did more to get your juices flowing than anything I might have done."

"How did you...? Fuck, fuck, fuck!" Rachel was actually blushing, something I never expected from this hardened street-fighter.

"I suppose I had a rather unfair advantage," I confessed. "After the last couple of days, my old-man juices are totally drained and so I could observe the action critically, without hormones getting in the way." *Being open is all very well, but there's no way I'm going to tell her that it was getting touch-and-go at the end.* "I could hardly miss the way in which you and Jimmy were staring at each other during the dirty deeds. However, don't worry, there's no way that your little kink bothers me."

156

"Well, what about you?" she retaliated. "You seemed happy enough to watch the lads reaming each other."

"Indeed, that bothers me not a jot," I smiled. "Pretty tame stuff compared to what my wife and I got into, back in the days of our youth."

"You're married?" This revelation seemed to have shocked Rachel more than her penchant for boy-love voyeurism being picked up. "No way! How could any woman ever put up with you?"

"Was married. Lasted almost ten years before we got divorced. Completely amicable it was, we simply decided that we had different needs and it was better that we went our own ways."

"So, let me try to get my head around this. You and your wife used to get it off watching gay sex?" The girl stared at me in amazement.

"Oh, no, nothing as mundane as that. We were part of the swinger scene and regularly participated in group sex sessions. These were in private houses or clubs and could get very wild. Anyway, I'm sure you know the kind of thing. Videos of these happenings are very common on porn sites."

Rachel rolled her eyes. "I wish you hadn't told me that. The thought that I might accidently come over images of you will keep me well away from all sites like that in the future."

"Even if they involve lots of man-on-man action?" I teased and was rewarded by a painful elbow in the ribs. "Anyway, enough of this banter. We should get ourselves sorted out and then think about finding somewhere for dinner. We should eat

157

soon and then hit the sack early. Our ride-share will be here back of seven tomorrow morning.

Rachel shook her head, but I could sense it was nothing to do with this banter. Her voice was steady and her eyes were closed as if she was doing something very difficult. "We've got to get serious about this caper. Today, you told the guys a lot of stuff without discussing it with me beforehand. Even worse, this included details that you hadn't yet seen fit to tell me."

"Mmm, I wondered when you'd bring this up." I couldn't help smiling, despite the danger of this setting-off my rather volatile compatriot. "What do you want to start with? Opening up to our shirt-lifter pals, the nuclear target or Miriam's compromised unit?"

Rachel gulped in surprise, clearly expecting me to be more on the defensive. "Well, why not start with Jimmy and Leroy? Why on earth would you want to get them involved? It was just asking for trouble."

"It's my fault actually," I confessed. "I told you to set up a ride share and just assumed that you'd be as paranoid as me. You clearly didn't do an in-depth search on the options available and hence didn't pick up Leroy's military intelligence links."

"Okay, maybe I'm not paranoid enough. But, so what? It's the Veep's mercenaries that're after us, not the military."

"Ah, that leads to the third point you wanted clarified. It wasn't just that there was a mole in Miriam's team, this crowd were actively supporting the bad guys. Your mother may have been technologically clueless, but there's no way that she wouldn't spot someone else playing in her sandbox. She's the one who was compromised. I'm fairly sure that she was actively supporting our opponents in some way. In the best case, she was hoping for the nuclear attack plans to develop to the point that, when she jumped in to save the day, it would be impossible to hide and thus she'd get a lot more kudos. The other option is that she was simply bought out by the Veep and intending to hold onto her coattails when that bastard woman builds herself up as the saviour who will eliminate the clear threat of nuclear disasters.

Rachel grimaced before responding. "I had already worked out that something wasn't right with what's been happening. It just didn't fit with the caper that Miriam originally described to me."

"And you didn't tell me?" I interrupted.

"Well, you were hardly open to me. In fact, it's only now that I'm seeing how much you kept to yourself."

"It was a rhetorical question," my grin widened, which must now be close to bringing out her psychopathic streak. "I'd already guessed that you're smart enough to spot that all wasn't kosher when these attacks on us kept on coming so quickly. Let's see if our conclusions match. I wasn't quite sure what way your evil mother was playing things until Banff. Before then, the aim could actually have been taking me out of the game – whether dead or alive. But Rimrock indicated that the bad guys wanted all of us off the board, including your mother."

"So you reckon that she wasn't working for the Veep, just trying to play her?"

"That's my interpretation. She was trying to move into a position to put pressure on the Veep and forgot how seriously those with power will respond to any interloper attempting to compromise them."

"You knew this, but didn't bother to tell me?"

"Ah, yes, but you didn't tell me that you suspected something of the sort."

Rachel covered her face in her hands. "Fuck! Okay. Fuck!"

"Is it okay or fuck? You've got to get your shit together now."

"Stop fucking provoking me. Poking me with a pointed stick, as you Brits would put it."

I couldn't smother a laugh. "Right you are, lass, a bit of pointed-stick poking."

"Well, gonnae no dae that?"

Now I almost choked and then recovered enough to laugh. *Chewing the fat*! Where the fuck did you get that?"

"My gran. I think I told you she brought me up until I was in my teens. She lived in Aberdeen and, although she spent a fair amount of time with us in DC, she never lost her accent. Few of our American friends could make out a word she said.

"Right, I seem to remember something about that. Actually, I'm sure your mum told me about her mother. But why the fuck? You were prepared to disdain classic Pythonesque stuff earlier and you're actually into a Doric so-called comedy?"

"I know it, but didn't say that I liked it," she responded, struggling to hide a grin.

160

"Then you're not irredeemable. But where the fuck were we before we digressed into the comedy of previous generations? With age, my ability to hold a clear thread of conversation was one of the first thing lost."

"My mum's nefarious plans that neither of us informed the other about," she reminded me.

"Yes, the information exchange process needs to be sorted out. So we agree now: *I'll show you mine if you show me yours.*"

"I wouldn't quite phrase it like that," she grinned, "but agree to the principle involved. You can start now by telling me how you narrowed down the nuclear threat. Not only location, but also the mode of attack, date and time of day."

"You already spotted that reprocessing plants are the obvious targets if you want to maximise the radiological consequences of an attack. I then thought through how I'd plan it if I was in Alice Beall's shoes and wanted to maximise the impact of an attack while avoiding any possible connection with me. What better than for it to look like I had a very lucky escape? I've already had a dark-web hacker rip into the Veep's trip plan. Her open schedule has her leaving Europe a week today, after golf in Scotland. However, there's an option in the Air Force Two flight plan for it to depart a day earlier. So, if some emergency comes up that forces her to cut her trip short, she could get out hours before the attack is scheduled to happen."

"Isn't that cutting it a bit tight? If there's any problem that grounds her plane, she'll get trapped in the fallout."

"That's the cunning bit. She's golfing in Ayr. It's home to many great courses, but not the very famous ones, like Saint Andrews or Gleneagles, where you'd expect someone like her to be found." I saw Rachel's frown and continued. "Not only is Ayr very close to Prestwick, where her plane will be based, it's also on the west coast with prevailing westerly winds. This means that any fallout from Sellafield would be minimal there. Nevertheless, on a map, it'll look like a very close shave and I'm sure she would play it up that way."

"And the attack, using a wide-bodied plane?"

"Sellafield isn't the hard target that a reactor would be, but still you'll need a big explosion to ensure that all physical barriers will fail. A large, fully-fuelled jet would be just the job. But, learning from 9-11, you wouldn't want the risk of heroic passengers buggering up your plans. A cargo plane would work and, even if you hadn't suicide-pilots to hand, coming from the west on auto-pilot you couldn't fail to hit your target."

"Really, it's as easy as that?"

I shook my head. "Not easy, but doable. It would take some fancy electronic kit to make a wide-bodied jet vanish from radar and, even if it was and then flying very low, there's always the chance of it being spotted visually. This risk is reduced if the attack is at night."

"Right, you've made a convincing case there," she grimaced, probably annoyed that she hadn't worked some of this out for herself. "Now we get back to Jimmy and Leroy. Why give them all this information if you could just as easily pass it on to your British security contacts?"

"Oh, I've already done that. They'll do a deep-dive into the threat and make sure that it's taken care of. They'll certainly find those directly responsible and it just depends on luck how much further up the command tree they'll be able to penetrate. The tricky thing is that I'm sure that there'll be nothing that'll stick to the Beall and her upper coterie. In fact, at some point, the Brits will need to share information with their Yank counterparts, so NSA will also be briefed."

"Now I'm even more confused. If it serves no purpose, why mention anything at all to *les boys*?"

"At some point, it'll be noticed that we're missing from the scene of the Rimrock attack and the Mounties will put out an APB on us. It's the kind of thing that Leroy would pick up, so it was better for us to pre-emptively muddy the water. In addition, the message about the threat shows us up as good guys, hopefully ensuring that they don't rat us out immediately. Leroy has the typical military distrust of security agencies, so that'll help. He'd love to see shit come down on an elite NSA team."

"So that was why you specifically named Miriam's unit?"

"I also hoped that this would take some heat off us, at least from the NSA folk who are working for Beall's hit squad. They'll quickly find out about our allegations and number one priority thereafter will be arse-covering. Also, the planned nuclear attack will now be dead in the water, so there's less incentive to find me. I've already done the damage that they wanted to avoid."

"Oh, so that's it? You're off the hook and can head off home?" She was fighting to hide it, but I was sure that this was something she dreaded. *Probably uncertain about starting anew without Miriam's controlling presence.*

"Much though I'd love it to be the case, the problem is that I've defused only this particular threat. I am sure that someone as driven as Beall won't just drop the entire idea because their first action was derailed. I suspect that there's a plan B somewhere in the background and that it'll get activated as soon as the upcoming shitstorm dissipates."

"So, what do we do now?"

"You first sort out somewhere for dinner and then you can get to work draining all of Miriam's black-op funds that you can lay your hand on. I'll give you a Swiss account that you can transfer the dosh to."

"So, we're stealing Government money now?"

"It's already been stolen from somewhere to ensure that it can't be traced. With a bit of luck, without Miriam at the helm, it won't even be spotted as missing. I don't need more money for myself, although I'll deduct my agreed consultancy payment before I transfer this into an untraceable war chest. This will then fund the dark-web hackers that we'll need to find out what other attacks are planned and then provide any support required to scupper them. With a bit of luck, there might even be a chance of taking down some or all of the ringleaders."

"I noticed you said *we*. So, I'm still with you for this?"

"Probably better the devil I know, rather than bringing in anyone new. There's bound to be a lot of fetching and carrying, so a brawny lass like you would be ideal."

And where are we going to be doing this? Back in Switzerland or the UK?"

"Well, certainly not anywhere in North America. The bad guys have just too many resources here. Much better if we just drop off the map until the dust settles. The EU is best for that, given open borders and tourist resorts that have hordes of foreign visitors, so we won't stand out in any way. To start with, I'll get you some identity papers that are good enough to get you to Paris. Then we'll travel by public transport – trains, buses, ships – until we reach our destination."

"Where'll that be?"

"I'll leave that as an exercise for you. See how long it takes before you work it out."

Rachel rolled her eyes. "So where is all the open exchange of information now?"

"Ah, this is something different. Part of your training." I gave her my most annoying grin and then headed off to lock myself in the toilet.

Chapter 18: Rachel

I identified Hvar as our final destination only when we boarded the ferry from Split. From Spokane it had taken us 4 days to get here, with travel going so smoothly that it seemed a bit of an anti-climax. We were now staying in an unassuming Airbnb flat on the western outskirts of the town. Jim had rented it for a month with the option of extending the stay for a further month. –This was easy as we were off-season and the number of tourists had decreased considerably. It seems that high season included large numbers of youngsters indulging in the local party scene, so we blended in well with the older generation of foreigners who now provided a good trade for the many bars and restaurants in the Old Town.

Our story, supported by our counterfeit documents, was that I was a niece travelling with my infirm uncle. *Not ideal, as far as I'm concerned, but much better than daughter with father or, even worse, young gold-digger with a rich, geriatric husband.* The apartment had two bedrooms. Jim annexed the big one with a nice view and an ensuite, with me shoved into the smaller with two small single-beds pushed together and access only to a shared bathroom. At least this bathroom had a shower, which I preferred to the bath in Jim's. *Probably needs his long soaks to keep his aged joints moving.* I smiled at the thought.

I had helped Miriam sort out the logistics for the Canada jaunt, so I had access to the account that she used for this. To my amazement, it contained over twenty million dollars, which I siphoned off into Jim's account. Then, to be on the safe side, I also emptied my private accounts and one that I shared with Miriam, converting funds into gold stored in a Swiss bank vault. Jim helped me set this up and provided me with an individual account containing some of the war-chest funds, which was to be used until we finally got things sorted out. *Whenever that might be.*

Given the cash at our disposal, I still wasn't sure why we were staying in this dump rather than one of the plush hotels or villas in the vicinity. Or even a yacht, as there were many available at this time of year. Jim's explanation was typical: "We don't do that as it's what I would look for if I was looking for someone like Miriam." *Well, it seemed to make sense to him in some way.*

At first, the novelty of the place was diverting. I have travelled throughout the world, but mainly work related, which usually ended up in major cities. For sun and sea holidays, it had always been Mexico or Hawaii. Hvar was so quaint, with such a long history, that I was often completely immersed in the ambience when simply looking at the buildings around the narrow alleys and steep staircases of the Old Town or exploring the corridors of the fortress. Now, after a couple of weeks, the novelty was beginning to fade and I needed to find some justification of being stuck here.

It's not that I've been idle. Jim's contract hackers had been ripping into the intranets of the government organisations and private companies that we suspected were involved in this plot. I had been gobsmacked about how easy this seemed to be. Most of our targets had been accessed at costs of only a few hundred dollars. Then another weird Jim ploy: everything ripped-off was immediately posted on a dark-web notice board, before we had even had time to look at the contents. The board was called *Green bastards want to steal our nukes* and, after he set it up, it started receiving further posts from anonymous hackers. Even better, the stuff that we uploaded was quickly analysed by conspiracy theorists – who were even more paranoid than Jim and, hidden within a lot of lunatic nonsense, we were able to pick out some gems that we would never have found on our own.

A novelty of Jim's board is that it focused on the Vice-president of the USA and not, like most of the other conspiracy boards, heads of states or major multinationals. Nevertheless, when Beall's close links to an industrial cartel were exposed, the conspiracy geeks went into a feeding-frenzy, exposing more and more material that could well lead to her early resignation, if not impeachment.

This was going so well that I had relaxed enough to finally start having some me-time. Our digs were about a kilometre from the town centre, but within a few hundred metres of one of the interesting beach bars. *HulaHula* was generally filled with big groups of stag-party guys or hen-party gals. However, other more interesting types were also to be found there. I fell in with Gabi on my third visit to the bar. She had been sitting alone, reading an ebook and radiating pissed off. It seemed at the time that we were the only folk in the bar not glued to their mobiles and so, in a move quite unlike me, I sat beside her and asked if she was okay.

Despite being a bit younger, in her early twenties, we hit it off immediately. She was Spanish and had come with a friend from the legal practice where they worked for a holiday filled with sun, sea and, hopefully, a lot of sex. It was supposed to be failsafe: they were both bi and, if a hook-up with some others didn't happen, they had each other. Unfortunately, on the first evening, her pal has disappeared with an older woman and had not been seen since. Gabi did admit that her buddy was slim, blonde and blessed with a truly huge chest, so classic catnip for lesbo-cougars. All I had to do was say I was much more into brunettes and buy a bottle of ridiculously expensive Champagne and she was mine. She tried to talk me into going back to her hotel room – a double room that she now had to herself – but I insisted in dragging her up the steps to my place. I just couldn't resist the opportunity of pissing Jim off.

Typically, he knocked the bedroom door next morning and asked if we'd like breakfast in bed. Gabi was disconcerted about my *uncle* finding me in bed with another woman, but I merely smiled and answered that breakfast would be just the job. *Bugger me, if he didn't shortly turn up with a tray, two glasses, a bottle of Krug and a jug of orange juice 'to keep us going until breakfast is ready'*. The problem was that he was clad only in a disgustingly small posing-pouch, which caused Gabi to break into a fit of giggles. Even worse, he then had to mix things up with my squeeze. "Sorry about that, lass, but I don't normally dress when I'm serving breakfast and it's all I had to hand."

I though Gabi was going to wet herself laughing and even I cracked a wry smile. "Okay, uncle, you pervy old bastard, go and get the rest of breakfast. We've been shagging like bunnies all night and need some sustenance."

Gabi looked gobsmacked when he merely nodded his head. "Yes, my dear, your wish is my command." Ten minutes later he appeared with another tray bearing coffee, plain and chocolate croissants, boiled eggs, toast, butter, jam and marmalade. *How the fuck did he manage to sort all that shit out?*

On the positive side, Gabi was well pleased. "Rach, when you're finished with your uncle, can I have him?" This comment was salt in my newly-opened wounds. *On the positive side, Gabi has been back to bed with me every night since then.*

Chapter 19: Jim

The dark-web notice board was a bit of a stab in the dark, but I knew that GCHQ – British intelligence communications – monitored these sites. This allowed me to keep MI5 up to date on what I was doing without risking any direct contact. This was especially important as, given how seriously compromised the US intelligence agencies were, I couldn't be sure that the UK would be much better.

Although the prime aim of these hacks, financed by my ill-gotten gains, was to identify further nuclear threats, putting everything on a conspiracy-theory notice board would inevitably put pressure on the Veep and her co-conspirators. As always with anyone in a powerful position, there were those who'd love to see her fall. This was balanced by her supporters in the NSA, who were already trying to trace me back via this site, while posting material that was intended to muddy the waters and discredit genuine hacks. Luckily, the conspiracy-theory geeks were very familiar with such tactics and did most of the work filtering out any such spam.

Even for the hacked material that I was sure was genuine, it was difficult to separate the wheat from the chaff and produce a picture of what the anti-nuke cartel were now planning. Beall's credibility within the group had clearly taken a knock as a result of the failure of the Sellafield attack and the arrest of a number of lower-level terrorists. Coming on top of the Rimrock fiasco, she must be under pressure to quickly implement a face-saving action. Europe was clearly on high alert, so another attempt there would be very difficult. With the growing impacts of global warming, nuclear facilities were springing up all over the globe, but the newer ones tended to be very robust and unlikely to assure the large-scale contamination disaster that she was looking for.

It seemed like we were stymied until a Japanese activist posted some confidential memos documenting a spat between Beall and the US embassy in Tokyo. Unsurprisingly, this was on how to respond to Japan's proposed introduction of the requirement that manufacturers of solar panels, rather than the facilities using them, should be responsible for bearing the costs of end-of-life recycling. The ambassador took the position that the Veep had too much of a vested interest to exert pressure here and resisted her attempts to use US influence to block this measure. He had, however, offered to discuss the matter face-to-face in Tokyo.

This was exactly the hint that I needed to provide a focus for my search engines and to guide further hacks. *It's got to be Rokkasho, I feel it in my water.* If a release of radioactivity from that huge reprocessing plant occurred in late summer, it would probably have limited impact on Japan, especially the mega-cities like Tokyo-Yokohama and Osaka-Kobe. Due to the typhoons that were increasingly common at this time of year, the contaminant plume could actually have a larger impact on China and Russia. The resulting international shitstorm would certainly magnify any radiological impacts. From the viewpoint of American right-wing hawks, maybe an even better outcome than Sellafield would have been.

Rokkasho would, however, be a much tougher nut to crack than Sellafield. Regulations after the Fukushima Daiichi accident had resulted in extensive engineering to increase its robustness, particularly with regard to seismic resilience and defence in depth in case of perturbations like total loss of off-site power. *Something like the planned UK attack with a jumbo jet would certainly cause a lot of damage, but would its radiological impact be large enough? The problem for the bad guys was that, if the attack failed to cause significant radiation releases, it acted as an own-goal, demonstrating that nuclear facilities can resist even such an attack.*

This fundamental problem bothered me, so I did my usual exercise of looking at it as if I was in Beall's shoes. *With the resources that I have to hand, how can I ensure that an attack will certainly lead to a major loss of containment? This target is so hard that even...* I groaned and put my head in my hands. *Surely not. Surely she wouldn't even consider using a nuclear weapon, would she?* However, I knew that, if it was the only way out of the mess she was in, she would not hesitate for a moment. It was an incredibly risky move, equivalent to a pre-emptive strike with a weapon of mass destruction. An act of treason that would certainly lead to a firing squad if it was revealed. This assuming that the attack didn't result in a war between the major global powers, which even the mega-rich would be lucky to survive.

Maybe time to bring Rachel in on this. I smiled while I considered interrupting her noisy post-breakfast shag. *Now, in that case, how would young Gabi react? Despite open displays of my aging body, the looks that I got from that minx indicated that she might be well into an AC/DC ménage-a-trois. Maybe better not to think about that and wait until they're finished and Gabi has left.*

Despite how much fun it would be to provoke Rachel, the potential impact of her possible retribution convinced me that it was not worth the effort. This was especially the case as I now saw how her role may be about to change. Beall was too much of a loose cannon and likely to become even more dangerous if another of her plots was scuppered. *Time for the kid gloves to come off and prepare from some pre-emptive retaliation.*

Chapter 20: Rachel

I was wearing only a minute tanga when I kissed Gabi goodbye at the door and then wandered out to the side terrace where Jim was working on a small laptop linked to his bloody PASS. *Linked by a cable! The old bastard is certainly consistent in using stone-age technology whenever possible.* He had also managed to obtain a military grade dish that provided a link to a satellite that had been set up by his dark-web hackers. *Again cabled to his laptop.* I could see no security benefit of this approach compared to the free WIFI in the flat or the usual mobile phone satellite links, when these were coupled to a TOR browser. *Anyway, if it makes the old bugger happy, it does no harm and the costs are trivial given the funds at our disposal.*

He looked pleased with himself, which was usually a bad sign. However, he just started with his usual banter. "It's nice to see that my sartorial elegance has finally begun to rub-off on you." I was confused for a moment before I realised he was referring to my underwear, which was indeed as skimpy as his posing pouch, which he was still sporting after the usual breakfast delivery.

I smiled and posed, hand on hip. "Not at all, just showing you the real point of such a garment. It's intended to show off a beautiful body, like the one that you're salivating over at the moment. In your case, a shroud would be more appropriate, in more senses that one."

He laughed and shook his head. "Ah, the younger generation. So much more concerned with the appearance of a package rather than its contents. Luckily, young Gabi seems a lot more appreciative. Such a wise head on such young, delectably-smooth shoulders."

I hid a smile and pretended to frown. "You just keep your filthy old paws off my young girlfriend. Any interest she may have in you is due to your apparent wealth and the way you wait on me hand and foot. That, of course, happening only when I'm in bed with her."

"Girlfriend, is it?" He grinned in his usual, annoying manner. "Is this the start of a long relationship?"

"Don't be daft, she leaves in a couple of days. Great fun, but really just a fuck-buddy. Admittedly a very enthusiastic and dirty-minded one."

"Dirty-minded, that's good. So she hasn't suggested bringing me into the action yet?"

She had, actually, on a couple of occasions, but I'm fucked it I'll even admit it to him. "Dirty-minded, yes, but not totally perverted. She'd suggest bringing you to bed with us only if her interest was necrophilia."

"Well, if I had to kick the bucket, there are probably a lot worse ways to go. Anyway, if you'd be kind enough to put on a t-shirt, we could get to work. I have limited-enough blood flow to my brain without diverting it to a massive erection."

I couldn't help spluttering. "Massive, you call that wee thing massive? There's more blood flow involved getting my nipples erect."

"Mmm, so I am having a similar effect on you. Should I put shorts on?"

"Your Alzheimer's getting worse: you're now totally delusional" My parting comment was thrown over my shoulder as I went to find a t-shirt. I did notice that he made no move to look for shorts. *Bloody typical!*

He looked rather grim when I returned and got straight down to business. "I'm reasonably sure that I know where Beall's crowd are going to hit next and, in very general terms, how the attack is planned."

"Wow," I sniped, "you're actually letting your partner know about this before you broadcast it far and wide?"

"Settle down, lass, as this is going to need some very gentle handling. Even a hint about what your nutty VP is planning could cause a major international incident."

Something about his tone of voice caused a cold shiver to run down my spine. He had this way of just switching from light-hearted banter to existential threats at the drop of a hat. *Probably bipolar or somewhere on the autistic spectrum.* Strangely, this thought cheered me up a bit.

Over the next half hour, I asked only a few questions for clarification while he painstakingly laid out the evidence leading to his prediction of a plot to use a nuclear weapon to attack the JNFL reprocessing plant in Rokkasho-mura. Although the evidence was compelling, I could not accept that even someone as inherently evil as the Veep would

177

consider risking World War 3 just to protect her commercial interests.

After Jim finished, I shook my head. "There needs to be another interpretation of the stuff that you've dug up. Even if that evil witch was mad enough to plan something like this, she needs to bring others onto her side in order to implement it. One lunatic at the top levels of US Government I could, at a pinch, accept, but not the numbers of them needed to pull off something like this."

He shook his head. "That was something that bothered me, but I think I've seen an option where shifting the blame could reduce risks of conflict with the USA and have some direct benefits when seen from a Western perspective."

I thought about this for five minutes, but drew a complete blank. "I can't see any way in which such an attack could be seen as a good thing, except in terms of the Veep's agenda."

"Yes, that was what I initially thought. However, I then focused on the technical issues associated with the attack itself. We have a very hard target here. In terms of practicality, my initial thoughts were leading me towards a suitcase nuke as the attack weapon, but then I realised that even something with that much power might not cause enough damage and, instead, emphasise just how high the protection levels of the site were. To be sure of success a much bigger bang is needed."

I frowned at this statement. "You're joking, surely. Something small enough to fit into the trunk of a car could have a yield of a couple of kilotons. That's Hiroshima scale."

Jim shifted into lecturer mode. "The Hiroshima bomb, Little Boy, was more like 15 kilotons, but I see your point. The thing is that Hiroshima and Nagasaki were air bursts against mid-20th century Japanese cities, where a lot of the damage resulted from the associated firestorms. A ground-level explosion near buildings constructed to nuclear standards would have much a smaller impact, especially if it had to be detonated at a location distant from the most sensitive facilities, where access by car may be possible. If I was Beall and really wanted to make sure of getting the job done, I'd want a device in the hundred kiloton range, higher even if that was possible."

I stared at my partner, wondering if he was taking the piss here. "That'd be at the high end of a lot of cruise missiles."

He smiled and nodded, as if I had said something sensible. "That's exactly what I concluded."

"But the Veep can't order that kind of nuclear attack on Japan. Even if she murdered the President and took over his role, there are too many fail-safes in play to stop that happening."

"Very true and, more seriously, this would certainly be enough to light the fuse on World War 3. So this was my problem, when I put myself in her shoes. How can I organise a cruise-missile strike on Japan that avoids this risk?"

"I don't think that there's any scenario where a nuclear attack wouldn't tip us over the edge. It's not as if you need only the weapon itself, you need all the infrastructure to ensure that it's effectively guided to its target. There are very few countries with this capability and none…" I ground to a halt as, all of a sudden, the pieces fell into place and a cold shiver ran up my spine. "North Korea! That's the only case where an attack would probably direct retaliation against the attacker with low risk of further proliferation."

"Well done, lass, you got there in the end. The cunning side of this plot is that fallout could potentially impact Russia and China, the only super-powers who might go out on a limb to defend North Korea. Indeed, they might be forced by public opinion to lead the retaliation, as there would be little risk that the West would interfere with them in this case. This especially here, when Japan would also strongly support such retaliation. And then there's the benefit to the entire world: a nuclear-armed North Korea was always completely unpredictable and a thorn in the side of even those who appeared to support this loopy regime. I'm sure Beall could sell this to her fellow-conspirators."

"Okay, you've convinced me. The only thing that I don't understand is how anyone can manipulate the Democratic People's Republic into doing anything as suicidal as this. At the very least, their nuclear arsenal will be wiped out along with their entire leadership."

"Yes, that's perceptive. I haven't yet nailed down how to get around that. But I'm sure that I'll find out what's going on when I focus my hackers on it. I know that there are quite a few dark-web anoraks in South Korea who would be very happy

180

to get paid to rip into DPRK military and intelligence sites."

"Well, it looks like your dance card is going to be pretty full for the next while. I guess I can focus on keeping fit, getting lots of exercise. Of course most of this will be between the sheets with dirty-minded Gabi."

"Ah, well, that's where I'm afraid I'm going to have to rain on your parade. I don't think you'll even have a chance for a last shag before you head off."

"Head off where?"

"Tokyo, via Guam."

"Tokyo I can understand, sort of. Although I can't see what I can do there to stop an attack coming from North Korea. But why the fuck Guam?"

"That's where you'll pick up the sniper rifle. They're much harder to source in Japan. Also tricky to smuggle into the country, so I've ordered up a model that disassembles into parts that should be difficult to identify, even if your checked-in luggage is x-rayed. With a bit of luck you won't get arrested." This with a smug smile that made me want to really punch his face.

"And what do I do with the rifle?"

"You're the assassin, I thought you'd be able to work this out for yourself."

"Okay, smartarse, let me make this clearer, who am I going to kill?"

"The Vice-president of the US of A, who else? Oh, if you get a chance, I'd appreciate if you also put a slug in that bastard Denis Buck."

What the holy fuck? I had offered to put down that bitch several times, but I had not really considered that there was any chance of it happening. "Honestly, you want me to leave immediately and pop off to Tokyo to assassinate the Veep. Are you even sure that she'll be there? I haven't seen anything about it on any of the usual newsfeeds."

"It hasn't been announced yet, but it'll be official by tomorrow. This is why you should get moving now. She's trying for the same play as before, leaving Japan only slightly before the attack takes place to maximise the impact of her resulting anti-nuclear message. It's just the Sellafield game plan remastered."

"That was kept under wraps, but a number of folk in the intelligence community are aware of allegations of her role in the abortive Sellafield attack. Won't this just raise suspicions?"

"If the attack clearly comes from North Korea, there's nothing to be suspicious about. It's just a strange coincidence. No matter what goes on the conspiracy-theory notice board, nobody will consider this hard evidence if the attack goes ahead, while the entire issue will be dropped if it doesn't. Only we know how dangerous she'll be if her second attack is foiled, especially as she'll be forced to move very quickly and we may not be lucky enough to intercept her again. Thus she needs to be rubbed out, and you're the only one I have to hand who can do this."

"Buggeration! Looks like I've got no choice. When do I fly?"

"In just under three hours. You have a private speedboat transfer from the jetty down in front of this apartment that'll get you to Split airport. Flights Split to Warsaw, Warsaw to Manila and then Manila to Guam. It'll be a long trip, but business class all the way, so not really tough for a youngster like yourself."

Fuckity-fuck. I'd better get packing then. I assume all my documents will be loaded onto my wrist comp."

"They already are." Again the smug grin.

"Also need to let Gabi know."

"I've also done that already. We're actually meeting for dinner tonight." His grin got even wider.

Now there was no chance of holding back and my slap sent him flying backwards to land on his scrawny arse. To add insult to injury, this only caused him to break into fits of laughter.

If that old cunt actually manages to bed Gabi, I really hope the inevitable heart attack finishes the fucker off.

Chapter 21: Jim

She really caught me that time. *I was sure that it'd be a roundhouse punch or a kick to the goolies, but she slapped me! Okay, it was hard enough to lay me flat out, but that's not a lot for my aged body. She's getting soft on me. From the work side, that's almost inevitable. But moving in on her girlfriend, even if she was only a fuckbuddy, should have caused a more extreme reaction.*

Whatever, in this case it was not simply a gratuitous provocation of my partner. I fully intended to shag young Gabi. Rachel had already done all the ground work, bringing her back to our digs and getting her used to me. *True, I could get a prostitute who would do all the necessary, but I want to have Rachel's girl. Now, was that because I'm just a truly annoying fuckwit or was there more to it?* I really hoped that the former was closer to the truth.

I could not help being impressed by Rachel's loyalty. I had just sent her off on a really dangerous mission that must go against a lot of the core values hammered into her during her time in the military. She accepted this without anything other than a check through the details of what exactly I expected her to do. *Would she have done this for Miriam? Am I simply a substitute for the dominating leader that she needs in her life?*

From the very limited time that we had spent together, discounting the period when I was doped out of my skull, I was sure that this simple interpretation was wrong. She was smart enough to look critically at the information that she was fed. Despite the controlling influence of her mother, she saw through the façade of Miriam's scheme and aligned herself with me. Nothing to do with our relationship, just a clever young woman. She was supposed to have a genetic component from me, so not so surprising.

This led me directly to the topic that I had been tiptoeing around. The more time I spent with this young woman, the more it was like looking in a mirror. Not physically, of course, but our banter was scary. We had the same sense of humour and tendency to populate our discourse with flowery language and obscure cultural references. This was not anything like Marion, but 100% me. It almost seemed to compensate for the psychopathic bits, which were 100% Marion.

I could objectively conclude that the Vice-president had to be assassinated and then send Rachel to do the dirty work. I was not sure, however, that I could kill anyone in the way that an assassin does. In the heat of combat, or when I was clearly threatened, I could pull the trigger. But someone surrounded by a lot of potential collateral damage? I just do not know. Rachel, however, would press a button that would wipe out a target together with their entire family without the slightest compunction. Was this inherent genetics or the result of long-term brainwashing by her bitch mother? I could never know for certain, but hoped it was the latter.

I rubbed my face to escape from such wool-gathering and return to the challenges that I had to face – both to defuse the imminent action against Rokkasho and to support Rachel in assuring that we could finally remove the threat of any further nuclear attacks. The latter was easier, so I focused on it first. The girl's flights were sorted out, but I had to organise digs for her in Tokyo, nail down the best locations for an assassination and then organise local logistics so that all would go smoothly and she could concentrate on getting the job done. Importantly, I had also to ensure that the subsequent extraction was resilient, with the flexibility to respond to the problems that inevitably crop up when any plan is implemented in real life. Here I had an ace up my sleeve. I knew the head of security at the British embassy in Tokyo and, indeed, had trained her in risk assessment a couple of decades ago.

Julia White was a very clever young lady... although by now in her 50s, I reminded myself. I drafted a mail to her that stated only that I had identified a credible threat on her turf and that we might be able to work together to neutralise it. I included a link that she could use to find my dark-web notice board and posted a notice on it from *Threat Assessment Wizard*, a term she had often applied to me. This simply noted a possible connection between several of the other postings, without specifying what it was. This would allow her to independently assess the evidence indicating that Beall was supporting anti-nuclear terrorist attacks. She would also now be able to use the notice board to communicate with me, without any risk of this being traced. So I just had to wait until she had time to digest this material and get back to me.

Next, I used my tailored AI tool to run over the specifications for the assassination and make suggestions for improvements, ranked by calculated probability of success. The problem is that the opposition had access to similar tools, thus being able to get the same output if they thought that there was a credible threat to the VP. Indeed, if they had enough gumption to turn their AI search engines on the dark web, they would know there were more than the usual suspects with the Veep in their sights. A classic hunter and hunted scenario. So how could I resolve this to assure high chances of taking out our target while minimising risks to the shooter?

Not surprisingly, the highest ranked options were based on the Veep's known penchant to play golf at every opportunity. *As already spotted by Rachel, a golf course is an assassin's wet dream.* Of course, her security team would know this, but the question was whether or not they were up to date on the latest developments of laser-guided smart bullets. When combined with a satellite image and differential GPS, a ballistic trajectory allowed targets to be hit at distances of several kilometres. An advantage of such attacks is that, when the target was tagged for a head shot, the conventional defence of placing objects – or agents – to block potential lines of sight can be bypassed to some extent.

The problem is that such munition is horrendously expensive. Two bullets, with the associated guidance package and a darknet assurance that the purchase would be untraceable, cost 18 million dollars, thus severely depleting our war chest. Nevertheless, it seemed like money well spent as long as we were assured a hit. I set up my search-engines to assess optimised shooter and target locations for the golf courses around Tokyo that might be used by a high-level VIP.

For the sake of completeness, I also checked golf courses near US airbases where Air Force Two might land. The most obvious options were Misawa and Iwakuni, with the latter being more likely as the former was rather close to Rokkasho.

Realising that all further work could run autonomously, I then checked the location of a pharmacy in the Old Town. This was located on the main square and thus conveniently close to a number of bars where I could eat lunch. In Croatia, I needed a prescription for Viagra, but it was easy to purchase a counterfeit e-script that would do the job. *The only question was whether or not Gabi would want me to use a condom, assuming of course that we actually got that far. Maybe better pick up some – maybe a dozen. If nothing else, if I leave the box lying about, it'll be sure to annoy Rachel when she returns.*

I tried hard to avoid wondering whether this should be *if* she returns. This was a very disturbing consideration.

***

My dinner with Gabi went as smoothly as I had hoped. She was already on cloud nine when I escorted her to Gariful, one of the best – and most expensive – restaurants in Hvar. We started with oysters and Champagne. I warned her about the aphrodisiac properties of the former but, regardless, she had nine while I restricted myself to three. We then moved to their signature *drunken lobster*, the 1kg crustacean shared between us. We accompanied this with a Corton - Charlemagne Grand Cru, an outrageously expensive combination that already had the girl panting. She had still space for one of their exquisitely crafted deserts and another couple of glasses of Champagne, while I managed most of my way through a glass of their best Hvar red.

Christ on a bike, how does she do that? I had already had three old-man visits to the toilet, while she hadn't budged from her seat the entire night. She was certainly well-built, but certainly not overweight for her muscular frame. I had hardly said a word while she chattered cheerfully and, although much had gone in one ear and out the other, I remembered that she was a rower who also did a lot of swimming. *Could her trained body alone burn the calories at a high enough rate? If not, what was I letting myself in for?* The hours of noisy lesbian sex that I had been forced to listen now had me worried. *Maybe a nippy-sweety would slow her down and give me a chance of surviving the night.* It didn't take much effort to talk her into a large Hennessy XO Cognac as a digestif, while I dithered over my red wine. Unfortunately, after

189

inelegantly slugging down this nectar, she was still bright-eyed and bushy-tailed.

I needed to save my energy, but Gabi simply regarded it as part of my natural generosity when we took a taxi for the short trip back to my apartment. As soon as I closed the door, she was already stripping off. *So much for all my plans to gently seduce this wench. She was ready for a good shagging regardless of whether I was capable of delivering it or not.*

***

Fuck me rigid, but that was a night I won't forget! Unfortunately, I was indeed fucked rigid and my knees buckled when I attempted to clamber out of the sweaty bed, no doubt also soaked with other bodily fluids. I literally crawled into the bathroom and used a towel rail to pull myself up from the floor. I wasn't going to be able to make it to the toilet, so flopped into the bath just in time before my bladder let loose. While still pissing, I bent over far enough to grab the lever for the shower, and could then lie back in a cleansing spray of lukewarm water. When my bladder was empty, I managed to bend forward again to insert the plug and then switch from the shower to the bath tap and increase the temperature of the water to just short of scalding. I sank back with a sigh and closed my eyes.

I could try to attribute my wrecked state to the pharmacological impact of overdosing with Viagra. However, deep down, I knew it was actually the physical impact of what the Viagra had allowed me to do. It was certainly nothing like Rachel's performance levels, but the young nymphet and I went at it like a pair of ferrets for a good hour or so. I had cheated, doing as much of the work as possible with fingers and tongue, but I had still been able to come inside her offered orifices once or twice. At least twice, I was sure of that, but it was very woolly thereafter. At some point she had talked me into trying some tailored party drug that she had to hand and I'd already been so spaced out that I accepted. *What the fuck it was, I have no idea, but it could well have contributed to my present feeling of having been run-over by a truck. Many times.*

After about a quarter of an hour, the bath had cooled down and I was beginning to feel that I might actually have the strength to climb out of it. To my amazement, I still had my PASS strapped to my arm and I was able to see that it was just after 7 am. If recent history was anything to go by, Gabi would sleep for another couple of hours. *Then again, that was after a marathon session with Rachel, so I can't be sure that will also be the case after my relatively feeble performance. However, the quantity of booze that the girl consumed, enough to render a rhino comatose, might balance that to some extent. Of course, it hadn't been enough to stop her shagging me into a greasy spot before I finally flaked out.*

Just as well I didn't actually try Gabi's desired threesome with Rachel. If so, I'd be stone-cold dead by now.

191

***

I was sufficiently recovered, thanks to some additional pharmacological support, when I heard Gabi wake and head immediately into the toilet. *First time since we started dinner, as far as I can remember. Either the girl has the bladder of a blue whale or I missed her visiting the bog after I flaked out.*

I had everything prepared so that, when she returned from the loo, I was waiting for her with the bottle of Champagne and a single glass on a tray. Apart from the number of glasses, the difference between this and my previous butler impersonations was that I had skipped the posing pouch. I was aware that I presented a less-than-impressive figure, but I had already picked up that Gabi regarded shagging a geriatric as one of the weirder options that she could now cross off her bucket list. She was fascinated by the idea of screwing her last lover's old uncle, someone who was older than her grandparents, as she had noted on several occasions. *I blame it on easily accessible video-porn, with its old-young sections. The younger generation think of this as something normal, rather than an inevitable consequence of the diverse prostitute market responding to client demand. But I can't complain after last night.*

Despite Gabi's offers to share the Champagne – and continue where we had stopped last night – I declined and went off to prepare her usual breakfast. Amazingly, given what she had eaten at our dinner, she polished off everything put in front of her, while sitting on top of the bedspread with her legs wide open and the offer of further bonking clearly still on the cards.

After I cleared away the breakfast things, my restraint broke down and I washed down two 25 mg Viagra tabs with a large mouthful of Champagne. *I have no idea what mischief Rachel is up to in Japan, but it's not likely to top this.*

Chapter 22: Rachel

After almost 3 days travelling, I finally arrived in Tokyo. Jim had booked me into the mid-range Park Hotel in Shimbashi. Although there were a number of bus, train and monorail options, I was so wasted that I simply took a taxi from Hanada airport. This was a much shorter trip than the transfer from Narita, the airport that I had used for my previous two trips to Tokyo.

The hotel was rather strange, with reception in an atrium on the 25th floor that looked up into the hollow core of the triangular cross-section of the *Media Tower.* There were paintings and sculptures everywhere, justifying its description as an *art hotel.* I had a room on the 31st floor, which, after I threw open the curtains, I could see looked over railway lines towards the Tokyo Tower. As far as I was concerned, its most attractive feature was the king-size bed. After a quick shower, I slipped between the sheets and slept like a log for five hours.

I was momentarily disorientated when I awoke in the dark room, lit only by the night glow of the Tokyo megalopolis that streamed through the window. I glanced at the bedside clock.

Nine pm and I'm now wide awake. Fucking jet-lag! I could have taken melatonin to reduce this, but I avoid any drug that could potentially impact concentration when on a job. *Okay, I'm awake, hungry and need a drink. Shouldn't be a problem to sort out in central Tokyo.*

There were a couple of restaurants and a bar on the 25th floor, but I decided that I also needed to stretch my legs, so took the elevator down to the 1st floor and ventured out into a wall of heat and humidity that came as a shock after the air-conditioned environment that had shielded me until now. My choice of shorts, t-shirt and sandals represented the lightest clothes I had but, within five minutes walking towards the skyscrapers of Toranomon, sweat was beginning to stream down my back. *Time to get back into aircon ASAP.*

I checked my wristcom and spotted that there was a craft beer bar in the immediate vicinity. This was more the kind of place that Jim would go for, but I felt really thirsty and so a beer might be the thing to start off with. After that, there was a craft gin distillery in one of the Mori Toranomon buildings, which I could head for afterwards.

I got a seat by the window in YonaYona, apparently the name of a brewery with a chain of bars. My wristcom automatically connected to their wifi and displayed an English menu that allowed me to remotely order drinks and food. I stayed away from some of the weirder sounding beers and settled for a relatively low-alcohol Pale Ale, adding a bowl of edamame *beer beans* to nibble on while I thought about what I really wanted to eat for dinner.

The girl who brought over my order gave me a strange glance. Only then did I notice that my t-shirt was sticking to my sweaty body and showing off nipples like acorns, a clear reaction to the aircon chill of the bar. *Really should have worn a bra, but what the fuck. Several of the girls in here have mini-*

skirts like pelmets and I've already seen a couple of flashes of white nickers. I was wondering if, actually, such a skirt wouldn't be a bad idea as it wouldn't stick to me the way that my shorts were, when I noticed that I also seemed to have attracted the attention of the Japanese couple sitting at the next table. The guy appeared to be in his mid-thirties and was wearing jeans and a denim shirt, which seemed a bit heavy for this weather. As a contrast, his partner was wearing a micro-skirt variant of what seemed to be a sailor-suit school uniform, which made her look about sixteen. In this rigout, she radiated Lolita-type jail-bait.

"Hello," the girl started shyly. "I hope you don't mind me interrupting, but are you okay? Your face is very red."

Shit, shit, shit. This fucking, bastarding allergy! "No, it's all fine," I responded. "I just flew into Tokyo this afternoon and crashed out immediately. There must have been down pillows, which I'm allergic to. Do I look terrible? *It wasn't my fucking nipples, it was the face like a beetroot that was attracting attention.*

The girl grinned, looking relieved. "No, you look lovely. It's just that your face is very red. It looks like you've been running or something. My face goes like that in a sauna."

Relieved, I grinned back. "Don't worry, this will go away quite quickly. I should maybe rinse my face with cold water, though, as that usually helps."

"The restroom is nearby. You go along the corridor facing the entrance to the bar and then I think it's on the left. It's well signposted anyway."

196

"Right, I'm off now and I'll be back in a minute." Sure enough, when I looked in the mirror, it looked like I had bad sunburn. I splashed cold water in my face for a couple of minutes and then it looked much better. Distinctly pink, but not disconcertingly so.

"You look much better now," my new friend observed when I returned. "Are you on your own? If you want you can join us."

I checked out her partner to see if it looked okay with him, but he appeared happy with the idea. I thus ended up spending a couple of hours with Toshi and Junko, just making small talk and sharing some snacks. I moved on to gin and tonic after my first beer, but the Japanese couple stayed with small glasses of beer, having a different one each round. By the time we were ready to leave, I'm sure Toshi's face was redder than mine had been. He was clearly one of the Japanese with a genetically low tolerance to alcohol. Junko, however, held her drink well and was getting increasingly flirty in line with her husband getting closer to falling asleep. As she squirmed about on the rather uncomfortable bar stools I was often treated to views of her skimpy panties and got the impression that these were becoming damp. This was enough to cause my nipples to perk up again.

Junko had clearly seen my interest and suggested that we went back for a nightcap to their flat, which was in one of the nearby Mori residential blocks. Although flattered, my immediate reaction was to back off before I got drawn into something I might regret later. Then, out of the blue, the thought of Jim screwing Gabi came to mind. *Fuck it! I'm here instead of shacked up with my Hvar fuck-buddy. Why the hell not?*

Before agreeing, however, I needed to check what I was letting myself in for. "That sounds great, Junko, but are you sure that Toshi will be okay with this? He looks very tired."

"Yes, he'll go to bed soon, so we can chat together, or whatever." She looked directly into my eyes and her message was crystal-clear. "You can stay the night, if you want and we can do what we want with Yoshi tomorrow. He's very obedient, you know."

Well, no doubt at all about who wears the trousers in this relationship. There was no way that I had been prepared to let Gabi drag Jim into bed with us but, after some fun with Junko tonight, a threesome including her husband might be just the ideal way to set me up for the rest of the trip. I'm sure this is exactly what Junko was aiming for from the start. So maybe it actually was my nipples that got her started rather than my red face.

***

The Takeuchis lived in a small but luxuriously furnished apartment on the 30th floor of the Atago Green Forest tower. *Clearly, the couple aren't short of a few dollars.* As predicted, Toshi immediately apologised and headed off to bed while Junko and I got settled on the settee with a couple of huge gins. She was turned towards me and her minute skirt rode up to give me a clear view of damp, almost transparent knickers that made it clear that her mons was clean-shaven. I was also aware that the sort walk from the pub had started me sweating again and my swollen nipples were on open display.

As if reading my mind, Junko grinned mischievously. "It was very sticky tonight. Would you like to take a shower? I think I also need to get out of my damp clothes." She kicked off her sandals and then pulled her top off, revealing a thin, lacy bra that did nothing to hide the erect brown nipples that crowned small but well-formed breasts. "I'm afraid that I've got no tits, but yours look very nice." She stroked my breasts through my t-shirt, circling one areola and then the other with the long, silver-lacquered fingernails of her left hand while her right cupped and squeezed my entire breast.

"Your tits look perfect to me," I stroked her breasts through the bra with the tips of my fingers, as my nails were cut short. "But you're right, I need to get my sweaty stuff off and have a shower." I lifter her hands away, peeled off my t-shirt and then pulled her hands back into place. "See how sweaty I am."

"Mmm, yes, you're very damp. Almost as damp as me." She now directed my left hand into her crotch. She was, indeed, extremely wet. "So, we should get out of these wet clothes and into the shower. It may be tight, but I'm sure we could both get into it." She extracted my fingers and sniffed them. "Yes, I'm ready for a shower, what do you think?" She shoved the sticky fingers into my mouth and smiled salaciously as I licked them. "Do you want to get wet?"

Junko stood and quickly stepped out of her skirt and briefs before pulling off her bra. By this time I had also shed my shorts and knickers. "Yes, definitely, I want to get really wet," I replied. "Although, how I can get much wetter than I am now, I'm not sure."

"Trust me, you've still got a long way to go." I looked into the Japanese woman's eyes and was sure that this would be the case. *Whatever that sad old bastard in Hvar is doing, it won't come close to this.*

Chapter 23: Jim

Gabi had now reunited with her work colleague and they had flown off back home. *I'm sure, trying to outdo each other with tales of their holiday experiences.* Anyway, I was glad to have that distraction out of the way as the details of both a response to the nuclear threat and the assassination of the Veep were beginning to come together.

On the DPRK side, deep hacks had revealed secret communication between Buck and the head of the Korean People's Army, who was strongly rumoured to be a target for replacement during the next purge by the volatile Supreme Leader. The Marshal had secretly approached the US to sound out their possible support in the event of a military coup to replace the Kim dynasty. This was a man who certainly had the power to launch a nuclear attack and would do so if this was part of a deal that was assured to cause the overthrow of Kim and his entire clan. This was good enough to confirm my assessment of the threat, but not sufficient to give any indication of a way to avoid it.

I also had hacked Beall's, as yet unannounced, trip plan. She was actually going for the more dramatic option of having Air Force Two land in Misawa, with helicopter transfers to and from Tokyo. She was again accompanied by Buck, which was probably not unexpected given his role in liaison with the Marshal. Golf had also been organised: near Tokyo together with the US ambassador and at the Gosser course in Misawa, with the Base Commander. The tricky bit now was to decide which would be the better option for the assassination. My gut feeling was that the Veep and ambassador together would result in very tight security, especially as this high-profile event would be well covered by the media. By comparison, in the vicinity of the Misawa base, things should be more relaxed.

With the blame for any attack inevitably being placed on the DPRK, Beall had no need to introduce the extra complications that would indicate that she escaped only by a fluke, so this could be initiated any time after she left Japan. Nevertheless, given her flair for the dramatic, I was sure that it would be within a day or two after her departure.

Even if not as urgent as the Sellafield case, the clock was ticking and I had just over a fortnight to find a way to defuse this threat. Preparation for the assassination was easier if we went for Misawa, I concluded. My focus here was not so much getting Rachel into place, but more ensuring that she could easily get clear afterwards. There was not only the risk of her being caught up in the nuclear attack if I wasn't able to prevent it, but also the clamp-down that would inevitable result from such a high profile murder – from base personnel and both the US and Japanese security services.

In the best case, the assassination of Buck might actually cause the Marshal to reconsider his coup and thus defuse the attack, It was a bit of a gamble, however, as he may already be committed and go ahead even without his promised support by the States. In this case, the attack might achieve his main aim of destabilising the present regime, especially if he had fabricated evidence in place that shifted blame onto the Kims.

Nope, too much of a risk. I need to have an option in place to protect the Rokkasho plant, even if the attack is launched. I'll work this out with Julia and she can link, as needed, with the Japanese Self Defence Force. We'll need to keep contacts very limited and tight. In particular, we can't risk anything leaking to any US intelligence agency, as these are probably all compromised.

The tricky decision that I had yet to make was whether or not to let Julia know about our plans for the Veep. She already had access to the evidence showing Beall's support of terrorist attacks, but this kind of hacked material would not stand up in any court and thus greatly limited the extent to which she could use it. In any case, there was no way that she could condone the assassination of such a senior figure, even if she personally agreed it would be a good thing. *The problem is, she'll know that I'm behind it as soon as she hears about the shooting. The question is thus: will she act on this knowledge or, knowing that solving the problem of Beall was now a fait accompli, just let it ride? Because she knows me so well, she could be more of a threat to Rachel than any of the players directly involved in this plot.*

***

Except for the day after my dalliance with the energetic young Gabi, I had established a routine of having a short swim in the sea each afternoon. The water was cool, but swimming reasonably hard for about 20 to 30 minutes was fine, especially if followed by a hot bath. The bay in front of the flat was fine when the sea was calm and I could use a concrete jetty to get in and out of the water. The alternative of access from a small pebble beach just didn't work due to my bad ankles and knees. When it was rougher or I was feeling lazier, I chose the option of the more sheltered President Bay, accessing it from below the Podstine Hotel. This variant had the advantage that I could have a post-swim drink in the hotel beach-bar, where I was getting quite well known.

During my swims I let my mind wander, as I found this encouraged lateral thinking. Today in President Bay, which was as flat as a mirror, my focus was on Rachel. *If the assassination is successful, northern Honshu will be like a well-stirred hornet's nest. So I need two things: an unlikely exit route and a diversion to focus attention elsewhere. This needs to be good enough that it'll even fool Julia, which is a very challenging task.*

As usual, I started by putting myself in Julia's place. After the event, how would she analyse the assassin's options? The obvious variants are go to ground in place and wait for the heat to die down, exit the immediate vicinity but stay in Japan, or get the hell out of Japan as quickly as possible.

The first option was tricky, especially for a foreigner who hadn't been in the area very long. They'd stick out and would certainly be closely checked. *She'd be fairly sure it was a foreigner, as the highly experienced assassins needed for a job like this would be very few and far between in Japan. They'll have military-trained snipers, but these will all be well known and easy to trace. No, she'd consider this option unlikely.*

Moving quickly to another part of Japan was a better option for a foreigner, especially as there is such a wide range of transport variants. The civilian airport in Misawa would get someone away quickly, especially if the flight was boarded very soon after the shooting, before any security cordon could be put in place. *Nope, too much risk of security getting their act together fast enough that, even if not at departure, any suspect could be picked up on landing.* Of course, this left Shinkansen, normal trains, buses, private cars, ferries and private boats. Private helicopters and planes could probably be discounted as too easy to check, while bicycles and walking would be too slow. *Again due to the risk of being picked up by the many CCTVs in stations, Shinkansen and other railway options would probably be considered unlikely as, after flights, these would be the next focus for security. This also applies to ferries and express buses. So this leaves private cars or boats, which could be purchased, self-drive hires or hired transfer services. These are inherently much harder to track, especially if cars avoid the freeways and their associated cameras. So, if it was me, I'd focus on likely escape destinations. Tokyo or one of the other large cities would be the best bet, as there are so many foreigners there that it'd be easy to lose one more amongst them. Sapporo is probably the nearest big city but, unless I was certain that the nuclear attack could be prevented, I probably wouldn't risk my asset in an area that could be heavily impacted by fallout and the subsequent chaos that would result from this. If I was sure that any missile could be intercepted, however, this counter-intuitive option would be ideal.*

I glanced at my PASS and noticed that I'd already been swimming for 30 minutes, but the sun was shining and I did not yet feel cold. *Need to keep going, one more lap around the bay gentle breaststroke should do it. I'll need to fill out details back at the apartment, but an option that would fit my needs is beginning to emerge. Motorway cameras read registration plates and can usually identify any passengers in a car. This is harder for motorbikes, especially if the rider is wearing a helmet with a tinted visor. In order to use automatic freeway gates, bikes have transponders that are picked up by the gate, but to trace a route using the roadside cameras, pattern recognition would be needed, which requires much more effort and would be done only if and when considered essential. It would be easier to simply identify the gates by which the bike joined and left the freeway. It won't be easy, but I can work around this, using the dark web. Rachel's bike could leave the vicinity of Misawa and appear to leave the freeway at Aomori city. In reality, she'd have swapped transponder codes with a bike from Tokyo and actually leave the road at Oma. There she can catch the ferry to Hakodate and then drive to Sapporo airport and fly somewhere distant, but still within Japan.*

I was getting a bit cold, but felt happy when I clambered up the ladder onto a jetty shared with the nearby dive school. I lay back on a lounger, warming in the sun while I waited for the friendly waitress to bring me my usual bottle of local beer. *It's all coming together now. I've got the concept and all it needs is fine tuning. And, of course, Rachel being able to take the shot and get away on her bike before the hue and cry starts.*

Chapter 24: Rachel

My first morning Chez Takeuchi had been an eye-opening experience. I awoke when Junko clambered out of our bed in the guest bedroom. "Need to go for a pee," she explained, while grabbing my hand. "Come on." Unbothered by our nudity, she led me though the master bedroom, where her husband was still sleeping, and into an ensuite bathroom that seemed over-dimensioned compared to the rest of the apartment. It was several times larger than the bathroom that we had used the previous evening. Half of this was taken up by a walk-in wet-room that boasted an overhead rainfall shower head, a hand-held shower rose and a hose attached to a distinctly phallic head, making me think of a water-powered vibrator.

She pulled me with her under the rainfall shower and turned a lever to dribble a low flow of cold water. "Fuck!" I gasped as she pulled me close, squirming to rub her smooth body against me while the shower rapidly warmed. "

"We can pee together in here. Would you fancy that?" I wasn't quite sure how to answer, especially when I saw that she was looking over her shoulder towards her husband, who was standing in the doorway, slowly rubbing a surprisingly large erection that seemed out of place given his slim frame. "Don't bother about him, he just likes to watch." Junko smiled lasciviously, hooked one leg around my waist and then I could smell urine and feel a warm flow of liquid run down my thigh. The

208

woman must have trained as a gymnast or be naturally double-jointed from the position that she finally got into, spraying pee directly towards my groin.

I'm not sure how I feel being watched like this. Somehow, it's completely different to the time in Radium with Leroy and Jimmy, much more explicit and also very intimate. There's no doubt that it works for Junko, though. Her nipples are rock-hard and her breathing is getting very deep.

When his wife finished, I heard Toshi sigh and noticed that he had come and spunk was now covering his flat, well-muscled stomach. Junko giggled in delight. "Don't worry," she whispered in my ear, "he always comes quickly the first time, but he lasts longer after that." She rubbed her hand into the space between our groins, licked her fingers and then pulled my head forward and stuck her tongue into my mouth. The slightest trace of urine was distinctly piquant.

Her leg released me and then she stood on tiptoes to rub her nipples against mine. "You're up now," she ginned mischievously as she manoeuvred my leg into place around her slim waist, something I was sure that I wouldn't be able to manage without her help, despite me being several centimetres taller.

Bladder pressure did the rest. *Not something that I'd normally be comfortable with, especially considering the voyeur husband, but Junko's so into it that it seems surprisingly natural.*

***

209

After washing each other under a greater flow of water, Junko reached for the dildo-shaped shower head. "We always do this before anal sex, but it's good fun anyway. Are you all right with it?" She raised her eyebrows suggestively.

"I've had anal douches," I admitted, "but not using a showerhead like that. It's kind of large."

Junko giggled. "So is my husband, as you might have noticed." I turned to look and saw that he had recovered his erection and it was as sizable as before. "Anyway, we have a lubricant gel that ensures that there'll be no problems getting it in. Or, do you want to do me first?"

Well, I've seen videos and all involved seemed to be having fun. Seems to be classic domme-sub roleplay material. In for a penny, in for a pound. "No, that's fine, go ahead so I'll know what to do later. Or will Toshi do you?"

"Oh, no. As I said he prefers to watch. Now if you'll just spread your bum cheeks for me…" I complied, twisting to see her kneel on a towel and then rub gel onto the index finger of her right hand. "Perfect, you really have a beautiful bottom. This is going to be a lot of fun for both of us."

I gasped when her finger slowly slid into my anus, rotating as it went so that I could feel her long fingernail inside me. "How's that? All okay for you?"

I had the impression that these were rhetorical questions, confirmed as she withdrew her finger, applied more gel and then shove two fingers into me. "Wow, I think that's probably enough," I grunted. "I've seen fisting videos, but I don't think my arse is up to that."

"I'm sure that all you need is a bit of practice," again her naughty-schoolgirl giggle. "But that's enough for now." She withdrew her fingers and absent-mindedly rubbed off excess gel in her groin before coating the exotic shower head with another fluid. "Both of these are edible, but this one tastes better," she explained.

I gave a louder grunt when I was penetrated by the shower-head. Junko twisted it slowly while she pushed further, continuing until I was sure that I must have a length of at least six inches within me. Then I gave a squeal when she turned on the water and I felt it filling my bowel. My roleplay mistress seemed to know how much water was needed before she withdrew the shower-head and encouraged the flow from my anus with her finger. From her position behind me, she was sprayed with brown-tinged fluid, but appeared completely unbothered, immediately repeating the procedure. I lost count, but must have had at least a dozen flushes before she licked my arsehole and confirmed that the job was done.

Then it was just the same all over again, but with me playing the domme role. Junko squeaked, squealed and writhed about during the procedure, but it was certainly just play on her side. She was still the mistress controlling the action, but I was happy to go along with her wishes.

Thereafter, tying her husband to a bed designed to facilitate this, blind-folding him, applying nipple clamps and then having our way with him seemed

211

quaintly conventional. Junko had insisted that we dress up in leather waspies with associated suspenders and silk stockings, which made the kink more obvious. *Despite the formulistic roleplay, this last touch was what tipped me over the edge. There was such a blur of sensory input – touch, taste, sound, smell and of course visual – that I maxed out and lost track of what I did and what they did to me. Given the preparation, certainly a lot of anal. Not something that I was into anything like Junko was, but by then I didn't give a flying fuck.*

***

When I eventually managed to escape from their apartment, feeling like I must be walking like John Wayne, I had been talked into coming back for dinner in the apartment the next evening. I tried to talk my way out of this, but the final straw had been when Junko suggested that we meet before this and have a swim together. Apparently the apartment had a pool on the 42nd floor that looked over directly onto the top of the Tokyo Tower. *How could I refuse that?*

The swim was great, in the formal Japanese way where there is a limit of 3 swimmers, each in their own lane. This was part of a luxury spa, with the lady's changing room incorporating a hot tub and a sauna. Unlike the pool, where we were the only swimmers for the half hour that we were there, the hot tub was packed with women relaxing at the end of the working day. There was a full spectrum, ranging from schoolgirls to elderly matrons, all chatting away while they rubbed each other down with rough defoliation cloths. I looked at Junko, myself and then the rest of those present, relieved to spot that erect nipples were obvious more often than not. I thus didn't need my pal to whisper into my ear that this was a regular meeting place for the lesbians in the building. She then surreptitiously slipped her hands between my thighs, grinned and clarified this. "Actually, not really lesbians as you think of them in the west. Most of these women are bi." She nipped the lobe of my ear to emphasise this and I noted both a gaijin matron and a Japanese schoolgirl spotting this and giving me knowing grins.

The rest of the evening was a replay of our first encounter. Yoshi had too much to drink, we had a Sapphic night of pleasure and then pervy, mild BDSM with hubby the morning after. It would have been a situation that I certainly could have continued longer, but that was not to be. The message from Jim broke into what I had thought was a secure hotel network. *I assume that you can ride a motorbike. If not, learn quickly.*

***

I tried to feel pissed-off that I was being ordered away from a dream sex situation while he was probably still shagging Gabi, but it just did not work. *I've passed on from Gabi and, to be honest, I'm getting saturated with the Takeuchis. They're fantastic folk, but I don't have the drive to shag close to the edge the way that they have. At least, not every day.* I smiled at this caveat. However, I was aware that I was doing my usual worry-avoidance wool-gathering that Miriam had warned me about on several occasions. *A motorbike, no probs. I can ride a bike, so how hard can this be? Apart from the fact that I hate the fucking things!*

The accident was a few years back, riding a scrambler. Admittedly going very fast downhill and on a track I had never been on before. I hit a rut that sent me over the handlebars to land on my arse. At first it didn't seem so serious but, as shock wore off, I realised that I wasn't in good shape. Luckily I had my wristcom, something I didn't always wear while biking, so I could arrange an emergency pick up. My pelvis was broken in three places and, although I was lucky enough to avoid surgery, I experienced excruciating pain, the like of which I have never encountered before or since.

I have ridden bikes of all sorts for half my life, so there was no way I was going to tell Jim that this was not an option. Nevertheless, I needed to check his plan to see if the bike could be replaced by a car or, indeed, any other form of transport.

***

After an hour of detailed analysis, double-checking all the links that he included to support his plan, I went to the mini bar, selected and mixed gin and tonic in a glass like a tooth-mug, and then slumped back with a sigh. *The plan was a work of genius. The crumbly, past-his-sell-by-date, opinionated, smug bastard had pulled it off!* I had realised from the beginning that an attack on such a high profile target was very close to suicide. The hit was doable, no doubt about that, but extraction would inevitably be touch and go. Even if this worked, it seemed probable that the massive resultant investigation would identify me as the killer and so I would be on the run for the rest of my life. Jim's plan would not only get me clear but, as a by-product, provide evidence that I could not possibly be the assassin.

God, if I didn't hate you so much, I could kiss you for this.

Chapter 25: Jim

Rachel admitted that she could ride a motorbike, as I already knew. But, even better, was prepared to do so despite her past accident, which I pretended not to know about. I now needed to set up the Japanese black-web contact who would play a critical role in my plan. I almost groaned aloud when we finally met by highly encrypted video link. Japanese as required: yes. Slim female as required: yes. Fluent in English: yes, completely. I thought that I had covered all of my bases when a goth who could have been a stand-in for the *Girl with the dragon tattoo* appeared on my screen.

Her handle was displayed beneath the image. "Okay, *Goodbye kitty*, we need to get this contract sorted out."

The girl smiled in a way that had *psychokiller* written all over it. "The contract is clear, I meet your bitch and then we set up a bike ride with a bit of techno-scrambling on the way. I can handle that."

"What you didn't get in the contract specification were the non-disclosure aspects. I'll pay you a further 50% on top of the very generous agreed payment for confirmation that you'll never talk to anyone else about this jaunt."

Her eyes narrowed. "This is something new. What if someone else was to offer me more than 50%?"

"In that case, I'd have to kill you."

"But what if they offered more than 50% plus protection?"

"Oh, so you're interested in the worst case scenario. They'd pick you up, torture you, and then kill you. As you see, they can offer a lot more than 50% for this option, as they'd never need to pay out."

We stared at each other for a couple of minutes, then she smiled. "Fine, I can work on this basis. It's just good to clarify what the boundary conditions are."

Despite her voice scrambler, her enunciation gave away her educated background. *Probably UK military background, or Australasian at a pinch.* The important thing is that I had enough for my AI tools to dig around and identify who we were dealing with here. The dark web tended to be a bit of a lottery, so some additional insurance would be worthwhile. Nevertheless, in my water, I was sure that *Kitty* was the right person for this op.

***

As far as Rachel was concerned, I oscillated between feeling that I was the protector of an asset and that I was more like an obsessively-protective father. *It must be the fact that I'm actually setting her up to be traceable – something which goes completely against the grain.*

Rachel's current identity, Lynn Smythe as specified in her travel documents, would hold up under normal circumstances. But it wouldn't withstand detailed analysis by police or security teams. As it will appear that she will be on the road north from Tokyo at the time of the assassination,

217

Smythe clearly could not have been the assassin who left Misawa on a bike headed for Aomori. So far, so good. If, however, Smythe was discovered to be Rachel, the trained sniper currently on the run from NSA, then this timeline would be checked in a lot more detail. This would certainly be the case if Julia revealed that Rachel's co-fugitive – myself – was aware that the Veep was linked to the attacks that had them on the run. So I had to create a credible background story that would, if exposed, show that I had actually intended to have Rachel carry out the assassination, but called her off when we were pre-empted.

After struggling for hours to come up with something that would work, I set off for a swim in President Bay, hoping that it would work its usual magic. Almost immediately after I entered the water, the links began to fall into place. Firstly, I needed to get a burner phone and have my best hacker work on it. This would contain a message from me, time-stamped to show that I called Rachel to abort the mission about ten minutes after the assassination. More importantly, it'll appear to be the phone that Kitty will be carrying when she actually receives this message while on the road, which could be determined by triangulation of radio masts.

That was the easy bit, but a dismantled sniper's rifle that appeared to have been purchased in Guam and this crushed phone needed to be dumped somewhere near the Oma ferry terminal. I could certainly find someone to do this, but any leak here would destroy the entire plan. *Fuck! There's only*

218

one sure-fire option that minimises risks: doing the job myself. The last thing I fucking need is to be back in the field, but there seems to be no other option.

I climbed out of the water after only fifteen minutes, aware that time was now very tight. I could do most of the other stuff en-route, but I needed to get a flight to Sapporo sorted out ASAP. Now I could abandon my usual circuitous routes and simply go for an option to get me there as quickly as possible.

***

To my surprise, it was very easy. Tomorrow I could fly Finnair from Split to Sapporo, with only a short transfer in Helsinki. Perfect in terms of getting to Japan, but touch and go in terms of getting hold of a sniper rifle. A delivery to either Split or Helsinki would be impossible, but I found an unusually cheap option of having one smuggled over from Russia to Wakkanai, which was only a 55 minute flight from Sapporo, so this would be doable. My hackers would ensure that, if anyone ever managed to trace this purchase, delivery would be recorded as to Guam 10 days previously. I would pick up the burner phone in Split and would get required hacking done en route.

I let the apartment owner know that I would take the option to stay for a further month and informed her that I would use the flat as a base for exploration of the surrounding islands, so that I would be absent for extended periods. *All being well, I'll be back in a week or so. If not, maybe I won't be back at all.*

Chapter 26: Rachel

The Veep was now in Japan and presently engaged in a series of meetings in and around Tokyo. Golf with the ambassador would be tomorrow afternoon, before some fancy reception at the Embassy. She would travel back to Misawa the day after and fly out that evening. *After what I hope will be her final game of golf.*

After breakfast, I met up with Kitty to buy matching bike leathers and helmets and rent a bike for me that matched the one that Kitty had stolen the previous day. Then a bit of hacking of the electronic memories of both bikes in Kitty's workshop and tomorrow I would be ready to ride to Misawa on my own bike, which would register as the stolen machine. This would be no problem, as Kitty assured me that the owner was abroad for the next month, so it would be a while before the theft was reported.

On the day of the assassination, Kitty would ride out of Tokyo on the stolen machine, which would then register as my rented bike when it joined the freeway and reset to its original registration before she left the highway through the barrier at the Aomori exit. She would dump the bike beside the main bus station, where she'd change out of her leathers in a toilet and then spend the night in a central business hotel that Jim had booked and prepaid for her. She'd crush the burn phone and distribute the parts between several different bins.

On the following day, she'd take the Shinkansen back to Tokyo.

The only weakness here lay in timing. We expected the Veep to play after lunch. It was an 8 hour ride from Tokyo and it had to be clear that Kitty, as me, couldn't possibly get to Misawa in time to carry out a hit that would probably take place mid-afternoon. Thus, she could not leave Tokyo before about 7 am. For the ideal case of a hit around 2 pm, this would work out perfectly as I could get to the ferry at a time consistent with a ride from Tokyo while Kitty would reach Aomori at a time that would fit with her having left Misawa immediately after the shooting. The more the time of the hit changed, the trickier making storyline fit would become.

If golf started late, Jim could get Kitty to modify her speed somewhat to fit in with my progress, but there was only limited flexibility here. I needed to get clear of the immediate area, but the evidence that the bike from Tokyo could not be carrying the assassin would get thinner.

It was even worse if Beall began the game much earlier than expected, especially if she cut it short, for example playing only nine holes. I would have to take the shot and then mess about somehow so that the time between the hit and the bike arriving in Aomori fitted the escape of the assassin. The longer that I was farting about to kill time, the more likely that I could be caught in the cordon around the attack site and the more complicated the messages to be left in the abandoned burn-phone would need to be. *Jim assured me that it'd be doable, but I really don't want to even think about it.*

* * *

I set off next morning. After I worked free of the congestion around Tokyo, I actually enjoyed the long run up to Misawa. My destination was actually Tsurugasaki, which lay across Lake Ogawara from the USAF Gosser Golf Course. This was going to make for a long shot – about 2 kilometres – but it was the nearest high ground in the vicinity. Most of the area west and south of the Air Force base was flat as a pancake, with a lot of trees blocking the view of the golf course. This made even a ballistic shot tricky. Tsurugasaki had the advantage of a slightly higher elevation and a clear view of some of the holes from across the lake, so this was my clear preference. It also provided a number of escape routes that avoided the built-up areas in and around Misawa town.

I stopped off to top up on fuel after 4 hours and again just before I reached Misawa. Unlike much of Europe, Japan had not yet fully implemented bans of fossil fuels for motor transport. Almost all cars and larger vehicles were fully electric, but hybrid motorbikes and small buggies were still allowed. I paid for fuel using an untraceable cash chip and, despite the temptation to enter the small restaurants linked to gas stations and associated rest areas, I restricted myself to sipping water and munching energy bars from my rucksack. This allowed me to keep my helmet on and minimised the risk of my face being captured by any CCTV that I failed to spot.

Despite the relaxing run, I was getting distinctly saddle-sore by the time I reached my destination. Guided by satnav, I made my way through a small village and then took a dirt track that brought me to the edge of a wooded hillside. First priority as soon as I hid the bike behind a pile of wood was to yank my trousers down and have a long pee. The first since I left Tokyo. "Fuck, but that feels really good," I sighed out loud. Despite having restricted intake of fluids since I awoke, my bladder had been uncomfortably full.

I pulled off my backpack and chugged a half-litre of isotonic drink. By this time, the world was beginning to feel a much better place. Then it started to rain. *Fuck, fuck, fuck!*

***

It was clear from the outset that I needed to sleep rough, but my backpack was already loaded with the rifle and its associated guidance system, while the helmet box contained food and drink for tonight and tomorrow. I thus trusted my leathers to keep me warm and dry, having only a thin, inflatable groundsheet to lie on. However, the rain was getting heavier.

The smart-bullet guidance system was military-spec, so it could happily sit in the deluge without risk to the connection providing a heads-up display on my helmet visor. In addition to the rain, it was getting dark, so now would be a good time to check

224

its targeting capabilities. First, however, I used the inbuilt web-link to check Misawa airport's most recent weather forecast. *It didn't look bad yesterday, but please don't let there by a storm front coming in so that golf will be cancelled tomorrow.* There was a plan B, taking out Beall as she boarded Air Force Two. This would, however, be a longer, more difficult shot and entirely fuck up my planned alibi.

To my great relief, tomorrow morning was predicted to be clear, with dry conditions throughout the day. *The bad fucking news was that it'll rain most of the fucking night! Fuck! I really should have tried to sort out a touring bike with panniers, instead of simply going with the option that was closest to Kitty's stolen machine. What I wouldn't give now for a small tent!*

Otherwise, all seemed to be good with the gun. I could access a false-colour image of the flag on the first hole despite the conditions and, when I painted it with the rifle's laser, the chances of a hit were presented as 98.8%. *Can't ask for much more than that, especially given that tomorrow it'll be clear daylight so the shot will be even easier.*

Chapter 27: Jim

Despite sleeping for a few hours during the flight from Helsinki, I felt distinctly spaced-out when I finally arrived in Sapporo. I collected my checked-in suitcase and then walked to the domestic terminal, where I put my case in a coin locker before checking-in for my next flight with hand luggage only – all done with an app on my PASS. I then located and checked into to the airport onsen on the fourth floor. This would kill time until I could catch the flight to Wakkanai. *How civilised is this? Sitting in a hot tub and soaking away my tensions while still in the airport. The West could learn a lot from Japan in this regard.*

The short flight to the small airport in the far north of Hokkaido took me over a landscape that looked increasingly like Scandinavia, with fields of cows and red barns rather than the tapestry of paddy fields typical of the rest of Japan. At the airport, the most notable difference was Russian being the third language on signs, after Japanese and English. Elsewhere in Japan, this would be Korean or Chinese.

I took a taxi to the nearby ferry terminal, where I met up with my dark-web contact. The Russian fishing-boat skipper looked like a caricature of his profession – tall and broad with a thick black beard and piercing blue eyes set into a weather-beaten face. His brown cap, which sported the logo of a Moscow-based construction company, confirmed his identity, as the rather gaudy Dallas Cowboys cap I sported confirmed mine.

As I approached, he pulled a large duffle-bag from below his table and then looked at his wristcom. My PASS authorised payment and he simply nodded at me when I picked up the bag and headed back out to the taxi rank. I was in time to check in the duffle-bag and catch the plane that was returning to Sapporo. If any of the crew was surprised to see the gaijin who had arrived only an hour before head back, they managed not to show it.

There were no problems in the Sapporo domestic terminal and thus, by mid-afternoon, I was in a taxi heading for my downtown hotel, the strangely named Royal Park Canvas, which was located directly beside Odori Park. My check-in was completely electronic and I could go directly to my assigned room and open the door with my PASS. There I assembled and double-checked the sniper rifle, despite the fact that it would never be used. *It would be silly to spoil my elaborate ruse by dumping what was a clearly defective gun.* I then checked on Rachel's progress, noting that she was in position and settling down for what would be probably be an uncomfortable night. *Nothing else for me to do. So, despite the threat of rain later, a good time to have a beer or two and something to nibble – although I'm not sure whether my body would think of it as breakfast, lunch or dinner.*

Typical of many cities in the far north, climate change was hitting hard but, as usual, with mixed pro and cons. Sapporo beer had been a central part of the city's culture for over a century and the sprawling Odori Park beer garden extended for about a kilometre along this strip of green, which formed the core of the city. In good weather it was always busy, clearly a great attraction for those wanting to celebrate before the turbo-charged winter arrived. The opening times for the beer garden extended year by year in line with Global Warming until, by now, they ran until the end of October.

It was just after five pm and already the sun had set. Nevertheless, the lights of the beer garden banished the darkness and space heaters removed the resultant chill in the air. The area that I selected had a distinctly Bavarian theme, with draft beer available in Steins and served by dirndl-clad waitresses. This ambience was a little spoiled by the limited beer-carrying skills of petite Japanese waitresses compared to the buxom Valkyries more typical of a Munich Oktoberfest. It was also noticeable that I was one of the few patrons drinking individual draft beers: most of the groups were crowded around high-tech *beer towers*, which maintained 5-litres of beer fizzy and at optimum temperature until they were finished.

Food also had a Bavarian focus, with pretzels, sausages, sauerkraut and the like, but some Japanese snacks were available. I went for the odd option of gyoza and a heavily salted pretzel, which went down very well with the beer. With the second beer, I had a portion of takoyaki. The octopus balls were so delicious that I considered a second portion, but decided that this was probably not a great idea if I intended to get an early night. I thus ordered a third beer, deciding that this would be my last.

I was halfway through my beer when a familiar figure came into the bar and headed directly towards me. *For fucks sake, what's Julia doing here?* I got to my feet and forced a smile. "Julia, lovely to see you," I gave her a fatherly hug. "What can I get you to drink? Or maybe eat? I've already eaten, but I can really recommend the takoyaki."

"Jim, you're looking good. A beer would be fine, a small Sapporo. I have a later date for dinner, but certainly time for a beer or two."

"I'm afraid half-litres are as small as they offer on draft here. Would that be okay?"

Julia smiled as she sat opposite me. "I suppose a half-litre would be small by German beerhall standards. Anyway, that'll be fine."

I ordered the beer using my PASS and then leaned forward, chin on my knuckles, and looked into her eyes. "It's really great to meet again in the flesh, but this is hardly a coincidence. What can I do for you?"

Her smile turned into a mischievous grin, which reminded me just how much restraint I had needed to avoid trying my arm with her when we worked together. Now a decade older, but every bit as attractive as before. *Just a shame I haven't aged anything like as well as she has.* "It's more what I can do for you. Saving you from yourself sort of thing."

I grinned back. "What exactly do you think that I'm up to, that you need to save me from?"

229

"Come on, Jim, I've been following all the stuff on your conspiracy notice board. You think the visiting Vice-president is a key person behind a planned attack on Rokkasho. I'm sufficiently convinced by this that I've already taken steps to implement counter-measures. Just to be on the safe side, I also put a visual identity check on older gaijin males arriving in Japan. This morning I was notified of your arrival in Sapporo, so I hopped on a flight up here. You are in a likely fallout zone if the attack was successful, so you must be up to some kind of mischief."

She stopped as the waitress came over with her beer, giving me a chance to formulate my response. After the girl left, I tried to look as innocent as I possibly could. "Me, a geriatric pensioner? What could I possibly be up to?"

Julia rolled her eyes. "Stop buggering around, Jim. I'm serious here. I know that you're up to something and I wouldn't be surprised if you were targeting Beall. The thing I don't understand is why you're here in person. Over the last ten, fifteen years, you've been a planner, not a doer. Which, given your age, is very sensible. I really hope that you're not intending to do something silly and go out in a blaze of glory."

I widened my eyes to parody surprise. "Me? Blaze of glory? You know that's not my scene. I'm looking forward to a long and peaceful retirement, pottering about in my garden and maybe getting round to the best-selling autobiography that I have always intended to write."

July snorted her derision. "You have always lived in a flat without a garden. Also, you hate writing and have repeatedly dismissed the biographies that I read as *supercilious, egocentric wank*, if I remember your wording correctly."

I lifted up my arms in a gesture of surrender. "Fair cop, you got me guv. I was planning to down Air Force Two with a little missile I've got in my hand-luggage. But, don't worry, I'll come quietly."

"Jesus, Jim, why do you have to be such a pain in the arse?"

"Because you look gorgeous when you're angry." I gave her a lascivious leer. *Good grief, for the first time this evening I'm actually telling the truth.*

Jim stop it!" She gave me a glare that indicated it was time to stop baiting her.

"Okay, let me start with the simple bit. I'm here to convince you to implement a variant on your reaction to the threat from Korea."

"But you don't know what our defence plan is," she interrupted.

"I would guess that the Japanese self-defence force, possibly with a bit of help from the Royal Navy, have set up an anti-missile shield that would make the chances of any weapon reaching Rokkasho negligible."

Julia looked a bit crestfallen. "Okay, given the info that you've provided us with, this was predictable, I suppose. Anyway, as you say, the chances of failure are already negligibly small."

I frowned. "Negligibly small isn't zero and, with the risk that any missile launch further

231

destabilises the already dodgy tensions between Japan, both Koreas, China and Russia, a bit of pre-emptive action seems justified."

Her frown matched mine. "So you've got a scheme that could block the DPRK missile launch."

"I think it might. You, the Brits, together with your Japanese national security counterparts, need to get pro-active. Inform the Chinese, Russians and South Koreans of a potential military coup in North Korea, which could result in attacks against its neighbours. You state that any long-range weapons fired in the direction of Japan will be regarded as an act of war and strongly recommend that the others ensure that their border forces are on full readiness."

"You haven't mentioned the Americans. How can we inform the others without including them?"

"Of course, if the information went through regular channels, this would be impossible. However, if somehow there happened to be leaks of a draft document being prepared for wider distribution, you could get away with it. Come on, MI5 knows how to do all this double-dealing spy shit."

Julia looked thoughtful. "Even if I thought it would work, this is an imminent threat, so are we sure that there's enough time to get everything in place?"

"Yes, it'll need some nimble footwork, so I'm glad we can go through this face-to-face now."

She raised her eyebrows. "Why do I get the feeling that me being here is actually part of your plan?"

I tried again with my innocent face. "I planned to contact you later this evening, as I didn't think you'd react fast enough to get here in person. So your presence is an added benefit from my point of view."

"I'm not sure that I believe you but, anyway, how do you propose that I play this now?"

"You should get the message drafted and leaked as soon as possible, as it'll take a while to get to appropriate decision-makers. You can get the draft filtering through your admin in a way that ensures it'll take ages before it's finalised. This'll give you deniability when the Yanks eventually pick it up."

She thought this though and frowned, "You know that this will also inevitably leak to the DPRK. Probably a lot faster than to the Americans."

"I'm banking on it. This should give the Supreme Leader a chance to intervene and, ideally, wipe out the leaders of the coup before they've a chance to initiate the attack."

"You don't think a change in regime in North Korea would be a good thing?"

I shrugged my shoulders. "It might well be, but I'm not convinced that replacing a dictator with a military Junta would be a great improvement. In any case, it'd certainly destabilise the region in the short term. The best argument for this action, however, is to block the plans of the antinuclear conspirators, who've probably already prepared for a regime change. Anything that fucks up their plans has got to be a good thing."

Julia spent some time thinking through this. "Alright, you've convinced me. I'll get onto drafting the note now. In the interim, can I be sure that you won't do anything daft? I know your propensity for putting out fires with gasoline and we've got a potentially huge bonfire here."

I smiled innocently. "Would I do such a thing? Or, more to the point, would I put my aging bod directly in the firing line? My presence here should convince you that we – or actually you – can defuse this entire thing without a risk of fallout. Either radioactive from Rokkasho or military, as even a blocked missile attack could lead to regional conflicts."

Julia smiled and then finished her beer. "I'm sure that you're up to something else, but you've always been a cautious bugger, so I suppose I'll just have to wait and see. I've got secure comms in my hotel, so I can get started there. Then I'll need to get back to Tokyo and link up with the Japanese to update them on what's happening."

As she rose to go, I stood and hugged her. "Thanks for trusting me on this, I owe you one," I murmured into her ear.

"If we pull this off, there'll be a lot of people in this area that'll owe you a lot more," She replied. "Of course, if all does go well, we'll bury this so deep that they'll never know."

"Well, that's the way I like it." I remained standing, admiring the movements of her tight buttocks as she strode out of the bar. *That went well. A shame that we didn't end up together in my bedroom, but I suppose I can't have everything. All being well, I'll be sharing a bedroom with Rachel by tomorrow night.*

Chapter 28: Rachel

I awoke to the view of a bulky body that blocked the sunrise from the patch of woodland where I had finally, very uncomfortably, fallen asleep. "Watchya do'n heer?" the monster asked in an accent so broad that it took me time before I worked out that it was supposed to be English.

I groaned, feeling all the results of my rough kip. "What's it to you? Why don't you just fuck-off?" I did everything possible to sound like a pissed-off Brit while I clambered to my feet.

"You just mind yur mooth," he slurred while he peered at my bike and the kit scattered around it. Then his eyes returned to my leather-clad body and he grinned. "Yur a spy. Yur here 'cause the veepee o' thu whole US of A's onna base. Yur ass is grass."

He pulled a phone from his jogging suit and glanced at the screen, just before I kicked it out of his hand. My bulky opponent wasn't happy. "Back down, bitch. Thatsa noost iphone you kin git onna base."

"Bitch, bitch is it? You've got such a big fucking mouth that I'm going to ram all your teeth down it. You've got only two options," I counted on my fingers to endure that the lug got the point. "Best option: give up and I'll immobilise you here with so little damage that your orthodontist can fix it so you can go back to the fucking Louisiana swamp that you were dragged up in. Other option: your future has only body-bag stamped on it."

His hesitation following this rant was enough for me to close in and let loose a jab to his exposed jaw.

This was casually swiped aside, letting me know that he wasn't a normal, body-building slab of beef, but someone with unarmed combat training. *Fuck, fuck, fuckity-fuck. I haven't even had a chance to get my early morning pee in the bushes out of the way.*

I forced myself to calm down and move into my *zone*, while I coolly listed my advantages over my opponent. Number one was my helmet, so I fell towards him as if I was off balance and, at the last moment, slammed my head into his chin.

This was enough to change the dynamic of the fight. We stood facing one another, sizing each other up. He had definite Asian roots, but was built like a brick shithouse in a way that made me think of hog-fed redneck from the Deep South. With amazing speed for someone so large, he tried a side-kick aimed at my head, which would probably have broken my neck if it had landed. I had only to twist outside the kick and use an open-hand blow against the inside of his knee to cause him to stagger backwards. *He's fast, but a show-off. It's silly to try such a fancy move against an unknown opponent.*

"God, but you're really fucking stupid," I smiled. "Did you really think you could land a kick on me? You're out of your class, boy, so give up before you get hurt."

As I knew it would, his attack was immediately repeated. *Works every time. A thug like him can't ignore any criticism of his manhood.* I repeated my evasion, hitting his knee harder with my knuckles. "Okay, fuckwit, the options have now narrowed down to you being in a body bag or being in so much pain that you wish you were dead."

"Yu tawk too much, bitch," he drawled, with a glare of hate that should have been able to strip paint. This time he feinted with a front jab, before he repeated his kick. Now I twisted inside his kick and punched him in the groin with all the power I could muster.

His gasp of pain was cut off by a back-roundhouse kick which, helped by my heavy motorcycle books, sent him flying backwards in a spray of blood. Then it got clinical as I proceeded to kick seven shades of shit out of his cowering body. He was semi-conscious when I drew my knife, ready to deliver a coup de grâce but, with a scowl, I forced myself to hold back.

Fucking hell! Some grunt goes out on an early-morning run and falls over me. Very unlikely, but typical of the shit that happens in real life. The best option would be to kill him. A little jab to the top of the spinal cord and the job's done. But if I don't kill him, could it fuck-op the entire operation?

The problem was that I had nothing with me that was easily usable as a restraint that would immobilise him for the hours until the hit. *Under ideal circumstances I'd have a knock-out injection and some ties, but I'm travelling light with only the minimum of kit. Fuck!*

To give me some time to think, I hit the back of my opponent's head with the pommel of my heavy knife, laying him out cold. Although such a blow could be fatal, this brute looked thick-skulled enough to live through it. *Now I just need to drag him into the woods and tie him up somehow.*

Dragging this hulk into the trees was no easy task. He must have weighed more than twice as much as I do, with the job made even harder by undergrowth that constantly snagged his massive frame. Despite taking off my helmet and jacket, I was drenched with sweat by the time he was out of sight from the track. The effort was also increasing the pressure on my bladder, so I had my delayed pee before going any further. I grinned when I spotted that the flow was splashing the side of his face. *Serves him right for forcing me to fight when I was bursting for a piss.*

When I was happy enough with the location, I checked that he was still breathing and then started to strip him of his shoes and jogging kit. I was glad to see that his trainers had conventional laces rather than any of the other fancier closing options, so that provided me with a pair of ties. His sweat-shirt was elasticated and he was wearing nothing below it. *Not really that he needs more clothing with the thick hair covering his body. Looks like a fucking bear.* I smiled at the thought and then pulled down his jogging-pants, which were again elasticated. My smile turned into a laugh as his pink boxers were then exposed. Not just pink, but covered with red hearts. *What the holy fuck possessed him to wear something like this? Must be a present from a girlfriend – or maybe a boyfriend.*

At this point, I saw that the boxers had a drawstring, so I hauled these off also. I winced

239

when I saw how bruised his groin was, with one testicle already swollen to the size of my fist. *Maybe as well that he's unconscious, 'cause that looks fucking painful.*

I balled-up the boxers and jammed them into his mouth, tying the gag in place with a shoelace. I then rolled him onto his stomach and used the other shoelace to tie his hands behind his back. The string from his boxers was long enough to tie his ankles together and then bind them to his hands. Satisfied with the knots, I stood to inspect my hogtied victim. *He might be strong enough to break loose when he eventually comes to, but it certainly won't be easy. Probably he'll lie there until someone finds him.*

This brought to mind my main concern: that he'd be missed and somebody would come looking for him. So the question was whether or not this risk justified me moving to another position. I swithered for a bit, but finally decided to stay put. I did, however, pull my bike further from the road so that it wouldn't be seen by anyone retracing the jogger's route. I then breakfasted on an isotonic drink and a couple of bananas before setting down for what would probably be a long wait.

***

The hit itself was a complete anti-climax. The Veep's party teed off at 1:30 and were soon on the green at the first hole. She was playing with two men, presumably Buck and the base commander, but these were hard to distinguish from the satellite images as they were of similar build and were both

240

wearing caps that prevented me getting a clear view of their faces. Anyway, Beall was unambiguous so I painted her with the laser and fired. Seconds later her head exploded. *No doubt about that being fatal.* "That's for my Mum," I muttered as I loaded the second bullet and painted one of her golf partners, who were standing in shocked confusion while security guards rushed towards them. Another head exploded. *50:50 chance of that being Buck.*

As planned, I then threw the rifle as far as possible into the wood and, after disconnecting the cable to my helmet, did the same with its guidance unit. It seemed a shame to dump such a superb weapon, but this was critical to our ploy.

I dragged my bike to the track and then rode off, taking small roads until I reached the highway. Now it would be a straightforward run to the ferry and perfectly timed to implement the switch of bike registrations with Kitty en route.

Chapter 29: Jim

Next morning I checked on Rachel, using only passive satellite images to avoid any direct link that could be picked up by anyone monitoring my accommodation with spy kit of the kind that I knew Julia had at her disposal. Even at highest resolution, my partner was very difficult to pick out. However, it was doable using top-end AI pattern recognition. *Of course, doable only because I knew roughly where she was. No way would she be picked up otherwise.*

I set up a smart-analyser on the image of the golf course, which would notify me when Beall's group reached the first tee. Then I checked the location of the transponder on Kitty's bike, which would currently appear to be Rachel's machine. Again all going smoothly there. *Time to have breakfast before I contact Julia to see how she's getting on.*

Over coffee and a tasty bacon and cheese hot-sandwich at a nearby Starbucks, I thought through the plan for the day, trying to identify possible glitches. *Developing a plan of action is the easy bit. Identifying all ways it could go wrong and preparing counter-measures for these is the real challenge.*

Back in my room, I was about to email Julia when she WhatsApped me, providing a link to a more-secure video-chat site. She was already in Tokyo and, after brief pleasantries, she overviewed progress with the leaked document. This seemed to have been picked up only by the South Koreans so far, who had quietly placed their border with the North on red alert. "This is good news," she finished, "as the DPRK has more intelligence assets in the South than in any of the big players."

"Yup, that's the ideal case. If the South has already acted on the leak, then the Supreme Leader will hear about it soon, if he hasn't already."

"Yes, that's the thing that worries me. What if the leaders of the coup also pick this up and move forward with their planned attack?"

"That's the advantage of Beall being in the line of fire. There must be guarantees that the attack won't take place before she leaves."

"That's just an assumption," Julia looked worried.

"Yes, but if I'm wrong, you're still prepared for the attack and can neutralise it if it occurs. If I'm correct, however, the leaders of the intended coup will either be running for their lives or are already pushing up daisies. I'm sure that the Marshal's agreement with Beall's crowd will have included some kind of parachute in case things went tits-up. Nevertheless, a dictator doesn't stay in power long without a plan for rapidly taking out anyone associated with the slightest hint of treason. I'd bet on fear of Kim being a bigger factor than any commitment to the Yanks."

"You're sure about this?"

"As I said last night, I wouldn't be here if I wasn't. And I'm still in Sapporo, as you know well."

"Okay, I'll take your word for that."

Like hell she will. There'll be at least a couple of agents tracking me. Plus a team following all CCTV and other monitors that they can access to trace my movements. Exactly as I hoped.

Julia looked at me as if she was awaiting some kind of reaction. However, she cracked first in response to my continuing silence. "So, I assume that you'll also keep me informed if anything unusual occurs."

"Scout's honour," I replied, tapping my head with two fingers in what I thought was the kind of Baden-Powell thing that scouts would do.

"Fine, let's go ahead on this basis and I'll let you know if there are any developments from my side."

"Brill! Toodle-pip and talk to you soon." I closed the link immediately and checked the app that had run in the background to assure no risk of an associated digital hack. I breathed a sigh of relief. All clear and running to plan. *I just need to locate the agents that Julia will have set up to track my movements and ensure that they do the job I want them to.*

***

I watched the satellite feeds with baited breath when the targets teed-off, knowing that the best option for a clear hit was the green at the first hole. I had five back-ups scoped-out, but these had increasing problems in terms of both the shot that Rachel would have to make and the complexity of her escape. As the latter was actually my biggest worry, I felt a weight lift from my shoulders when Beall went down. *Looks dead and without any hope of resuscitation.* I was also watching when the base commander's head exploded. My AI had been tracking the party since they left the Lakeside Grill after lunch. *Fuck, she's mixed up her targets. Anyway, girl, get the fuck out of Dodge ASAP.*

I waited for a few minutes and then sent the first message to Kitty in her role as Rachel. *Cancel hit. Target already down. Looks like US black ops. Divert to primary escape route.* This was intended to be intercepted on receipt and used to pinpoint where Rachel was supposed to be. Nevertheless, there was a chance that Julia could detect it being sent and decrypt it, despite the secure TOR service I was using. Now I had to give the appearance of responding to this unexpected change of plans.

Although I already had the information needed, I went through the process of checking travel options on the internet and then booked the afternoon flight to Hakodate. I then sent another message. *Will arrive at H airport about 6 with change of clothes.* The last job was to reserve a ticket on the ferry for Rachel. Although it was rather short notice, I knew that, for a motorbike, there would be no difficulty getting a place on the boat. I would have over 2 hours to wait for Rachel to arrive there, but that would give me plenty of time to pick up a rental car at the airport – again making it look as if I was reacting to a surprise development.

The interesting bit now was to identify the agents who Julia will have staked out and then, while appearing to make my travel as difficult to trace as possible, ensure that I didn't actually lose them until they had seen me meet up with Rachel.

Chapter 30: Rachel

The timing of the hit was almost perfect, so that Kitty was informed of it before reaching Hachinohe and then, as me, could take a route north to avoid Misawa. At Towada, she would change back to her bike's original transponder and thus, as the assassin, turn northwest towards Aomori city. I would also ride through Towada, and there change my bike registration back to that of the hired machine. Then I had a run directly north to the smaller port of Oma and would have plenty of time to catch the ferry leaving just after 5.

During my ride to the ferry, I picked up Jim's text in a window of my visor. This noted that he would meet me after I arrived in Hokkaido. *What the hell's that stupid old bugger doing here? I know the plan was to have support to help plant evidence to support our storyline, but this should be someone like Kitty who was hired via the dark net, not Jim himself. There'll no doubt be some convoluted reason to justify this, but maybe he's just worried about me.* I smiled at the thought.

Although it was a much shorter run, the long trip yesterday and my night sleeping rough made the ride increasingly uncomfortable, especially as I had to make it appear that I arrived just in time for my boat. I was very happy to finally dismount on the ferry and head first to the toilet and then to the bar for the rest of the short, 90 minute crossing.

As I relaxed with a sandwich and an isotonic drink – the strangely named *Pocari Sweat* – the

247

enormity of what I had done began to sink in. A sniper must switch out all thoughts about the victim when preparing for the shot, but afterwards this inevitably sinks in after the adrenalin high has completely burned out. There have been four US presidents assassinated – Lincoln, Garfield, McKinley and Kennedy – but no VPs until now. If my identity ever became known, the US justice department would not be able to rest until they had tracked me down. *This is why my cast-iron alibi has to be established – even if it does result in me being identified as someone who was actually preparing to take the shot. Hopefully, this will be well buried by any agencies who ever uncover this, given the associated links to black ops run by the Veep.*

I smiled when it suddenly dawned on me that this wool-gathering was really intended to keep my mind off the somewhat more immanent threat of being downwind of a nuclear facility facing a possibly devastating attack. Jim had convinced me that the risk was minimal. Nevertheless, although the probability was low, the consequences for me personally could be severe.

I should feel reassured that Jim himself is on the same firing line. Given his age, though, he's got a lot less to lose than me. Despite that, I'll bet the bastard has iodine tablets with him. That's something I should have thought of packing…

***

Just as I returned to my bike, shortly before the ferry docked, I got another message from Jim. *I am now at the port. Meet me at Orix car rental.* The attached map showed that this was very close to where I would disembark from the ferry.

The couple of bikes on board were directed off before the cars and trucks, so I was at the meeting point ten minutes later. Jim waved at me as I approached and directed me to a spot beside a rather slick-looking saloon car with heavily-tinted windows. After I clambered off my bike, he quickly moved up to give me a hug, which allowed him to whisper into my ear. "Right, girl, all your luggage onto the back seats as soon as you like. Keep your helmet on. I'll brief you when we're underway."

I scowled, but silently obeyed. *He's acting as if we're under observation, which can't be right. If there was any risk that he was being tailed, it'd be better for him to keep well clear of me.*

We drove in strained silence until he accelerated onto the E5 highway, when he switched on the music system that I could see was cable-linked to his bloody ubiquitous PASS. "Fine, we can chat now. Even if someone is good enough to keep a laser scanner on a window, my system will scramble our conversation."

"For fuck's sake, Jim, why did you pick me up if you're being followed? Even if you were incapable of losing them, you could simply have messaged me an escape route."

"Ah, yes, you'd think that, wouldn't you? However, part of my cunning plan is to pretend that I don't know that I'm being followed. This allows us to strengthen your alibi."

249

I took off my helmet and threw it into the back, shaking my head to loosen up crinks in my neck. "Christ, Jim, why do you always have to make things so bloody complicated? Should I get a gun out in case they decide that following is too passive now that they've seen that we're together?"

I glared in response to his annoying grin. Nevertheless, he clearly decided to put me out of my misery. "You don't have to worry about them. These are good guys: security from the British embassy."

"If that's the case, why are they following you and why do you have to make sure that they can't overhear us?"

"They're following us because my embassy pal, Julia, doesn't trust me. Thus, we need some privacy so that we can get organised to plant the evidence that'll support the storyline that I'm building. You need to clamber into the back and strip off, changing into the clothes that I've packed for you. You also need to wash down all external surfaces of your leathers, boots and helmet with the magic fluid in the blue bottle. It'll destroy any traces of gunshot residues and any pollen or dust that could link you to the location where the shot was taken."

"How does it turn out that, any time we get together, I end up taking my clothes off?" I couldn't hide a smile.

"Luck, I suppose," he grinned. "Anyway, you need also to get the broken down rifle from my pack and make sure that your fingerprints are on it. Then give it a quick wipe down – as if you were trying to

250

clean it but were too rushed to do it properly. There's a rest area in about 10 kay where we can dump your helmet and the rifle stock. We'll spread the rest during stops over the next couple of hours. After that's done, we can find a roadside hotel to crash out in."

I switched on a light in the back and then started wriggling out of my kit. Even though the car was relatively spacious, this was still a bit of a struggle. Then there was the chore of decontaminating the surfaces and cramming different items into poly-bags for disposal. By the time I was finished, I was coated with sweat – which didn't improve the conditions of the bra and knickers I'd been wearing for the last thirty-six hours.

As if reading my mind, Jim called back. "You'll find wipes and clean underwear with the other clothes. Dirty stuff you can also pack for disposal."

I'm sure the sad old bastard is watching, but it's not as if he'll see anything he hasn't seen before. It was, however, a pleasure to strip and wipe myself completely clean. *We'll be in a hotel soon, but the feeling of fresh clothes is very welcome.*

I was dressed in t-shirt, jeans and trainers and had the material for disposal sorted out when Jim pulled into a quiet rest area and parked beside a line of bins for different kinds of waste – glass bottles, cans, paper and one labelled *general garbage*. I threw my helmet and the rifle stock into this, along with dirty underwear. A few seconds later, I was in the front passenger seat and we were heading back onto the highway.

"Will the guys following us be able to pick up that stuff?" I wondered aloud.

"Not unless they want to risk losing us. They'll certainly note where we stopped, though, and there'll be someone sent out to investigate as soon as possible. The other option is that someone jumps out to have a look and gets left behind, but I suspect they won't go for that option if they're unsure if we have dumped anything other than rubbish from a snack."

"Okay, so we're dumping the evidence showing that I intended to carry out the assassination, but was pulled out when I was beaten to the punch. You thus need someone to find it, but ideally not the local police and not too soon."

"Exactly. Julia needs to be convinced that you couldn't possibly have fired the shot. Once she has the evidence to support this, there's no benefit to her muddying the water by bringing this up, especially as it might lead to exposing the role that we had in setting up the defence against the Korean attack. It'll certainly leak out at some point, but by then the focus will be on the likely role of CIA black ops. As news of the assassination spreads, my conspiracy hackers will flood websites with a mixture of real evidence of the Veep's schemes and fabrications on a building reaction to this within the CIA. The top brass is then caught in a clinch: they could actively deny this, thus implying that they either didn't know what Beall was up to or they actively condoned it…"

"Or simply keep their heads down," I finished in response to his pause. "It makes a crazy sort of sense. If the Veep's actions were treasonable, they would need to do something, but an exposé could do a lot of harm to US credibility."

Jim nodded. "And, before anything else, they'd need to be sure that this wasn't actually a CIA action carried out by some loose cannon. The problem with plausible deniability of dirty deeds is that they get somewhat disconnected from the normal chain of command and thus there must be a lot of executive-level spooks shitting themselves about what may result from opening this particular can of worms."

I sat back and closed my eyes, letting this convoluted plot sink in. *What kind of twisted mind is needed to come up with something so Byzantine? Anyway, I'm glad he's on my side. Especially as it looks like I could actually get off with this extremely high-profile murder.*

After another stop to quickly dump more evidence, Jim switched on cruise-control and relaxed back with a sigh. "We've got twenty minutes until our next stop, so we should probably get the debriefing out of the way while everything is still fresh in your mind."

"Before we get to that, there's something that I've just thought of. We are cleaning my kit of any traces of the crime scene. But what about my bike? If someone thinks to do a forensic analysis of that, then maybe I'm scuppered."

"Yes, I thought of that. It's why I had you dump the bike outside that car hire place. They'll contact the hire agency in Tokyo and arrange to have it picked up. I invented a story about a family emergency back home in the US. I also paid them to give the bike a good wash beforehand, explaining that, in your rush to meet up with me, you'd had a bit of an accident. Lady's bladder-control issues, that sort of thing. Anyway, the bike will get a good steam-clean that should remove any evidence in the very unlikely case that anyone decides to have a look."

"Ah, bladder control, good that you brought that up. I did have to pee at my hide-out, so maybe there's a chance that a good forensic analysis would pick that up." *I don't need to mention that some of that could be sampled from the grunt that I beat up.*

"You got your drinks and snacks for your trip from Kitty, didn't you?"

I frowned at this non-sequitur, but simply mumbled a confirmation.

"Then you'll be clear. These contained an enzyme that'll scramble any DNA in your urine. It's one that's used by the CIA, so it will again help to thicken the plot. So, as long as you didn't have a crap…"

"Come on, I'm not that daft! I managed to make it until the toilet on the ferry, although I must admit it was getting a bit touch and go. A bit less self-control and the bike might really have needed a good clean." I couldn't help giggling at the thought.

"Fine, so was there anything else significant to report?"

"Well, I did get spotted by a jogger at my bivouac early this morning. A guy from the base. I took him down but left him breathing. He'll have been found by now."

Jim grimaced. "Fuck, we could have done without that. You're a psychopath, remember! Why in God's name did you leave him alive?"

"It was just a guy in the wrong place at the wrong time. Once he was down, he was no threat, so I didn't need to kill him."

"Well, I take it from that, that he couldn't identify you?"

"I had my helmet on the entire time and, with the tinted visor, there is no way that he'd make out my face. It was clear that I was a woman, but I tried to use an English accent, so he wouldn't get much from that."

"Oh, well, we just live with it. What did he look like, by the way?"

"Big, and built like a brick outhouse. But not body-builder bulk, he could move. I'm sure he was trained in some kind of marital art and would be relatively high grade, black-belt of some sort."

"That, at least, is a bit of a blessing. Someone like that is very unlikely to admit to being taken down by a girl your size. Even in his own mind, he'll have bulked you up quite a bit. This might even play to our advantage, although I could really have done without the extra complication."

"Extra complication?" I spluttered. "Your schemes are labyrinthine in the extreme! They couldn't get more complex."

He grinned and tapped me on the head in a most annoying manner. "Schemes need to be complex, because reality is also complex and inherently uncertain. The trick, however, is to hide all the minutiae below a superficial story that seems simple and obvious. Anyway, you can ponder these words of wisdom while you get ready for the next drop: the rest area is coming up in 500 metres."

***

At the last dump site, Jim included his mobile phone together with the last of my kit. He had snapped it in two, but didn't remove either the chip or the battery from the phone. "Right, now we make it hard to be followed." The car shot off and, in contrast to cruising just below the speed limit as we had done until then, he accelerated to 20 kilometres per hour above this limit. After only ten minutes, he took the turn off for Lake Toya and then slowed down to stick to the signed speed limits.

It was almost 9 pm and already dark with low-lying cloud when we finally pulled into the covered forecourt of the Hotel Grand Toya. With only a small backpack remaining from our combined luggage, we checked into a room in the new annex, which had been pre-booked and in which a couple of other bags had been dropped off by one of Jim's dark-web contacts.

In addition to toiletries and a couple of changes of clothes for each of us, we now also had a secure laptop and a small dish antenna that could directly link to satellite re-routers. I was about to set these up when I glanced over and saw that the old fart had started to strip off his clothes. "What the fuck are you up to now, you perverted old sod?"

"Well, I don't know about you, but I'm starving. I've booked a small, private onsen and food will be served as soon as we get settled. Here's your yukata," he threw a cotton robe over to me, "so you can come along or get something sent to the room. Your choice."

The mention of food reminded me that I had eaten nothing but energy bars and the sandwich on the ferry, the thought causing my stomach to rumble. "Oh, what the hell. At least you could turn your back and pretend not to be ogling me."

By now he was naked, but obediently turned his back. Only when I was wrapping the belt around my yukata did I spot that he had positioned himself such that he had a clear view of me from a mirror on the back of the door. I rolled my eyes and gave him the finger, but he merely laughed in response.

The lock of our room door and that of the private hot tub at the end of the corridor were both biometric, so we set off without even a key – apart from the robes and zori sandals, there was me with only my minimum jewellery and the old codger with his daft PASS.

The private spa had a small changing area, where we hung up our yukatas and left our sandals. We then moved on to couple of low stools, with associated hand-held sprays and bottles of liquid soap, set beside a huge wooden tub containing steaming water. Jim reminded me of the washing protocol for these places and then we sat on the stools and washed ourselves three times before entering the scalding water.

I sank down onto a low bench in the tub which brought the water up to neck height, sighing with pleasure as the heat released tension that I wasn't even aware of previously. I couldn't help thinking back to Canada, with Jimmy and Leroy. It seemed like only a short time ago and here I was, on the other side of the globe and now one of the hunters rather than the hunted. *Assuming, of course, that I don't get fingered as the assassin and end up on a most-wanted list, with half of the world's security agencies and bounty hunters on my tail.*

Gradually, I became aware that my partner-in-crime was looking at me in a strange way and turned to him, raising my eyebrows as a silent question.

He wasn't sitting quite as deeply as me, so I could make out indicators of tension in his scraggly shoulders and neck. "Right, I suppose that it's my turn now for the debriefing. I can confirm that the hit was a success and the Veep is no more."

I shook my head at this statement of the obvious. "I could have told you that, as I saw her head explode. A large calibre bullet does that. You can't just put a band aid over the hole, because her brain was distributed over a large part of the first green."

"But," he frowned at me, "you missed the secondary target. Buck is very much alive and kicking."

"You're joking! I also saw the mess of his skull after the round impacted. He's got to be pushing up daisies by now."

"Yes, I spotted the mix-up. It was the base commander that you took out, not Beall's co-conspirator."

I put my head in my hands when I suddenly remembered the confusion caused by the chubby guys in matching baseball caps. "Fuck! Sorry about that. I probably should have done a better job of checking the target but, having just killed the Vice-president, you can understand that I wanted to get moving ASAP."

"It's okay, I'd have done the same in your place." Once again, I got a condescending pat on the head. "It's a bit annoying, but here we also have a bit of *Gluck im Ungluck*, as they put it in the Big Canton."

"That's German for something like a blessing in disguise, isn't it? So, what did we gain out of me missing by secondary target."

"I haven't got all the analysis sorted out, but the main message is that Buck seems to be a much bigger player than I thought. What this tells us…" Jim stopped speaking when a knock on the door was quickly followed by two kimono-clad waitresses who entered with large trays. "…is that it's dinner time," he improvised.

The women were clearly unbothered by the contrasting naked bodies in the bath and set up the trays on a low table sitting in a niche at the other side of the tub. One of them also opened curtains which now showed that this dining area lay beside a window, presumable with a panoramic view over the caldera that I knew was outside.

After the waitresses left, Jim resumed where he had left off. "My conspiracy team picked up a message from Buck about an hour after the hit. It was on a link that he considered secure, but which was being copied directly onto my dark-net message board. He reiterated his support of the coup and told his tame marshal to set up the missile attack for tonight. Any time after 11 pm. This would be just after Air Force Two was scheduled to leave Misawa with the Veep's body. As you see, he's still sticking to the old playbook, taking advantage of his cousin's assassination to provide an excuse for leaving Japan just before the attack."

"So, taking Beall out has brought us nothing?" It was difficult to keep disappointment out of my voice.

"Au contraire. Not only has one of their most important pieces has been removed from the board, but we now also know – rather that guessing – that Buck is a major player. I must confess that I had my doubts that he was intellectually capable of being a ringleader. I was convinced he was likely to be just a pawn. In fact, I wanted him rubbed out mainly because he's a twat. It seems that I'm wrong, though. He stepped into Beall's shoes immediately after she hit the deck."

"My God!" I placed the palms of my hands on my cheeks feigning shock. "You're actually admitting being wrong, are you? Tell me it's not so."

Jim scooped up hot water in his hands and poured it over my head, causing me to splutter as I had started to laugh at the same moment. "This is a good lesson to learn. I'm not infallible. Nobody is. It's easy to over-rate me, because I'm very good at my job. However, every now and then, I fuck-up and you need to be aware of this, questioning every suggestion that I make. I'm fairly sure that this wasn't a message that you ever got from your bitch-mother. If it had been, she might still have been on this mortal plain. It's clear that you're not as daft as she thinks... thought you were."

"That's the best that you can do, damning me with faint praise?" I couldn't help smiling at this as, after so much time in his company, I realised that any praise at all – no matter how faint – was so unusual that it should be treasured.

"Not only faint praise, but I'll award you with a cold beer if you get your bare arse out of the tub. We can grab something to eat while we drink the beer, which is certain to be Sapporo Classic. There will also be some local sake if you prefer that."

He climbed out to set an example and to my surprise, dried himself with the small cloth that we had used for washing rather than the large, fluffy towels that hung in the changing area. Spotting my frown, he explained. "The Japanese guy who introduced me to onsens claimed that a wet cloth dries you better than a dry one and, to my surprise, it works. Just wring out the little cloth regularly and you'll be dry enough. If you want to put on your yukata but still feel damp, finish off with the big towel, but you shouldn't go dripping into the changing area. As you see, the seats by the table are plastic-covered, so we'll be fine in the buff if that works for you. After I have something to eat, I'll

261

relax for a bit and then have a last soak before going back to the room."

The small, damp towel worked as claimed, but I decided that I would be more comfortable eating with the big towel wrapped around me. I also brought the other towel from the changing room and chucked it to Jim. "Here you go, you wrinkly old bugger. Get that round your waist so that the sight of your aged bod doesn't put me off my food." To my surprise, he obeyed without demurring, seemingly more intent on something that he was reading from his wristcom.

I opened a couple of the large bottles of beer – Sapporo Classic – and poured glasses for both of us. While looking over the wide range of small, beautifully presented delicacies, I located the sake and poured some of this into very small cups. "Cheers!" I raised my beer and extended it towards him.

"Kampai!" he responded, finally looking directly at me before sinking his beer in a long swallow. "Well, I think that we've now got something to celebrate." He then proffered his brimming sake cup to me and I clinked it in a silent toast before he again polished his drink off in a single gulp. "Okay, lass, get us topped off and I'll let you know what's going on."

He munched sashimi while I complied and then drank both his beer and sake before starting to speak. "That was just a short message from my pall Julia at the Embassy. I'll read it to you. 'You got lucky there, you jammy bastard. If you hadn't been beaten to your target, I'd have no choice but to let you – or at least Rachel – go down for it. Whatever, just get the fuck out of Japan before you get into any more trouble.' That was nice, wasn't it?"

"Wait a minute, why did you tell your *embassy pal* my name. If there had been any slip-up, I could have ended up in deep shit."

"I didn't tell Julia anything about you, but she's a smart cookie and certainly has access to everything the Canadians have on our eventful visit there. Knowing that you were with me then and that you're a trained sniper wouldn't make putting a name to my selected assassin very difficult. Because she's been working so closely with Japanese security on this threat, she'll have been able to pick up all the breadcrumbs that I left for her. The final evidence will be any bits of the unused sniper rifle that she's been able to find. By now, she'll also have seen the intercept of Buck's message to North Korea, which will lend credence to our manufactured material indicating that the CIA black-op was run via his military contacts. This may make the Veep look more of a pawn than she actually was, but it's probably lucky for Buck that he's heading home before someone here in Japan gets the balls to try and investigate his role in today's actions."

All of a sudden, I remembered something that Jim had said before the waitresses appeared. "Shit, the missile attack is scheduled for tonight. I know there are supposed to be interceptors organised, but it is always possible that it could get through. I remembered today that I forgot to pack iodine tablets. Have you any?"

His smug grin made me want to slap his face. "Oops, I guess that I forgot to tell you that news of a failed coup has already leaked out of the DPRK. It seems that their Ministry of State Security guys were also monitoring our conspiracy notice board and Buck's message was the final straw that initiated action. This means that the missile interceptors – and iodine tablets – are now superfluous."

That was a final straw for me, so I did my best to slap him, but my low seating position and the bottles on the table meant that I didn't manage more than cuffing the side of his head. This caused him to laugh aloud.

"You cunt! You must have known that I'd be worrying about this…"

"Yes, but you should have been able to work out that, if I'm relaxed and happy that you're literally getting away with murder, then there's no chance that we'll be waking up to fallout tomorrow morning."

I sulked in silence for the next half hour while we nibbled on excellent food, downed icy-cold beer and sipped a dry, slightly aniseed-flavoured sake. My nemesis was clearly unbothered and spent the time filling me in on his trip to Japan and his encounter with the mysterious Julia. The more I listened, the more obvious it was that he really respected this woman and actually regarded her as the major threat to our plans. She had been the focus for his complex web of misdirections and hence the reason for celebration of his success.

After we felt our food had settled, we entered the hot tub for a further 15 minutes and then headed back to our room. Maybe it was relaxing hidden tensions in the bath but, as soon as I entered the room all I wanted to do was hit the sack. In contrast, Jim seemed full of beans and settled down at a laptop with a beer from the mini-bar. After a quick visit to the bathroom, I shucked off my yukata and clambered into the side of the huge bed closest to the window. I don't even remember whether I cursed him for not, at least, booking a room with twin beds.

Chapter 31: Jim

The girl was clearly knackered and went out like a light as soon as her head hit the pillow. I grinned and looked at the beer I had selected – a pale ale from the Hatachino craft brewery, called DAiDAi ale for some obscure reason. Seemingly it was an indigenous Pale Ale – so an iPA rather than the usual IPA. Tasted fine in any case.

My laptop was cabled to my PASS and the satellite uplink, allowing me to contact Julia with minimal risk of my location being picked up. As I expected, she was clearly still working and responded to my ping immediately.

"So, Julia, still burning the midnight oil I see. Don't you have underlings for that?"

She scowled at me before responding. "From the yukata, I guess you're still in Japan. You really need to make yourself scarce ASAP. Although your underling didn't make the shot, it's equally clear that she was intending to."

"Who, me?" I tried to look offended at the suggestion, but spoiled this with a laugh. "Anyway, there's no evidence to suggest that Rachel intended to shoot anyone."

"What about the sniper rifle that you've dumped bits of around southern Hokkaido?"

"Oh, that. Just intending to do a bit of hunting. There seem to be both deer and wild boar needing culling up here."

"Apart from that rifle being over-kill for game, the hunting season hasn't started yet."

"Yes, well the girl was a bit rusty and thought she would get in some practice on ranges before she goes for the real thing."

"If that was the case, why dump the gun?" My pal was clearly getting annoyed with all this tap-dancing around the topic.

"The fact that you're contacting me shows that, following today's assassination, suspicion might fall on anyone in possession of a gun capable of such a shot. We decided that we just can't be bothered with the hassle of possible interactions with the local constabulary if the actual shooter isn't found soon. If it really was US black ops, they're bound to have a pretty good extraction plan. Is there anything on this that you can share with me?"

Julia drummed her fingers on her desk before answering. "The Yanks have a witness of sorts but, as yet, haven't allowed him to be interviewed by anyone off-base. I suspect that he'll leave for the States on Air Force Two later tonight. The American decision to handle all aspects of the shooting themselves has not only pissed-off Japanese police and security agencies, but has also stoked the fire under a host of conspiracy theories."

"Mmm, you must have more than that. US bases are notoriously leaky and I expect you'd monitor that place pretty closely." I could see from the way that she grimaced that I had hit a nail on the head.

"Okay, it's all hearsay at present, but the shooter appears to have been a woman, but someone a lot bigger and more powerful than your girl.

Apparently with a funny accent, which the witness thought might be Canadian."

I laughed aloud. "That's the US for you: when in trouble, blame Canada! Considering that few can tell the difference between accents from the northern US and southern Canada, this does little to discount CIA black ops."

This brought a smile to Julia's lips. "Right enough. Seems a bit strange that it was a single shooter rather than the usual black-ops team, though."

"Maybe they've learned from the fuck-ups in British Columbia. I was on the receiving end there and saw how things got more out of hand as the teams got bigger."

She nodded. "Could be. Anyway, without any help from the US, we've managed to trace the assassin as far as Aomori city before we lost her. We've got the best AI image recognition combing through CCTV for images of foreign women who might fit the profile, but it's a bit of a needle in a haystack."

Excellent, searching for foreign suspects will never pick up a resident like Kitty. It seems that we've certainly benefited here from Rachel's unfortunate encounter. "Do you think the Japanese really want to catch the culprit? If it does turn out to be a US agent, there'll be an unbelievable shitstorm, which can't help but damage relationships with Japan. As the US base isn't cooperating, the best option for you might be just to turn a blind eye here."

"Do you really think this or are you just happy that someone saved you the bother – and risks – of taking out the Vice-president?"

"Well, to be honest, I can only celebrate Beall's demise. The woman was a total megalomaniac. However, given the choice, I'd have been happier for her to suffer a bit – or a lot – rather than a clean kill. Anyway, the planet is a very much better and safer place without her."

Julia gave me a weary smile. "Yes, I guess things have probably turned out for the best. But, please, if you're going to get up to any such nonsense in the future, do it as far as possible from wherever I'm posted."

"Well, look on the bright side, it's got to be better than the northern part of Japan glowing in the dark, with the Chinks and Ruskies trying to decide who gets to wipe out North Korea."

"Yes, that near miss is going to give me the heebie-jeebies until my dying day. So, thanks for all you've done here. Despite all the clear evidence against it, I can't help suspecting that you had something to do with the assassination. But, as it is, better to let sleeping dogs lie and simply wait for the dust to settle."

"Thanking your deity that it's not radioactive," I couldn't help adding. "Anyway, time for me to hit the sack. Tomorrow, I'll set about organising a replacement hunting holiday. Maybe in Scandinavia: what do you think?"

"It's on the other side of the planet, so I think that'd be perfect. So, safe travels."

"Thanks. But I do think that you're overworking a lot here. Maybe you'd like to join us on our wee trip?"

She smiled. "That's a nice thought but, if I was intending to relax, I'd be heading for somewhere remote in the middle of the Pacific."

"Also a nice thought. We should meet up somewhere like that sometime. Anyway, nighty-night."

"Goodnight." She closed the link and I sank back in my chair with a sigh. *Looks like we're in the clear. This'll actually tie in nicely with heading back to Europe via Helsinki.* I immediately checked tomorrow's flight and saw that it was surprisingly full. Nevertheless, a couple of business-class seats were free, although these were rather distant from each other. I booked them separately, using different accounts for payment, even though this would do little to hide the fact that we were travelling together. *Making it easy to see that we're leaving Japan will make Julia happy, so why not. It's when we get to Europe that we'll need to go into deeper cover.*

Realising that my bottle was now empty, I rooted through the other beers in the mini-bar. At the back, there was a can of Hokkaido-brewed beer – an Otaru Pilsner – that seemed just right to finish the evening. While I sipped that, I skimmed through the Conspiracy theory notice board. Several satellite images of the Veep's assassination were now posted, along with several detailed ballistic analysis to identify the position of the shooter. These were generally very close to Rachel's hide and, in one

270

case, the type of gun used had also been correctly identified. I grinned. *The dark-web denizens may be nut-jobs, but their technical abilities are shit-hot.*

As I expected, my original suggestion of this being CIA wet-work had been widely accepted and led to a major hack of the US embassy in Tokyo. I shook my head. *There'll be a lot of red faces there when the material posted on the notice board is found by the media.* Particularly damning was a heavily encrypted message sent from the Ambassador to Langley, clearly via a personal link to the Director of the CIA. This would have been very hard to pick up, much less decrypt. Unfortunately for him, the original mail was stored on his computer and was now available for all to see. *You can do what you want in Dallas, but if you mad fuckers are behind an attack on Japanese soil that I wasn't even warned of, I'll have your balls on a plate.*

As I read this, I choked on a mouthful of beer that I was just about to swallow. *If he had wanted to fire-up conspiracy loonies, he couldn't have phrased it better!*

A couple of decades ago, such material would immediately lead to an enquiry by a Congressional Committee. In the age of fake news, however, there would need to be a lot of investigations before things got so far. Nevertheless, this snowball was rolling down a slope and many at the top of US security agencies would now be focused on making sure that they had plausible deniability just in case this action was the result of loose cannons within their own organisations.

We've stirred up a hornets' nest, so now's the time that Buck's allies are most vulnerable. The conspiracy theorists will be hacking everything they can, but it may be worth adding some fuel to the fire by posting bounties for anything more linking Buck to the Veep's actions. I set this up while finishing my beer.

Realising that there was nothing more that I could do here, I got ready for bed. As I was about to climb in on the opposite side to Rachel, I was greatly tempted to lift the sheet covering her to have an illicit ogle at her naked body. Realising how sad this was, I managed to restrain myself, but memories of sharing the hot tub with her distracted me for a quarter of an hour before I eventually drifted off to sleep.

Chapter 32: Rachel

Following our flight to Helsinki, we spent three weeks travelling around the EU using a range of identities and means of transport, reminding me of the procedure to lose trackers following our original arrival in Europe from Canada. During this time, I was required to repeatedly change my hair colour / wear wigs and sport spoofed contact lenses. However, the paranoid old sod did nothing more to hide his identity than wear really silly hats and different sunglasses. I repeatedly observed that he stood out more as a result of such disguises, looking like a pensioner who had lost his mind, but he assured me that this was part of his cunning plan.

Unlike the hotels, guesthouses and Airbnb places that we stayed in during this time, when we arrived in Switzerland by rail and picked up a *mobility* hire car at Basel station, Jim directed me – his chauffeuse for any such cases – to drive to converted industrial buildings on the outskirts of the town of Baden. Only then did he deign to inform me what he was up to.

"Well, lass, it seems like it's time for you to earn your keep. It'll give you a chance to let your inner psychopath off the leash for a bit."

"What are you gibbering about, you old nutter? You make it sound that we're about to attack someone."

Jim grinned in his usual annoying manner. "Not quite. Actually, someone is about to attack us.

I'm sure you'll be able to handle it, as it'll probably only be a couple of hit men. Three or four, tops."

Despite the rabbits he had pulled out of hats previously, I was beginning to wonder if he had finally cracked under the strain. "And just how did you come to that conclusion?"

"Well, the first thing is that, despite the difficulties involved, there's been a team tracking us since Helsinki." He clearly noted my scepticism. "There's a reason I've been wearing these Joe-90 specs." He spotted that I was losing him completely. "I mean these glasses with the big frames. Never mind about the name, that's just fanboy shit from well before your time. Anyway, they're not a fashion accessory," he shook his head when I rolled my eyes, "but actually the support for a couple of high resolution cameras and the associated AI-image mapping shit. I download this to my PASS each evening and it clearly shows that three individuals have been captured on at least two different occasions."

I was unconvinced. "Strange coincidence maybe?"

"Is it also strange that all three, two men and a woman, have special forces training of some kind or other?"

"You were able to find this out on your own?"

"Don't be daft, lass, that's not the kind of shit that I do. The dark-web hacker-wallahs have a call-off contract to do this for me."

"Okay, say you're right. Why do you think they're going to hit us?"

"I have an alarm that warns me in real time whenever they appear. This went off in Basel station, with all three of them in shot. Although they're not obviously together, it's probably prudent to assume that they are. This wasn't completely unexpected, so that's why we're here."

A shiver ran up my spine. "There's more than that, isn't there, you twisted old fucker. You're setting us up!"

"You're not as daft as your mum," he started, in his typical way of slagging me with a back-handed compliment. "I've been sniffing about to see who these folk are and why they're after us. The action is probably driven by someone in the CIA or NSA, but they're using foreign mercenaries to make it difficult to trace. So, this being the case, it seems best to clear the air. What do you think?"

I could have decked the stupid old fuck. "You're setting us up for a hit, just when we've nothing to defend ourselves with. I've being going on to you about getting kitted-up since we arrived in Finland. Despite this, what do I have? A fucking hunting knife and a hatchet! And you've only got your daft walking stick!"

"It's actually an antique sword-stick…"

"No, that certainly can't be described as a sword. It's nothing better than a fucking walking stick. If you want a sword, get a katana, or a broadsword, or a fucking scimitar. Anything but that daft walking stick."

"Alright, Rachel, you've got a point there. But that's why we're here in Oederlin."

I was confused for a second until I saw the neon sign proclaiming that this old warehouse was indeed called Oederlin. "And this helps us how?"

"Well, this is where I normally live." My look of distain made him quickly move on. "As you may have noticed, I'm more than a little paranoid, so the defences here should be adequate. There are also some weapons in my humble abode. So just park the car here and let's get upstairs. We should have a bit of time, as I'm sure the attack won't come until it gets dark.

***

I carried our limited luggage up a flight of external stairs to a heavy steel door, which opened silently as Jim approached it. This led into a huge, high-ceilinged room that was clearly originally constructed as an industrial fabrication area. The left hand side had a row of windows looking onto a river, while the windows on the right side were blanked off with steel plates. Despite modernisation, it still tended towards steam-punk gothic, with all kinds of bits and pieces of ancient metal-working kit scattered along the walls. These archaeological relics of the early 20th century contrasted with a niche in the far left corner that was filled with top-end electronics set around a black leather gaming chair with inbuilt control panels in the arms. Jim immediately settled into it and the screens around him came to life when he set his PASS into a unit that was clearly crafted to hold it. In addition, background classical music came on, evidently from a high quality sound system. *Maybe Stravinsky's Firebird suite.*

"I'll just run a defence check and see if I can trace our opponents," he muttered, "so be a good lass and make me a coffee. Triple espresso would be just the very dab."

So much for bodyguard: I spend most of my time with this old sod acting as general dogsbody. I looked around and saw nothing that looked like a coffee machine. "So just how do I do that? And how can you live here: there seems to be no residential infrastructure?"

"As should be obvious, this is my office. The living area is through the door there." Without taking his eyes off the displays in front of him, he nodded his head in the general direction of something that I had thought might have been the entrance to a walk-in industrial oven.

As I approached, I could hear the sound of heavy bolts withdrawing and then the massive door whispered open, revealing that it was set in a concrete bulkhead that looked to be about a half-metre thick. *More appropriate to a vault or a bomb-shelter rather than a living room.* I looked inside and grinned, taking in the minimalist, but very modern, open-plan kitchen, dining area and bed in a space that was at least as big as his *office*. Even the toilet, shower and large, freestanding bath were separated only by a glass wall. *Only a man living on his own would be happy in a place like this.*

The kitchen had both an inbuilt traditional espresso machine and a little capsule coffee-maker. Although the former had beans already loaded into

277

the grinder, I chose the latter and filled the water reservoir before selecting a capsule at random from a rack and putting a medium-sized cup below it. While the machine warmed up and started gurgling to produce the first espresso, I took advantage of the privacy to empty my bladder. *Bad enough sharing bedrooms with him, but I'm not using that toilet any time he's present.*

After the third espresso had been added, I set a cup in place for myself and then took the coffee through to my personal albatross. "Okay, here you go. Anything else that you need? Polish your shoes? Peel you a grape?"

"Stop waffling, lass." He took the cup and had a careful sip of the scalding fluid. "Do you want the good or bad news first?"

Considering how confident he had seemed previously, this was a worrying question. "I'll have the good news, but save it until I've got my coffee." I went back to the kitchen and made my espresso a double, taking time to prepare myself for very bad news.

As soon as I returned, Jim got directly to the point. "The good news is that I've located the bad guys – well, actually, guys and gals – and they seem to be holding off until nightfall, pretty much as I expected."

Already sensitive to bad news, I broke in. "Wait a minute, guys and gals? You said two guys and one gal."

Jim smiled. "So, you've learned to listen carefully to what I say. That's also good news, I suppose. But, as you've spotted, there's more than

278

one gal. And, in fact, more than two guys. That's the bad news."

"You're still holding back," I pointed out. "How many of them are there?"

"They've made things easy for me, as they are now grouping in a car park nearby the Leibstadt nuclear complex. They're in two large SUVs…"

"How many, for fuck's sake?"

"At present eight: five guys and three gals."

"All fully tooled-up, I suppose."

"I'm sure. They arrived separately and the SUVs were waiting for them. As both vehicles have tinted windows, it's difficult to be sure what weapons they have, but it'll be best to assume the worst."

"So, what's the plan? Scarper off sharpish, I assume."

"That would be the worst plan. We'd just be postponing the attack and it'd happen somewhere without the infrastructure that we have here."

"Jesus, but there's eight of them. If we now know who they are, we could just pick them off one by one."

"But here we have the home advantage. With eight opponents, or maybe more, we'll have to play hard-ball. You may want to have a glance in the green cabinet over there. It's marked *tools and spares*, but has a selection of weapons."

That's a start but, with eight experienced mercenaries, it'll need to be some very heavy armament. The cabinet opened as I approached it and my jaw dropped. "Fuck, Jim, we need weapons – real guns – not these fucking toys." I lifted out a

279

contraption that was an ultra-modern take on a crossbow.

"Not a bad toy that. The Teflon-coated ceramic tips on those depleted uranium bolts will go straight through the best of body armour. Completely automatic with a ten-shot magazine."

"That'll be just peachy against an assault rifle with a hundred-shot drum magazine."

"It's a precision weapon, not something for spraying an area with no thought about collateral damage. Anyway, if you want a gun, open the box at the bottom of the cupboard."

In the box were a couple of old-style automatic pistols. "Getting there, but not what I'd choose to go up against machine guns."

"Those are Glock 18s and you should find a rack of extended 33-round magazines in there, which will let you spray bullets about, if that's what you want. However, if all goes well, we won't need any of that shit. These weapons are only for the case that anyone gets into the building and I've no intention of letting that happen. But help yourself if it makes you happier."

"Much happier," I muttered while selecting a belt with two holsters for the automatics and a dozen fast-release clips for the magazines. After adjusting the belt to fit comfortably and loading it up, I also grabbed the crossbow and a couple of evil-looking throwing knives.

Jim finally took his eyes of his screens, looked around at me and laughed. "It may be a comfort blanket for you, but are you seriously going to wander around encumbered with all that shit? It's only mid-afternoon, so we've got hours before anything will happen. I propose an early dinner, but maybe a little Apéro first will help to calm you down. I'm sure that I've got a rather nice, old Meursault premier cru in the fridge that would be perfect. There should also be some pate there, so get a baguette out of the freezer and pop it in the oven."

"Bugger that! There's no way that I'm getting pissed if we're going to be facing a bunch of professionals in a few hours."

"It's exactly because of this bunch that I want to drink some of the best wines that I've been holding onto for special occasions. It'd be a shame to kick the bucket and leave these undrunk."

This old tosser just goes from bad to worse. "You're a nutter, you know. At least tell me that you've got some kind of alcohol clear-up drug to hand."

"Of course, I'm not that daft. I'll certainly need it after polishing off the Opus One with a large bison steak."

The temptation to strangle the annoying bastard was almost irresistible. *If I didn't need him to run his defences, I'd be working out ways to dispose of his corpse.*

Chapter 33: Jim

I could see that Rachel was getting twitchy after we finished a deliberately drawn-out dinner and so I restrained myself from teasing her further by suggesting a post-prandial digestif. I reckoned that we still had a couple of hours, but passed her a tablet that would accelerate metabolism of the alcohol in her system. I noticed that she had drunk considerably less than me, but recommended that, after her food settled, she combined this with some exercise on the multi-trainer in my office, while rehydrating with isotonic drinks.

"Fine, but first of all I need to hit the loo. So would you please bugger-off back into your office."

I couldn't help chuckling. "So, it seems that you're a shy assassin, even after all the time we've spent together."

"I'm not shy, but I'm not doing my business with you watching, you fucking old perv."

"As I have previously admitted, guilty on all counts. Although the amount of fucking has been very limited of late, I'm sorry to say. Anyway, I don't see why I have to leave the table even if you're not in an exhibitionist mood at present."

"You're looking straight into the loo just now. Haven't you noticed that the wall is glass?"

"Of course it's glass, but all you need to do is press the button beside the sink and it goes opaque."

"Oh…"

I enjoyed her look of surprise, before anticipated her next concerns. "The entire area is very well ventilated and covered by an anti-sound curtain. There may not be a door, but you're as private in there as you want to be.

When Rachel disappeared into the bathroom, I took a last glass of wine back into the office to check on how my dark-web cronies were getting on with preparations for the aftermath of the attack. *Always better to be an optimist and have everything ready for the best case. In the worst case, it won't make any difference as I'll probably be pushing up daisies.*

***

When Rachel joined me in the office after about half of an hour, she was dressed for mayhem. She had managed to find my flack-jacket and somehow adjust it to fit her very much smaller frame. As this came down to mid-thigh on her, she wore her belt over it. Both pistols were holstered at her side, with spare magazines at her back and knifes fit into sheaths set in front of her stomach.

I chuckled. "You look like a girl wearing her assassin-father's clothes. Anyway, a sensible choice, even though the aim is to avoid needing that kind of protection. In the worst case, the bad guys will come through the door, which will be open if they get that far."

Rachel frowned. "Open? It looks pretty heavy duty, so why not let them fight their way in."

"Do you know how much that door cost?" I feigned horror at the question. "Anyway, if they get

283

that far, we're better presenting them with a setting that'll maximise their confusion."

"Well, it's certainly confusing me. But, first of all, what have you got that'll hold them back?"

"Well, assuming that they drive down the ramp to this building, I have a mine that'll take out one of the vehicles, no matter how well armoured it is."

Rachel frowned. "So, you take out the first one, blocking the road. They'll need to slog around it on foot."

"That would be an option, but I'd rather take out the second one, making it harder for those in the first car to escape."

"A bit optimistic, but that'd certainly even the odds a lot if there are no survivors."

"There won't be. I'm using a shaped charge backed with an incendiary. Even without the ammunition that they'll be carrying, it'll be a funeral pyre for anyone inside."

The grin showed that her inner psycho was awake and ready to rock and roll. "Then what?"

"I've made sure that they know about this office, so it should be their target. As you noticed, the stairs up to the door are metal. I've got a super-capacitor fully charged and, when they're on their way up, I'll hit it with about 100,000 volts. With a bit of luck, that'll be end-game."

Rachel looked disappointed. *Maybe worried that she won't get a chance to get her hands bloody.* "What if they don't want to come in the front door?" she asked hopefully.

"It'll be a lot more difficult for them and, for that case, I've a number of booby-traps in place.

Nevertheless, I'm sure they'll come up the stairs – at least initially."

"And, what if your electric shock doesn't work?"

"That's when the door opens and then you're up. I suggest you upend the heavy work-bench and place it to the side of the door into my room. You're going to need your back to the wall if you're going to be firing those guns on fully automatic, and the table will give you protection if you need to duck for cover."

"Won't do a lot against armour-piercing rounds," she pointed out.

"True enough, but better than nothing. I addition, you'd better take these." I handed her a wrap-around visor that looked like high-tech cycling shades and a pair of ear buds.

"Armoured glasses are sensible, but I already have combat earphones."

"Not like these. They have smart sound blockers in addition to normal com functions."

Rachel rolled her eyes. "And I need these for what?"

"I was getting to that. As soon as anyone comes through that door I'll hit them with both directed ultrasound and blinding lasers. The sound is especially brutal and even the bounce-back could be enough to damage your ears. Hence the plugs."

My in-house assassin seemed to like the idea and her eyes gleamed. "But there's more to it, isn't there?"

"Yes, well I'm a feeble old man and need all the protection I can get…"

"As you would say, cut the waffle," she interrupted and gave me a wicked grin.

"Yes, well, immediately after the laser and sound barrage, all lights will go out."

"These fuckers won't be scared of the dark and, in any case, their night vision will switch in immediately."

"That'll be perfectly timed for the infrared flares that'll light them up."

"Maybe being paranoid isn't so bad when you come up with shit like this. I do believe that we actually could pull this off."

"I'm glad you're feeling confident, as I can see that they're now moving out. It's a bit earlier than I expected and, if they head directly here, we can expect them in about twenty minutes."

"No probs. Let me just set up the killing field and work through some scenarios. I just need to know where you'll be."

"Me, I'll be back in my room. I can follow the action and guide things there with an interface linked to my PASS."

"You and your fucking antiquated wristcom! That's not cheering me up a lot."

"But you've got to look on the positive side here. I'll be completely safe and, as my bodyguard, you won't be distracted by concerns about me."

I ignored her theatrical groan, transferred all data to external stores and locked down my computers. Once I closed the door of my room, I was in an effectively impregnable fortress. *Nothing at all to worry about now as the girl is completely capable of looking after herself.* I should be reassured, but somehow a nagging doubt remained in the back of my mind.

***

I patched Rachel's visor into a webcam viewing the approach ramp. As planned, I activated the mine as the second SUV passed over it. My monitors in the office picked up Rachel's gasp when the heavy vehicle leapt about a metre into the air and then burst into a fireball that blinded the camera. A second cam then showed the leading SUV blown forward into our hire car by the blast wave. For several seconds nothing further happened apart from a rain of burning debris, then four doors opened simultaneously and camouflaged figures burst out and threw themselves into cover, scanning the surrounding area.

My AI was monitoring hand-signals and providing me with a reasoned interpretation. "It looks like they're leaving a rear-guard, so probably think that there may be someone in the vicinity who took out their buddies," I informed Rachel while switching to a split screen showing several views of the stairs. "So that's one… two… and three on the stairs. Zapping them now!"

The only impact of my weapon was a cascade of sparks as charge earthed in various places. "Fuck, they must have some kind of Faraday Cage protection in their suits. Okay, girl, you're on now." I hit the button to open the external door and saw our opponents backing down a few steps, clearly trying to work out what this strange development meant.

I needed no interpretation to work out that the leader of the team was waving the largest of his underlings forward through the door, while he and the other mercenary took up positions on either side of it. Just before the big guy crossed the threshold, firing blindly ahead, the other two sprayed shots into the room, which ricocheted about at random.

Rachel was unfazed and coolly emptied a full magazine into her attacker's chest before the lights went out and the ultrasonics kicked in. My multi-spectral scanners showed us her victim dropping to his knees, but still alive despite the battering that he had taken. I noted that Rachel simply dropped the gun she was holding, drew the second, and fired a further full round into his helmet. "Their armour is something special, beyond anything I've seen previously," I pointed out, just before his two partners threw themselves into room, diving to opposite corners of the far wall.

"Fuck! I'm not sure that these guys are being seriously impacted by any of my defences. Watch out!" I quickly confirmed all three targets and then left further monitoring to my AI. Only now I noticed that my software had identified one of the attackers on the stairs as the woman that I had spotted in Basel. *Right, now I can take the kid gloves off.* I switched to my external intrusion defences and selected a laser that would normally be used to blind attackers. I used a virtual joystick to guide it onto the rear-guard while I diverted all available power to the laser and switched off all its

288

protective over-rides. The millisecond pulse fried the laser, but also put an industrial-strength beam through the head of my target.

Ignoring fire from the others, Rachel was still blasting at her first opponent. One more full magazine into his visor and then he made a fatal mistake, reaching up to steady his helmet. Rachel had reloaded before he realised his error and was able put another full magazine into his armpit, knocking him to the floor in a spray of blood. *Joins are an inherent weakness in all armour, as protection has to be sacrificed to allow flexibility.* But my psychopath's obsession with a kill had also left her open. Although the two remaining attackers' fire had been all over the place, a burst caught her full in the chest and threw her back against the wall, where she slumped in an immobile heap.

"I shouldn't be doing this," I whispered to myself donning visor and earbuds before grabbing the crossbow and ordering the vault door open. My IR flares were strobing at my back while lasers and ultrasonics targeted any raised helmet, but the two fuckers were working their way along the sides of the room, taking advantage of the shelter provided by the various pieces of industrial junk scattered about. *Stupid idea, leaving that crap in place. Anyway, the advantage is that I can see them clearly and they probably don't even know that I'm here.*

I crouched down and slid along the wall to the left until I could see the leader crawling towards me, helmet first, facing the floor. *That'd work well for the lasers and IR.* I grinned as I sighted on the top of his helmet and sent a bolt straight through it.

Lots of little bullets are all very well, but don't have the power of a single, heavy projectile specifically tailored for penetration.

My direct view across to the other side of the room was blocked, but the heads-up display in my visor presented a synthesis from all monitors available and clearly showed where the last mercenary was sheltered behind an ancient lathe. Despite all my attempts to blind him, he was still firing bursts from an assault rifle in the general direction of Rachel.

Assuming that his concentration was entirely focused on his target, I stood up and ran forward until I had a shot. All that was exposed was part of his right leg, but my bolt went straight through his knee, eliciting a scream of pain. *Or maybe her knee, it sounds more like a woman.*

I was cautiously approaching my victim when she was tackled and thrown onto her back, a figure astride her. *What the fuck's Rachel up to?* As they were now superfluous, I stopped all active counter-measures and switched on the lights. Although my partner was much smaller than her opponent, she was in a better position – especially after emptying her pistol into the mercenary's gauntlet at point-blank range, disarming her and probably completely mashing her hand.

By the time I got to their side, Rachel had dropped the gun and was now stabbing the side of her victim's neck with one hand, searching for a weak point under her armoured collar, while the other wrenched at the bolt that still protruded from the mercenary's knee. Although our attacker was pummelling Rachels ribs, her continuous screaming indicated that she was in extreme pain.

"Move back, Rachel, I've got this."

"Fuck off!" she grunted, redoubling her efforts to stab her opponent.

"Christ's sake, girl, the woman's done now. You're just a fucking cat playing with a mouse."

"Just fuck off!"

"We don't have time for this nonsense." I moved into position and put a bolt through the mercenary's visor.

Rachel's glare caused me to move back. It looked like she was ready to transfer her pent-up rage towards me. "I already told you to fuck off!" she screamed.

I glanced at a timer running at the edge of my visor. "Rachel, calm the fuck down. It's now almost five minutes since I blew up that jeep. The police and fire service will be here soon. We have a bit of time as it'll take them a few minutes to get the burning wreck extinguished, but I guess police and maybe even anti-terrorist forces will be at our door in ten, fifteen minutes max. That's how long we've got to set up the shoot-out scenario."

I don't know if it was the tone of my voice or the message that I was communicating, but I could see Rachel's breathing slow as she fought to control herself. "So, what's this fucking scenario?" she asked, with an obvious threat conveyed by her tone of voice. "Something else that you haven't told me about, is it?"

"Look, I'm making this up as I go. But we need to get moving now."

291

She closed her eyes for a moment and then opened them to look directly at me. "Okay, I'll do what you want," she conceded with obvious reluctance. "But you've got to let me know what the fuck's going on."

"Fair enough. As you know, I identified three folk following us at Basel Hauptbahnhof. In addition to the automated alarm, my AI ripped off the IDs from their wristcoms. I spotted the woman on the stairs; actually that's her that you're presently sitting on. I was hoping for this, so I had already prepared the hack that would replace her ID with the one that I used to hire the car out there."

Rachel seemed to have only now remembered that she was sitting on a corpse, so climbed to her feet without taking her eyes from mine. "Jesus, this is typically convoluted. Just get to the fucking point."

"Okay, the storyline is that this woman came here with the others on her tail. She was the one who set off the mine and killed the others, but it was a Pyrrhic victory as her hideout was exposed and she died trying to defend it. We need to set up the bodies to fit this storyline."

The challenge helped to get Rachel focused. "This isn't going to be easy, given the range of injuries that they have and the profile of damage to the room."

"It doesn't need to be too explicit. It'll seem an open-and-shut case, as long as there is no evidence of anyone else entering or leaving the building this evening. That's my job to sort out."

"We're just going to hang about, are we?"

292

"Indeed, we'll just lie low next door for a few days. My living accommodation is as heavily shielded as is possible with current technology. After we've closed the bulkhead door, we'll never be found. Helped, of course, by the fact that nobody will be looking."

I saw her frown, then added some explanatory background. "This office is rented by someone who will soon seem to match our woman here. The living area is owned by me or, at least, the main identity I use in Switzerland. This is my registered address, where I pay tax and shit like that. There should be nothing to link the two properties. Enough chatting now. We've not got long and you need to work on the shoot-out details. All the rest we can go over once we're safely locked away and the police are doing their thing."

I turned my back and left, trusting the girl to do her assigned job – while fervently hoping that she could restrain herself from shooting me in the back.

Chapter 34: Rachel

As the old cunt turned away, the temptation to shoot him was almost overwhelming. Noticing that I had already raised my gun, I smiled wryly. *Shooting him would be too quick a death. And I've got to sort out this room PDQ.*

I started dragging bodies about, working on how evidence that both the defender and one of her attackers were killed by crossbow bolts could be part of a credible story. *She killed one with the crossbow, but the other attacker got a hold of it somehow or other. He shot her leg with it, but they then got into a tussle. She managed to shoot him in the armpit, but he then was able to fire the crossbow a last time before he bled out. Very contrived, but maybe good enough.*

"Hey, auld yin," I shouted, "I don't suppose you've got an option for torching this place, have you?"

"Thought you'd never ask." I could hear amusement in his voice. "I left a remote on my desk that'll start a thirty-second timer. When you're finished, push the button and put the gizmo in the woman's hand. Then get in here quickly and I'll shut the door.

A gizmo, how fucking quaint. Why would anyone use anything like that when they've got a wristcom? As I struggled to work out where best to place it, I realised that I could answer my own question. *It's just a box with a single function and a big red button. No chance of mixing it up with anything else in the chaos of combat. Maybe not so stupid.*

I pressed the button and rushed into the living area, reluctant to trust the accuracy of the timer. The door had started to shut when I registered that I had just been asked to confirm that everything that needed to be in the room was left in place. "Of course it is, do you think I'm completely stupid…" At that instant I realised that a sheath on my belt held a bloody knife. I had no memory of putting it back there, but managed to grab it and hurl it though the remaining gap before the door closed with the sound of bolts slamming into place.

Typically, Jim had seen this frantic move. However, he simply grinned and raised an eyebrow. *Annoying bastard. I really should have shot him.*

***

"Okay, lass, I'll talk through the scenario that I'm developing for the investigators so that you can act as a control and pick up anything I may have missed." He glanced at the sheath on my belt to emphasise his point. "The police are already here with a couple of fire engines and an ambulance. As yet no press, which is a shame. I hope they get here before the NDB…, the Swiss Intelligence Service," he explained in response to my quizzical expression.

"Is it already so clear that there's a terrorist link," I asked.

"They'll certainly bring in the NDB guys when they start counting bodies and see how they're

295

kitted up. Then there's also the fact that the SUVs were decked out in CD plates, suggesting a link to the Russian embassy."

I grinned at the thought of the can of worms now opened. "That wasn't very clever."

"Nope. I guess we were thought of as a soft target and so, with the overkill on the attacking side, it should have been a quick operation that'd run under the radar. The CD plates are fake, but would have helped to keep police at a distance if that was required to ease a rapid escape."

"Jesus, almost as much of a fuck-up as Rimrock Hotel."

"The only bright side for those who are responsible for this fiasco is that none of the attackers were captured. The bodies will be identified as internationally-known mercenaries, but there should be no obvious link to whoever ordered the hit. They did, however, score an own-goal by meeting at Leibstadt before hitting us here."

I wrinkled my brow in concentration while Jim waited for me to pick up the point here. "Ah, it's nuclear. There are reactors at Leibstadt."

"Exactly, with more reactors, high-level waste storage and other nuclear facilities just a few kilometres downriver from this point."

"This can't help being linked to Sellafield and Rokkasho by anyone who knows about those two failed attacks."

"Unfortunately, it'll also be linked to me by anyone who, like the Brits, know of my involvement and that my digs are here. Luckily, I will seem to be travelling about Europe and there should be no indication that I'm even back in Switzerland, much less at home. But the bad guys tried to take me out once and could be preparing to try again."

I tried to see how this would fit with the way in which I'd been organising the corpses of our attackers. "So, you're making a story about the woman being somehow on our side, despite being kitted up just like the others. I can't get my head round that."

"We don't need an explanation, just a clear scenario. The investigators will need to make sense of the details they uncover. I should have said that my dark-web team are currently working on the webcam covering the stairs. This'll be a key piece of evidence."

"You already made it look like she hired the car we used and they'll find it here," I interrupted. "But I'm sure you said that the webcam was switched on only after we arrived, so there was no record of us arriving."

"Indeed, this is where the hackers come in. There's a back-up memory unit in the cam to cover 12 hours in case of loss of external power. My guys will edit this record to remove the image of the woman entering with the hit squad and instead show her entering when we first arrived."

"Are you sure that this kind of editing will stand up to detailed forensic analysis?"

"It probably wouldn't, although my guys are very good at fake videos: it's one of their main bread-earners. The thing is, why would anyone bother? The storyline is self-consistent, so I guess most effort will go into identifying the bodies and trying to work out who was behind this action and what their goal was."

I tried to find other loose threads in this story. "You said the woman will be shown to have rented the office, which just happens to be next to yours. How does that work?"

"Again, we don't have to specify a path through this labyrinth, just leave some suggestive breadcrumbs to suggest an answer. The rental will seem to have started two months ago, which will be just after I went for what I hoped would be a relaxing vacation in the Alps."

I began to see what he was getting at. "So this might be coupled to the attack on you there. Setting up a base for action in case that assassination attempt failed. But surely this would suggest that the woman was linked to our opponents."

The Machiavellian old bugger gave me an annoying smirk. "So, what additional evidence would be nice to suggest that there might have been some sort of schism in the opposition?"

While he was waiting for a response, I thought over the last few weeks, trying to assess the perspective of the leaders of this plot. "Well, Beall was singularly unsuccessful. Setting up the reprocessing plant attacks must have taken a lot of work, which has ended up doing more harm than good for their cause. Beall's hand is also off the tiller, so maybe some of those involved are getting cold feet. After all, if their actions are exposed, they're guilty of treason and a death penalty is very likely for their particular case."

"Yes, that's something that would occur to anyone who is in the know about past actions – which must be the case with the NDB. It was a Swiss military chopper that picked me up after my holiday home was bombed and this occurred so quickly that I'm sure the British embassy spooks must be keeping their counterparts in Bern fully informed. With this background, what would serve a suitable breadcrumbs to support the hit team going after a rogue member?"

By now I was beginning to lose patience. "You've already done something, haven't you, you annoying bastard. Just tell me."

"That's not how this works. I don't want you to simply confirm what I've done is sensible, I want to see if there's anything that I missed. If you had access to all the tools that you know that I have, what would you do?"

"If it was up to me, I'd shoot you now, using these tools to cover up my escape. I'd also rip off all your accounts, to set me up in luxury somewhere I'd never be found. Tasmania, Bora Bora or some fucking place like that."

Jim laughed. "I had hoped that you'd miss that option. However, you have a greatly inflated view of my financial worth: it wouldn't keep you for long even if you relocated to a bothy in the wilds of the Scottish Highlands. Anyway, you're drifting off topic. You're supposed to be sorting out the story behind your incinerated victim next door."

I glared at him. "Your victim, actually, you interfering fuckwit. Anyway, remembering how you fabricated the evidence to show I couldn't have been the Veep's killer, I guess you could fake some incriminating messages. This could be tricky, though, as you'd need to backtrack the woman's movements for days or weeks in order to provide a basis for an organised hit like this."

"Yup, that's the essence of what I've done, but I was able to do this without any kind of trace of her movements."

"Stop being fucking annoying and tell me what you've done." I reached towards my holsters, before remembering that both pistols were now slag in the next room. I then remembered that I still had one throwing knife and drew it. "Remember, murdering you is still an option for me."

Indicating an evident death wish, he laughed again. "Okay, lass, have it your way. My computer – well, supposedly her computer – has an ultra-hard cache memory which stores sent messages that are being routed through it. This will contain a number of messages to scrambled addresses, but several of these will be identical to posts on our conspiracy theory board. These will be ones pointing out a potential role of Buck in the plots. It thus kills two birds with one stone: showing our girl is a loose cannon and further implicating daft Denis in this retaliation."

"That's clever," I conceded. "It's just a shame that your computer will be a pool of molten metal with traces of burnt plastic if your incendiaries are indeed good enough to remove all traces of our DNA from the room."

"The computer, certainly, but this cache really is ultra-hard. They may have difficulties extracting it, but it'll be readable when they do."

"If that's the case, will anyone find it? It wouldn't be obvious in the wreckage that's now your computer corner."

"It has a radio-beeper, signalling once an hour. That's only to ensure that it'll be found as long as those involved aren't totally clueless. It really isn't so hard to find when you consider the incentive. A trace of the woman's communication might be the clue that solves the problem that they're faced with."

"Christ, Jim, listen to yourself. You're assuming that someone will be digging into this who is as paranoid as yourself. Would any normal team dig so deeply?"

"You're completely correct, lass. Only someone as twisted as I am would be digging into such fine details, Luckily, I'm fairly sure that someone like that will be supporting the investigation here."

I suddenly saw where this was leading. "That'd be your pal Julia from Japan, would it?"

"Indeed! Well done girl. You're not as loopy as your berserker tendencies would otherwise suggest. I'm sure that, given her role in uncovering the Rokkasho plot, the Embassy will offer her aid here."

"That'll take a while though. I guess they could quickly bring her in virtually, but it would require a day or so to get her to Switzerland."

301

"I don't imaging there will be a great rush, as the evidence suggests that the entire hit squad has been wiped out. Now it's just post-mortem work, trying to discover what was behind this action and, more to the point, who organised it."

Now that the adrenalin rush was receding, I realised that we were tiptoeing around the fact that the hit targeted us. Someone was convinced that we were still a sufficient threat to justify siccing this pack of killers on us. "So, who was it? Who's trying to kill us?"

There was a smug look on Jim's face that was just asking to be slapped off. He had some more information and wanted to force me to beg for it. *Bastard.*

"There's certainly some folk after us, but why do you think that they want to kill us?"

"Well, bursting into the room that we were supposed to be in with guns blazing is a bit of a give-away, don't you think?"

"That's not very friendly, admittedly. But don't you think it's strange that, with your more primitive armour, you were able to walk out of that firefight?"

Bugger! Now I think about it, it was strange that there were no attempted head-shots. Initially, I thought it might be due to the disruption to the attackers caused by Jim's lasers and ultrasonics, but someone was compos mentis enough to put a full magazine into my chest. Modern assault rifles should definitely have penetrated the old vest that I was wearing. "Maybe it was just luck," I responded just to be provocative, but immediately realising how unlikely this was.

"Luck would be possible. But we'd have also needed to be very lucky that, in the time we've been traced, nobody has gone for the simple option of taking us out one-by-one, or even both together. With the kit that this squad is able to access and the support they have, that shouldn't have been a problem even if it required assassination in a public place. Instead of that, they waited until we were somewhere isolated, even though they knew that I was then on home ground."

"So, you think they were trying to capture us?"

"I think that's the most likely option."

"And you've suspected this for some time?"

"A while. But, of course, I couldn't be sure. We can check this, though, if you can dig out any of the rounds that are caught in your vest."

I stripped off my oversized body-armour and dropped it to the floor, only at that point fully aware of the pain in my chest. I lifted my t-shirt and inspected the dark purple bruising that was rapidly developing. "Well, they may not have wanted to kill us, but damaging us a bit didn't seem to be a problem."

"Ouch, that looks sore." The old bugger's smile contrasted with his soothing words. "Anyway, you're still breathing, so you should look on the positive side."

"Easy enough for you to say, as you seem to have escaped without a scratch."

"Maybe so, but remember that I came in to save you. Very much against my better judgement, I should add. You're supposed to be guarding my old body, not vice versa."

When I thought about that, it did seem a strange thing for Jim to do, especially armed only with his stupid crossbow. "So, you came to my aid because you knew that there was no risk of you being killed?"

"Hardly that. Remember you were the one with the bullet-proof vest and it was certainly live ammunition they were using. Had I been hit, I'd have a lot more than a wee bit of bruising."

"A wee bit of bruising! Have you looked at this?" I pulled my top higher to display the state of my upper body, black and blue from groin to neck and visible even though my sheer sports-bra.

"Yes, it's very colourful," he conceded. "But why don't you check if there're any bullets in your vest. I'd bet that they're soft-points or something similar."

Pulling my t-shirt down with a theatrical groan of pain, I bent over to pick up the old ballistic vest. Sure enough, it held the flattened remains of 3 rounds. They were exactly as I wouldn't have expected if the hit squad were tooled-up to go against opponents who might well have vests. "You seem to be correct," I admitted with great reluctance. "However, if these hit any unprotected part of a body, they'd cause a real mess. Not what I'd call non-lethal."

"I suspect that the aim was to take us alive, if possible. Nevertheless, they were prepared to accept the chance that either of both of us wouldn't survive. The ace they had up their sleeve was their incredibly high-spec armour. They could let you blast away with munition that would penetrate a normal vest and be confident that they risked nothing more than a wee bit of bruising."

His smug smile as he finished this sentence was almost enough to drive me over the edge. However, just before I finally lost control and gave him a well-deserved kick in the goolies, the anomaly of him coming to my rescue came back to mind. "But you came to help me armed only with your daft crossbow. What was behind that?"

"I had seen how little impact your bullets were having, so I realised that I needed something with a lot more penetrating power. The bow has two settings, one with increased rate of fire and another that maximises draw – effectively the speed of the bolt. This latter setting is usually used to increase the weapon's range but, close up, it'd allow the bolt to penetrate a thin steel plate. Or, of course, any kind of practical helmet shielding."

"And you were sure about that?"

"Fairly confident. It seemed worth the risk anyway."

Now I was flustered. "This was to save me when you saw me going down? Don't tell me that you're finally getting all paternal on me."

"Not at all," he grinned. "It's just that I happen to need an assassin and this saves me the bother of training up a new one."

I'm not convinced he's really so objective about this. But, more importantly, who the fuck else does he need me to assassinate?

Chapter 35: Jim

I still had lots to tell the girl, but there was plenty of time. We would be locked down here until the heat died down, which would certainly be a number of days; possibly even a week or more. The apartment was well set up for this and it wouldn't be a problem from the point of view of logistics. It would, however, get a bit claustrophobic and Rachel would need to calm down and get over her adrenalin high from the combat. I struggled to hide a smile when I thought about the way that violence affected both her and her mother. *Need to give her some space for masturbation before it gets so bad that she's tempted to jump even my aged bones.*

While she was still struggling to get her head around my chivalrous rescue action, I waved her towards the bathing area and opaqued the dividing wall. "Before anything else, you should have a long soak in the bath. I'll set it up with some salts that should help. Also, you may want to have a strong drink now. What do you fancy?"

I could see that she had more questions for me, but recognised that my suggestion was sensible and meekly started to remove her combat boots. "I think a large brandy is needed. The ultra-expansive one that you were glopping down earlier."

"The Louis XIII cognac that I was delicately sipping, you mean. I'll get you one of those. Just throw your kit on the floor, I'll get washing and storage sorted out later. Go on, into the tub with you." For a moment I was tempted to offer her some sex toys so that she could also sort out her other needs, but realised that might set her off again, reminding her that she was within an inch of giving me a good kicking. Probably something else that she might find cathartic.

I heated a huge snifter glass with steam from my coffee machine, while I dug out a local craft beer from my booze fridge. After a long swallow of the hoppy ale, I dried the snifter and, with only a small shudder due to awareness of the cost, poured a large portion of the golden spirit into it. *It could be worse; she could have asked for coke with it.*

Despite her evident stiffness, Rachel had stripped-off quickly and her clothing was thrown into an untidy pile just outside the bathroom. I could now hear small gasps, indicating that she must be lowering herself into the hot bathwater. When these ended with a long sigh, I took her drink in to her.

"What are you doing, you perverse old bastard? Can't I just have a soak in peace without you ogling me?"

I smiled when I noted that there was little fire behind her ritualised complaints. "First of all, there's not much to ogle, as you're up to your neck in bubbles. As I knew you would be," I added before she had a chance to respond. "I programmed the foaming bath oil and the gentle massage jets, so it couldn't be otherwise. Anyway, I thought you were in need of this drink."

Appeased, she gave me a smile. "This bath is actually just what I need, so thanks for suggesting it. And the drink, of course." She took the glass from me and gulped down a large mouthful without waiting to sample its exquisite aroma. I closed my eyes and shuddered.

Her smile widened. "I guess from your reaction that this really is the very expensive stuff. I don't suppose you've got any ginger ale to go with it, have you?"

I thought about pushing her head under, but realised that this would just spill the drink. I thus restricted myself to a groan before I headed back to my beer, hearing her laugh behind me. Spotting the pile of clothing, I gathered it up for washing. I was amused the way that her combat trousers contrasted with her lacy panties and, without thinking about it, lifted these to my nose. The smells of sweat, female musk and traces of urine were quite intoxicating. *Maybe, given the choice, I'd go for that aroma rather than the cognac.*

Forcing myself to concentrate on the job in hand, I took everything over to a small laundry niche, where I loaded clothes into the washing machine, slipped boots into a rack and started to hang up the flack-jacket before remembering how antiquated it was. I then chucked it into a bin and made a mental note to order a more modern replacement. Or maybe two.

I was settled at the dining table, finishing my beer, when Rachel hollered from the bathroom. "That brandy wasn't terrible, so I'll have another one. I think this time with Champagne. Soon as you like, James."

"That wee bitch is enjoying this far too much," I muttered under my breath as I stood up and went in search of the cheapest brandy and fizz that I had to hand, struggling to remember the additional components needed for a classic Champagne Cocktail.

***

I had a shower after Rachel eventually emerged from the bath, having downed a further 3 cocktails during this time. I offered her a bath robe, but she had decided to simply wrap herself in a thick, white bath towel. She was reclined on a leather settee in the sitting area when I joined her, clearly having refreshed her drink yet again. *I hope she stuck to the cheap plonk that I left out and hasn't broken into my good stuff.* I grimaced at the thought of what she might have done explicitly to annoy me and, to divert myself, rummaged in the fridge for an alcohol-free beer.

In any case, the woman was now relaxed. *Probably due to being half-pissed.* I tightened-up the yukata that I was wearing and carefully sat down in the leather reclining-chair opposite her. Rachel was evidently much less bothered about propriety as her towel had ridden up until it almost, but not quite, revealed her groin. *Could be accidental, but maybe she's just being a provocative bitch.* The options seemed equally likely to me.

Rachel stared at me in a concentrated way that suggested that I was off the mark in my estimation of her degree of intoxication. "While I was soaking, I've been thinking through what happened. As I was fitting pieces together, there's something that I now recognise as strange. It seems to be general knowledge that you purchased and live in this

309

apartment, but the ownership of your office next door seems to have been well-concealed. You suggested that it was rented and that you could modify records to show that the woman had taken it over a couple of months ago." She paused, clearly waiting for input from me.

"Yes, that's a perceptive observation. I own that property also, but the record is buried within a property management organisation. This should look bona fide as, whenever I don't need it, short-term leases are often taken out by local groups. These are usually artist collectives organising shows or workshops. As many of the events that they organise are well publicised, it diverts attention away from any times when it appears to be empty."

The minx nodded and settled in a way that moved her hem a few millimetres higher. "That's very clever but, remembering that your hack to fabricate the lease to our victim happened only while they were underway, why did our attackers go straight next door rather than here? Maybe more to the point, why did you expect them to do so?"

"Ah, even more perceptive." I couldn't help squirming, as it was increasingly obvious that I had once again badly underestimated how smart this young woman was. "This was based on a suspicion that been building up for some time now..."

"One that you hadn't told me about. I thought we had an agreement based on complete openness, but it seems that your assurance here was, once again, a lie. This *suspicion* wouldn't be in any way linked to your feeling that we were targeted for capture rather than assassination, would it?"

"There is a link, I must admit, but it's very sensitive and, when I tell you what it is, you'll understand."

She was clearly unconvinced. "This is just more of your typical circumlocutory obfuscation, isn't it?"

"Circumlocutory obfuscation, not something that I'm often accused of…"

Rachel was now getting annoyed, with the result that her towel was riding higher, making it even more difficult for me to concentrate. "Just spit it out, for fuck's sake. What or who do you really think is behind all of this."

I sighed. "It's a who, I'm afraid. The way the opposition has been sticking to our heels despite my best efforts indicates that the op is now being run by someone who knows me very well. This was confirmed when, as you cleverly noted, the bad guys went directly to my office where, under normal circumstances, I'd organise the defence of any attack on this apartment, which is the obvious target. There's only one person who I'm sure knows about the office."

Rachel frowned. "You mean your pal Julia? Surely, she can't be on the other side."

"I actually wish this was the case but, unfortunately, I'm sure that Julia has no idea about the office."

"Then who…?" Her face suddenly went pale. "Wait a minute, you can't think it's her… We both saw her die."

"She certainly was very seriously injured, but we didn't have a chance to check further. We legged

311

it and, from the records we've seen, the body disappeared in the one helicopter that escaped Rimrock."

"You mean my mum? It can't fucking be!"

"Now you can see why I didn't mention anything to you when there was still a shadow of doubt. Of course, I can't be 100% certain, but it's the best explanation I have for what's happened since we left Japan."

Rachel put her head in her hands. I had no idea if this was shock or some kind of relief that her mother was still alive. I waited in silence for almost ten minutes until she looked up. "So, if it is my mum behind the attack, she was at least aiming to capture us rather than simply taking us out."

"The hit-team were using munition that could be considered non-lethal, but only for the case that the defenders were well armoured. Your jacket proved to be good enough, but a few rounds of those dumdums into your legs would seriously fuck you up and a head shot would certainly kill you stone dead."

"Well, it does sound like my mom. It's not like the risk of her daughter being killed would distract her from any goal that she had."

The girl sounded so miserable, that I moved over and put my arm around her shoulder. "You can see now why I didn't want to say anything before I was reasonably certain. We had enough on our plate without you being distracted by this."

"Distracted? I suppose I might have been. It was somehow easy to accept that she'd been killed when one of her dodgy schemes went belly-up. But the bitch surviving and then moving over to directly support the evil fucks that we're fighting against – it's worse than a clean death."

"Miriam's ethics were always flexible and she was always happy to fuck someone up – often literally – if she saw a benefit to herself."

Rachel shrugged her shoulders. "I suppose that I always knew this. Somehow, though, I couldn't really see myself being the one fucked."

"Well, at least we're walking out of this in one piece. Even if it is a rather tenderised piece in your specific case," I grinned. "Actually, thinking about your battered bod, I have some analgesic cream that might help. If you just strip off and lie on the bed, I'll rub it on for you."

"No you don't! You're not going to change the topic of conversation by being gratuitously provocative. I clearly remember that you claimed that you rescued me only because you needed an assassin. Was this to kill Miriam?"

Shit, I wish I didn't have to do this now. "Well, actually, it's not just one person. I do have a list – or, at least, a first draft of a list…"

"Cut it out, you annoying old fuck! Is she one of your targets?"

"Well, for the case that she really was alive and working for the opposition, she was on the list."

"How high on the list? A straight fucking answer this time."

"Well, after Buck, she's number 2."

I could feel a shudder go through her body. Then, after about a minute of silence, she got to her feet. "Fine then, but this time you've got to keep me

313

in the loop, regardless whether it could be distracting or not."

"Excellent. We need a good night's rest but, thereafter, we can start planning assassinations together."

"Sounds like fun." She then dropped the towel, walked over to the bed and threw herself backwards onto it, propping her head and shoulders up on a pillow. "What are you waiting for? You can get going on the rub down with a soothing lotion that you promised me, just after you serve me up another of those fizzy drinks.

I groaned and scurried off to obey her commands. *She's indeed a pain in the arse but, all in all, that could have gone a hell of a lot worse.*

Chapter 36: Rachel

Once again, we've beaten the odds and live to fight another day. Although I'd never admit it to the fossil, the pain in my chest is a reminder that I'm still alive, as I probably wouldn't be if he hadn't come to my rescue with his bloody crossbow. After I'd been knocked down, I was completely open to the fuselage of bullets that were ricocheting all around me. They wouldn't all have hit my vest. Of course, it was all due to their fucking body-armour. If not for that, I'd have taken them all out.

Following the shoot-out, I was trying to think positive thoughts. However, the tricky area was, naturally enough, sex. There was no way that I could hide the inevitable urges resulting from our violent dispatch of a top-end, black-op team, even if Jim hadn't already been aware of the kink that I had inherited from my mother. He had been nothing but a gentleman when he applied a soothing balm to my bruises, but he couldn't have helped notice the results of his hands sliding over my naked skin. Apart from nipples like acorns, the smell of my flowing juices would have been unmistakeable. Nevertheless, he finished up and quickly scooted off to the loo with only the slightest trace of a physical reaction.

I thought back over the last few days and smiled. *Probably hasn't able to get it up since he visited that so-called massage parlour in Colmar. That was three... no two days ago. I guess their body-body massage will ensure that I won't need to put up with the sight of his feeble erection for a few days yet. Now if I just had Toshi to hand, or even Junko...* Unconsciously, my legs opened and I began to stroke my clitoris while salacious memories of Tokyo replayed in my mind.

An indefinite time later, I was deliberately holding myself on the edge of an orgasm when a stage-cough brought me back to the present. "Just to let you know that I'm climbing into the sack now and will be out cold within minutes. I doubt that you will, but if you need any toys, there're some in the bedside drawer there..."

I glanced over at an open drawer by my head, but realised that I certainly didn't need any help at present. I could feel him slipping between the sheets and was sure that he had turned to watch me, but I was beyond caring. *Or, at least, I hope it was that and not the extra frisson of knowing that he was watching me masturbate to a very noisy climax.*

***

The next morning, I awoke to find that I had fallen asleep on top of the bedding, with my sticky fingers still between my thighs. I think I actually blushed when I realised that Jim was walking towards me with a tall glass in his hand. "I thought the smell of coffee would wake you, but maybe Buck's Fizz would be the way to kick-start your day." In response to my groan, he smiled his understanding. "Yes, the hangover should be beginning to kick-in now, but there's a secret cure in this drink that'll sort it out instantly."

I grabbed the glass from him and, with shaking hands, downed it in one inelegant gulp. I immediately burped but, to my amazement, felt the throbbing pain behind my temples immediately begin to dissipate. "Thanks for that, but couldn't you have waited until I got myself sorted out a bit?" I shoved myself into a seating position against the headboard and, a little late, dragged a quilted bedspread over my upper body.

"Sorted out?" he displayed an exaggerated frown. "I thought that you looked fine as you were. Anyway, I'll get your breakfast now." A couple of minutes later I had a tray on my lap that matched the spreads he had prepared to impress Gabi – including another large glass of Buck's Fizz."

As a reflex, I sniffed my fingers before realising that he had spotted the motion. "Fuck! Okay, maybe you should just wait a minute until I have a quick shower."

He laughed and shook his head. "Why now? The last time in Hvar you and young Gabi were coated head to toe in joy-juices and neither of you showered before breakfast."

I couldn't help smiling back. "True, that. Very, very true. Fuck it to hell! It just adds a little je ne sais quoi, don't you think?"

"A petit soupçon thereof," he agreed and we both laughed aloud.

After that point, my regular masturbation needs were merely a source of amusement for him and no longer an embarrassment to me.

***

We actually spent ten days locked down, gradually establishing tacit guidelines to allow us to coexist peacefully in these close conditions. There was no way I could convince him to wear anything in the bed that we shared, or even just remain clothed at all times when he was up. However, he did finally accept the requirement to switch on all privacy features any time he entered the toilet – even when this was for his regular visits during the night. He also allowed me complete access to his computer link to the outside world, although I had to agree to limit any outgoing communication to dark-web posts on noticeboards. Here he emphasised that it was certain that Miriam and the cabal would have extensive monitoring established and that I should bear this in mind. I expected him to also insist that he first checked any such messages and, when this did not happen, I invited him to carry out such checks anyway.

His other major concession was to allow me to cook dinner occasionally. He clearly fancied himself as a gourmet and showed off his abilities in the kitchen for the first few days. I saw that his expectations were low when he finally gave in, which was just the incentive that I needed. Despite the limitations of cooking out of a fridge, I produced a Sri Lankan-style curry that he evidently enjoyed and had started complimenting me on before he realised that he was falling out of his self-assigned curmudgeon persona. "Well, actually not bad," he managed as a compromise. We were both grinning like idiots, so the barriers between us were certainly beginning to crumble.

***

When we finally left, carrying only backpacks, we were able to join a noisy group leaving an evening jazz concert in a microbrewery that was also part of the Oederlin complex.

I was again tasked with working out our final destination, but it was easy to guess Hvar as we neared the border to Croatia. Although monitoring the dark-web kept me up to date with the activities of his teams of hackers and other conspiracy fellow-travellers, Jim wouldn't come clean with an explanation of why we were going back to where our Japan adventure had kicked-off. The only hint I had was when we picked up another sniper rifle in Split, where we had dropped-off our hire car and were now spending a night before an early ferry next morning.

Unusually, this hotel room had only a shower so Jim had to make do with this rather than his usual soak in a bath. He was being his usual annoying self thereafter, wandering around in his truly offensive, wrinkly birthday-suit. When he then asked me to check the gun out, my already strained patience reached breaking point.

"Fuck it, Jim, what're you up to now? Beall is a historical footnote, Buck has gone to ground and, after two monumental catastrophes that are now well known to intelligence agencies worldwide,

319

there's no way that anyone is going to try another attack on a nuclear facility."

"Not for a while, certainly, but I don't like leaving a job half-done. There's also the fact that, despite having lost yet another hit-squad, I can't imagine our opponents giving up and leaving us to live happy ever after."

I had to concede that point. "Especially not my mom. Her entire career is now well screwed and her only chance of pulling any coals out of the fire is to hang onto Buck's coat-tails and hope he can provide her with some kind of alternative. For that, she needs some kind of win." For a second, I almost felt sorry for her – but then this quickly disappeared and was replaced by hatred for all she'd done. "Yes, to be honest, I'll be able to relax only when that cunt is six feet under. Next time I think she's dead, I'll put a stake through her heart, cut off her head, set fire to the corpse…"

"I can't really disagree there," Jim grinned. "However, I think her evil nature didn't require selling her soul to the devil, so a head-shot would work for me."

"Okay, that explains why we have a rifle now. But why the fuck are we heading back to Hvar? You don't have my little Spanish nymphet still shacked up in that naff flat, do you?" I could feel myself scowling suspiciously.

He laughed in a typically annoying way. "Ah, young Gabi. She certainly was an enthusiastic lass, wasn't she? Unfortunately, she had to return home. Nevertheless, a night with me seems to have cured her of her lesbianism."

My slap knocked him off his feet and onto the double bed in our usual shared hotel room. It didn't stop his guffaws, unfortunately. "You fucking, despicable, old paedophile. I bet you shagged her just to piss me off."

"Well, it worked then." His smug grin was just asking to be smacked off his face. "But, to tell the truth, it was all Gabi's idea. Personally, I found her a bit on the chubby side."

Realising that I still had the rifle in my hand, I slowly aimed it between his eyes. "You tell the truth as often as my mom does – which means never." With a smile, I pulled the trigger. We both knew the gun was not loaded, but the click made me feel a lot happier.

"Yes, girl, you're definitely learning." He still had the smug look on his face, but this vanished when I raised the rifle and prepared to club him with the buttstock. "So, Hvar... If not for sexual delectation, why would we be heading back there?"

I was distracted by this question, frowning as I lowered my weapon. "Mmm, why indeed? Actually, I never did work out why we chose to hide ourselves there in the first place."

With unusual alacrity, he bounced off the bed, grabbed my shoulders and kissed me on the brow. "Yes, that's the key. If you answer the second question, it also covers the first."

"Okay, I can do this." My threatening glare gave him some warning, but I had grabbed a good hold of his scrotum before he had a chance to escape. "If there was a question that I needed to answer and I knew somebody who had this answer,

I'd just torture it out of them. Easy-peasy." I squeezed his testicles and was rewarded by a high-pitched squeal of pain.

"Fuck, you might be learning from me just a little bit too quickly," he gasped. To my surprise he actually seemed pleased with me rather than pissed-off, confirming my suspicions about his inherently masochistic tendencies. I loosened my grip a little and he continued in a more natural voice. "Yes, as you've now guessed, Hvar wasn't a randomly-selected destination. I had a general idea that could have levelled the playing field a little from there, but Rokkasho cropped up before I had worked out anything more concrete."

"You're waffling again," I warned him, giving his balls an encouraging squeeze. "Just cut to the chase."

"Ouch!" he squeaked, rising to his toes to reduce the pain. "Fuck, that's sore!"

I started to ease off when the old bastard slipped around under the arm holding him and somehow managed to slam on a wrist lock, causing a shock of pain that forced me to my knees. "Christ!" I screamed as another twist of my wrist drove my face into a rather mouldy carpet. The sneaky fucker was now kneeling on my shoulder blades, immobilising my arm using only a couple of fingers. As my other arm was trapped below my belly, still holding the stupid bloody rifle, I was helpless when he slowly ran the fingers of his free hand down my neck, clinically locating the various points where he could inflict further pain or simply render me unconscious.

"Well then, love, should we continue this lesson?" he whispered into my ear.

I started to tense up in preparation for a counter-attack, but he spotted this and another shock of pain caused me to scream.

"Quietly now, lass, we don't want to disturb the neighbours. Although, in this day and age, it'll probably just be written off as a bit of SM fun. So, are you tapping-out now?"

With greatest reluctance, I gave a grunt of agreement.

"And you promise to be nice to your beloved sensei and never again even think about grabbing his goolies?"

I thought about this for a moment, then quickly agreed when I felt him begin to twist my wrist.

"Good girl." He kissed me on the back of my neck and then staggered to his feet.

The desire for revenge was almost overpowering. *How the fuck does he do this?* I rolled to my side and then onto my feet. *Jesus Christ, the old fart can hardly even stand without help.* I threw the rifle onto the bed but, before I could do more, he turned towards me with open arms, palms up.

"I know that you're straining on the leash now, desperate to kick seven shades of shit out of me. Which, of course, you'd have no problems doing in a fair fight. But you should be focusing that rage on our real enemies. I realise that I can be a little tricky to live with..."

I snorted angrily, which caused him to grin.

"Okay, right, I'm a complete fucking pain in the arse. But, despite that, I've only got your best interests in mind."

"So a bit of humiliation is in my best interest?" Even as I said this, I couldn't help remembering the occasions when he'd gone out of his way to protect me, even if he did always manage to find a convoluted excuse for it being self-interest on his part.

"It is, actually. Despite our time together, you still often forget that your superior speed and strength gives no guarantee of winning a fight against a weaker opponent. You're a smart woman, but your military training lets you down. It's not completely beyond the bounds of possibility that, at some time, you could be confronted by someone like me. I hope that you now realise that fisticuffs shouldn't be your first response."

"Okay, smart arse, if you were me in such a position, what would your approach be?"

"A high-velocity, large-calibre shot from a great distance."

Well, I couldn't argue with that. "But, remembering where we started off here, what if I just needed to torture some information out of you?"

He frowned and tapped his finger against his bottom lip for a while. "That, actually, is a very good question. My experience with torture to date has been on the applying it side rather than being on the receiving end." He evidently saw my look of surprise and continued. "But, in the very few cases that I had anything to do with what your spook buddies call *enhanced interrogation*, I was completely unimpressed with its effectiveness. I'm sure that your evil mother would disagree, but I've found that bribery, when an option, is much more likely to produce reliable information."

"Mmm, interesting." I thought about it for a moment and then pulled my t-shirt over my head and then peeled off my bra. "So, if I promised you a truly mind-blowing shag, then you'd give me all the gen on Hvar, would you?"

Jim looked momentarily flabbergasted, then burst into laughter. "You had me going for a moment there. I immediately thought of Marion, but then I spotted the twinkle in your eye. You've moved on to another useful interrogation approach, conning your victim into liking you and making him want to give you whatever you're looking for. Very clever." I started to reach for my bra, but he reached over to stop me. "At least let me savour the view while you collect your winnings."

I shrugged my shoulders. "Up to you, but the sight of my tits is hardly something novel after all we've been through together."

"True, but it's not something that I'm ever going to get bored with." Then he ruined the compliment by flopping back onto the bed and closing his eyes. "This is all about Denis. As I previously admitted, I considered him mere window dressing, but he seemed like an easy target when we were last in this neck of the woods. I thought that taking him out might rattle the rest of his co-conspirators and make it easier to set up hits on them."

"Fair, enough, but why Hvar?"

"Oh, right, I guess I forgot to mention that. Denis has a holiday villa on one of the nearby islands. Villa might not do it justice, it's actually a sizable estate. He's also got a yacht berthed here. Again the term yacht may make you think of a wee boat with sails, but in this case we're talking about a floating gin-palace, about 70 metres, with all the on-board sybaritic pleasures that a multi-billionaire would expect."

I stepped out of my sandals, peeled off my shorts and lay down beside him, trying to work my way through this new information. "So, he's mega-rich and thus probably has lots of properties. Why do you think he'll be here now?"

"That was the problem when we were last here. He was spending most of his time in the States when not jetting about with his cousin, the Veep. He has apartments in New York and Washington DC and estates in California, Florida and Hawaii. However, the estate here is his only property outside the US of A, where he is currently persona non grata. So, this time, I'm fairly sure that he'll be here. We just need to ensure that we get him before he gets us.

Chapter 37: Jim

It was strangely comforting to get back to the little apartment in Hvar. This was probably due to being able to settle down somewhere without any requirement to keep on the move, but also with freedom to wander around outside our digs without any special precautions. Rachel claimed the main highlight for her was finally having her own bedroom and, to be honest, that was also a factor for me. There was no doubt that we had managed living on top of each other in Oederlin relatively well, but now having more space for ourselves definitely contributed to making the atmosphere more relaxed.

It was the third day after our arrival and, finally, it had stopped raining. After serving my trainee breakfast in bed – a rather domestic ritual that I had somehow fallen into – I had adjourned to the somewhat cramped front balcony to catch some rays. Although probably overkill, I was using PASS-cabled ear-buds to listen with eyes closed while my AI assistant summarised developments over the last 12 hours. A throat-mike allowed me to make notes and, in a couple of cases, initiate responses to developments. The chances of anyone attempting to eavesdrop here were negligible, but better safe than sorry. *And it sets a good example for Rachel.*

The Oederlin debacle was still a primary focus for my smart search engine. It could not be played down, especially as the information that I leaked on the dark web notice board had caused a conspiracy-nut feeding-frenzy. Despite lack of any hard evidence linking this team of multinational mercenaries to the US, the Swiss were very seriously pissed-off and raising hell, not only via the usual diplomatic channels, but also much more visibly in the UN and the IAEA. Rachel was convinced that this was the result of another of my labyrinthine plots but, despite the temptation to simply accept credit, I had to disabuse her of this rather flattering notion. Just as I was thinking this, drops of cold water hit my brow, causing me to jerk up in surprise.

Rachel stood above me, grinning, with a dripping face-cloth in her hand. "Fuck it, girl, you could have given me a bloody heart attack."

Her grin became wider as she wriggled her naked body onto the other sun-lounger, which faced mine. "That can only happen when you have a heart, you annoying old sod."

I raised my eyes to heaven and opened my arms wide. "See, God! See how the ungrateful wench treats her ancient teacher. I wait on her hand and foot, from dawn to dusk, and this is all the respect I get."

Rachel giggled in a disconcertingly girly manner. "You don't believe in God, you geriatric coffin-dodger. Or, if you did, you'd believe that you were God's incorporation in flesh."

I used my right index finger to wipe moisture from my brow and sniffed it suspiciously. "This isn't piss, is it?"

Another giggle. "That's just wishful thinking on your part, you perv."

328

Now it was my turn to grin. "I thought wet sex was actually your thing. Indeed, AC/DC water sports with a bit of kink on the side."

Rachel's smile vanished and she glared at me. "Now, why would you think something like that?"

Oops, let my mouth run away with me there. "That's a topic that we can come back to some other day. For now, there are some developments on the assassination front that we have to discuss."

I could see that she was not happy with me changing the topic like that, but the magic word *assassination* assured her attention. "So, you've got the hit set up already?"

"Not yet, but there's background to it that we need to go through." She settled back to listen, but, from her rigid nipples, I guessed thoughts of violence were already going through her head.

"The first key point is that the last attack on us has proven serendipitous. I wish I could say that it was a consideration when I lured the hit squad to Baden, but the area around there is the nuclear heartland of Switzerland. A brutal firefight involving heavily armed terrorists couldn't help being linked to Sellafield and Rokkasho, where involvement by some rogue group associated with the US Government and some parts of their intelligence services is now well-established in the minds of most important actors here. From hacks into a range of intelligence agencies, it seems now generally accepted that the mercenaries were actually part of a third attempt to attack a nuclear site, which backfired more by luck than by judgement."

Rachel frowned. "So, despite you owning the property next door, you don't feature here? How does that work?"

"As I noted previously, we don't need to provide the entire picture – just provide enough jigsaw pieces that the story seems obvious from what is available. Even without further false information from me, a wide range of credible nuclear attack scenarios have been developed from the starting point of this terrorist team. They have now all been identified and there is no doubt that they represent the top-end of the soldier-of-fortune market. Especially, if you're looking for psycho-killer mercenaries with absolutely no scruples."

"When you put it that way, it's actually amazing that we survived..." She frowned at me before adding, "...suffering only a few little bruises."

"This again puts me on my hobby horse. I'm sure that things wouldn't have gone as well if we had our own hard team and went against them head-to-head. However, a powerful force like that against a pensioner and a girl – what could possibly go wrong? We had some degree of luck in Osoyoos, Clearwater and Banff, but you can't depend on that. Oederlin was a massacre, because that's what it was carefully planned to be."

"I don't remember you being quite so confident at the time."

"Over-confidence is a bad thing under any circumstances, but the opposition really had little chance. This doesn't mean that a lucky shot from their side couldn't have been very bad for us, but

330

the overall risk was acceptable low. Now this brings me back to your original question. With all these professional killers running about, why would anyone expect a retired consultant to have anything to do with the resultant carnage? Even for the very few people who know that I have a tame assassin in tow, they would hardly expect that you alone would go up against those lunatics."

I could see that Rachel was about to object, so I threw her my glasses, which were linked to my PASS via a short-range, tight-microwave beam. She could now view the CVs of our attackers, appearing to her as a hologram that seemed to sit on her lap. Although probably difficult to read in bright sunlight, she sat in silence while she quickly flicked through it. Despite her tan, she seemed rather pale when she finished. "Christ Almighty, that's one bunch of truly dangerous motherfuckers. But, wait a minute, you had profiled them before they turned up on our doorstep. Why didn't you say anything?"

"I had basic background on a few of them, but it didn't make any difference in terms of what we needed to do."

Rachel bit her lip as she pondered my response. Then she sighed. "Okay, I suppose not. But I've realised that you're doing your usual wandering off topic. You were supposed to be telling me about the hit."

"Ah, yes, good girl. The old brain doesn't manage to stick to the thread of an argument the way that it once did. I suppose that it's…"

"You're doing it again! The hit!" Suddenly she smiled. "You were just winding me up there, weren't you? God, but you're an annoying old cunt."

"A, finally, you acknowledge my divinity." I was stopped by the balled-up, wet cloth that hit me between the eyes. "Right, the hit. This is something that we need to schedule as soon as possible. This latest pressure on the US has forced the White House to set up a bipartisan, bicameral Commission to investigate the involvement of the Vice-president in terrorist actions, which will be a real three-ring circus for both domestic and international media. All in all, this must be the worst case scenario for those who were mixed up in this conspiracy. If they had been covering arses previously, they'll now be moving towards identifying fall-guys who can be thrown in front of this runaway train."

"Well, they've got Beall. In any case, the Veep must be worth a lot as a fall-gal," Rachel grinned.

"A good start, but she couldn't have done all of this alone. Maybe, just after Rokkasho, they could have focused on rogue agents in national security, but Alice was already cold in the morgue when this last attack must have been getting planned."

"Now I see it," her grin was beginning to look distinctly feral. "Denis must be the key suspect. Although the evidence for his links to North Korea should be convincing, he has enough power to muddy the waters and argue that all of this could be fabricated, all part of a campaign against him."

"Yes, the law doesn't work for the mega-rich in the way that it does for mere mortals. Think about Trump and you see how impotent normal processes are when facing an ex-President, even when it was recognised that he lied more often than he told the truth."

"So, you think Buck's going to be able to escape justice?"

"Ah, that's where things gets interesting. If it was only a normal investigation, he'd have a good chance of selling some kind of cock-and-bull story. But now we have a Commission at the very highest political level and he's close to the top of the list of those summoned to appear before it."

"That seems to be a good thing. The evil fucker must be shitting bricks."

"Yes, well, being summoned and actually appearing in front of the Commission are two very different things. It's not yet common knowledge, but I've picked up that he's setting up the basis for being able to claim that he's unfit to travel. The weaknesses in his cyber-security that we were able to exploit in the past have been sorted out, but it was easy for my AI to spot two of the world's top cardiac surgeons suddenly flying to Split yesterday and disappearing without trace thereafter."

"Well, I suppose that would give him some breathing space. But doesn't it only postpone the inevitable?"

"Completely correct, lass. That's actually the key message. The only way he can be sure of getting out of this mess would be if he died. Or, at least, if he appeared to die."

"And, with his resources, he can then be resurrected in another persona."

"Exactly! Even he can't be sure that he'll escape charges of grand treason, but he can ensure that his death isn't examined too closely. Indeed, from the US side, his appearance before the commission could open a very nasty can of worms and his death will be a great relief for lots of folk in high positions."

"So that's what we need to do: kill him before he dies?"

"Exactly. If not, we'll need to start the entire process of finding him from scratch."

***

A couple of hours later, we were examining satellite images of Vis, the nearby island where Buck was holed up. His estate was south of the small town of Komiža and, although I had the coordinates of his villa, it was impossible to make out clearly as most of the building was actually built into sea-cliffs. Easier to spot were the jetty and the huge luxury cruiser moored just off it. On top of the cliff were vineyards and olive groves that belonged to the property. There appeared to be nothing but drystone dykes delineating the estate, but I was sure that it would be well guarded electronically. Regardless, access to the villa seemed to be entirely by sea. Within the estate, the only stairs that led from the top of the cliffs to the shoreline dropped into the next bay, separated from Buck's cove by a rocky headland.

Rachel scowled. "The golf course was a sniper's wet dream, but this is a fucking nightmare. There's no chance of getting a clean shot from the clifftop and getting into position for a shot from sea

334

would be extremely bloody obvious. If I was Denis, I'd have a counter-sniper set up – which makes that option suicide. If we had some cannon fodder – like those guys in Oederlin – a frontal assault might work, but even that would be chancy."

"Good, you've confirmed my assessment of the situation. I had hoped that maybe you'd see a cleaner option, but it looks like we're going to be forced into playing hard ball here." I stopped and grimaced, having problems going further. *This isn't me, it's not what I do. This is pure fucking Miriam.*

"Are you okay, Jim?" Rachel sounded worried. "You're not having some fucking old-man breakdown are you? Should I call a medic?"

I forced a grin. "Nothing that a good blowjob wouldn't sort out. Ouch!" The well-deserved slap of my ear was half-hearted. "Anyway, when I talked earlier about letting your inner psycho loose, I hoped that it really wouldn't be needed. Unfortunately, I was wrong. You're going to have to take out Buck's yacht, so there'll be a lot of collateral damage here. It's likely that some of the victims will be completely innocent, with no knowledge at all of the evil that their employer has been up to."

"And I'm going to do this with a sniper rifle?"

"Of course not, it'll be a laser-guided missile. I've ordered it already. Actually it was much easier to get a hold of than that smart bullet kit you used in Japan. And a hell of a lot cheaper. Don't you find that rather scary?"

"I find that convenient. So, when will you have the kit?"

335

"In a couple of days. We'll need that time to set up our alibis in any case. Even if Buck's guilt is accepted, you can't make an attack like the one that I'm planning without rattling a lot of cages. As with Misawa, it needs to be crystal clear that we weren't involved because, otherwise, our very presence here will be enough to put us high on the list of suspects. Even better, we should shift the blame towards a credible culprit, one who won't be in a position to deny responsibility."

"I am sure that you already have lots of details thought through, but I guess you're going to keep me on tenterhooks for as long as possible."

"Some vague ideas, that's all. That's why I'm off for a swim now. I'm sure I'll have more ideas when I get back." *And, hopefully, you'll be a bit more relaxed after some self-abuse. The shorts that you're wearing look like you've pissed yourself.*

336

Chapter 38: Rachel

I managed to last until Jim had pottered about and finally departed with his swimming kit before I stripped off, threw my shorts and knickers into the laundry basket, and scampered into my bathroom. Just the sound of the shower was enough to take me back to Otago and it took little tactile manipulation to bring me to a shaking orgasm. *Shit, that was close. I saw that Jim was perfectly aware how turned on I was about this hit and it was so tempting just to go for it while he watched. But it's definitely better for our relationship this way.* Thoughts of pulling down my shorts and having at it with an audience like the humping guys from the hot springs were already having an effect and so, still damp from the shower, I took a towel to my bed and threw myself backwards on top of it, legs wide open. This time the climax built up slowly, taking so long that the thought of Jim arriving back before I finished added an extra piquancy to my second orgasm.

I had showered but was still only wrapped in a towel when Jim got back. "Jesus, autumn is approaching and the water is getting chillier by the day."

"So, have you got the details of the hit for me now?"

"Not yet but, more importantly, I think I've got a concept for our alibi. I'm off for a long soak in a hot bath, but you can start thinking about any options you have to get a hold of something owned

337

by your mother and have it shipped here within the next few days. The challenging bit is to ensure that the transfer is completely untraceable."

I was initially confused, but then smiled. "Miriam's going to be the one to take the fall for this, isn't she? You're going to set it up so that she gets all the blame. The idea is good, but how do you know that she won't have a cast-iron alibi?" I trailed after him into his bathroom and sat on the toilet seat while he stripped off his swimming trunks and t-shirt and started to run a bath.

"Yes, well I've got some ideas about that. Maybe the bath will sooth me enough that I can nail down some details."

"Yes, well, while you're waiting for the bath to fill, maybe you can expand a bit on a throwaway comment from this morning. You know, about my interests in water sports…"

I almost laughed aloud at his discomfort as he forced himself into a quarter-filled bath that was clearly too hot. "Oof, wow, that's warm. This morning was it? That's a long time ago."

"Water sports, wet sex," I reminded him.

"Ah, water sports, like scuba. I did a lot of diving at one time and there are quite a few places here…"

I leaned over to take a wrinkled nipple between middle finger and thumb. "I promised never again to crush your balls, but that doesn't cover nipples…" I squeezed hard and he squeaked like a cartoon mouse. "Actually, there are a lot of other vulnerable parts of your anatomy not covered by my promise," I looked down at his shrivelled dick.

"Right, wet sex, golden showers and all that urophilia stuff. Increasingly popular, I believe, given its prominence in web-porn."

"Which you implied is a kink of mine. Why would you think that?"

"Well as a child of the liberated 21st century, at least one who lived where such liberation wasn't prosecuted by religious loonies... Fuck, that's really sore!"

"You made the comment, then changed the subject immediately. Why would that be?"

"Fuck! Why did you do that again? I haven't said anything."

"It was going to be a lie or some kind of side-track." I pinched his nipple again. "You know, there's a cheese-grater in the kitchen and your willy is looking very vulnerable there.

"Okay, I give in. I was keeping an eye on you when you were in Tokyo and spotted your dalliances with the couple from Toramon."

Somehow this did not come as a surprise, but I was well fucked-off regardless. "So you didn't trust me and felt the need to spy on my personal relationships. You've got absolutely no respect for my privacy or my right to have any kind of life that's not under your control."

He sighed and settled back into the bath. "I'm well aware that you're a big girl..." He caught my glare. "You're a grown woman and I have neither the right nor the intention to spy on any part of your private life. Quite frankly, your sexual preferences or kinks don't interest me at all. But you were on a highly sensitive op and here your past military

339

experience helps you not a jot. Although it may not be very probable, when somebody picks you up in a bar, you always have to consider if there might be more to it."

"Well, that's clear in your case. Anyone picking you up would certainly be a very dodgy character. But I happen to be a good-looking woman and this isn't at all unusual for me."

"Yes, that's clear – for example young Gabi. Although I believe that it was actually you picking her up in that case."

"Whatever, there's no reason for you to think that I was going to get into trouble."

"You travelled to Japan on documents that I was fairly sure wouldn't raise any flags, but we've not tried to disguise your appearance at all. If someone had enough computing power dedicated to tracing you, getting spotted at the border is a definite possibility. In such a case, it's just a matter of following you – either electronically or with bodies on the ground. Given that there are some very powerful people who consider us a threat, we need to be on our toes."

"And you really think I was vulnerable to an attack? In downtown Tokyo, of all places?"

"Unlikely, it's true, but you went home with a couple shortly after meeting them. At the very least, something worth checking on to see if it was kosher."

"And was it?"

"Yes, it seems so. It wasn't hard for my cyber-gophers to dig into the Takeuchis. Typically Japanese, they've done nothing to hide their

340

membership of a swinger group that comprises mainly young professionals in central Tokyo. Their listed profile focuses on mild bisex bondage, with explicit preferences for urolagnia and anal play. It's clear that the wife – Yoko or Junko, I seem to remember – was the Domme in that relationship. This fits with her picking you up."

"Fuck it, Jim, you were monitoring me the entire time!"

"Well, given that I organised your flights and the hotel, it was trivial to have a few key CCTVs hacked so that I could watch over you. In that pub, you were in full view of a webcam behind the bar. There was no audio, but it was easy to follow what was going on."

"And you had nothing better to do than act as a peeping Tom?"

"Evening in Tokyo is mid-afternoon here, so I just had the video running in the background. As I said, I quickly determined that you were in little danger from that couple – despite your surprise decision to go home with a pair you had known for only a few hours. At worst, you seemed to be risking a well-tanned bum. Probably before, after or even during a golden shower."

I felt a shiver when I realised that the old voyeur had the capability to hack into any cameras present within the Takeuchi's apartment. It was bad enough him possibly watching me masturbate, but the idea of him being a fly on the wall while Junko was easing me out of my comfort zone was seriously creepy.

"You don't have to say anything," he added. "I can see your discomfort and I can assure you that I made no attempt to monitor anything you did behind closed doors in Otago. I did once have a quick glimpse when you and your pal were swimming, but again that was effectively open CCTV."

"So, this is what you want me to believe? You could have indulged your voyeuristic tendencies, but chose not to out of respect for me. Despite this, you seem to have a good idea of what we were up to."

"I can assure you it wasn't hard to guess. Your Domme must have been delighted to find a unicorn and would have made the most of it."

"A unicorn? What are you babbling about?"

He grinned. "Ah, that's an old swinger term. A unicorn is when a couple find a willing bisexual woman who is interested in a sexual encounter without any emotional hang-ups."

"But why a unicorn?"

"Because they're very rare and, when you find one, the experience can be magical." He laughed and then broke into a choking cough, probably caught up in memories of his perverted youth.

I frowned, but couldn't help being attracted to the idea of being magical. "So unicorns are all female?"

"Yes, at least back in antediluvian times when my wife and I were part that scene. Nowadays, I guess the term might be applied to anyone in the full male-female-other spectrum. Anyway, your Tokyo fuck-buddies seem to lie on the vanilla side

342

of the kink range, so I'm sure that they must have been delighted to meet up with you."

I still wasn't completely convinced. "So your degenerate past was sufficient for you to know exactly what I got up to with Junko, with no electronic intrusion at all."

"My well-rounded experience of the world allowed me to make some guesses, but it was your reactions to them that gave me the confirmation that I needed. So, when Junko was pissing on you, did you like the taste?"

My slap sent him flying backwards, spilling water from the now-filled bath onto the floor. As I stomped out of the bathroom I heard his chuckle. "See what I mean!"

***

I needed to clear my head, so went out for a walk, following the path along the shore to Hvar old town. Although the sun was shining through thin clouds, the heat of summer was long gone and, when in the wind, it was rather cool. I found a sheltered table in a bar facing the harbour where the ferries from Split docked and ordered an Irish coffee. I watched the tourists go by and half-heartedly attempted to guess their nationality while I replayed my confrontation with Jim. Gradually, my annoyance began to fade as I realised that him looking out for me was more a guardian angel effort than any kind of intrusion of my privacy. The fact that he managed to work out what I had been up to with Junko was rather embarrassing, but I had to admit that he didn't seem shocked in any way. *I wonder if golden showers were included when he and his wife were getting up to bi-swinger high jinks. Somehow, it wouldn't surprise me in the least.*

Just at that point, I was distracted by a pair of very beautiful Spanish girls who sat at a table two-away from mine. *Probably early- to mid-thirties, but could be late twenties, especially from the way that they chatter simultaneously while managing at the same time to scroll through the screens of their mobile phones.* They were both black-haired with lovely deep tans, but the contrast in their somatotypes was dramatic. The shorter girl had a wild mane and was well rounded, with a massive bosom and sizeable buttocks, but an amazingly slim waist. A real hourglass figure. *Definitely built for comfort rather than speed.* Her friend had her hair cut very short and had a slim, boyish figure. Nevertheless, her androgynous appearance was extremely attractive. *Now if I had to choose between that pair, who would I go for? Of course, the obvious answer if they did turn out to be a couple was choose them both. I wonder if they have any interest in a unicorn.*

Unfortunately I had been sipping my coffee when this thought made me laugh – so it transformed into choking as the very alcoholic beverage went down the wrong way. When I recovered I was aware that most of the patrons of the bar were looking in my direction, including the two young Spaniards. I wiped my face with a napkin and waved my hand in a manner that I hoped indicated that I was alright. Both girls smiled at me,

344

but the way that the short-haired one scratched her head and raised one eyebrow seemed to indicate more than an interest in my health.

Wow, could it be that the magic unicorn rides again? A lesbian threesome could be just the very thing to cheer me up. Maybe I should see if they'll come back to the apartment with me, just to annoy Jim. I can't see him curing either of these ladies of their lesbianism.

I glanced away for a moment, steeling myself to getting up and approach them, when I froze in shock. Although she was wearing a wide-brimmed hat and a scarf over her face, the woman walking past me had to be my mother. My hands were shaking and I could feel my pulse racing. *Get a fucking grip, it's just somebody that looks like her.* But, from the woman's posture, gait and annoying laugh, I knew this wasn't the case. The bitch-demon from hell was not only alive, but also in Hvar, of all places. *Small world coincidences are all very well, but this is fucking ridiculous.*

Miriam was walking along the harbour towards the area where super-yachts were berthed, her arms linked with a younger man on one side and an older woman on the other. I carefully positioned my wristcom so that I could grab a video of her retreating back. I thought about sending it to Jim, but realised that, if my mum was wandering about openly, she probably had some kind of backup cyber-security. So, assuming that I hadn't already been picked up, I needed to get back to the apartment without showing up on any of the CCTVs scattered about the town.

Miriam and her partners stopped for selfies by one of the huge cruisers, then climbed the gangplank and vanished into it. *Must be Buck's boat.* Because of the other yachts tied-up around it, it was tricky to tell how large it was from my seating position, but it could well be 70m.

Fuck, fuck, fuckity-fuck! I couldn't work out if the worst shock was confirmation that my evil mother was actually alive or if it was the evidence that she was definitely part of Buck's entourage.

I jerked upright when someone touched my shoulder, then relaxed when I saw it was one of the Spanish women rather than one of Buck's goons. I shook my head in response to a mouthful of rapid Spanish. Then, seeing my confusion, the tall, slim member of the pair switched to slow, stilted English. "Are you okay? You were first coughing, choking, then you looked like you had a shock. Do you need a doctor?"

I tapped her long, thin hand while taking the opportunity for a closer look at this very pretty woman. "I'm fine, honestly. Thanks for your concern, but I just saw my... ex-wife," I added quickly, frantically trying to come up with some credible explanation for my behaviour. "It was a really bad break-up, she moved in with my father, you see. She's a total bitch."

"And your father, he must be a total cunt. Oh, I mean a total bastard. Is that right?"

I smiled. "You're completely correct. He is a complete, fucking cunt-bastard. But, anyway, I'm fine now."

I was rewarded by a glowing grin. "Why don't you come over and have a drink with us? My fiancé and I do not get much of a chance to practice our English." I noticed her glance at a small diamond ring, so I guessed the engagement was recent.

"Well, why not? But you've got to let me buy you a drink. I'm here on holiday with a rich uncle. For me it's really to get over my divorce, but he needs help as he's very old and really can't be trusted on his own.

I was almost able to forget my mother while I spent a most enjoyable hour with *las chicas salvajes*, which I guessed meant something like *the wild girls*. The willowy one was called Consuella – or just Connie – while the bounteous one was Maria. Although they were clearly devoted to each other, their approach to holidays reminded me of young Gabi: a chance to party, with the option of some sex on the side seen as a benefit. While they flirted with me, I made my interest clear but, remembering the unicorn definition, also noted that this would only be sex. I had no aim to get into another relationship in the near future. This seemed to fit perfectly with their plans.

I was about to suggest that we met up again for dinner when I remembered that I needed to try to avoid being spotted on my way back. "Well, chicas, we've got a few hours of the afternoon left. How do you fancy coming back to my apartment? I've got a nice big double bed and I'm sure we have some Champagne lying about. There's a nice restaurant close by and, after that, there's a fancy club down on the shore."

347

To my surprise, Maria agreed immediately. *Wow, I'm definitely channelling my inner unicorn here.* Connie, however, seemed unsure. "Are you certain that it will be okay? You are staying with your uncle, after all. Most of my family are okay with Maria and me, but the older ones, especially the Catholics, are not so happy."

I grinned at this opportunity for calumny that I had been handed. "Oh, that's definitely not a problem. My old uncle Jim is gay, with a special kink for domination by well-endowed black men. He often dresses up in suspenders, stockings, waspies and stuff like that: the entire lady-boy kit. It looks very weird on his old flabby body, but he's completely harmless." The girls burst into giggles at the thought.

"Alright, let's go then," Connie grinned. "I hope that he is wearing his kinky clothes." This started Maria giggling again."

I'd be happy if he's wearing any clothes at all. I fit myself in the middle of our group, arms around the waists of my new friends and ensuring that Connie would be between me and Buck's yacht, just in case Miriam was in sight. "Actually, sometimes he wears nothing but a pink ribbon tied around his penis. I don't know how he manages that, as his dick is extremely small and his eyesight isn't very good."

More giggles and now I could feel Maria's hand slip under my t-shirt and then move downwards, surreptitiously stroking my bum. "There was another time that I arrived back and he

348

was dressed as a cat. Although that involved only cat-ears and a butt-plug with a cat's tail on it."

"A butt plug. What is that?"

I explained and then allowed myself to be talked into describing his amazing collection of such toys. I was enjoying giving my fantasy free rein and, from their increasing unsubtle groping, it was getting my girlfriends into the mood. *Me as well. This is going to be a fun afternoon. And it'll piss-off the old fucker so much.*

To my surprise, and the girls' clear disappointment, the apartment was empty when we arrived. Nevertheless, this allowed us to head straight into my bedroom, shedding clothes as we went. When nude, the contrast between the bodies of my new lovers was even more dramatic. They were almost like manga caricatures, Connie looking almost prepubescent with her small conical breasts, shaven mons and boyish hips while Maria was like a raven-haired Marilyn Monroe, with the addition of rings in her nipples, navel and glinting from her bushy pubic hair. I had intended to offer a choice of my toys, but we immediately ended up in a writhing heap on the bed, working hard with fingers and tongues. For a few moments I felt guilty that I had made no attempt to tell Jim about my surprise encounter in Hvar town, but that vanished as I abandoned myself to the simple joys of uninhibited Sapphic sex.

***

349

It was about an hour later when I heard a knock on the bedroom door. The three of us were sprawled on top of the bed, Connie and I gently nuzzling Maria's nipple-rings. My chicas immediately struggled to drape a distinctly damp and smelly bedspread over themselves while the door slowly opened. "Hello, ladies. I waited until the shouts and screams died away, so I hope that you're ready for a break." Jim brought over a tray loaded with a bottle of Krug in an ice-bucket, 3 tall flutes, a small dish of caviar with the usual horn spoon, slices of lemon, a dish of sour cream and a pile of blinis. "If you'll just sit up a bit, I can put this over your collective laps."

Jim was, typically, wearing only a posing pouch but, as it was a rather lurid pink, it started Maria laughing and I knew that both Connie and I were grinning like idiots. "It's okay. He may have a weak heart, but the sight of some bare boobs isn't going to finish him off. Not female ones anyway."

I managed to get all of us sitting against the headboard with the bedspread thrown back, but modesty preserved by a sheet pulled up until it covered our groins. "Okay, Jim, that's us sorted out now. You can serve the fizz."

"Certainly, love," he carefully set the tray down and quickly popped the cork on the Champagne. After pouring the first glass, he offered it to Connie. "I hope you enjoy this, Chief Inspector, the Grand Cuvée was considered the world's best non-vintage Champagne in pre-warming days and I think that it's still eminently drinkable."

Connie's intake of breath was followed by an uncomfortable silence as we stared in confusion at our butler.

The second glass went to Maria. "Here you go, Inspector, it sounds as if you probably need a drink by now. Shagging does tend to give you a terrible thirst."

I took the third glass from him and stared into his eyes, wondering if he'd finally gone loopy.

"Okay, give me a shout if you need anything else."

He turned to leave, but I grabbed the string of his tanga and hauled him back. "No you don't! What's all this Inspector stuff?"

"Oh, that." He was trying to look innocent and failing miserably. "I guess you were in such a rush to get at it that you didn't get around to introductions. So, we are lucky indeed to have two high-fliers from the EU counter-terrorist centre gracing our humble abode. I'm sure that they're well aware that we've been targeted by such terrorists in the past, so having them to protect us has got to be a win-win situation, n'est-ce pas?"

Connie had a quick gulp of her drink, gave me an apologetic glance, and then sighed dramatically. "Your uncle has something of a reputation in intelligence circles, which is clearly well deserved."

"But you think we're terrorists?" I interrupted. "That's why you're staking us out?"

Connie sighed again. "It's not that. It's more that you – or maybe your uncle – seem to be a magnet for mad assassins. He had a holiday cabin bombed and there were at least two attacks on you

351

in Canada. Two definitely, but we suspect a third. You were in Japan when the Vice-president was assassinated. Things seemed to be dying down, then there was OK Corral just next to his Swiss apartment. There's nothing to suggest that you were anywhere in the vicinity in that case, but it seemed like a very strange coincidence."

I couldn't help noticing that Connie's English had suddenly become more fluent, almost colloquial. "So you were just monitoring things. If so, how did you end up in my bed?"

"It wasn't something that we planned from the beginning," Maria contributed, her English also much improved. "It was just that, in that bar, you looked very interested in us, so it seemed like a good chance to get to know you."

"And you get to know the folk you're spying on by shagging them?"

Maria was clearly trying to hide it, but couldn't help smiling. "Not always. Actually, never until this afternoon and that needed a lot of improvisation. But it was rather fun, wasn't it?"

"Actually, it was," I smiled back.

Jim gave a stage cough to attract our attention. "Well, I'm glad that's all sorted out. Have at it, ladies, and don't hesitate to call if you need anything."

***

After Jim's bombshell, things were rather uncomfortable while we struggled to find small-talk, focusing more on drinking very nice

352

champagne and grazing on the caviar. It was Maria who finally addressed the elephant in the room. "Right, okay, we're spooks who are trying to find out what you and your weird partner are up to. We would have taken any opportunity to have a chat with you, it's what undercover agents do. I'll also come out and admit that, given the chance, I would have been more than happy to go to bed with you under any circumstances. I do really like how you look and act. Also, what we've manged to uncover of your CV is impressive. We regularly encounter the maniacs who make up US black-ops teams, but you're nothing like them."

"Maybe it's the calming influence of... my uncle," I quickly added to avoid going into tricky explanations. "He was dragged into this action by UK intelligence and then passed to the US, without any chance to opt out." I stopped when I realised that my mouth was running away with me – probably just exactly as these agents wanted. "But I guess you already know about all of this."

"The US has been less than helpful, but we had a very detailed briefing from the Canadians. As you can imagine, they were completely horrified by the cavalier way that the Yanks had been crashing about in their country."

"Yes, the pooch was well and truly screwed there." I noticed a couple of frowns. "I mean, the maniacs responsible for these actions fucked-up royally."

Connie nodded. "Although there was no indication that you were in any way responsible for the carnage in Banff, the Mounties had identified both of you as persons of interest that they would like to talk to. This was fairly low-key, so it ran through Interpol rather than the usual intelligence units. In Spain, we have a TV programme that each weekend highlights some people who the police are searching for throughout the EU. Most of the responses we get are from publicity-seeking time-wasters, but we received a very interesting contact from a young woman who had just returned from holiday…"

"Gabi!" I groaned, putting my face in my hands.

"Yes, indeed, Gabriella Montero. She was actually concerned that you might have been under some kind of threat." Connie smiled. "Although she reckoned that you were tough and very sensible, she was worried about your uncle – who seems to be very lovable, but very frail. She wouldn't go into details, but it seems like he overdosed on Viagra and she thought he was going to have a stroke. He wouldn't let her call an ambulance, but it seems that she's been worried since then."

Maria laughed. "So, maybe he's not completely straight gay?"

What an unbelievably stupid old fucker. "He probably talked Gabi into servicing him with the huge black dildo that he keeps by his bed. The absence of an over-endowed stud was what probably required the Viagra…" I realised that I was rambling and stopped.

Connie looked concerned. "I am guessing that you didn't know about the Viagra. Anyway, if it doesn't kill you immediately, an overdose is unlikely to have long-term impacts."

There's going to be long-term impacts on his scrawny arse before this day is out. I closed my eyes and took a deep breath. "He may be – or have been – very intelligent, but he can be stupid as fuck sometimes. So, to get back on theme, you were going to tell me why you just happened to be sitting close to me in that bar. You knew that we had been in Hvar, but presumably also that we had left."

"Well, we know from British intelligence that you were both in Japan at the time when the US Vice-president was assassinated."

"And you think we did that?" I tried my best to look horrified at the thought.

"Not at all, the evidence points to some rogue CIA hit squad. But there's a funny coincidence here: nuclear threat levels were raised to high in Japan while you were there, just as they did in the UK when you were being chased around Canada and then in Switzerland when the battle occurred near your uncle's place. And, of course, his area of expertise is terrorist risk assessment, especially if anything nuclear is involved."

"So, you think we're lone wolfs, out to attack some nuclear facility?"

"Not at all, we think you're working with the Brits, or the Swiss, or both possibly. Neither country has admitted this but, very interestingly, they haven't denied it either. We would have rather approached this in a less surreptitious manner, but the bottom line is that we want to know what you're

355

up to and if there are likely to be more nuclear alerts in the future."

Shit! Jim hasn't done as good a job of covering our traces as he thinks. "Well that seems eminently reasonable. I hadn't realised that communication channels in Europe were so poor. I tell you what, let's finish the plonk and have another roll in the hay and then I'll get Jim in and he can give you all the details."

Maria was evidently keen to go, but Connie clearly less so.

Maria provided clarification immediately. "Um, as I said, this wasn't quite as we planned. Following our information from Gabriella, I was hoping to get picked up by you and then break the ice a bit. I'm afraid that Connie just got swept up with this – she really doesn't play for our team."

"Wow, she definitely fooled me," I scanned her lovely slim body. "She played the bit about being newly engaged to perfection."

"Yes, that's the thing about undercover work – it's something that you need to do."

I took a hold of Connie's left breast and rubbed a rapidly hardening nipple with my thumb. "I suspect that, if we tried really hard, we could cure her of her poor lifestyle choice."

"Maybe we could," Maria agreed. "Anyway, I've always fancied my boss, so it would be a shame to miss out on the second opportunity to have my evil way with her." With that the buxom wench pushed her face between Connie's thighs.

Within a short time, any reservations that Connie may have had vanished while Maria and I worked together to use our tongues and fingers to bring her to the noisiest climax of the afternoon. Thereafter, it took only a little soixante-neuf for us to reach our own shuddering orgasms.

Chapter 39: Jim

I had been monitoring Rachel's walk into town, but got distracted when I spotted Buck's cruiser in the harbour. I knew that he would be lying low in his villa, but hadn't really thought about his family and house guests using the boat. Thus, by the time that I returned my attention to the bar she had stopped at, Rachel was already chatting to a couple of women. It didn't take long to identify them. *So maybe it's just the old honey trap: get the girl between the sheets and hope that she lets something slip when basking in post-coital bliss.*

The question was if she would go back to their digs or bring them here. I was fairly sure that Rachel would push for the latter – just to annoy me – and it was likely that this would be the agents' preferred option, as it could give them a chance to snoop around the apartment. *I just need to play this carefully and see if there is any way of turning their presence to my advantage. The key thing will be to get them off-guard and it'll help a lot that Rachel still has no idea of what exactly I'm planning for Buck and his retinue.*

I called a taxi and set off for a top-end gourmet food and wine boutique that serviced the superyacht community. *This is going to be expensive, but that's what the war chest's there for, after all.*

Although costing in excess of 5,000 euros, the food and wines fit easily into a couple of large, hemp carrier bags supplied by the shop. I killed time while shopping by sampling a few wines and grazing on free nibbles, aiming to ensure that I got back to the apartment after the girls had settled in.

I opened the front door as quietly as possible, but the chances of me being heard seemed slim. From the shouts, screams, grunts and groans, the women were having a high old time. Typically, Rachel had left her bedroom door slightly ajar, ensuring that I was left in no doubt about what was going on. Even if not for the noise, the smell was completely unmistakable.

I checked through the CCTVs that I had hacked to monitor Buck's yacht and was able to watch live as it departed. I left my AI kit to work over all the recorded video and see what could be determined about its passengers.

Okay, sounds like the ladies have stopped slaughtering pigs, so I better get a tray ready. I swithered about going in au natural, but compromised with the smallest posing pouch I possessed, which was a truly horrendous pink colour. *I've no idea why on earth I purchased that, but I'm sure Rachel will have been regaling the agents with stories of my eccentricity, so it'll fit in well.*

I rapped on the door and then pushed it open without waiting for permission, delighted to watch the chaos as naked anti-terrorist agents attempted to cover up. I managed to restrict myself to the faintest of grins while I waited for the women to sort themselves out. *Rachel has really hit gold-dust this time: these women are drop-dead gorgeous. Especially the one who looks like a dark-haired Annie Lennox.* I could not help a pang of jealousy, but was sensible enough to realise that a woman like that would not come within a mile of an old fart like myself.

The confusion and discomfort was tangible when I revealed the names and backgrounds of Rachel's new fuck-buddies. By playing it low key and making it appear that I welcomed our surprise visitors, I hoped this would give the required hint to Rachel, so that she could defuse the inevitable tensions.

Much though I would have loved to stay longer and enjoy the view, I forced myself to leave as soon as was polite, carefully closing the door completely. *Fuck, why didn't I put a camera in the girl's bedroom? Okay, I wanted to give Rachel privacy, but had no idea that she was going to bring home EU intelligence. Or, maybe more importantly, that they would be so fucking tasty.*

***

After about half an hour they were at it again, if anything even noisier than before. I was relieved about that, as it indicated that Rachel had forgiven her new friends' subterfuge – at least to some extent. *Now I just needed to sucker them into providing a perfect alibi for my next attack on Denis and the bastards supporting him.*

Again, after the noises died down to post-coital groans, moans and sighs, I knocked the door and stuck my head into the bedroom. This time, the huddle of sweaty flesh sprawled on the bottom bedsheet did not even try to cover up. It would have been difficult anyway, given that all other bedding had been kicked off onto the floor.

"Well, ladies, that's indeed a sight for sore eyes. I must say, the EU does a fantastic job of anti-terrorist protection. It makes me wish I needed this as much as young Rachel. Anyway, you must have burned off a lot of calories by now and, by the look of the sheet, also must need a bit of rehydration. What will it be? I have some very nice pâté de foie gras, local cheeses and salami, fruit and fresh baguettes, crackers and brioche. There's also more champagne, a nice Meursault and an old Sauternes, which might go better with the foie gras. Of course, also beer, fruit juice or mineral water if you've got a thirst."

With a groan Connie dragged herself into a sitting position and gave me a suspicious stare. "You're not trying to bribe us in some way, are you?"

Maria was still lying spread-eagled on her back, but turned to look at me. "Bribery sounds good to me. Champagne, fizzy mineral water and any of that food would be perfect."

Rachel had been struggling to extract her torso from under Maria's right thigh and, when she managed this, looked me in the eyes before bending over to nuzzle the chubby woman's groin, making slurping noises that made the Spaniard giggle in embarrassment.

I smiled. "I don't have beaver on the menu, but this seems also to be an option. I'll bring in a tray of food and you can just help yourself. I'll also bring in Champagne and mineral water and leave them in

361

ice-buckets on the table here. Of course, I can serve you drinks whenever needed."

Rachel lifted her head and licked her lips in a decidedly risqué manner. "May as well bring in the Sauternes, also, as it's supposed to be good with goose liver, although I haven't actually tried it before. And some still water." I had turned to go when she added, "and some orange juice."

"Grapefruit, if you've got it," Maria chipped in just as I reached the door.

"The whole works, it is," I confirmed, heading off to the kitchen where I had already started to load up the biggest trays that I could find.

***

Late afternoon gradually transformed into early evening while the girls gorged themselves, doing a lot of damage to the food and polishing off both bottles of wine in addition to a couple of litre bottles of mineral water. Needless to say, trips to the loo became increasingly regular as time wore on but, following Rachel's example, they did not bother closing the toilet door even when I was in the bedroom playing my wine-waiter role. I felt as if I was being treated like a eunuch in a harem, but the job certainly had its perks for anyone with voyeuristic tendencies.

Rachel had mentioned that her original plan was to take her new pals – or watchdogs, as they now seemed to be – for dinner nearby, so I had reserved a table for the four of us at 7:30. Although I was beginning to feel peckish, I couldn't imagine that the ladies would be able to eat a morsel more. Nevertheless, when I checked at 7:15, they seemed keen to give it a go and scurried off to the bathroom together.

Despite my expectations of what they might get up to in the shower, they emerged only 25 minutes later and quickly dressed, now completely unbothered by the fact that I could see them through the open door to the kitchen, where I was finishing tidying up.

The nearest restaurant, *Primi Piatti*, was billed as an Italian Pizzeria, but actually included a number of traditional dishes from the island, with a focus on seafood. Although there were a number of people eating on the balcony, a rather cool breeze led the ladies to choose eating indoors. Apart from us, the only others eating inside were a group of elderly Brits at the other end of the restaurant, so we had enough privacy to chat freely.

The wine list included a good selection from local vineyards and I selected a premium Pošip as an aperitif while food options were discussed. After much toing and froing, the girls decided to try *Gregada di Hvar*, a kind of fish and potato soup, while I went for a meaty pizza. My companions appeared little impacted by their alcoholic afternoon and the Pošip was gone before our meals arrived. I thus ordered a dry white Bogdanuša to go with the fish and a heavy, red Plavac Mali for myself.

The atmosphere was strained and, as soon as our food was served and the waiters adjourned to the kitchen, Rachel could hold back no longer. "I told my chicas here that you would explain why

363

we're back in Hvar. Given the number of attacks against us, it seems sensible to get someone else on our side in case something else crops up. In principle, they've got the entire EU security force behind them."

I hacked of a large chunk of pizza and had a mouthful of wine before I answered. "Maybe the Swiss and UK intelligence services have reasons for not sharing everything fully with the EU, but I don't give a shit about that kind of pettiness. Just ask any questions that you like and I'll do my best to answer them."

The two agents looked at each other in amazement, while Rachel focused on filling her bowl from the large tureen that the soup had come in. "Right," Connie swallowed nervously, "let's just confirm that we have the very top level issues sorted out properly. Was there really a plot to attack Sellafield?"

"Yes." I raised my eyebrows to indicate she should continue.

"And, was the Vice-president of the US involved in this plot?"

"Certainly, she was one of the top-level conspirators."

"Did you assassinate her?"

Rachel stopped with a soup spoon halfway to her mouth, holding her breath.

"I set up a dark-web notice board that exposed the conspiracy and it was inevitable that she would need to be eliminated to avoid links to the rest of the cabal being exposed. So, I effectively shot her in the head and I have no regrets whatever about that."

"And was there another nuclear threat in Japan?"

"Yes, with the same team involved."

"But how were both these threats neutralised?"

"I certainly helped there, but I was supporting the UK in both cases. I gave them some background, but they did the heavy lifting."

"So, what about Switzerland, was that another nuclear attack?"

I munched the very tasty pizza while thinking about the best way to handle this question. I had a sip of wine and then was ready to respond. "I'm sure that I've said nothing so far that you didn't already know, but now we're getting into areas where there aren't easy yes-no answers. So grab some food before it goes cold and I'll fill you in here."

Another bite of pizza and mouthful of wine and then I felt that I had my yarn straight. "So, a nuclear attack on Switzerland: to the best of my knowledge this was not planned." I saw that Maria was keen to break in, but waved her down. "The general threat to nuclear facilities remains, but after two failed nuclear attacks and conspicuous failures to eliminate one of their main obstacles – which is me – the US plutocrats behind this plot are beginning to fall out. Of course, the assassination of the VP could either be a final straw for them or actually might be a result of splits within their ranks. I'm fairly sure that I was the main target of the mercenaries in Baden, but I was able to play the two sides of the conspirators against each other and help ensure that nobody walked out of that fiasco. They would have shown me no mercy, so I have no regrets about anything I did. Certainly, like the case of the VP, you could argue that I'm directly responsible for their deaths due to the way that I played the game."

Connie frowned. "That's interesting. I was never convinced that even a hit squad comprising those very tough mercenaries would be a serious threat to any of the major nuclear facilities in Switzerland. However, if you were the target, it actually looks like overkill."

I attempted to smile while chewing pizza, then needed to top up my glass before I washed it down. "Yes, overkill is the best way to describe it. But I assume you've seen the details of the Banff attack. Using a fucking helicopter gunship, of all fucking things. I'm sure that those at the top of this plot are smart, but the next level down seems to be peopled by lunatic psychopaths…"

"Who dislike you intensely," Maria added with a smile.

That was actually a very good point. The attack in Switzerland could be explained by Buck's desire for revenge after I had both scuppered his plans and exposed his role in North Korea, but there was a lack of hands-on control that seemed atypical of him. Even Miriam, who was happy to have others do her dirty work for her, would have wanted to follow the action and would surely have prevented her heavy team walking into such a trap. She knows me well enough to realise that I am not going to be caught with my pants down, especially on my home turf.

Luckily my wool-gathering had not been noticed. Based on the background that I had prepared for her, Rachel was able to fill in further details, even admitting that we had passed by to checked out my apartment en route to Croatia, just in case they had some way of back-tracking us over the last few days.

I concentrated on eating until the tricky question eventually came up, surprisingly from Maria rather than Connie.

"Yes, that's all understandable, but why did you come back to Hvar?"

"After we got back from Canada, we were simply focused on losing anyone who may be trying to follow us, so Hvar was just random. It did, however, seem like a good option for lying low – a small, low-season, tourist spot. It certainly would have worked well if not for the stroke of bad luck due to young Gabi spotting that TV programme."

Maria narrowed her eyes, clearly suspicious. "That explains your first visit, but why come back?"

"As I'm sure you know, one of the probable leaders of this conspiracy is a cousin of the recently departed Vice-president, Denis Buck. He has been summoned to Washington to account for himself, but is currently holed up nearby, on the island of Vis."

"Wait a minute," Connie interrupted with a frown, clearly struggling with this as a justification for coming to Hvar. "If Buck has the role that you are accusing him off, he was probably behind the last attack on you. Coming here seems to be equivalent to strolling into the lion's den."

367

I grinned. "Not at all, there's probably nowhere safer that we can be. I'm sure that Denis would love to have me removed from the chessboard, but he'll be much more worried about anything that could shine light on his presence here. A fire-fight on the neighbouring island would be a nightmare for him. It would be shitting on his own doorstep in the worse kind of way."

"Mmm, I suppose that you've got a point there. Although, if he does go to Washington, your position here won't be as secure." Connie still seemed unconvinced.

"I'm fairly certain that wild horses couldn't drag Denis back to the States, but if that did occur, then having the protection of your team could be invaluable."

"And there's nothing else that you're up to while you're here?"

I had been expecting this, but tried to look uncomfortable, maybe not very successfully if Rachel's rolling of her eyes was any indicator. "Well, I'm still digging up further information to make Denis's guilt more obvious. Which is very serious, as I'm sure that what was intended would be classed as a crime against humanity. I wouldn't be surprised if someone or other didn't use this to simply take the law into their own hands and snuff the bastard. Just like they did his cousin."

"Shit!" "Fuck!" The two agents cursed simultaneously.

"Indeed, if you look at it this way, maybe it explains why the Brits and Swiss haven't been as open with you as they should. Both these countries

368

feel threatened and would be very happy to see Denis six-feet under."

"You really think that either of these security services would arrange an assassination in an EU country?" Maria was clearly sceptical.

"The Swiss probably not, but the UK might. In any case, if they had any indications of a third party planning a hit, you can be sure that neither of them would do anything to block it."

"That actually makes sense." Connie was deep in thought, which made her look even more distractingly cute. "There are rumours that the Brits were a major support to the Japanese during the crisis there. Given how good their intelligence was, it's quite credible that they knew about the plan to assassinate Mrs Beall, but chose to let it go ahead."

Time to add gasoline to the fire. "Now that you mention it, this would fit with the fact that the Russians, Chinese and even Koreans knew about the nuclear threat before the Yanks did."

"Well, Jim, you've been very open here and I think we now have a better picture of what's going on. How do you suggest we play it from here?" I could feel all three woman waiting for me to answer Connie's question.

"I can see that you've got a problem here, as you don't want to have a high profile murder on your patch. You'll also see that, despite the fact that I'd love to see the man publically humiliated before being executed for grand treason, I wouldn't lift a finger to prevent someone quickly taking the bastard out in the near future, as it reduces risks to Rachel and myself. What I'll do is continue to put everything I find out on the dark web notice board – you know the one?"

Both women nodded, but Connie frowned. "Will this be everything, though? From what you've just said, you wouldn't post anything that would allow us to stop an assassination, would you?"

"I'll post anything I find out about third-party threats, but you've got to realise that both the Brits and Swiss monitor anything posted and so they'll know if any of their plans are compromised and change them appropriately. In any case, I suspect that you really don't want any serious conflicts with your allies, so maybe your first action should be to try to build some bridges here. I know that there are some at top levels who enjoy inter-organisation pissing contests, but working together on this one would be win-win, I'm sure."

I guess that my openness had really broken down barriers, as the three women now discussed how we could collaborate most effectively. As a first gesture of goodwill, Connie promised to organise military satellite surveillance of Buck's estate and send us a link to it. I had to hide a smile at that point. She was clearly unaware how easy it was for my black hats to access that. She was also going to organise a quick response team with a couple of choppers at the Lora naval base in Split. We would get a 24/7 panic button that would allow their immediate mobilisation any time needed. Again a very nice gesture, which I was rather profuse in thanking her for. Nevertheless, a raised eyebrow from Rachel confirmed my feeling that, for most likely scenarios, by the time that a squad flew in from Split the shit would have already hit the fan and hence it would be useful for clean-up only.

Better for my plans, and to Rachel's evident delight, Maria agreed that she would move in with us for the next few days. This was ostensibly to allow better communication, but I'm sure that Connie's aim was to monitor our actions more closely. I guessed that she had expected some sort of objection from me, but she was in for a surprise. "That'll be just perfect from my side. As I'm already retired – well past my sell-by date in a manner of speaking – I like to work together with the younger generation. I've already been training up young Rachel and I think she'd admit that she's learned huge amounts from me in the few weeks that we've been together."

"Yes, despite that decrepit façade, there's a brain in there that's accumulated a huge amount of real-world experience over decades in the field." Her kind words contrasted with a death-stare, which the others wouldn't see. "Anyway, Maria can work together with me and that'll ensure she gets updates as soon as I do."

Connie seemed to be struggling to find a response, so I jumped in. "Of course, I normally charge for mentoring underlings, but I can accept your support team in lieu of payment. More importantly, you seem to have finished eating. How about desert?"

To my total amazement, the women pounced on the menu, looking for one or two or, maybe, three options that they could share. Having still a couple of slices of pizza and almost half a bottle of

371

wine to finish, I left them to it while I went off for my usual hourly pee.

By the time I returned, they were tasting another bottle of wine – apparently suggested by the waiter based on their selected deserts. *How do they do it? I've eaten a fraction of what they have, but they're slim and trim while I'm distinctly podgy. Fine, Marie is buxom and maybe tending towards steatopygous, but she has a very slim waist and radiates fitness. Must be lesbian sex, keeps you trim no matter what you eat or drink! If I have the luck to be reincarnated as a woman, I'll have to remember that!*

***

After the meal, which Connie insisted on paying for, the agents resisted Rachel's suggestions about going back to her bed for round three. Thus, after linking mobile phones with her, they set off back to town in a taxi. It actually wasn't a long walk but, finally, the two Spaniards seemed to be showing some signs of the huge amounts of alcohol that they had imbibed since they first met Rachel in the bar. I was sure that they'd take drugs to sort that out as soon as they were out of sight, but holding their drink in Rachel's presence seemed to be a matter of honour to them.

I had been slipping rapid alcohol-metaboliser into Rachel's drinks since mid-afternoon and so, although distinctly happy, she was nothing like drunk. Actually, as we walked arm-in-arm back to the flat, I could feel her supporting me on several occasions. *So busy looking after the girl, that I've been careless about myself. Anyhow, she can get me home no problem as long as I can keep my bladder under control. Should have had a last piss before we left the restaurant.*

We just managed to get to the flat, before I shot off to the nearest loo – the one we thought of as Rachel's – and barely managed to unzip my fly before I let rip.

"You better not be dripping all over the place, you dirty old bugger," Rachel shouted after me. From the sounds from the kitchen, she was sorting through bottles in search of the makings of a nightcap.

My loud sigh of relief drowned out whatever else she was saying. *This is going to be tricky, I've got to get her to buy into my plan for the attack on Buck, without telling her exactly what I'm doing. This will not make her a happy bunny.*

By the time I got back to our living room, Rachel had stripped down to a sports bra and panties and was sprawled inelegantly on the sofa, sipping what smelled like Calvados from a huge snifter. "What a fucking day," she sighed. "You'll never guess who I saw before I had the luck to get picked up by the randy secret-agents…"

"Ah, that'll be your mum." I smiled when she choked on her drink.

"How the fuck could you possibly… Shit, that'll be because you were spying on me."

"Just looking out for you, in my usual, over-protective manner. It's important to pick up whoever is taking an interest in us. Unlike your

373

kinky couple in Tokyo, in this case the women were actually targeting you. Knowing who they are lets us make best use of them while they think that they're actually monitoring potential attacks and generally keeping us out of mischief."

"So that means that you spotted Miriam by luck, does it?"

"Of course not. Because you were in town alone, I was keeping an eye on you in real time. When I saw your look of surprise, I went through the output of the expert system that monitors anyone coming off or boarding Buck's yacht any time it's docked in Hvar. That's when I spotted that it was actually Miriam. Honestly, given what she was wearing, I'm not sure that the AI would have identified her on its own. But when focus was narrowed down to a small time window, it was quite straightforward."

"You don't seem surprised about this. What aren't you telling me this time?"

"We already strongly suspected that Miriam was working with the opposition, so it isn't really very surprising that she's now shacked up with Buck – accommodation-wise, if not in the biblical sense. In fact, this also confirms my suspicion that Denis is now the main figure in this conspiracy, because that's who you'd expect your fucking ambitious mother to be with."

"I suppose that makes sense. But I'm amazed that she's up and about. Even if she was able to survive her injuries, I'd have expected her to still be in intensive care somewhere."

"Her face was certainly messed-up and a chunk of rotor-blade sticking out of your chest is not going to be a trivial injury, but she probably had access to the very best medical care and you know how jammy she is – the devil does, indeed, look after his own."

Rachel frowned. "Do you think this means that the EU team also knows she's here?"

I had already been thinking about this. "I think it's quite unlikely. Miriam was reported to have died in the Banff attack and I'm sure that the US spooks will have generated enough evidence to support this. She was too closely linked to the fucked-up attacks to be allowed to remain alive. Either she would have been snuffed, in which case her body would provide supporting evidence of her death, or she'd be given a new identity and her apparent body removed beyond any possible subsequent investigation."

"She was reported to be cremated and her ashes scattered at sea, as per the wishes in her will."

I grinned. "I hadn't actually checked that as yet, although I suspected that you would."

Rachel shook her head. "As expected, she made no attempt to let me know that she was okay."

I think the fact that the Oederlin hit team went in soft is as about as much as you could expect in terms of a maternal instinct."

"That's soft for a bunch of psycho-loonies. If you hadn't been prepared for the attack, I'd certainly have been seriously injured, if not dead."

"Yes, that's certainly a consideration when planning what we're going to do now."

"You've got the smug look that suggests you've worked out one of your labyrinthine plans."

"Yes, that's the good news."

"And the bad news?"

"I can't tell you what it is."

At first I thought that she was tensing up to attack me, but then she shrugged, had a large gulp of her drink and then sank back with a sigh. "It's Maria and Connie, isn't it? You want to ensure that I don't leak anything to them."

"Clever lass. You're now getting the hang of playing both sides against the middle. As you remember from Japan, if anything ultraviolent happens in our vicinity, you can be sure that we'll immediately come under suspicion. We thus need an airtight alibi for our next hit – which will really rock a lot of boats, in more senses than one. What better than you being shagged mindless by one – or both – of our guardian agents and me being next door when the deed is done."

"Basically sounds doable," she frowned, "but that requires getting in another trigger man – or trigger gal – which will increase the risk of leaks."

"Exactly. This means that we've got to move very slowly and carefully – although we do need to take Denis down before he can set up his *death* and vanish immediately thereafter. In this regard, did you manage to get a hold of anything personal of Miriam's?"

"I've got a friend who has a key to my apartment in DC. She'll go in and pick up a makeup bag that my mum left at my place in case she ever had to stay over."

"And how do you plan to get it to us?"

"I thought about her FedExing it to a post box in Split."

"You've got the right idea, but it would be better for her to send it to the UK embassy in Bern. I'll send you address details. They owe me big time and I'm sure that they will DB it to me care of the Consulate in Split."

"DB? What's that?"

"Sorry, diplomatic bag. I can organise to get the package transferred without any official record of it existing. I'll need to call in a few favours to ensure that it isn't opened or interfered with in any way. I'll also need to pick it up in person, but it shouldn't cause any suspicions as I can combine this with a briefing of their security team on our latest findings."

"Jesus, Jim, you never do anything simply if there is a vastly more complex option available."

"Good tradecraft," I smiled. "So we know what we need to do now, do we?"

"Keep monitoring Denis and his retinue so that we can build a better picture of their comings and goings. Even if not all details, I guess I can let my chicas know that we're doing this."

"Certainly, it's an ideal topic for pillow-talk. Because you also need to build up a regular routine of afternoon sweaty sex with *les girls*."

Rachel put her wrist to her forehead and sighed in a theatrical manner. "The things I am forced to do so that we save the world from nuclear catastrophe. Me doing all the heavy lifting while you play on your laptop."

"Well, if you need a hand, I'd be happy to take care of young Connie for an hour or two."

"Don't be daft, you nearly had a heart attack the last time you attempted to shag a real woman. Stick to grandpa porn and then maybe you'll last long enough to actually implement your cunning plan."

Very sadly, she did have a point there.

Chapter 40: Rachel

I've had some strange relationships in my time, but that with Maria really takes the biscuit. On the physical side, it's just about perfect, as we both like regular sweaty sex and enjoy experimenting that takes us a bit beyond vanilla lesbianism, especially during Connie's occasional visits. But shagging an anti-terrorist agent when I know Jim is next door setting up assassinations is downright weird.

It was now just over a fortnight since our first encounter and we were getting comfortable with each other – despite our relationship developing in close proximity to my pseudo-uncle, as I increasingly thought of him. Typically, he was the perfect gentleman whenever Maria was with me, although occasionally forgetting to dress before serving us post-coital drinks and snacks. I tried to convince my girlfriend that this was perverse, disgusting and totally offensive to the eye. However, she though it was *quaint*.

I now accepted that he needed to keep me in the dark in terms of his plans. He had already proven how easily he could read me and we had to assume that the agents would be at least as good in this regard. Indeed, this was a cornerstone of his plan. I could tell my chicas that I knew nothing about any planned attack on Buck and Co and they would be able to tell that this was the truth. They would certainly have profiles on both of us and might even have been able to winkle some background about our apparent role in Japan from

379

the Brits. This had never been brought up explicitly, but I did not try to hide my intense dislike of the ex-Veep and the fact that I considered her assassination a very positive development. The picture was thus established: I was the dangerous sniper, which seemed to get Maria's juices flowing, while Jim was the eccentric boffin in the background – weird, but fundamentally harmless.

I was actually thinking though this after an energetic mid-afternoon shag, stroking Maria's thick hair and enjoying the feel of her sweaty body lying against mine, when Jim burst into the room. "Denis's fucking boat has been hit. From the size of the explosion, I'm guessing maybe a cruise missile. I know that the Yanks wanted him out of the picture, but this seems a bit extreme, even for them."

Shit, have we been pipped at the post here? Suddenly, I realised the inconsistency here. "Was Buck on board? He's never left the villa until now."

"Not a Scooby. But I guess someone thought so."

Maria stumbled and almost fell as she scrambled in search of her clothes, which were scattered about the room. "Fuck, I need to get back to the office. Connie will be going ballistic."

"I wonder if she's heard yet," I started, just as Maria's mobile rang.

"I imagine she has now," Jim smiled at me, making my hackles rise. *The bastard knows more than he's letting on."*

It was clear that shit had hit the fan in Connie's office. We could hear only one part of the conversation, but Maria reported that Jim had known about the attack as quickly as Connie, and that he was suggesting a possible US cruise missile.

"Or a drone," he contributed. "Actually, the more I think about it, a drone is more likely as it has less of a signature to be picked up by satellites. It could be launched over the horizon from the target – either a sea-skimmer or smart torpedo. Your chances of picking it up would be negligible in either case."

Maria relayed this information back to headquarters, something I found incongruous when looking at her naked body, still glowing from the effects of an intensive, drawn-out orgasm. She listed for a while, then turned to Jim. "Is that it? Are those the only options?"

I was now aware that I was beginning to be able to read him to some extent. This was the question that he had been waiting for. "Well," he rubbed his chin to emphasise how deeply he was thinking about it, "the missile and drone options are those that would be selected if you had access to military resources, but I would imagine that the US must finally be getting cautious about any action that could be seen as them carrying out an attack on EU territory. If they had a good enough assassin, like the case in Japan, I suppose they could go for a shoulder-launched missile or a drone set off from land. The attack was just north of the island of Vis, so this probably isn't such a smart option, as you'd almost certainly be able to pick up the terrorist on satellite images."

Maria had her phone in one hand as she struggled to pull a very small pair of panties over her sweaty thighs. I went to help, which also allowed me to hear more of the other side of the conversation. It seemed that protecting us was no longer a priority, so the helicopter held in Split was being ordered to drop a squad to initiate ground searches and then carry out low-level sweeps over northern Vis. Despite Jim's caveats, the lone attacker scenario seemed to have been seized on by Connie.

By the time that Maria finished her call, I had managed to help her into her bra, blouse and shorts, forcing myself to resist the temptation to grope her while I was doing so. She then kissed me quickly, pulling back as I tried to force my tongue into her mouth, and then turned to leave. "I'm sorry, mi amada, but I've got to go. I'll get back as soon as possible, but it may be a few days. There's probably a killer on the loose and we can't guarantee your protection under the present conditions, so please be very careful. Both of you." She blew a kiss to me and then rushed out the door. I guessed a car would pick her up before she got to the end of our road.

"Wow, Jim, you really have been a busy little beaver. I assume that you can now let me know what kind of badness you've been up to."

"Maybe you should dress – or, at least, drag on some underwear. Despite your exertions of this afternoon, you're probably going to be very wet when you find out just how bad."

***

As Jim hadn't yet performed his usual butler service, I grabbed a glass and a bottle of local white

382

wine from the fridge before I settled down on the settee in the living room. I had ignored his recommendation about clothes, but he picked up a t-shirt and threw it to me. "I've already crossed a few self-imposed boundaries and don't need to be tempted to get into further mischief." He smiled while taking the bottle from me and attempted to take off the screw cap while I pulled on a small vest that actually concealed very little.

After he struggled for a bit, I retrieved the bottle and easily broke the seal. "Stop faffing about and tell me what you've been up to." I filled my glass and handed him back the bottle. To my surprise, instead of getting a glass or going for a beer, he took a large mouthful of wine directly from the bottle. *Very unusual. He must be in urgent need of some Dutch courage.*

"Well, as I said, Denis's yacht has been wiped out by a massive explosion."

"Come on, Jim, stop pussy-footing about. You blew the boat to fuck."

"Yes, I did. It was a tele-operated missile-launcher that I controlled from my laptop here. Today was the first time that I could be fairly sure that my attack would achieve all its goals, so I just went for it."

I immediately remembered Jim's analysis of the assassin option. "Wasn't that a bit risky. Whenever you set up the weapon, you had a high risk of being caught by satellite survcillance. There's almost no ground cover on that bloody island."

"Yes, I worked through my dark web contacts to ensure that there was no way I could be linked to purchase of the missile system, but I couldn't trust anyone else with setting it up."

"Okay, let me try to get my head around this." I frowned as I thought over the last few days. "After you picked up Miriam's stuff in Split, you've been to Vis only once, about a week ago. This was so that you could do your scary naturist sunbathing stuff without disturbing anyone with a sensitive stomach. You were dropped off in a little cove that's accessible only be sea and rarely visited this late in the season." I quickly looked at the map of Vis showing the attack location that was still displayed on Jim's monitor. "I suppose you could have climbed out and it wouldn't have been far from where you needed to set up, but there's still the risks of being picked up by satellites. Actually, thinking about it, that isn't possible because you contacted me after you were dropped off and gave me a link to a local webcam. I checked and could see you making the call – with your horrible dangly bits in full view. Maria was most amused."

"Exactly! And maybe you even looked in on me later in the afternoon?"

"We might have had a glance or two, just to check you were okay. Maria's idea that was," I hastened to add.

"Excellent, so all went to plan." The smug look on his face was just asking for a slap.

"So, how did you get the attack set up, you annoying bugger?"

"Easy! I snorkelled along the coast and set everything up in one of the large caves that are found all along that coast. These are just the job, often containing large, flat slabs of rock that are well above high tides and completely invisible from the air. It was a bit of a struggle swimming with all the kit and dragging everything into place, I must confess. However, the return swim was very easy."

"But you were in view of the webcam..." I suddenly remembered Oederlin. "So you must have hacked it so that you appeared to be present the entire time."

"That's it. The place I appeared to be lying was under some trees, so my absence won't be spotted when someone eventually has a check on this. You would have seen from the webcam that I have had two short swims, returning to my sun-bathing area each time. The first was when I originally entered the water, when I was sure that no satellites were overhead, and the second when I returned – when I again knew that I couldn't be picked up. So it's clear from the webcam images, which are automatically backed up by the local police, that there's no way that I could be involved. What do you think?"

I was still frowning. "I don't know. It seems a bit overly complex. Wouldn't it have been easier to have someone else put the weapon into place for you?"

"Too risky, especially as it needed to be set up in a very special way."

"So there's even more to this Machiavellian plot?"

"Indeed. Because, as you noted, my carefully constructed alibi might not hold up if anyone looked at it very carefully. For example using top-end forensic analysis of the webcam video. So I need a diversion that ensures that all analysis goes in a completely different direction."

I thought this through while Jim waited expectantly. "The stuff from my mum. You've set it up so that she appears to have carried out the attack!"

"Yes, that's the key here. It's actually also why I had to be the one to press the trigger."

This seemed like a non-sequitur, but then pieces seemed to fall together. "You were not only setting her up to take the fall, but she was also on the yacht. You think I wouldn't have been able to take the shot if I knew Miriam was in the firing line."

"You probably could have, love, but it's even trickier than that. I wasn't aiming at the boat, your mum was the primary target."

"Why? I know you fucking hate her. Shit, I fucking hate her. But was she so much worse than anyone else on that ship?"

"I can't judge who's better or worse than anybody else, but my aim was to vaporise her. This was essential to sow confusion about who the shooter was. The missile was set up to detonate on soft impact and it hit her between the shoulder blades while she was drinking on the upper sun-deck. So far there's no indication of anyone surviving, which is how it was planned. The yacht was fragmented and sunk immediately in deep water. They'll undoubtedly try to recover what they can, but there will be little, if any, evidence that your mother was on board. There will be some satellite images, but remember how wrapped-up your mother was because of the damage to her face. I'm fairly confident that there'll be nothing that's unambiguous. Certainly nothing as clear as the evidence linking her to the attack weapon."

"I think we need to back up a bit," I wiped my face with my hands as I struggled to imagine the impact of a high-yield warhead on Buck's huge yacht. "You can be sure that Miriam is dead, but even a large explosion couldn't be assured to kill everyone on board. Anyone who was below decks, far from where my mother was, would have a chance of surviving. And any survivor could then confirm that she was actually on board."

"Yes, that's why my second missile hit the hydrogen tank. These eco-yachts avoid fossil fuels and are very safe because, even under accident conditions, the hydrogen storage units are amazingly robust."

I grinned, again seeing more pieces fall into place. "But not robust enough to withstand a direct missile impact."

"Yes, the resulting explosion is very spectacular. That why, based on the explosion alone, something with the yield of a thermobaric cruise missile is an obvious interpretation. Following more detailed analysis of satellite images, however, this will change to missiles fired from the island."

"Wow, you weren't pissing-about here. That's worthy of my evil mother. I thought that you were the one who avoided collateral damage."

Jim's face dropped and I almost felt sorry for him. "I can assure you that I thought long and hard about that and came very close to just dropping this option on several occasions. Apart from the crew of twelve, who probably had no idea what Denis was up to, there were four security guards. It's not clear if they knew anything or not but, in terms of their chosen profession, I can't say that I care a lot. But there was also Denis's wife, daughter, son and baby granddaughter. I can't imagine that the adults were completely blameless, but murdering a baby, for any reason, makes me sick to my stomach." He lifted the wine bottle and gulped down another huge mouthful.

"Shit, sorry man, but you know what they say about omelettes and eggs." From his glare, this was clearly the wrong approach. "I know you don't like it, but something like this was inevitable. It would be either you pulling the trigger, or me, or someone that you pay to do the job for you. An atrocity like this is the only way to break the plutocrats behind this conspiracy. They think they're above the law and that, due to their wealth, they and their nearest and dearest are sheltered from the consequences of anything that they do. Now, finally, they know that this isn't the case and they'll be running for cover, with little interest in anything but protecting their own hides."

Jim shivered and took another swig from the bottle. "I'm not so befuddled with age that I don't know that. I also realise that I'm being a hypocrite: I've already sent you to carry out an assassination that I hadn't the guts for."

"Or the ability," I reminded him. "Anyway, we've only done what was necessary to protect a vastly larger number of people, the murder of whom would not cause a single sleepless night to a cunt like Buck. Finally, he's seeing things from the other side, suffering from the deaths of members of his family. But you don't think this will cause him to repent, do you? He's just going to go to ground until he has the chance for revenge against anyone who dared fuck with him."

"Yes, lass, you're completely correct. I guess this sentimentality must be one of the signs of my slow slip towards dementia. Anyway, your chicas will leave you alone for the next few days, so we need to nail down the next stage."

"Which is?"

"Assassinating Denis of course. But you're the lead on this – I'll just provide the logistical support that you need.

***

That evening as I lay in bed, my mind was buzzing with thoughts of the upcoming action. I had been sorry to miss out on the attack on the yacht, but I could understand why Jim played things as he did. Even now, I was uncertain whether I could pull the trigger with my mother in the crosshairs. Buck, however, was going to be a pleasure. My fingers automatically slipped into the warm wetness between my thighs. *Just as well Jim's being careful, I could even fuck him in my present mood.* I smiled and reached into the drawer of my bedside cabinet. *Girls are lovely but, at the present moment, I need something long and hard – and I want it now.*

Chapter 41: Jim

Although Denis had greatly improved his cyber-security, the chaos following the destruction of his yacht and the assassination of most of his immediate family allowed my hackers to incorporate a virus within one of the host of messages of sympathy that he was receiving from the great and the good. Although I had no access to the dedicated personal server that contained his most sensitive documents, I could now read everything on the laptop used by his personal assistant, Alice, who also turned out to be his niece. *Very typical of the nepotism within these plutocratic dynasties.*

It was never explicitly mentioned, but AI interpretation of her email correspondence made it clear that Buck was moving his simulated demise forward, presumable as a heart attack would be quite understandable given the pressure that he was now under. *Also certainly playing on inevitable sympathy that will now restrict looking into his death in too much detail.*

I had a draft of his updated will which, as expected, specified cremation and dispersal of his ashes from the beach of his estate. It had also been modified, following the death of his wife and children, to make a cousin in Australia the heir to most of his estate. Even without my dark-web team, I was able to trace this woman, Violet Buck, despite her minimal electronic footprint. She was actually the step-sister of the Veep, a daughter of the brother of Denis's father from his second marriage. Like her sister, she also owned a company in the sustainable energy sector, with a focus on the antipodes and Far-East markets. One interesting piece of recent news was that, after two decades of a monogamous relationship with her wife, Violet was reported to be bringing in a husband to form a polyamorous group marriage, as recently allowed by Australian law. It was extremely difficult to find any information about man involved, a reclusive billionaire from the British Virgin Islands, so I set my hackers loose on him.

The obvious interpretation here is that this secretive BVI plutocrat is actually Denis's new identity. *It's not unknown for those involved in shady dealings to have some kind of backdoor escape route in case this is ever needed. Of course, if you know your way around, these can also be provided as a service in the dark web – but this is never completely secure. As the BVI is notorious for tax evasion, I bet Denis kills two birds with one stone here – having a nice, little tax-free nest-egg decoupled from his known fortune in the USA.*

Although Buck's assistant's laptop did not have all details, it was clear that Denis still had good links to someone highly placed in one of the US intelligence agencies – or, possibly, a politician who was briefed by them. He was thus quickly informed when the cave where the attack was carried out was found and, later, when evidence came to light suggesting that Miriam was somehow associated with this. By a stroke of luck, Denis received the latter news when he was meeting with Alice and within range of the laptop's microphone.

Initially, both Denis and Alice were very sceptical about this analysis, as Miriam had been living with them for several weeks and they knew that she was actually aboard the yacht. It was only when Alice observed that this was now the second time that Miriam had been *killed* that Denis became unsure. I watched with great amusement as Alice checked logs of comings and goings on the estate and spotted that Miriam often went off for a "sail along the coast" with one or two others. It was an open secret that this was a superficial cover that allowed her to indulge her passion for al-fresco sex, which had drawn in several of the house guests, his son and a couple of the security guards.

It's amazing how little is required to create a story that explains some coincidences. Miriam and also several of her fuck-buddies disappeared when the cruiser went down. Combine this with circumstantial evidence that Miriam had something to do with setting up the attack and the question became not whether she was actually involved, but if she had somehow managed to escape the attack or if she had been literally hoist by her own petard.

I updated Rachel on developments and had her check in with Maria to see how things were going with the EU investigations. After some uncomfortable circumlocution, Maria finally admitted that there were some indications that Miriam could be involved in the attack. "I know she was reported dead, but there are some traces that indicate she could have been in contact with the weapon that was used," she added.

Rachel did a good job of veering off the topic, as if it was painful for her. She then finished by asking when Maria might be able to visit.

It was clear that Maria really wanted to be with her friend, but evidently that this was extremely tricky, given this latest information. "With a bit of luck it might be cleared up soon, as we've now got Yanks crawling all over us and they're pushing the line that we're the victim of a focused disinformation campaign. As Buck has refused to meet with them, they are insisting that we get a warrant to search his property. Given that all evidence suggests that, despite anything else he may have done, Buck is the victim here, Connie's doing everything possible to block them. This has already caused a media frenzy and we really don't need to add fuel to the flames."

Rachel looked at me and shrugged. "Okay, love, it'll be great to see you whenever you can get free, but I completely understand your position and realise that it'll be a while. So, back to self-abuse for a bit," she sighed. "We'll keep a low profile, but I'm going stir crazy in this small apartment. I talked Jim into renting a little motor-boat, so I we'll cruise around the islands for a bit and maybe along the coast of the mainland towards Dubrovnik."

"That's a good idea and I really wish I was going with you. This office is a madhouse at present and I can see Connie is having yet another fight with the bloody Yanks, so I'd better go now." She and Rachel exchanged video kisses and closed the link.

"Excellent," I smiled. "Now we need to work on the story you spun to Maria in order to build ourselves clear alibis. I can do that while list up the additional kit that you'll need for the hit."

Rachel gave me her feral, assassin grin. "I take it that you're thinking of doing the shooting from a boat."

"That I am. I'll try to get something reasonable large, but it'll be tiny compared to Denis's ship. It's also likely that the hit will take place sometime during the night."

"Okay, so I need a gyroscopic stabiliser and night sights. That should be no problem given the contacts that you have."

"Just let me have the specs and you'll have the kit within a couple of days. I'll need to get some of the local bad-boys to steal me a small cruiser – something with an absent owner, so that it won't be missed for a while. I can have it moored in one of the uninhabited coves hereabouts when we're ready to use it. I'll also need some charges so that we can scuttle it after the job. Also a couple of isolation suits so that we minimise any traces that are left on board."

"So that means that we're doing this together?" Rachel was visibly sceptical about the idea.

"Yes, I'm afraid so. We won't be able to anchor, so you need someone steering the boat while you make the shot."

She shrugged and her grin widened. "Of course, on an operation like this, I'm the lead, so you need to do what I tell you."

"I guess I can live with that," I smiled. "You're in charge as soon as we get on site. Of course, at other times, I'm the captain of the boat."

"Well, that'd work for me. But remember, I make the final decision on the hit and, if I don't like it, we abort and try again some other time."

"I wouldn't have it any other way. Despite my great age, I'm not ready to be a martyr for the cause. But bear in mind that, if we miss this chance, our next opportunity is likely to be in Australia."

"That's definitely an incentive. I hate fucking Oz. Not only has the place a fucking awful climate and is fully of deadly creepy-crawlies, but it's also infested with macho, beach-bum Ozzies."

I smiled. *Nothing I'm going to disagree about there.*

***

A week later, Denis's health was reported to be deteriorating rapidly and Alice set up a private jet which was supposed to bring his cousin out for a last visit. As I expected, Violet would appear to be accompanied by her wife and husband. In addition, her retinue included two assistants and a couple of security guards. As I followed the logistics of setting up this visit, I tailored our attack plan appropriately.

The first complication was that, after landing in Split, two helicopters would be used to ferry the

396

visitors to and from Buck's villa. In addition, a third chopper with a security team would accompany them. *Well, that buggers up the easiest attack option.* If there had been only one aircraft, the easiest option would be to take it out on their return flight, just after take-off and I had ordered some sabot rounds to do that job. With three targets, the chances of success drop so much that I decided that this option was better discarded. Unfortunately, this meant getting closer to the villa and going for Denis directly. *Certainly a trickier target, but with the advantage of less collateral damage.*

At this point, we were wending our way along the coast of Mljet and I had Rachel set up a chat with Maria so that she could show off the picturesque village of Sobra in the background and report that we were now aiming to arrive in Dubrovnik within a few days. Immediately thereafter, I set course back for Hvar aiming to anchor in quiet harbours during the day and cruise at night. With blackout shades on our running lights, the boat would look normal when viewed from sea level, but would be difficult to spot from a satellite. *There's no way that we can hide from a targeted search, but the main aim is to ensure that nobody will ever think to look for us.*

Violet and party would arrive tomorrow, so my hope was that their stay would be brief. Knowing Denis, I was sure that he would want to disappear as quickly as possible. Trying to imagine being in his shoes, I thought through various timelines, with a focus on when his apparent death would be announced. Although coupling this with his cousins visit could make things easier to hide due to the inevitable chaos that would result, such an option would delay her leaving as she would be expected to stay until the ceremony of scattering his ashes, which would take days to organise. So a flying visit by Violet and then his death announced around the time she gets back to Perth. A deathbed video telling her not to bother coming back would then appear to link well with the subsequent announcement of his death.

The more I thought through this, the more I was convinced that this was exactly how it would play out. The problem was, based on all my history with him, this was just too slick for Denis. It now couldn't be Miriam's involvement, so again I was left with the uncomfortable feeling that I was missing something. *Fuck it! Paranoia is a good thing, but I'm now jumping at shadows. I need some relaxation, but there's no chance of fitting in a prostitute before we go into action. Fuck!*

Chapter 42: Rachel

Buck's cousin had arrived two days ago and Jim's hackers provided full details of her planned departure tonight, so all was moving ahead smoothly. We transferred over to the stolen cruiser – not very large, but significantly bigger than the small motor-launch that we had been living on for the last fortnight. It did have primitive stabilisers, but I was definitely going to need the gyroscopic rifle mount to cope with the choppy sea. The good news was that clouds obscured the moon, but the bad was that squally showers were forecast.

Three hours before Violet's pick-up was planned, the time set for a period during the night when no military spy-satellites covered the target area, we cast off. The boat was almost completely automated, so Jim was easily able to handle the controls while I set up the gun and its support kit on a canvas-roofed sun-deck. We were sailing without running lights, but bottom-mapping sonar combined with occasional radar pings ensured that this presented no risks. Jim kept our speed down and, as we neared our target with half an hour to go, switched to a small electric docking motor that reduced us to crawling speed but was effectively silent.

By now the rain was a continuous downpour, but the island sheltered us from the wind. Our isolation suits included face masks with inbuilt coms, so I could hear Jim counting down the distance to our target. With the high-end optics built into the gun, I could clearly see the three helicopters, but visibility was not good enough for the shots that I needed to make. "No option, Jim, but we've got to get a targeting drone in there. I know that it greatly increases the chances of being spotted, but I've no chance of hitting anyone without it."

"I guessed that would be the case, so the drone is already set up. I'll just get it in the air now."

I heard only the slightest hum, hardly detectable over the sounds of wind and rain, and an indication of a shadow that instantly vanished into the murk. "That's impressive, I hardly saw it go, even though it was only metres away."

"Yes, lass, that's the best stealthing you can get on the black market: top-end military-spec, made in Israel. It's a skimmer, so only about a metre above the waves. I would expect Denis to have defences facing the sea, but these will be partially blocked by the helicopters."

I grinned into the rain. "Actually, the weather could be on our side. It'll make the shots tricky for me but, if I was Buck's security guy, I'd have a couple of counter-snipers set up high on the cliff. A targeting drone is no good to them until they're under attack and know roughly where to direct it."

"But they'll certainly have radar, so it might not be as simple as that. I've removed the radar reflectors that were mounted on this boat and have some very basic EM stealthing, but I imagine that we'll be picked up at some point."

"I depends on how extensive their radar coverage is. I would guess that it's more a back-up, with satellite imagery used to provide preliminary risk assessment. To avoid anyone else analysing images of the party leaving, we're now in a window when they've lost that option."

"It'll depend if they managed to track us at any point since we set off from Hvar. Anyway, lass, we're just about to find out how good they are. A group has just left the villa, heading for the choppers."

I had already spotted this and had the drone linked into my targeting system, providing a clear view behind the helicopters. A couple of guards were making for the furthest away helicopter, leaving Violet's party in full view. They were struggling with umbrellas, which dispersed the group and allowed me to spot Buck and set him up for the first shot.

Suddenly Jim distracted me with a shout. "No, girl, the primary target is the little female beside Denis. Take her out first, then Denis, then whoever gives the easiest shot."

"Fuck, a bit late to change plans," I mumbled while I fixed the small woman indicated in my cross-hairs and immediately fired. I did not even wait to see the result before making the slight correction that gave me a head-shot on Buck. By now guards were throwing themselves towards the rest of the party, but I managed to get in a shot at the cousin and a last one at the fuel tank of the nearest chopper, just before Jim jammed the throttle to full and the cruiser took off. Only now, as I raised my head from the rifle siting screen, could I see the muzzle flashes from the cliff. "Ah, the counter-snipers. It looks like there are two of the buggers. Not much chance of them… Fuck!"

I rolled onto my back, trying to avoid screaming as pain shot through my right arm. *Law of fucking conservation of luck. We got lucky to get the shots off and now some jammy bastard has managed to hit me when he's probably just wildly spraying shots in our general direction.*

I then realised that Jim had abandoned the helm and was now crouching at my side. "How bad is it? There's a lot of blood, but I can't tell if an artery has been hit." He opened a first aid kit and clamped some tissue against the wound on my upper arm, causing me to squeal in agony.

"Fucking hell, what're you doing? First morphine and then you can bugger about with the wound."

The effect of the injected analgesic was almost miraculous. Pain rapidly died away without the spaced-out feeling that I associated with such drugs. As if reading my mind, Jim had a look at the tag tied to the syringe. "Seems to be a battlefield-tested ketamine variant. How is it?"

I could see how worried he was and gave him a weak grin. "Pure, dead brilliant, as they would say in your neck of the woods. Anyway, you can poke about now and see how fucked-up I am."

I watched as if it was happening to someone else. He cut my suit free from elbow to shoulder and swabbed my arm with some kind of antiseptic fluid. A gash was bleeding heavily, but not with the gushing flow of a hit artery. After applying some kind of spray that notable reducing bleeding, he added a gauze pad and a pressure bandage. "Okay, that's as much as I can do for the moment." He pulled over some form of cushion and laid my arm on it. "Just lie there for a bit. I need to get back to check if there's any sign of anyone on our tail."

After getting back to his feet, he proceeded to throw the rifle and the associated targeting kit overboard. "Maybe better getting incriminating evidence out of the way, just in case," he muttered.

"You know that there's going to be my blood on that," I reminded him.

"That's an acceptable risk. Even if they're tracking us now, they won't have any clear images in this weather and the water here is deep enough that the chance of anyone being able to find the gun is negligible." He then struggled to push a partially-deflated raft off the stern, another one of his nutty ideas aimed to muddy the water when the attack was analysed.

Soon afterwards, I dozed off and the next thing I knew he was gently shaking me awake. "How do you feel now, love? We need to get you onto our wee boat and scuttle this thing. I'm afraid that I'm not up to carrying a sonsie lass like yourself, so you'll need to move under your own steam."

I cautiously rolled onto my hands and knees and then, distaining his helping hand, slowly rose to me feet. "The pain in my arm is building up, but I don't think walking will be a problem."

"Fine, but just be careful. It's finally stopped raining, but the deck is wet."

"So what, it's a non-slip surface," I pointed out. "Let me just get transferred as quickly as possible and then you can dose me up with a bit more of that magic painkiller." Despite my bluster, I had difficulty keeping my balance due to irregular swaying of the smaller boat. Nevertheless, I was able to drag myself down into the main cabin using my good arm. I sat on a bench, where a first aid kit was lying with a syringe sitting on top. Using my teeth to remove the protective cap, I injected myself and at sank back with a sigh. Moments later I had dropped off again.

***

It was light when I came to, noting that I was lying on the bench with a blanket thrown over me and a pillow below my head. It was a bit cramped, but I realised that there was no way that the old bugger would have been able to carry me to my bunk in the next cabin. Although my arm was again painful, a more immediate issue was the pressure on my bladder. I managed to scramble my way to the head, but then realised that stripping off the one-piece isolation suit was an impossible task with one arm effectively immobile. I had almost resolved just to piss myself when I remembered the small stiletto strapped to my calf. It was touch and go, but I managed to cut the crotch of the suit clear just in time, plonking down onto the loo with a sigh of pleasure.

I was just finishing when Jim looked in. "Bugger! Sorry, I should've removed the suit earlier."

"Fuck off! Can't I even have a pee in peace?"

"If you wanted privacy, then closing the door might have been an idea. I just wanted to be sure that you're okay."

"At the time, closing the door was low on my list of priorities. I was bursting."

"Ah, due to my old man bladder, a predicament that I know only too well. You had lost a fair bit of blood, so I had you on a drip for a few hours. A full bladder after that isn't so surprising."

"Fine, so what are you still hanging about for? Is this one of your voyeuristic kinks?"

"I'm sure I don't need to remind you that you're the one with the history of golden showers."

I got ready to punch him in the groin. "You're treading on thin ice here."

"Yes, whatever, but I thought you'd want me to help you out of that suit as soon as possible. After you were hit, you did lose bladder control. Not at all unusual, as you well know. But anyway, now that you've finished piddling, I'll get you stripped off and into the shower. As you've already started with the work," he shamelessly looked at my groin, it'll be easier to cut you out of the rest. I've also got a plastic cover that I can wrap around the bandage, so that'll make washing easier."

I grimaced and then stood up. "Righty-ho! Just do what you've got to do. But I'll need some more painkiller first."

Using a pair of surgical scissors, he carefully cut away the suit and also the remnants of the pair of nickers I had been wearing. He then covered the bandage and headed back out to get the analgesic.

405

As it was so commonplace, I had hardly noted that Jim had previously been wearing only one of his tiny posing pouches. When he returned, however, even that minimal piece of clothing was missing. "What are you up to, you pervy old fuck? In my weakened state, the last thing I need is a view of your horrible old willy."

"Well, first I'm going to give you this pill," he handed me a yellow capsule which I immediately dry-swallowed. "The stuff I've been using up until now is acceptable for battlefield conditions, but you need to go onto something weaker now. I'll then help you wash, which is why I'm in the buff. It'll be very much easier for you if you just stand in the shower, legs and arms just a little bit spread, and I'll do the rest."

He was gently moving me into place in the tiny shower and, to my surprise, I found it easier just to go with the flow. *Must be the drugs, as I can't imagine why I'd let him touch my naughty bits otherwise.* I smiled as this term brought back memories of the lads in the hot spring. "So, how did I do? And, come to think of it, why did you change the primary target at the last minute?"

He started washing my hair and then moved on to my shoulders before answering. "Do you really want to have the debriefing now? You should wait for that until you're having breakfast. Although I guess that, by now, this would be brunch."

"Mmm, that's good." His fingers were kneading tension out of my neck muscles. "Just give me the highlights, the details can wait. Firstly, the primary target."

Again a pause while his hands worked lower. "Yes, the primary target. Remember I'd been going on about how Denis's plans seemed both clever and uncharacteristically vicious, in a sloppy kind of way."

"Stick to the point. You're waffling again."

"Yes, well I recognised who was with Denis and a lot of loose ends suddenly fell into place."

Even though he would not be unable to see it, I rolled my eyes. "Just tell me who the fuck it was."

"Anne McCabe. Remember her?"

"Fuck, the name seems strangely familiar." I could not remember details, but the woman seemed to be linked to something that we discussed in Canada. "Was she someone that you though was more likely than Denis, when we were trying to work out who was involved?"

"Exactly. I always thought that she was more the type to be planning large-scale atrocities than Denis. Denis is completely amoral, but he seems to lack a truly evil side. Something McCabe has in spades."

"Wasn't she supposed to be dead?"

"Yes, but remember so was your mother. Both Denis and his cousin, the ex-Veep, have the tendency to stick with a plan if they think it's sound. So it's not really so improbable that he ends up supported by two truly evil women, both of whom have the advantage of being officially deceased." Jim slowly worked lower, now focusing on the muscles in my lower back and buttocks.

"I get it that she could be the mastermind behind the attacks, but surely Denis is higher up the food chain than she is."

"Yes, certainly. Denis has the wealth, political clout and contacts in the military and security services required to support these actions. But, following his losing streak, I suspect he'd move to Oz and lie low for a decade or two if left to his own devices. However, as a result of our actions, McCabe is going to be fucked-off beyond belief and would do anything to restore her standing in the conspiracy. Even if Denis was out of the picture, she'd just find another sponsor and the whole thing would start again – which would also mean both of us as prime targets to ensure that we can't get in her way again."

"Okay, that's one question answered. Now the key one: how did the hits go?"

Again a pause while he moved even lower and started working on my thighs. "Well, as you were hit, I had to focus on first aid and wasn't able to properly check the video records until a couple of hours ago…"

"You're waffling," I growled. "Just answer the fucking question."

"Okay, you hit McCabe just below her throat. I don't know what munition you were using, but it blew her entire bloody head off."

"Sabots with soft-nose flechettes, just in case I also need to go for a chopper," I answered automatically. "What about the others?"

408

"Denis was hit full on the face. His brain exploded out of the back of his head. I think you can take that as another confirmed kill."

"And the cousin, Violet, did I get her?"

"She was already turning away, but you appeared to hit her between the shoulder blades. If not dead, she'll certainly be seriously crippled. The helicopter you hit must have leaked fuel everywhere. All it needed was the security guards blasting away towards the sea and it went up in a spectacular fireball, which also destroyed the second chopper. I don't know what further casualties or damage that caused, but there was certainly no way that the attack could be hidden. Both emergency services and EU agents arrived within a half hour or so and the place had been a total zoo since then."

I turned around just as Jim was about to progress on to washing my arms. My breathing was already deepening when I looked into his eyes. "You know what you fucking need to do now, so get to it."

"Buggeration!" he murmured, "I told you it'd be better to do this after your shower." Nevertheless, with a groan and a distinct creak of his knees, he crouched down to comply.

Chapter 43: Jim

Fuck, fuck, fuck! Fuckity-fuck for fuck's sake, as the girl would say. I told her that it wasn't a good idea, but I'm as much to blame as she is. I knew this would happen. She may have some genetic input from me, but there's 50% from her psychopathic mother and another chunk that came from a totally loony Irish terrorist. *Why she hasn't yet murdered me is a mystery. Anyway, she's now out cold in her bunk, so I've time to work out how the merry fuck we go on from here.*

The good news was that the hit had gone to plan. Rather amazing, especially given the way that I was reworking it in real time. The global threats have been neutralised for the moment and, given how much Denis was a thorn in the side of the big-nobs in the States, there will be huge amounts of pressure to bring an end to this entire fiasco. Given the evidence linking Miriam to the destruction of Buck's cruiser, she'll certainly be a suspect for organising the assassination of Denis and his cousin unless any proof that she was aboard the sunken cruiser emerges. It will help a lot that, given the inevitable confusion, there is little chance that anyone will pay special attention to McCabe being targeted. So my *Conspiracy Theory* site will be able to push her involvement well before anybody on Buck's side thinks to start a cover up. It might be that one supposedly-dead woman in Denis's coterie might be explainable, but two should blow the entire thing even further open.

410

I was painfully aware that our alibi for the assassination was thin, depending a lot on whether efforts to cover our movements over the last couple of days would be sufficient in the event that anyone wanted to look at us as potential culprits. *To reduce the risk, I need to throw someone under a bus.* Or, in plain text, screw someone before anyone else has a chance to screw us.

After a mental debate about which agent would be the best option, I called Connie. "I've just heard about the attack on Denis Buck's villa, so I guess shit is hitting the fan back in Hvar at the present moment."

I was clearly someone she did not have time for. "Jim, nice to hear you stating the obvious. But, as you can imagine, I've absolutely no time for chit-chat."

"Sorry, Connie, but you may want to hear what I've been picking up via a hack on Buck's villa..."

"For fuck's sake, Jim, you know we can't use that, it's..."

"Yeah, yeah, but even if you can't use it directly, it might help your investigations. Buck's assistant, Alice something or other, has been setting up a scam to allow him to appear to die and move his fortune to his Australian cousin. This was the one who was visiting. I don't know why, but she seems to be the source of the information that was needed for this hit to be set up. Maybe with all the specified heirs dead, she'll get something out of it. She's his niece after all."

The silence drew out to the point that it was becoming painful, then Connie gave in. "So, Jim, you had all this information and didn't let us know? I thought we had an agreement."

"Sorry, love, but I had only bits and pieces that were as likely to be nonsense as truth. It was only when I picked up the news about this attack that everything came together. Do with it what you will, but I'm just updating you as I promised. If it was up to me, however, I'd grab the assistant's laptop before she has time to scrub everything sensitive."

"I'm actually at Buck's place at the moment and have seen the girl that you're talking about. She seems completely shell-shocked, but I'll get the laptop anyway. By the way, is Rachel there? Maria would like to talk to her. Not about getting together this time, but more to get her expert opinion on the equipment that the assassin would have needed." I could hear the faintest trace of a smile in her voice.

"Unfortunately, she's not on the boat at present. We needed a couple of days on our own, so she's off doing a bit of hill-walking. Actually, given how much she's been missing Maria, she's probably shacked up in a brothel or a lesbian commune. You've got her link, haven't you?"

"Yes, but if she's chilling out, she might not have heard about the attack yet."

"Probably not. I know that you're up to your eyeballs, so I'll contact her."

"Fine, but, from what you've told me, it might be useful if you could provide support here. How soon can you get back to Hvar?"

"From here, in this rust-bucket, probably about a day or so. There's no autopilot and I'm not the youngest, so there's a limit how long I can sail each day. It'll actually go faster if I pick up Rachel first, then we can spell each other conning the boat."

"Fine, pick her up and get here when you can. It probably isn't time-critical, but sooner would be better than later. "

"Not that I'm refusing, but why do you want an old fart like me anywhere near your crime scene? I can provide my technical input remotely."

"One reason, and one reason only. The fucking Amis are demanding that you're kept well away from the investigation."

"Ah, well, in that case I'll be with you as soon as humanly possible. They can be total cunts."

I dropped the call after a couple of minutes of hearing what complete cunts they were. I then accessed the backdoor to Alice's laptop, seeing that she was already in contact with Denis's lawyer back in DC. Just in case she received instructions to delete everything in the machine's memory, I activated a routine that my hackers had already set up for me. This changed the password and then caused the laptop to switch off. I then mailed Connie to tell her what I had done and gave her the new password. Unless Alice was smart enough to physically destroy the computer, clearing the memory was no longer possible. Just to cause further confusion, I sent a text to her private mobile, which would appear to come from the lawyer. This simply stated that Alice should comply with the police and security agents: the legal team would ensure that nothing sensitive was obtained. I then sent the lawyer a text that would appear to come from Alice, stating that the EU team was now monitoring all communication and that she would not be able to get back in contact until she was allowed to leave the estate.

***

Although it probably was not required, I set course for the harbour at Sabor and docked long enough to have a coffee in a nearby café. This would not stand any close examination, but could be superficially interpreted as me picking up Rachel. It will be tricky explaining her wound when she finally gets together with the agents, but the first priority was getting her looked at by a medic. After swithering for a bit, I prepared a report for the UK intelligence guys. This covered everything that I had provided to Connie even though, if she had made contact herself as I recommended, they would already have most of this material. I finished with a low-key report of another attack on us, with Rachel being nicked before she disposed of our assailant, presumably a freelance bounty-hunter. I thus requested the Split consulate to arrange to have a doctor flown out to meet me at Hvar when I got there. *On balance, a better option than trying to sort out something myself.*

The next job was to produce a notice board entry suggesting McCabe had been seen in Hvar. I ran this through a couple of AIs to ensure the style would suggest a past contributor from Canada. As both the EU and the Brits would be monitoring the site, I would need to go no further. Indeed, as I expected, it was not long before the tinfoil-hat brigade started to find more links between the supposedly-deceased McCabe and Denis's extended family. I smiled at the thought. *Once this snowball has started rolling downhill, there'll be no stopping it. So now the cunts bothering Connie will receive yet another faceful of fan-delivered shit.*

It was now late afternoon and, despite my shades, I was getting blinded by the slowly-sinking sun, which was now full in my face. As I had been following along the coastline, I decided to stop for the night at the town of Orebić. I then contacted the Split consulate to have them divert the doctor to the nearby Hotel Crystal, where I had booked its top-end luxury suite. After tying-up at my allocated slot in the small marina, I decided it was time to wake Rachel. *Can't put off facing the music any longer.*

***

Rachel had managed to throw off the quilt I had covered her with and was now sprawled on her back, with one leg dangling out of the rather narrow bunk. I took a moment to admire her naked body before I gently touched her shoulder. "Time to wake up, lass. You've been sleeping for the best part of sixteen hours, and it's now time to get you off this boat."

She groaned and tried to bring her hands to her face, wincing as she moved her wounded arm. "Fuck! I definitely need more of that pain killer stuff."

"If you can manage without for a wee bit, that'd be better as I've got a doctor lined up and he'll probably be able to provide you with something more appropriate."

"Shit, okay, that's doable. Help me up and we'll see what I'm like when I'm on my feet."

Holding onto my arm with her good hand, she pulled herself up with a grunt and stood upright, swaying slightly.

"You're probably light-headed due to loss of blood. Just take things slowly."

"I'm okay. Just let me steady myself on your shoulder and then we can head for the galley. I'm dry as a bone and beginning to feel more than a little peckish."

After I got her settled down at the dining table, I fetched her a pint glass filled with a mixture of orange juice and sparking water. She downed it in one long swallow. "Another one of those and a coffee, if you don't mind. Actually, I'd prefer Champagne instead of the mineral water, but I don't suppose that's on the cards."

I forced a smile. "Probably not the best idea at present. Nevertheless, after I get you to the hotel and the medic has looked at you, I don't see why a nice dinner with top-end Champagne wouldn't be on the cards." I refilled her glass and started the machine to produce capsule-coffee.

"A hotel: indeed that would be nice. It's definitely a bit cramped on this boat."

I handed over her coffee, set the machine of to produce one for me, and then updated her on what I had been up to over the afternoon. She smiled when I told her the story that I had produced for Connie to explain her unavailability for calls. "A lesbian commune, sounds like exactly what I need at present. If I'd had one of those, I wouldn't have needed you to scratch my itch."

Unfortunately, I was sipping my coffee when she said this, so immediately started choking, to her great amusement. *I just hope that I'm not fucking blushing.* "Look, about that, I'm really sorry. I should have been more careful. I wouldn't want to take advantage of anyone who's in a vulnerable state. Least of all you."

She laughed aloud. "Jim, for fuck's sake, stop babbling. I can't say that I was thinking clearly myself, but I definitely bullied you into giving me the details of the hit and the consequences were inevitable. Of course, you could have left me to masturbate, but that certainly wouldn't have worked out so well. Me, with a bad arm an' all," she added in a reasonable Scottish accent.

"Well, as long as you're not traumatised by the experience."

"Nothing traumatic about it, probably because I couldn't see your horrible old body." She laughed again. "Oh," she suddenly seemed more serious, "you're not beginning to think of me as your daughter, are you? The incest taboo went out the window yonks ago: as long as it doesn't end up with resultant kids, of course."

"Incest, as such, bothers me not a jot. It's the way in which it can involve manipulation of impressionable children that I find completely objectionable."

"So, you think of me as a child, do you?" Now Rachel sounded pissed-off.

"Not at all. It's the aspect of old folk, seniors, taking unfair advantage of their position of power. Teacher-pupil, professor-student, boss-underling, whatever." I squirmed uncomfortable. "I consider myself as your mentor, for some obscure reason. So that means I can bonk lasses even younger than you, if above the age of consent, but…"

"My God, you really are a dopy old fucker," she interrupted, her smile reappearing. "You may not be as daft as I originally thought that you were, but if you think doing as I commanded was you manipulating me, you're slipping into Alzheimer's faster than I expected. Nevertheless, it's not a bad thing, as it shows that, at the very least, you're finally learning to do as you're told. Before long, though, most of the instructions will be reminders to put your trousers on, zip up your fly and go to the toilet before leaving the house."

Jesus, that went better than expected. "Ah, you're a hard woman, making fun of my honourable nature and increasing frailty. Anyway, do you think you can walk to the hotel or should I sort out a taxi? I reckon it's only about 400 metres."

"Actually, I'm so stiff that I'm sure that the walk would do me good. But I need a piss first." She elbowed me playfully, but painfully, in the ribs. "Do you want to watch again?"

"I wasn't…" I started before she started laughing and I realised that she was winding me up. "Okay, I'd love to watch but, instead, I'm going to get you some clothes. You may have forgotten, but you're still in your birthday suit."

418

"So I am and, for a complete change, you're fully clothed. That's a turn up for the books."

"Well, from the grief that you're giving me, I'd say that you've recovered faster than I expected," I conceded. "Although I think I preferred when you were comatose," I added sotto voce, but loud enough that I was sure that she heard me. However she refused to rise to the bait.

***

The doctor arrived at the hotel about an hour after we checked in, so the Consulate must have pulled out all the stops to set this up. Although he said very little when he arrived, his tattoos indicated that he was military and I guessed SAS. "Large calibre: lucky that it didn't hit the bone or take out more muscle", he muttered after he carefully removed the bandage on Rachel's arm. "What were you using for an analgesic?"

I told him and he grimaced. "I'd use that for a serious injury in a combat situation, but it's a bit over the top for this little scrape."

Rachel looked like she was going to hit him. "I can tell you that this hurt like fucking hell and bled like a bastard."

I put a hand on her shoulder to try to calm her down. "Yes, well it was a...., well a rather critical situation and I've got nothing other than basic first aid training."

The medic seemed to be mollified. "Okay, I suppose that, under those circumstances, better to be safe than sorry. As long as you can live with it, I'd

419

stay away from opioids and go for something mild like paracetamol or ibuprofen. Now, for the wound itself, there are two options…"

"Which will get me back in action faster?" Rachel interrupted.

The doc grinned. "How did I know you were going to say that? *Semper fi* and all that shit."

"That's the fucking marines," Rachel growled. "So let's get on with *who dares wins* and all that shit."

Rachel had come to the same conclusion as me with regard to the doctor's background and his widening grin seemed to support that.

"Okay, tough girl. If you were sensible, you'd let me pack the wound and take you with me in the chopper. Back in hospital with proper kit, a plastic surgeon could do proper repair work. For fast, I can just staple this up and cover it with synth-skin and a pressure cover. You'll have a hellish-looking scar, but you could get back in the field immediately, as long as you avoid stressing your upper arm. Avoid anything that needs a lot of biceps or triceps, but pulling a trigger should be fine."

"The girl will go for the fast option," I got in quickly. "She's not the pulling triggers sort, but as long as she can type, that'll be fine."

Rachel and the medic looked into each other's eyes and smiled. "Aye, right, a typist," the doc muttered and got to work.

Fuck, I hope this guy gets his job done quickly. From the hungry way she's looking at him, she's ready to jump his bones at any moment.

The SAS guy was indeed fast, but also extremely neat and I thought that, given what the original wound had looked like, the scar might not be too bad. After he left, we had a room-service steak dinner with all the trimmings, accompanied by a bottle of Veuve Clicquot Grande Dame and the most expensive Bordeaux on their rather limited wine list. Thereafter, feeling well stuffed, we stripped-off and carried glasses of cognac from the mini bar to the private Jacuzzi on the terrace, which I had already filled with water that was as hot as I could handle.

After I had carefully clambered into the tub, I helped Rachel – making sure that her injured arm was kept well clear of the water. I noticed her rolling her eyes and silently acknowledged that she was probably less likely to stumble while entering the bath than I was.

After getting ourselves comfortable, with her head against my shoulder, Rachel turned so that she could look directly into my eyes. "Well then, Jim, is that it now? We've wiped out all the bad guys, so we can just go back to our normal lives."

Bearing in mind what happened the last time, I need to keep well away from any discussion of murder and mayhem. "Um, I suppose that any immediate threats have been removed. Both threats to nuclear facilities and to ourselves. There are, however, a few loose ends that I'd like to clear up."

She turned away and leaned back against my shoulder. "So, who else do I need to kill?"

"Oh, no more killing," I responded hurriedly. "The main problem is the wealth that will, somehow or other, be inherited by other members of Denis's plutocratic dynasty. As long as their main source of further wealth – non-nuclear power generation – is under threat, there's always a possibility of one of the heirs deciding to take a page from Denis's playbook. Either an heir or, I suppose, some other member of the original conspiracy group. I'd prefer to kill that option before birth."

"Well, we could just assassinate the lot of them. A hitlist of plutocrats, that's a cool collective noun! It would definitely make the world a better place."

"I can't argue against that conclusion, but it'd be really difficult to do. There's lots of them and they're scattered all over the world. Better to hit them where it really hurts."

"Grandchildren," she suggested hopefully. There's fewer of them and it would really gut even such powerful families."

"Somehow, I doubt that. It's a Sisyphus task anyway. Even if you take them all out, they can then just produce more."

"Okay, wise one, what would you do?"

"Hit them where they will really feel it – in the wallet. Have their entire wealth confiscated. Beggar them and have them thrown out of their grand villas, estates and townhouses. That would do it."

Rachel was silent for several minutes while she thought through this idea. "That's fine in theory, but it just wouldn't work in the US. Just think about OxyContin. There was good evidence of the Sackler

422

Family's responsible for more American deaths than the Korean and Vietnamese wars together, but the billionaire dynasty could effectively block full legal retribution and not a single one of the key actors known to be responsible was prosecuted. So, you see, Buck's empire is simply too big to be punished by the law."

"Yes, you're a clever lass. The theory is indeed good. But, as it was put by the immortal sage Yogi Berra: 'in theory there's no difference between theory and practice, in practice there is!'" I was rewarded by a snigger from Rachel as she thought through this aphorism. "The thing to bear in mind is that there is one big difference between greedy pharmaceutical companies and what Denis and Co have been up to. OxyContin predominantly killed people in the US, due to the ineffectiveness of the agencies that were supposed to protect the public from such abuse. There are so many ways to move blame in this case that, with sufficient legal power, justice will never be served. Denis was, however, supporting terrorist attacks on foreign countries. That's an entirely different kettle of fish and could, if played correctly, completely bypass the non-functional US legal system."

Rachel sounded impressed. "Right, you old fart, I'd give you a score of ten out of ten for hubris. But how exactly are you going to do that?"

I turned my head and kissed her on the forehead. "That, my love, is an exercise left for the student."

423

Chapter 44: Rachel

Jesus suffering Christ on a bike! That old fucker is doing my bloody head in!

Despite pleading, threats and a number of bites to his shoulder that must have been very painful, I could not get anything else out of him on his latest cunning plan.

I must admit that, after fifteen minutes in the hot tub, my eyes were getting heavy, so I probably was not at my best last night. But even now, enjoying a long-lie while Jim was sorting out breakfast for me, I could see absolutely no way around the inherent inequity of the US legal system. This being especially difficult in this case as, at both national and state level, odds were always stacked in favour of the mega-rich and politically powerful.

Before attempting to squeeze more information out of my unbelievably annoying colleague over breakfast, I performed my morning ablutions and pulled on the robe that was provided by the hotel. Jim was sitting at a table set up on the terrace and finished pouring a Buck's Fizz for me when he saw me emerge.

"A cheery good morning to you, my love. Look at this gorgeous, sunny, autumnal setting. Doesn't it make you feel better, just looking at the view?"

I had to concede that the view over the sparkling Adriatic was spectacular, but I deliberately put on a grumpy face. "Are you ready to tell me your plan yet?" I leant forward to give him a good view of my tits, which were on the edge of falling out of my robe. *His entire body may have the testosterone content of a very small dormouse, but a glance of nipple will be enough to distract him. If I was completely nude, this wouldn't work for some strange reason. Men!"*

He blinked, clearly trying to focus on the question. "Nope, that's not how it works but, if all goes well, you'll have worked it out before breakfast is over."

"You know, I really hate you." I pulled the robe closed around my chest, but moved my thighs apart so that it opened below my waist. The table was glass-topped, so he wouldn't be able to miss this. "I've already thought through what you said last night and there's no possible way of subverting the entire US legal system. It's just impossible. It's actually set up to be that way."

Again a pause as he dragged his attention away from my groin. "Is it really? I'll give you a hint – think of the most fucked-up President in the entire history of the USA."

"Trump? What's he to do with anything? He's been dead for years." I drained my glass and passed it to Jim for a refill. As if I was unaware of what I was doing, I scratched the landing-strip tailored-pubes above my shaven *naughty bits*. I quashed my tendency to smirk whenever I thought of that term.

"Mmm, yes, well maybe not so much the actual person…" He glanced down and then forced his eyes back up to my face."

All of a sudden, I saw what the twisted old bastard was getting at. "The President! An executive order can cut through all the red tape that's specifically designed to stop unpopular legal cases moving. You're going to put the screws on the President of the US of A! You're off your bloody head."

"Of course that wouldn't work. That's why you're going to be the one putting the screws on him. Come on, you've already assassinated the Vice-president, so how hard can that be?"

***

To my everlasting embarrassment, I was so shocked that the glass slipped out of my hand and smashed on the tiles flooring the terrace. "Me? Fuck off, you mad old cunt. That's just not happening."
"How no?" he grinned, getting his revenge for me previously slipping into *chewing the fat* nonsense.
"Just gonnae no," I responded automatically. Then grinned like a lunatic. "So, am I also going to shoot the President? That would be cool as fuck!"
Jim grimaced while he cleared broken glass. "No you are not, under any circumstances, going to assassinate the sodding President. As far as I can see, he's one of the few folk in the administration who seems to have the slightest clue about the rule of law."
"He chose Beall as his Vice-president," I reminded him.
"He had little choice, given the power brokers who financed his election campaign. Nevertheless, I'd bet that he'd shake your hand if he knew you were the one who took her out of play."

426

"What, you're going to tell him that?" I could hear the panic in my voice.

"No, of course not. But I'll be prepared to admit that I played a major role in setting up the assassinations of both Beall and Buck."

"And that's supposed to be credible? Look at you, you've hardly got the strength to lift a rifle much less the ability to hit anything with it?"

He laughed while he poured me a replacement drink. "Yes, that's fair. I'm not going to say that I carried out the hits, but just that I manipulated others opposed to the conspiracy so that they did the dirty work for me. You were only my trusty bodyguard, who stopped Denis's mercenaries from achieving retribution for these actions."

"Wait a minute, I'm merely your lowly bodyguard. So how come I'm the one putting the screws on the President?"

"Ah, that's because of my progressive Alzheimer's. I'm starting to dribble and wet myself, so you've been forced to take charge of the entire operation. This is your military and intelligence training coming to the fore."

"And this operation involves what?"

"Dragging the permanent members of the UN Security Council together, supported by the EU, Japan, South Korea and Switzerland, so that the President has no choice but to do what you tell him."

***

We were already back on our little boat heading back to Hvar before I was able to start getting my head around the job that had been dropped in my lap. The SAS doc had done a great job and not only was I feeling a lot fitter, but my head seemed to have cleared considerably as the heavy-duty analgesics flushed out of my system. I settled into the little cabin with my laptop linked up to Jim's bloody wristcom and started digging through the briefing files that he had prepared for me

Actually, it was not quite as bad as it first seemed, as Jim had already started sounding out his friend Julia in the Tokyo embassy and, following Rokkasho, she was well linked in to top levels of the Japanese, South Korean, Chinese and Russian intelligence agencies. Already Russia and China had initiated first moves to formally bring a motion of censure against the US at the UN Security Council. Having the unexpected support of the UK and France was warmly welcomed, as was Switzerland, which always tended to punch above its weight in international politics. My main job was thus to bring the EU into the fold. This would kick-off later in the day when we finally reached Hvar.

There was no doubt about it, the President and his Cabinet would be under enormous overseas pressure but, even then, I was not convinced that this would be sufficient to mobilise action against the oligarchs who formed the core of the plutocracy that was the USA. I could imagine a long drawn-out process resulting in heads rolling in the military and intelligence services and some token hand-slaps for the great and the good, but not the major shake-up that Jim seemed to be looking for.

Bugger! The cunning old bastard's got another card up his sleeve. My immediate response was to stomp up to the wheelhouse and give him a bollocking, but I gritted my teeth and held back. *This has got the feeling of another one of his fucking tests. Now, if I was going to add the final push that would force the President to react, what would I do?*

The President of the US has vast individual power as Commander in Chief, but if he wanted to implement some major security action, backing by the National Security Council would be important. *Would they bend to external political pressure if there was no direct physical threat to the country?*

I felt a shiver run up my spine. *Jim, what the fuck have you done now?*

Chapter 45: Jim

"Jim, you bastard, what the merry fuck are you up to here?" Considering her injuries, I was impressed both by the speed she was moving and the fact that she'd rumbled me already.

"Cool down a bit, love, remember that you're an invalid," I smiled at her in a paternal manner, which probably only fanned the flames.

"As you'll soon also be, you old cunt. You've already set up something to force POTUS to take real action against the Washington elite."

"Well spotted! I was sure that you'd notice eventually, but you're much faster than I expected." Rachel was clearly confused by my admission of guilt and held back the punch she was preparing for me. "Maybe you've also worked out what this might involve?"

She frowned in a way that was almost cute, in a scary kind of way. "Well, it would need to be a direct threat to the US. But there's no way that even nutters like Denis would do that." She spotted my smug grin. "But you wouldn't hesitate for a minute if you were certain that you could pin it on the bad guys. For Christ's sake, surely not a nuclear attack?"

"Well, sort of. But a bit better focused than the grandstanding events that McCabe dreamed up for the Veep and Buck. Did you know that the Pentagon has an SMR and there's also a micro-reactor under the White House?"

"No way! You can't put reactors in place in complete secret. And, even if you could, why?"

"Mmm, for the why, you need to think back to the way that the US was split in the twenties. Insurrection or even civil war were scenarios wargamed at that time, when it was recognised that both the Pentagon and White House were vulnerable to any events that caused complete loss of external power for extended periods of time. That vulnerability can be easily removed by setting up a small reactor in the basement. The how is simple – these things can be transported in standard shipping containers through the tunnels existing below both locations and then installed by security staff with minimal technical knowledge."

Rachel was clearly unconvinced. "Even if that's the case, these things would be failsafe and robust as hell. There's no way that you could threaten them."

"Yes, you'd think that, wouldn't you? However, Trump's sabre-rattling during his first term had NATO and some allied states already dreading what a second term would involve. The US had gone from the West's main defender of democracy to its greatest threat. Of course, NATO could do nothing about this, but this didn't stop some national intelligence agencies preparing for a worst case."

"If it was very sneaky, then that would be the Brits I suppose."

I nodded. "Yes, with a bit of help from Mossad, as Israel had their own problems with a would-be dictator at that time."

"This has got to be ultra-top secret. You couldn't know about this unless you were involved."

"Oh no," I shook my head, "I'm not even close to that security level. All I ever did was carry out some risk analyses of hypothetical scenarios. But it wasn't so hard for me to fill in gaps and develop an overview of what was going on."

By now Rachel's ire had completely dispersed as she was drawn into the story. "So, hypothetically, what did your spooks put in place for the super-horror scenario of a US President completely losing his shit and preparing for nuclear war."

I shrugged. "Hypothetically, there may be a self-destruct function built into the reactors at both sites."

I watched the colour drain from her face. "You call me a psycho, but you've set up a weapon to kill everyone in both the Pentagon and the White House."

"No, no, of course not. I had no direct involvement at all. In any case, these would just be wee reactor melt-downs. Probably wouldn't kill anyone at all, but the disruption would be immense. Also, these aren't the kind of things that you can cover up, so the Government would almost certainly fall as there would be nuclear crap on their very own doorstep."

"Wait a minute, just hold your horses here! If this ever came out, in any way at all, it would cause a shit-storm of apocalyptic dimensions."

"Yes indeed, love. So it can't come out. This is for the President's ears only. Well, of course, he'll need to bring in the core of the National Security Council to set up a kill list – what you Yanks prefer to call a disposition matrix, I believe."

I could tell from the evil glint in her eyes that the penny had finally dropped. "Your black-hat buddies have already set up links that will allow all these actions to be traced back to the veep's co-conspirators. Luckily, the NSC can't dig too much into these, as this risks the entire fiasco being exposed. Better just to organise a few fatal accidents to take out key actors and then a series of high profile legal cases to completely bankrupt their dynasties, thus ensuring that this conspiracy cannot be repeated."

"Indeed. With full NSC support, this will probably increase the President's standing and make him a shoo-in for a second term, even without the usual required support from vested interests. Not only that, we can finally get rid of those fucking self-destructs, which I was never happy with in the first place."

Despite trying to hide it, I could see that the girl was impressed. "If there was any justice in the world, you'd get the Nobel peace prize for this bit of political legerdemain."

I laughed aloud. "The last fucking thing that I need. Anyway, this was all technical stuff – risk management shite – and techies like me stay in the background. You, however, could be up for the Presidential Medal of Freedom. That wouldn't do your career any harm."

Rachel stood in shocked silence for about a minute, then finally shook her head. "I think we're getting ahead of ourselves here but, in any case, there's no way that I'm taking credit for the work that you did."

"Ah, lass, I'm afraid that you've no choice. I've already scripted out the next couple of steps, which will require some pillow talk with your little EU bit of fluff. I suppose that I could do it, at a pinch, but I'm sure that she'd rather be shagging you."

"Who wouldn't," she giggled. "But why is any pillow talk involved here."

"Yes, well, that's the thing. We need to present discovery of this plot as something that you have come over alone and want to communicate to the President without me knowing about it. You're a loyal US citizen and ex-military and would do anything to avoid threats to your homeland. Indeed, you've narrowly avoided being killed by these conspirators on several occasions. You can paint me as a geriatric wild card, who has helped more by luck than judgment, mainly due to the exposures on my dark-web site."

"Okay, that last bit will be easy, as you are indeed a geriatric wild card," she grinned. "I just can't wait to see the rest of your script that is going to pull all of this together."

I grinned back and patter her on the head. "About that, grasshopper. I'm afraid I'll show this to you only after you've drafted your version."

A almost managed to avoid her slap, but it was clearly pulled as it hurt only a little.

Chapter 46: Rachel

After a bit of toing and froing, we eventually dropped Jim's ideas of contacting the President via the EU, especially as they had already decided to support the UN censure motion against the US. Instead, we decided that it would be easier to go through the US ambassador in Bern. As we had removed all immediate threats to ourselves and ensured that any of Buck's remaining supporters would be keeping their heads very low, there was no time pressure and so we could move slowly and methodically, ensuring that our tracks were well covered.

Back in Hvar, we were met by both EU agents at the harbour and were briefed on progress during the short helicopter flight to Buck's estate. The remnants of two helicopters had been pushed to the side so there was just space for us to land beside another, larger police machine. I smiled at Connie when I spotted a US navy chopper hovering offshore. "Fucking Yanks," she grimaced. "Just won't fucking back off. They seem to think that just because a rich American was shot that they have some right to take over the investigation. You'd have thought that there were enough murders in the US to keep them busy. Wankers!"

I took advantage of Connie's distraction to surreptitiously caress Maria's bum. Jim grinned and added fuel to the fire. "Yes, I'm fairly sure the main reason for that is to facilitate any required cover-up of their own involvement. It was a bit convenient for Buck to be knocked-off just as he was trying to fake his death in order to escape a Congressional hearing. Anyway, Rachel, you were trained as a sniper. What do you make of this?"

I hesitated for a moment, to make it seem as if this question had caught me by surprise. "From what you've told me about weather conditions at the time of the attack, this had to be a professional team with very sophisticated weapons. From the number of targets hit when under fire from the shore, I'd guess at least two shooters. They'd need a stable firing platform, so maybe a submarine."

"What about a raft?" Maria asked.

"Mmm, I guess so, at a pinch. A large, stabilised cruiser would be best, but I'm sure that you've been able to eliminate that option."

"Yes, no chance of anything big," Connie responded, "although there could have been a couple of smaller boats in the area."

"Well, that's also possible. But, again, the key thing would be access to top-end military rifles and associated support kit. At the very least, some targeting drones – especially if the shooters were low in the water."

"If I had to guess, I'd say US navy SEALs," Maria nodded in the direction of the American helicopter. "It seems rather suspicious that they just happened to have navy resources in the area. In fact, if they had been just a little faster, they might have recovered that raft before we found it."

"Ah, so it was a raft. I'm surprised that you found it, though. They should have either disposed of it or taken it back with them as SOP."

436

"Sop, what's that?" Maria frowned.

"S – O – P: standard operational procedure. I did actually train with SEALs a few times when I was in the Marines. They definitely have black ops guys who could carry this off."

Connie sighed. "I've got a feeling that, no matter what we suspect, it'll be impossible to prove US involvement here."

"But circumstantial evidence is mounting to the point where it can't be ignored," Jim pointed out. "Attempts to kill us in Canada, assassination of the Vice-president, fire-fights in Switzerland and now the two attacks here. This can be managed only by a large organisation with sophisticated technical resources."

I clambered out of the helicopter and turned just in time to catch Jim as he stumbled down. "Thanks, lass, old knees don't work very well," he mumbled, taking the opportunity to rub his hand down the front of my t-shirt. "You feeling the cold, or just missing Maria," he whispered in my ear.

Sleazy old fucker. However, I then noticed that, indeed, my nipples were like a couple of acorns and quickly pulled my denim shirt into place to cover them. He met my glare with a smug grin. *Shit, I should have realised that this would happen when I visit the scene of my last hits.*

Luckily the EU agents seemed oblivious. Connie was now talking us through the situation on the beach as it was when first-responders appeared on the scene. She had already shown us video-clips during our flight, but a clearer picture emerged as she gave us her interpretation of events, including

437

here some relevant background from interviews with staff.

"The first shot seems to have missed Buck and hit the woman with him. We haven't yet identified her, as the preliminary DNA results seemed screwed up." Maria opened a pad and showed a series of snaps of the decapitated corpse.

"Yes, well I know why that is," Jim interrupted. "It's because she's dead."

On cue, I cut in. "Of course she's dead, you silly old bugger, her head's been blown off."

"No, she died years ago. Or, at least, she seemed to. That's Anne McCabe and it's exactly the way I want to remember her. She was a truly evil swine."

"What?" "You knew her?" In their surprise, the two agents talked over each other.

"I've had run-ins with her in the past. She fancies herself as an eco-terrorist. Was supposed to be killed while making a bomb, but I was never convinced."

"What the fuck would she be doing with Buck?" I asked, beating the agents to the question."

"I've not a Scooby," Jim grinned, "but you can be sure she was up to no good. Anyway, her terrorist links are yet another nail in Buck's coffin."

"Yes, well, Buck will certainly be needing a coffin," Connie continued her exposition. "The second shot blew his brains all over his personal assistant, the pretty Alice. We haven't been able to get much out of her, as she's still in shock."

"But you've got her computer," I asked.

"Yes, forensics are working on it now. I know that Jim has already hacked it," she frowned in his direction, "but we need to go through the motions so that everything is admissible in court."

"And what about Buck's computers?" Jim asked. "They were completely shielded, so I had no chance to get near them."

"When we had physical access, our geeks were able to hack into a desktop and a couple of linked tablets, but there's clearly a lot of memory missing." Maria answered. "Probably on a high-capacity drive or uploaded using a private satellite link."

Jim frowned. "I'm sure all the key material for Buck's business empire is moved by his own satellites, with hard backups in each of his regional offices. Anything related to the conspiracy would be too sensitive."

"I don't suppose that you found anything on Buck's body, did you?" I wondered out loud.

Connie checked her tablet. "We found three micro-drives in a compartment within that gaudy belt-buckle that he always wears. Our team hasn't gotten around to looking at them yet."

"Those could be important, but you'll need to be extremely careful as they'll be as tamper-proof as it's possible to make them." I scratched my head. "What about the cousin?"

Again Connie showed us photos. "She was badly wounded, but might have survived if she hadn't tried to drag herself towards her wife, who was drenched with aviation fuel when the first chopper was hit. They both died of their burns, along with the helicopter pilots and four of the security guards. Another half-dozen guards and villa staff suffered burns and shrapnel injuries, but all should survive."

"Well, the attackers weren't worried about collateral damage, that's for sure." Jim raised an eyebrow in my direction and I buttoned my shirt to be on the safe side.

Connie shrugged. "That's painfully obvious. Although I dragged you here mainly to piss-off the suits in the Navy chopper, it was useful to see that Rachel's analysis of the scene fits well with our own. Now that you're here, however, is there anything else you want to look at?"

I swithered for a moment. "Well, I suppose a place like this has CCTV monitoring, at least in the common rooms and covering approaches to all access points."

"Yes, video storage is in the block where the guards are housed and other passive monitoring is carried out." Maria answered. "We've already secured all hard drives and image analysis is ongoing. However, for some strange reason, everything prior to the attack on Buck's yacht had been deleted. We haven't been able to get to the bottom of that as yet."

"Well, could I have a quick look in that area?"

"Why don't you have a look with Maria," Jim suggested. "It might be worth Connie and me having a look in Buck's office to see if there's anything there that might help."

Thank you Jim. I'll never call you a useless old bastard again. There just better be nobody in the

440

guard quarters, as I'm going to shag Maria senseless.

***

As I had expected, all security staff had been removed from the villa and their residential wing of the villa was completely empty. Apart from the security centre and a server room handling all external communications, there were six double bedrooms, a dormitory capable of sleeping another dozen, a canteen, a gym and a recreation centre. Maria explained that the property was fully staffed only when guests were present, which was generally only for a couple of months each year. A skeleton staff, which included two couples covering security, were in residence at other times.

I rushed Maria to one of the bedrooms that had not been in use, blatantly groping her as we went. The young Spaniard was clearly bemused by my urgency, but happy to go with the flow. Within a minute we were naked on the bare mattress of a double bed, going at it like rabbits. I came quickly and noisily, but then was able to slow down a little and concentrate more on pleasuring my bed-mate.

Although not as desperate as I was, Maria had clearly missed me – or at least missed our regular sessions. It thus took little effort to bring her to a squirting orgasm with my fingers and tongue. As we cuddled in post-coital bliss, I became aware that the room now smelled like a well-used French brothel. "I just hope nobody comes in here in the next few

441

days, as it'll be quite obvious what's been going on," I murmured.

"Not much risk of that," Maria responded sleepily. "The place is now locked down, but all the forensic work is focused on the beach, the main lounge and Buck's private apartment. As we already have all the surveillance records, there's no reason at all for anyone to come into this block."

"That sounds perfect, so we can mess about for a bit longer," I squeezed a prominent nipple and was rewarded by a positive-sounding moan.

"We can't be too long, though, or the others will wonder what we're doing."

Jim will know fine well and I'm sure that Connie will suspect, but another fifteen minutes should be okay. Without any discussion, we moved into soixante-neuf position and I enjoyed a very tasty and relaxing quarter of an hour of Sapphic fun.

***

We quickly showered before dressing and heading back to the main building. I doubt that it really made much of a difference, but at least we were making the situation less obvious.

In the large lounge, Jim and Connie were sitting together on a settee, leafing through a large, leather-bound album. When he noticed our entry, Jim waved us over.

"Good old Denis, covers up his goings-on electronically, but then prints out incriminating material in glossy hard copy. Like many of his peers, I guess bragging about sexual prowess is part

442

of his alpha-male role. Unlike those with a string of mistresses hidden from his wife, young Mrs Buck seems to be an active participant in his escapades.

Maria and I hurried over to look over their shoulders at the pair of A4 prints of a wild bi foursome. "The Bucks and one of the couples in their permanent security team," Connie noted.

Just as well we didn't see this beforehand, or Maria and I would still be hard at it now. "Interesting," I admitted, "but not really incriminating. The fact that he's buggering one of his employees while his wife and another employee are sitting on his face might be considered some form of sexual exploitation, but both of them seem to be well into it."

"And probably also get a large bonus for services rendered," Jim nodded. "But, look here…" he quickly paged back to a spread featuring Buck with three women."

"Wow," Maria sighed and I noted the slightest trace of a blush. "That's the missus again, with McCabe and… It's his niece, Alice, isn't it?"

"Indeed, a bit of incest to add to his peccadillos," Jim smiled. "But there's no way now that his close link to the miraculously resurrected McCabe can be hidden."

"Seems like a stupid mistake to make," Connie frowned. "I can understand him having all security video deleted after the first attack, just in case he came under investigation. I'd also expect that all the more recent stuff would have also been scrubbed after his planned fake death was announced. But why the picture album?"

Jim continued turning pages. "I'm sure this is just one of a number of albums recording his conquests. He's a collector, documenting the notches on his bedpost. Nowadays, everyone focuses on cyber-security and most are aware that anything digital that isn't isolated within a Faraday cage is vulnerable. But why would he worry about this album? I'm sure he planned to have it shipped out to Oz along with especially treasured personal items from his other properties."

"The arrogance of those who consider themselves above the law," I added, while I goggled at the diverse range of group snaps that seemed to cover most of the kink spectrum for groups of usually four but up to eight participants. There was something about this voyeurism that was strangely addictive and we gazed in silence while Jim slowly paged through the album.

Suddenly he stopped, with a sudden intake of breath. I peered more closely. "Oh, fuck!" I gasped and closed my eyes.

"Shit!" Connie was also closely inspecting the photos, then turned to face me. "Is that your mother? The one wearing the strange veil."

I could only nod, but Jim stepped in. "Indeed. We can now add necrophilia to Denis's kinks as there are two dead woman in action there."

I squinted. "Fuck, I think you're right."

"Yes, that's the shooting victim you call McCabe," Connie confirmed.

Jim laughed. "He's got the real axis of evil there – one sitting on his dick and the other fingering his arse while his wife eggs them on with a riding crop. Only a shame that it's not something more painful, like a cat o' nine tails."

Maria patted me on the back. "Sorry that you had to see that. Are you alright?"

"A bit of a shock, but it's nothing that I'm particularly surprised to see my mother get up to. Anyway, I guess finding that album was worth the effort of dragging us out here."

Connie nodded. "We'd probably have seen it eventually, but it wasn't on the list of things that we were looking for. I just wonder if such evidence of a relationship between Buck and these women makes interpretation of the attacks more difficult.

I shook my head. "There's no indication of a relationship here: they're just fucking. They'd do that even if they really disliked each other. In fact, knowing my mother and from what I've heard about McCabe, I could easily imagine that it would be hate at first sight for that pair."

Jim grinned. "You took the words right out of my mouth, love. And, if you look closely, you'll see Mrs Buck isn't holding back with that riding crop. I bet she detests both of them."

Maria was evidently baffled. "If that's the case, why are they shagging?"

I shrugged. "As they say in North England, 'there's nowt so queer as folk'."

Jim laughed. "Again, the very words taken out of my mouth."

Chapter 47: Jim

We chilled in Hvar for a week, simply enjoying the lack of pressure. Rachel spent every possible moment with Maria during the five days until she and Connie transferred to Lyon. There, they would liaise with Interpol on drafting reports of the two attacks and agreeing responses to them.

When not performing my butler role, keeping the lesbian lovers supplied with food and drink and, between sessions, clean bedding, I was setting up Rachel's video-meeting with the President and putting together the material that would support this play. Here I needed to carefully find a balance between providing so much evidence that POTUS was forced to make some very difficult decisions that would shake up the Washington status quo and minimising required recognition of serious crimes carried out under his watch. *Assuming, of course, that he isn't part of the conspiracy.*

I gave the girl a day to recover from her marathon sex sessions and then we spent our last day in Hvar going through the files that I had prepared. Here, in particular, I wanted Rachel's opinion on whether we should include instructions on how to kill the self-destructs on the SMRs in our initial message or if it might be better to hold this for later.

Rachel frowned for several minutes before cautiously giving her input. "If it was up to me, I would give all technical background we have on how the reactors were compromised, but let the US specialists in this area do the rest for themselves."

"I can see where you're going with this," I admitted, "but what if they fuck-up? Even for these resilient SMRs, a melt-down is far from trivial."

"Come on, Jim, these guys aren't daft and will be painfully aware of that. They will, however, have full responsibility for getting things right rather than having the solution presented to them on a plate. This will create a more visceral reaction against those involved in weaponising these reactors."

"I think you're right," I conceded, "so let's go ahead on this basis. We can give hints to indicate who we think is responsible, but let them dig into the material available and interpret that for themselves. I'll put all the associated evidence and supporting information together on a secure chip and we can take it to the embassy in Bern as soon as we get back to Switzerland. I guess we'll be back to the Embassy a couple of times, so I'll book us a hotel in downtown Bern."

Rachel smiled. "Somewhere nice, I hope. Not one of the dingy places you usually choose."

"I think we're justified in going up-market and, at present, there shouldn't be anyone actively looking to rub us out. Leave it up to me."

***

Instead of travelling with the usual ferry, I organised a private speedboat transfer to Split airport. Despite the short flight time, we flew business back to Kloten, which Rachel took full advantage of, drinking Prosecco in the lounge before boarding, followed by Champagne during the entire flight. Although far from drunk, she clearly had a nice buzz on when we disembarked into terminal 1.

To my surprise, there was a couple waiting for us at the end of the jet-bridge, a young man in a suite with a tie and lapel badge that indicated that he was something to do with the airline, while the woman with him was dressed as a traditional chauffeuse. Rachel also appeared bemused by this pick-up, which seemed to have been organised by the US embassy.

The guy from Swiss asked where we were staying and promised to pick up our checked in luggage and get it delivered to the hotel. The two of them relieved us of our hand-luggage and we were then led through a security gate and down steps to a bulky Cadillac limousine that was sitting just below where our flight was docked. It certainly looked the part, with the stars and stripes proudly displayed on both car flagpoles.

After we settled ourselves in the back of the vehicle, bringing our small pieces of hand-luggage with us, Rachel moved closer so that she could whisper into my ear. "Are you sure this is kosher? This isn't something that you've mentioned to me."

"I can assure you that it's a complete surprise to me. I'm just checking now…" I fiddled with my PASS for a bit while we drove over to the VIP building and then through a security gate without any obvious identity checks.

We were already on the motorway, when I settled back with a sigh. "Yes, it's from the Embassy right enough and, as you notice, we're getting the diplomatic Full Monty." Only then Rachel seemed to notice that Swiss police cars with lights flashing were moving over to bracket us in.

"Wow, that's nice, she grinned. "We've got everyone clearing the fast lane for us and I'm sure we're doing well over the speed limit."

"Assuming no traffic jams, we should be in Bern in just over an hour. Is there anything that we need to go over beforehand? It seems that they've fast-tracked us to meet the Ambassador."

"Shite! You may not have noticed, but we're in casual travelling clothes. I had intended to have a shower and get changed into something more formal."

I shrugged, despite the fact that, in my scruffy cargo pants and ancient craft-beer t-shirt, I made my partner look dressy by comparison. "The ball's in their court, so we just play it by ear." With that, I dragged a tablet from my backpack and linked it to my PASS, having a quick hack into the less secure parts of the embassy internet to find if there was more there about what to expect.

Rachel had started to root out her tablet when there was a click and the driver's voice issued from speakers in the panel that separated her from us. "If you want privacy, please press the green button located in your armrests. Press again if you want to talk to me. There are drinks and some snacks in the cupboard facing you. Please help yourselves."

We looked into each other's eyes and nodded. There was no way that the back of this car wouldn't be bugged, so we did not even bother to push the green button. "Thanks for that, something to drink would be just the very job." Rachel opened the polished mahogany doors of the cabinet and was evidently delighted to see that, in addition to a range of spirits, a half bottle of Champagne was sitting in an ice bucket. "Right then, auld yin, what do you fancy? A little drop of sparkly?"

As I am sure she expected, I shook my head. "Maybe a beer?"

She rummaged about in the little fridge. "They've got all the classics: Bud, Bud light, Coors, Coors light…"

I shivered in horror. "Fuck no. Maybe I'll have a glass of fizz after all."

"Actually, there's something here called Anchor Steam."

"Right, that'll do."

"Excellent, all the more fizz for me," She handed me the beer bottle, which had a ring-pull top. "Do you want a glass?"

"I think that would be a bit more civilised, seeing as how we're in this swanky limo. Maybe also something light to nibble on?"

"Okay, I can pull out this tray and shove a selection onto it. Then I need to get to work on the booze, if it has to be polished off before we arrive."

I groaned. "Well, don't get too drunk. Remember, you're supposed to be leading this op."

"Fuck, I'd forgotten about that. Anyway, all we need to do is hand over the chip and, after that's

450

been transferred to POTUS, arrange a time for a discussion. Assuming that he'll wear it, of course."

"Well, this reception indicates they're taking us seriously. Despite my many years in the game, I've never had this kind of VIP treatment before. Of course, this may be because I always work in the background. I actually feel a bit exposed travelling like this."

She grinned. "Yes, you'd rather be taking some indirect route using public transport or a cheapo hire car. Me, I've got no problems with this luxury drinks-cabinet-on-wheels."

"Enjoy it while you can. I don't think this is likely to happen to you again."

"Maybe not, but carpe diem." I watched as she rummaged around, ignoring a bowl of fruit and looking for more hedonistic snacks. Another fridge contained a tin of caviar and a few cheeses. Also a range of half-bottles of white wine, including a sparkly. "Oh, there's something here called Le Rêve Blanc de Blancs. Do you think that would be any good?"

"I've heard of it, but never tried it myself. It's supposed to be up there with the better English wines."

"Sounds a bit like damning with faint praise," She smiled. "So maybe better to stick with the real thing."

"No, really, due to global warming they're struggling to make good Champagne in France and a lot of the big producers now have estates in countries like Chile, New Zealand, the States and even Canada."

Rachel lifted out the bottle and examined the label. "You're not bullshitting, for a change. The producer here in the Napa valley seems to have links to Taittinger. I guess I should force myself to have a wee taste." She poured the remnants of the Champagne into her glass and slurped in down in an inelegant manner before opening the Californian fizz.

"Come on, love, it's not so far to Bern. You need to screw the nut."

"We're just going to hand the chip to some embassy underling and then go on to the hotel. Nul problemo."

There was a click and the driver broke in. "I'm sorry that we didn't make the protocol clear. You will be met by the Ambassador and get formalities sorted out. The video meeting with the President will be about half an hour later."

"Jesus Christ," Rachel groaned, pushing the opened wine to the back of the shelf loaded with snacks.

I grinned. "Shit, that's me blindsided for the first time in a while. I'm just glad that I'm too far gone with dementia to provide any input here. Shouldn't let that fine wine go to waste though." Just to be annoying, I then poured half of the little bottle into my empty beer glass and slumped back with a sigh.

Rachel's death stare was a classic. *If she gets through the rest of the afternoon without a heart-attack, she'll be just in the mood to kick my arse black and blue.*

Chapter 48: Rachel

We were clearly expected and drove directly into the Embassy compound and down a spiral ramp that took us into a very new-looking garage. The limo stopped in a parking area in front of a large elevator. Two soldiers in full battle kit flanked a pair of contrasting women in grey business suits – one tall and statuesque in a short skirt and heels while the other was small and slim, almost elfin, wearing trousers and what looked like plain, black trainers. The chauffeuse rushed to open doors for us while the Amazon came forward to greet us.

"So, Rachel and James, we finally meet. I hope that you don't mind skipping all the usual formalities and just get straight onto first name terms. Going per du, as the Swiss would term it. I'm Shelly, the Ambassador, and this is Shania, my science attaché. Normally, we'd have a few of the intelligence folk here as well but, as you can imagine, that is something that the President has specifically forbidden."

It was strange for the focus to be on me instead of my older, male partner. "Shelly and Shania, nice to meet you. I can understand the need for us to move quickly and informally, so can I start by giving you this chip, which has all the background to the present problem. I'm sure you know how sensitive this is, so it has to be couriered directly to the President. It's quantum-locked and tamper-proof, but will be vulnerable as soon as we unlock it."

Surprisingly it was Shania who spoke up. "We've been analysing everything that has happened recently and didn't expect anything else. However, if you unlock it now, we can transfer it directly to POTUS without a risk of interception." She waved a blocky chip-reader in my direction.

Remembering how effective Jim's hacker-wallahs were, I raised my eyebrow sceptically.

Shania picked this up. "No, really, this is completely secure. Encryption is based on a one-time-pad approach, with packets of the signal randomly distributed within the data-fluxes of eight different secure military channels."

I glanced at Jim, who gave a small nod. "Okay, that would work. You need biometric input from both of us now. I assume that thing includes a retina-scanner."

The Ambassador frowned. "Retinal scans? Can't those be hacked?"

I smiled, remembering how I had exactly the same question when Jim suggested this option. "Yes, indeed, normal ones can. But we're both wearing smart contact lenses, which are linked to bio-monitors. We both need to be in the conditioned physical state set for decoding, otherwise nothing happens. We also have pre-set states that will erase all contents."

Shelly frowned. "I've heard of this technology, but wasn't aware that anyone had implemented it."

I nodded. "That's what we were hoping. This version is a bit of a home-brewed lash-up, but it seems to work. Anyway, let's try it."

The chip was inserted into the reader and I stared into it, mentally going through the preparation for the one time that I did a sponsored fire-walk. A green flash indicated that it had worked. Then Jim was on, looking into the reader with a wicked smile on his face. *I dread to think what experience he was using here – and must remember never to ask.*

Another green flash and the release of tension from the Ambassador's shoulders was visible. "Right now guys," she announced, "that's the foreplay out of the way. Let's get out of this dismal garage and into somewhere more gemütlich."

***

Jim had already briefed me on Professor Shelly Landstrom, someone he had never met but who seemed to have impressed him. Unlike political appointees, who were selected for a cushy holiday paid by the taxpayer as a reward for support of the President's election campaign, Shelly was a career diplomat with a purely academic background as professor of political science at Yale. Reflecting her family's Nordic roots, she was unusually polylingual – an ability that was greatly appreciated in multilingual Bern. It was this background that led Jim to select her as our contact rather than going through London or the EU.

The woman had evidently done her homework. When we emerged into her plush office, a waitress was standing beside a table of drinks. Shania mumbled an apology and scurried off while Shelly slumped into a leather chair that faced a matching settee. "We need to wait a little until those above the clouds have gone through your material. So what do you fancy, Rachel, a glass of wine? Maybe something fizzy? I have a Swiss one from Aargau which is very good." I had only to nod and within seconds both of us had elegant flutes filled to the brim.

"And you, James, I believe you are more of a beer man. How about something from your hometown? An IPA from MischMasch?"

"That'd be perfect," he replied and settled back with his beer while Shelly's focus returned to me after the waitress had discretely left the room.

"I can't overemphasise how sensitive this meeting with POTUS is. You will be the only one at our end: this goes far beyond even my security clearance. I'm afraid that it also means that James is excluded. We are aware of how closely the two of you have worked together, but you're American with both military and intelligence security clearance, while he is a foreigner with known links to spy agencies in other countries."

I looked over to Jim who merely shrugged his shoulders. We had already discussed this as a possible scenario. It was just that a situation where I would have to perform without preparation while half-cut hadn't come up as even a very low probability option. "I can understand this and, as he's not in the best mental condition, it's probably for the best. Nevertheless, although he may not be able to remember what he had for breakfast, he's still able to function as a risk assessment whizz on his good days. I can't come close to him in that area."

"That's fine. We can keep him in the background so that he'll be on call to provide any supporting background that you need. In any case, he'll need to sign a non-disclosure agreement."

I struggled to avoid grinning, knowing how little Jim would be restrained by such a silly paper tiger. "Whatever works for you will be fine for us. In any event, I'll just be happy to be well shot of this entire zoo. From the very beginning, everything has been far above my paygrade and nothing would make me happier than walking away and never hearing about it again."

Shelly nodded. "I don't know all the details, but I can well understand what you mean. Despite that, I suspect that you may get an offer today that you might find difficult to turn down."

I looked at her in confusion, as this was something else that I hadn't thought through properly. "Formally, I'm still attached to NSA – although my mother's group was very low profile, almost black-ops level. Since the attack that seemed to kill my mum, I guess I'm formally AWOL. Although how that works when teams in your own organisation are trying to assassinate you, I can't get my head around."

The Ambassador smiled. "There, at least, I know that POTUS is fully aware of your situation. As you see, the usual spooks are missing from our meeting – which you can be sure they're really pissed about. Similarly, the President will be joined only by the Joint Chiefs, with nobody else from the Security Council present."

Shit, this really is the highest level that we could have wished for. I could feel sweat running down my back and was even more conscious about how scruffily I was dressed.

Shelly must have picked up signs of my discomfort. "I guess that you're a bit nervous about this meeting, especially as you've been dragged here directly from your flight. Would you like to pop into the washroom here," she pointed to a door that I hadn't previously noticed.

"Don't you have a fresh t-shirt in your backpack?" Jim asked, glancing down at my chest as I turned in his direction.

Fuck, fuck, fuckity fuck! Although I had a tight sports bra under my top, my nipples looked like a pair of thimbles. "Um, Madam Ambassador, I wonder…"

"Shelly, call me Shelly," she grinned. "I guess you'd like to borrow a jacket."

Jim laughed and I gave him my most severe glare. Then I couldn't help seeing the funny side and also laughed. "Yes, that would be greatly appreciated. I guess it must be nerves."

"Okay, I'll organise that." The ambassador whispered something into her wristcom. "If you hang on for a few minutes, there will be some fresh clothes – including a jacket – waiting for you in the restroom. There will also be pills that will help speed up alcohol metabolism and, if you want, something to calm your nerves."

I smiled wryly. "I think having a quick shower and then getting into something more formal will sort out my nerves. How much time do I have?"

A quick glance at her wristcom and she answered. "Twenty minutes or so. Maybe you should get yourself sorted out now. I can just have a quick chat to James in the interim. We will stay away from whatever it is you need to discuss with the Commander in Chief, but I'm curious to know how he actually got involved in the first place. According to the files that I've seen, he's supposed to be retired." I quickly headed for the toilet with my backpack, dreading to think about the bullshit that Jim was likely to come out with.

The *restroom* was far beyond my expectations – more of a dressing room with a huge en-suite bathroom containing both a shower and a Japanese-style deep bath. I stripped completely and shoved all my sweaty clothes into a laundry bag that was hanging beside a rack decked with a black suit, similar to the one that the waitress had been wearing. I wished I had time to try the bath, but made do with a quick shower that immediately made me feel much better. The embassy had also provided me with underwear and a blouse, but I settled with fresh undies and a t-shirt from my rucksack. The jacket fit perfectly and I was torn between the matching skirt and trousers. Finally, I decided for the skirt but ignored their choice of shoes and simply put on my original grey espadrilles. *It's a video conference, after all. They'll see me only from the waist up.*

I returned to the ambassador's office to find Jim spouting some nonsense about his support being the result of an agreement between British and US agencies that focused on him have a training role, occasionally mentoring younger staff. "As you can imagine, at my age, I shouldn't be in the field at all. It's not just the arthritis, high blood pressure and cataracts, but I get very forgetful nowadays. I can remember jaunts from the '80s in detail, but yesterday morning is distinctly hazy. If it hadn't been for the attacks in Canada, I'd have been be back at home in Baden within a week, watching daytime TV and working on my memoires. Just as well that I had the girl, um, the fit one, yes, Rachel looking after me."

I couldn't help smiling, remembering him taking out the plane in Osoyoos and the helicopter pilot in Clearwater. He was laying it on thick, but Shelly seemed happy to listen. "Okay Madam…, Shelly, I think I now look and smell a bit more presentable. How is it looking for the meeting?"

The words had hardly left my mouth when Shania bustled in. "Okay, Rachel, we're ready for you now. I'll just take you to the secure-comms room now."

"Fuck!" I mumbled under my breath and glanced at Jim, who gave me an almost unnoticeable thumbs up.

Shelly waved. "Best of luck. Once you're settled in, Shania will join us here but we'll all be available if there's anything you need at any point."

The science attaché was already halfway down a corridor when I left the office and I had to run to catch up with her. *Thank fuck I didn't go for heels.* I grinned at the thought and realised that I now felt completely calm. *Battle training. I may fuck-up in front of the Leader of the Western World, but that's got to be buttons compared to a bullet to the spinal cord.*

The comms room was dimensioned for much larger meetings, with a horseshoe shaped table that could have sat about twenty facing a huge video screen that was showing the seal of the President. I was shown to the head of the table – probably the ambassador's chair under normal circumstances – and then a ten second countdown immediately commenced. "If you need anything, press that switch," Shelly pointed to a red panel on the arm of my chair before she sprinted from the room, slamming the door behind her.

Now time to give POTUS a roasting. I swallowed and squirmed in my seat.

***

The President was in an even larger meeting room which, to my amazement, had only two other participants present. They both wore medal-bedecked uniforms and I recognised the older black man as the Chairman of the Joint Chiefs of Staff and hence guessed the small woman, with an appearance that indicated Asian roots somewhere, was the Vice-chair. I was still trying to get my head around this when the President spoke up. "Special Agent Isaacs, I'm glad we could get a hold of you

461

so quickly. To make things easier, would it be okay if I just call you Rachel?"

"No problem at all Mister President."

"Excellent. I should also let you know that this meeting has the very highest security classification and a record will go only to the participants at this side. You aren't formally cleared for anything even close to this level, but we'll get that sorted out later. The key thing is that I want you to be completely open, without any fear that anything you say could come back and bite you."

I took a deep breath. "As you know, there have been attempts to assassinate my partner and me, all of which were authorised at a very high government level. Not to mince words, by the Vice-president herself and a group of her co-conspirators who have either immense political influence or are highly placed in our intelligence community."

The President winced. "Yes, we're painfully aware of this. Nevertheless, so far, you've had no indications of involvement at top military levels, have you?"

The two Generals looked uncomfortable until I answered. "No, none at all. Direct attacks against us have involved mercenary units used for intelligence black-ops. There may have been some involvement of specialist military units who also do such work, but I imagine the initiators of these actions were within NSA or similar organisations. This is supported by the planned attack against the Pentagon, in addition to that on the White House."

462

There was a shocked silence. After a painful hiatus, the President grimaced. "What attacks would these be?"

I opened my eyes in surprise. "The reactor melt-downs. This was outlined in the chip that I provided."

POTUS looked at his military advisors and saw only blank stares. "We were hoping to get your input on the degree to which key organisations are compromised, so we scanned quickly through the files you provided, focusing on the evidence against Denis Buck, his family and their compatriots."

"Yes, that's described in detail. But didn't you look at the assessment of future threats?"

The President squirmed. "I remember a file on that, but we thought that the priority was to clean house now, before we have the UN crawling all over us."

I shrugged. "Well, I can understand that. I think the present probability of the threats I'm talking about is quite small, but the consequences are so large that a bit of pre-emptive action seems justified."

"You've got my attention. Why don't you talk me through this?"

"Okay. This is a last-resort option that the conspirators cooked up to provide a defence in the event of their plots being uncovered. I can go into detail, or Jim, Mister Forsyth, will give you even more technical background, but basically it involves self-destruct triggers built into the reactors under the White House and Pentagon."

"The what?" The President interrupted. "Why would there be a reactor in my basement?" POTUS glared at the two generals as if it was their fault.

"Just in case of emergencies," The Chairman whispered.

"In any case, inherently safe," the Vice-chair contributed.

I wiped my face theatrically and sighed. "Right, I'll give you the condensed version. All the details are in the file that I sent." I talked for almost 10 minutes while my audience sat in silence, seemingly aging about a decade during this time.

"Damnation!" The President had gone red in the face and looked ready to explode. "I know that some of these Washington power-blocks and lobbying groups think that they actually run the country, but when they're actually planning to blackmail me in case their nefarious schemes fail..." He ground to a halt, clearly at a loss for words.

"Well, at least that's something that you can easily counter. As far as we've been able to determine, the SMR triggers are very simple, intended to be robust and undetectable rather than tamper-proof. Nevertheless, to be on the safe side, I'd recommend that you simply ship them out to some remote location and defuse them there. After that, they can be safely reinstalled. If you do this using only a trusted team, the conspirators may think that they still have this bargaining chip and hence be less likely to panic."

"I think we can do that." The President looked over at the generals, who were both working on palmtops. "So, I hope that there wasn't anything else like that in your future threats appraisal."

"No, most of the rest of the file develops some ideas on how to remove future temptations that could motivate similar groups. The bottom line is that the US is drifting further towards a plutocratic oligarchy, with all traces of anything like a democracy slowly disappearing. This is, of course, not unique to the States, but now you have a chance to strike back – which could also help us gain some of the international credibility that was lost when the Vice-president's role was exposed."

"I am almost afraid to ask, but what will this involve?"

Now let's see if POTUS has the balls to really rock the boat. "Based on the information that you now have, the best option would be to arrest everyone who has any links to this conspiracy and charge them with treason. This would be linked to a call for the death penalty for anyone found guilty and immediate freezing of all their corporate and personal funds, including all of those held by family members or kept overseas. It will be important to keep compromised intelligence agencies well clear of this action, focusing on resources available to the police and the military."

"Wow, you don't lack ambition, do you?" The line went dead for a few minutes while POTUS had a quick confab with the generals. "We'll need to think about this, but there does seem to a strong case for action, maybe even something as radical as you suggest."

I couldn't help smiling as he took the bait. There was not even a mention of possible errors in the material that we had provided. "It certainly needs careful consideration, but this has to be done quickly, if at all. We have tried to keep everything related to this topic as secure as possible, but leaks are inevitable. If forewarned, some of the culprits have the ability to initiate pre-emptive blockage of actions against them while, at the same time, dispersing their resources to make freezing or eventually confiscating them as difficult as possible. Quick action has the additional benefit that it will probably be enough to block the upcoming UN Security Council censure of the States."

"Well, Special Agent, you've evidently had more time to think this stuff through than we have. We'll work through your ideas and then will want to speak to you again tomorrow. I can set up an air force transfer that will get you to Washington by tomorrow morning."

"Ah, Mister President, if it is okay with you, I might be better remaining in Switzerland tonight. I need to brief my colleague and bring together all the background material that he has, but which we didn't have time to include on that chip. I guess I could fly out tomorrow. Of course, in any case, I'm available by video whenever you wanted me."

The President flicked through a tablet and then smiled. "Actually, that could work well. The plane that was serving as Air Force Two is currently in Germany and would be available to fly you out tomorrow morning. On that plane we'll have all the secure communications tech that we might need."

"That would be fine with me. I'll be ready to move tomorrow. Just let me know where and when."

"Excellent, and thank you again Special Agent," he smiled. "To facilitate security clearance, you are now an executive White House consultant attached directly to me. I guess we're going to be seeing a lot of each other in the near future, but bye for now."

Before I could say anything further, the link went dead and a few minutes later Shania entered the room. "Well, that was originally scheduled for 20 minutes and you ended up with the best part of an hour. Now the ambassador has instructions to organise your ultra-VIP transport to the States. You must have really impressed POTUS."

We strolled together to the Ambassador's office, where she was still chatting to Jim – somehow having moved on to the topic of Swiss wines. As soon as I entered, Shelly turned to me and smiled. "I've been instructed to be your travel agent now, but I wondered if you would like to stay in the Embassy overnight. It might make logistics easier."

I looked at Jim who gave a minimal shake of his head. "That's very kind, but I think it'll be easier if we just go to our hotel now. Our luggage should be there and we can just chill for a bit before I'm on the move again."

"That's fine. I thought this might be the case, so a car is waiting to take you to the Schweizerhof now. It's a very nice hotel and I can recommend the spa. After a grilling by POTOS, you probably need some relaxation."

"Indeed I do." *And a couple of drinks ASAP.* I waved at Jim. "Let's go, I need to decompress in a hot tub." I said my goodbyes to the Ambassador and then Shania escorted us to the limo.

Chapter 49: Jim

Our VIP treatment continued at the Schweizerhof hotel. Check-in formalities were ignored as the embassy had already arranged to pick up our bill, so we were led to a 2-room suite where our luggage had not only been transferred, but also unpacked, with clothes hung up or placed into drawers. *So, plenty of opportunity to bug the place.* I scanned the rooms with an electronic sniffer while Rachel spent the time telling me how thrilled she was to have met the President, but highlighting her misgivings about transferring to DC.

I found rather obvious pinhead video monitors in both bedrooms and the lounge, but also noted much more subtle audio-only bugs in each location that would not be picked up by most tools. *Good to know that these are here, but maybe we gain more by pretending that we haven't spotted them.*

"Okay, that's the embassy eavesdroppers switched off," I announced.

"Are you sure that it was the embassy and that you've got them all?" Rachel raised an eyebrow and I winked back, letting her know that we were still being recorded.

"Well, whether it's the embassy or not, better to err on the safe side. It's impossible to be sure about finding all bugs with the simple kit that I have with me, but it's only for tonight so I guess we can live with it."

"Okay, but now I need to get your assurance that everything that we've done is kept completely confidential until it's cleared by the White House."

"Until the hit on Buck, everything that I had was shared with the UK, Swiss and EU security services. You've now passed all of that to the President's team, together with some work of your own on risks to the US and possible pre-emptive measures. I'm perfectly happy, as long as you don't give me details of any of that stuff."

"Yes, well the problem is that, despite your regular *senior moments*, you're especially good at pulling together the entire picture on the basis of very limited bits and pieces of evidence. What we don't want – and I agree with POTUS here – is for any internal problems in the US to be communicated further. Even to partner organisations."

I pondered over this for a couple of minutes. "I can see your concerns and would like to help, but a blanket agreement to avoid communicating further on this topic is too much like an open cheque as far as I'm concerned. It's true that I'm retired, but I still might take on the occasional little job if it seems interesting. Such jobs are likely to involve nuclear threat analysis, but how can I even get started if there's no way that I can tell if there is potential to overlap with your secret concerns or not?"

Rachel frowned. "I hadn't thought this through. Assuming I take this proposed White House support role and it has some long-term perspective, it won't be an issue for me. I don't suppose that you'd consider something similar?" The girl actually sounded as if she wanted me to take this bait.

I laughed. "In all honesty, I can't think of anything worse than being drawn into the Washington spook system. I'd rather have my piles cauterised with a red-hot poker. And that's before considering the location: why the fuck would I want to be in an armpit like DC when I could be living my twilight days in Switzerland?"

"Bugger. I had a feeling that this would be your response. So, how do we sort this out?"

"Oh, that's easy. You just need to think about how such problems are handled in commerce: you put me on a retainer. This can be as formal as you want, but with technical details deliberately vague. You pay me enough to cover any lost work and I commit to allowing you to vet any job offers that I get. I will be upfront about such vetting, which will probably mean that some work won't even be offered to me. Nevertheless, I'll have a nice nest-egg to cover my extra-curricular activities to fight off senior-citizen boredom."

Rachel groaned. "So I just need to organise a large enough budget to cover your gallivanting, while you commit only to not doing work we want you to stay away from. Looks very nice from your side."

"Well, it's got to be better than me cramping your style in the White House. I would have imagined that you'd be very happy to be shot of me by now."

Her wry smile indicated that she was not quite as happy as I had expected. "I suppose having time

471

for myself will be good but, on the other hand, who's going to give me breakfast in bed?"

"As a government high-flyer in Washington, I'm sure you'll be able to find someone to handle that role. Anyway, let's get serious. You've been in the room for almost a quarter of an hour and still haven't had a drink yet."

"Fuck, I must be more shell-shocked than I thought. I had been thinking about visiting the spa, but there's a nice deep bath, so I'll run that while you sort out my drink."

"Champagne, I suppose."

"You suppose correctly. Soon as you like, auld yin."

***

I left my tablet in the lounge, running an app that produced the sounds of typing on an old-fashioned keyboard. *The kind of thing they would expect me to use.* This also generated the sounds of breathing and muttering, to provide the required evidence of my presence. I then tiptoed into the large bathroom and closed the door quietly.

"Okay, as far as I can tell we're completely secure here."

Rachel was up to her neck in bubbles, waving the empty glass in her hand. "That's convenient, wouldn't want my new employers to think I'm a lush, after all.

I topped her up from the bottle that we had discovered in the huge *mini-bar*.

"There's another glass here, so fill it and get your horrible old body into this bath. I suspect that you need a long soak as much as I do."

I filled the glass and then hesitated. "I know that it's usually murder and mayhem that turns you on, but you seemed to be either feeling the cold or ready to rock and roll when we arrived at the embassy."

"You don't need to be scared, I'm not going to jump your decrepit corpse," she shivered in a way that I supposed was intended to represent disgust.

"Okay, but just keep your hands to yourself." I smiled, stripped off and slowly lowered myself into the other end of the bath. My legs slid along outside of hers, so her feet ended up close to my groin. *Just as well this bath is long as well as deep.*

Assuming that we couldn't be overheard, Rachel then summarised her chat with the President. "I can't imagine how it could have gone better," she concluded. "It was a bit of a thrill, though. Deceiving POTUS is almost as much of a kick as shooting him would be."

Buggeration, this doesn't sound good. "Yes, look at the positive side. You'd only be able to assassinate him once, but you're probably going to be stringing him along for the foreseeable future."

"About that... I was in a position where I couldn't possibly refuse a request to provide support getting this clusterfuck sorted out. But a special consultant in the White House is far beyond anything I expected. I don't think I'm actually capable of doing the job."

I gently massaged her feet. "Don't worry about that. At least half the folk at that level are political appointees rather than chosen for their abilities. With the experience that you've gained working with me, you'll have an insight into many key problems that's quite unique. And, of course, I'm always on call – providing at least a little input to justify my huge, gigantic, totally-enormous retainer."

"Well, we'll just see how that works out. But what are you going to do now? You're going to really miss me, you know."

"Aye, like a dose of…" I hesitated. "Well, strangely enough, I think I will. You've been a complete pain in the arse, but I've gotten used to you. Maybe it's mainly the nymphets that you bring home…" Her heel pushed forward against my testicles. "Ouch! Anyway, it's been a bit of a learning experience for me. After we first met, I gave myself a week before I strangled you in your sleep."

Rachel grinned. "A week? I was sure that I wouldn't last anything as long as that before I gave you a good kicking."

"Well, you did try a couple of times, but they didn't work out so well for you. Fuck!" Her heel pushed even harder. "Anyway, what I'm going to do. I'll go back to Baden for a bit and decide whether it's cost-effective to re-establish Oederlin as my Swiss base or move somewhere else, just for a change of scene. After that I'll need a real holiday, somewhere warm. Maybe a month or two in the Caribbean."

"Funny you say that. Maria told me that was high on her bucket list. Maybe we could meet up with you there?"

"Why on earth would you want to meet up with a sad old pensioner when you could be cruising the nightlife and assured decadence of the adults-only resorts in that neck of the woods? For example, I could recommend Hedonism II in Jamaica, one of my ex-wife's favourites."

"So you don't want to meet up with me?" She scowled at me as her toes started to rub against my scrotum.

"Certainly not in Hedonism. I think I'm at least a decade or two beyond being able to check in there. I usually just rent a villa somewhere quiet, within walking distance of a small town. The kind of place full of fellow geriatrics. You'd hate it."

"So I guess we could have a week at this Hedonism resort and then pop by to see you for a few days."

I sighed. "I suppose that would be a possibility, especially as, after a week of high-octane swinging, you'd probably sleep for most of the time. But think of the alternatives. What about taking young Maria to meet up with your kinky pals in Tokyo?"

After about another fifteen minutes of discussing ever more outrageous holiday options, Rachel leaned forward and tweaked my nipples. "Righty-ho, enough of this nonsense. I'm starving and could eat a horse."

I grinned. "You might be in luck there. I think fillet of foal is one of the house specialities. That

475

would go well with an aged Bordeaux or a super-Tuscan."

"I think I'll stick to beef, but maybe horse could be something to try sometime in the future. Anyway, thank god that I didn't use a more Glaswegian expression – like 'I could eat a scabby-heided wean'."

"Mmm, long-piglet. That might also be good."

"Enough, already. Stop wittering and get out, dressed and ready to hit the most expensive dining that this hotel offers."

***

What a very pleasant evening. Dinner featured excellent food and wine, complemented by excellent service and tasting even better when we were informed that the embassy was also picking up this tab. Rachel was understandably nervous about her immediate future, but buoyed by the fact that we had actually survived the last couple of months and come through almost unscathed. Now, in retrospect, this seemed almost miraculous.

Aware that our conversation was almost certainly monitored, we stayed away from sensitive topics, but chatted about our trip. This was focused by snaps that Rachel had received from Gabi, Maria and Junko Takeuchi. I was strangely touched that the girl was now relaxed enough to share these with me and happily respond to the banter they initiated.

We followed dinner with a nightcap in the Lobby Lounge, by which time I was struggling to keep awake and even Rachel was beginning to fade.

Back in our suite, I declared that it was time for me to hit the sack and, despite pressure to have another drink, retreated into my bedroom. After rushing my night-time ablutions, I quickly stripped and slid into bed. I was out cold as soon as my head hit the pillow.

* * *

It was about one thirty when bladder-pressure forced me awake. There was sufficient light from a full moon streaming through my curtain to allow me to stagger to the loo without putting on the bedroom light. It was thus only when I returned that I spotted that Rachel was asleep on the other side of my bed. *Fuck, how long has she been there?*

I slowly squeezed back into bed, trying my best to avoid disturbing the girl. I was now wide awake, lying on my back but trying to remain as still as possible. Inevitably, I could feel the first twinges of cramp in my calves, which forced me to turn onto my side, facing away from Rachel. I had just started to dose, when I felt her move closer and spoon against me with her breasts squeezed against my back. *Lucky for me, there's no chance of this leading anywhere after the amount of alcohol that I've imbibed this evening. Although, if I had thought to replace my stocks of Viagra, who knows...*

Chapter 50: Rachel

I awoke to the *urgent* ringtone on my wristcom. "Fuck," I moaned when my hangover immediately kicked in. I was sufficiently compos mentis to mutter "camera off" before I answered. "Who's this? Do you know what time it is?"

"Hi, it's Shelly and the time is just the back of seven."

"Oh, sorry Shelly, it's dark outside and I thought it was earlier than that."

"No problems. Just to let you know that we have found a window for your flight to depart from Zurich, which means that you need to get moving soon. The car is waiting for you downstairs."

"Bugger! I'm actually still in bed."

"That's OK. We'd just appreciate if you pack and get to the car as soon as possible. You can breakfast en route to Kloten and then shower and change on the plane. How much time do you need?"

"Well, I didn't actually get a chance to unpack last night, so I guess I can be down in 5, 10 minutes."

"Perfect. I'm actually in the limo and can update you there."

"Okay, see you in a jiffy." I fell back onto my pillow with a groan.

The toilet flushed and Jim emerged with a glass of Champagne in one hand and a pill in the other. "I'm afraid you'll have to pass on my bespoke breakfast and put up with whatever the embassy has

478

for you. I'm sure that they'll also have something for your hangover, but this will get you started off."

I dragged myself out of bed, gulped down Jim's offerings and, after a quick pee, headed off to my bedroom, where the clothes that I had been wearing yesterday were piled on a chair. By the time I got into the lounge, Jim was waiting for me with both my check-in bag and my backpack, which he had evidently repacked with my toiletries.

"Okay, lass, this is probably better than some drawn-out goodbye." He pulled me into a hug and kissed me on the forehead. "Look after yourself and don't hesitate to contact me if I can ever help." He then moved back and opened the door to the corridor. "I would see you off the premises, but few have a strong-enough stomach to view me in my birthday suit."

As I left I could have sworn that I saw tears in his bleary old eyes. *Probably a trick of the light. Or maybe related to whatever is giving me the sniffles. Fucking coronaviruses.*

***

Just over two hours later I was sitting in the lounge of the presidential jet, belted in my seat and with a glass of excellent champagne in my hand. Suddenly, it occurred to me that I had now achieved everything that my bitch mother had fought for during her entire career. This all despite never having even considered this a possibility in the past. *What did Miriam do wrong? Was it just her nature – the fact that she was an evil cunt who would stop at*

479

nothing to achieve her goals? Or was it the fact that she constantly under-estimated Jim, considering him only one of the many pawns that she could exploit. She did recognise that he was brilliant at what he did, but thought she could make that resource readily available when she planned to create me? I'm sure now that I have inherited a lot of abilities from him, but these only came together when we worked together. Nevertheless, he put me through hell and I'll get my own back when we meet again. As we certainly will.

THE END

www.ingramcontent.com/pod-product-compliance
Lightning Source LLC
Chambersburg PA
CBHW011737010726
47496CB00010B/2970